Two Sisters of Coyoacán

Roberta Satow

COPYRIGHTED MATERIAL

FOR RICHARD, MATTHEW AND JASON

Roberta Satow

Roberta Satow wrote her undergraduate honors thesis in political science at the University of California at Berkeley about Trotsky. When she learned that Ruth Poulos (the person Lilly Abramovitz is based upon) was a fellow psychoanalyst, she felt impelled to write a novel about her role in Trotsky's assassination.

She is the author of *Doing the Right Thing: Taking Care of Your Elderly Parents Even if They Didn't Take Care of You.* She is Professor Emerita of Sociology at Brooklyn College and the Graduate Center of the City University of New York. She is also a psychoanalyst and writes a blog for *Psychology Today.*

PART I

Prologue

Joe Hansen, one of Leon "Lev" Trotsky's private guards, and Melquiades Benitez, the handy man, were on the roof of the Trotsky compound connecting the siren that had been sent from sympathizers in Los Angeles after the failed Siqueiros raid. Joe, with his Rottweiler eyes, saw Jacques drive up to the house in his rented black Ford. It was a bright, clear afternoon although there were threatening clouds off in the distance. Jacques usually parked facing the wall near the garage, but this time he parked parallel to the wall with the car facing toward Coyoacán.

Jacques got out of the car, waved to the dozen policemen milling around their guard house and yelled up to Joe and Melquiades, "Has Gertie arrived yet?" They didn't know Jacques or Gertie were coming, they had just stopped by the day before.

Joe shouted back, "No, not yet," opened the iron doors to the garage and continued working on the roof. Harold Robins, another guard, greeted Jacques when he got to the patio. Jacques walked over to Lev who was feeding the chickens as he did every afternoon after five o'clock tea.

"You look terrible," Lev said, pausing to look at him. "What's the matter with you?"

"Oh, I had the flu or something nasty. But I'm feeling better now," Jacques said. "I was hoping you would read my revised article because Gertie and I will be leaving tomorrow."

"Really, where are you going?" Lev asked.

"We're going to Acapulco for a few days," Jacques said, "and then back to New York."

"I have to finish feeding them," Lev said, pointing to the chickens." Turning back to the chickens, he said, "Come on, *bubelehs*."

Natalia Trotsky walked over to Jacques and said in French, "*Hello. How are you? Why are you dressed for a storm?*" She laughed.

Looking at the ground, Jacques responded in French, "*I'm awfully thirsty. May I have a glass of water?*"

"Get him the water," Trotsky said to Natalia in Russian. *"He wants me to read the stupid article again."* She smiled and walked to the kitchen. Lev called after her, *"They're leaving tomorrow."*

Lev sighed and said, "Well, why don't we go over your article?" He walked toward the house with Jacques following behind him. Trotsky was six feet tall, broad-chested and physically powerful. Jacques was shorter, and his broad shoulders were slightly stooped. He had lost a great deal of weight since his arrival in Mexico.

The Old Man sat down to read the article while Jacques sat on the edge of the desk with his khaki raincoat over his arm. Lev thought the article was incoherent and unoriginal, but he didn't want to be rude. He suggested a few changes. "I think you could specifically mention the traitor Dwight MacDonald's muddled article in *Partisan Review* when you argue that the standard Marxist categories apply to Hitler and that fascism is the most developed stage of capitalism."

Jacques got up from the desk and stood behind Lev as if he were reading over his shoulder.

"What are you doing?" Lev asked, wiping the sweat off his forehead without looking at Jacques. "Why don't you sit down? You're making me nervous."

"I'm just anxious to hear what you think."

"If you want me to read it," he said, tapping his fingers on the desk, "sit still."

Jacques did not sit down. He shifted his weight from one foot to the other.

"Damn it, what's wrong with you?"

Jacques' raincoat fell to the ground, and when Lev turned to see what he was doing, Jacques plunged a pick ax into the back of Lev's head. The Old Man shrieked, got up from his chair and tried to grab Jacques. Lev pulled him down to the floor, blood pouring from his wound onto Jacques' shirt and all over the magazines and newspapers piled on his desk. He stumbled out of his study and collapsed in the hall.

Natalia rushed to him, his face covered in blood, and screamed, "Mon dieu!"

"Jacques," he whispered.

Joe and Melquiades were still on the roof when they heard the screams. Melquiades grabbed his rifle and aimed it at the window of Lev's study, but Joe yelled, "Don't shoot, you could hit Lev!" Jumping down from the roof, Joe ran to the house. When he saw Lev on the floor, alive but badly wounded, he raced back up to the roof and shouted down to the police in the guard house, "Get an ambulance, hurry." Joe and Harold entered Lev's study. Chairs were overturned and broken, papers and books were scattered on the floorboards, the Ediphone was lying on the ground in pieces intermingled with the lenses of Lev's glasses and their twisted metal frame. Jacques was standing in the middle of the room in a daze, his arms at his side. Harold hit him in the head with the butt of his revolver. Jacques fell to the floor, yelling, "They made me do it!"

Joe grabbed the pistol out of Harold's hand. Then he noticed what he realized must have been the murder weapon—it looked like a prospector's pick. One end was pointed, while the other was flat and wide; the long wooden handle had been cut down so it could be concealed under Jacques' raincoat. The sight of the bloody pick sent Joe into a frenzy. He punched Jacques in the face and kicked him in the head. Jacques cried, "Kill me, kill me, I want to die!" Lev whispered, "Don't kill him, don't kill the Stalinist bastard! He must talk!"

1

Lilly lugged two shopping bags filled with condoms; Miriam carried a carton filled with pamphlets, *"What Every Woman Should Know."* They had picked them up from the contraception center at the Brownsville settlement house where they met as volunteers six months earlier. It was a gray early November morning in 1932—a few days before the election of Franklin Delano Roosevelt. A light wind wrinkled the puddles in the gutter as they walked along Pitkin Avenue in Brooklyn looking for a site to distribute their supplies. Lilly stopped for a moment to put on the gloves Mama had knitted for her. She inhaled the egg-rich aroma of fresh challah and the sweetness of pumpernickel with raisins that drifted onto the street from Bessie's bake shop.

"Come on already, Lilly," Miriam said over her shoulder. "It's heavy."

On the corner of Junius Street, a group of unemployed men argued, their voices rising above honking cars trying to pass the junkman's wagon. A young father cursed Hoover in Yiddish as he pushed his crying infant back and forth with intermittent "shushes"; a man with skin like a worn leather glove responded in Russian, waving his arms for emphasis. "You can live on this? It's nothing," a third man huffed. Lilly and Miriam knew they were referring to the city lowering public relief to $2.39 a week per family. They also knew they could no more put these men to work than make the sun shine on a cloudy day, but they could offer their wives a way to lessen their desperation over yet another mouth to feed.

Threading their way across Ralph Avenue, they took care not to step in the manure droppings from the iceman's horse. On the other side, they were greeted with the acrid smell of Sour Shlomo's cucumbers, green tomatoes and sauerkraut pickling in a big oak barrel. It competed with the dizzying odor from the shoemaker's shop.

"Wow, did you take a whiff of that?" Miriam said.

"Yes, it's heady stuff. What is it?" Lilly asked.

"Glue, I think, for attaching the soles on shoes. We can't stop here, I'll faint!"

They finally settled on a spot in front of Fat Gussie's Knishes. She made potato, kasha and cabbage knishes. The savory smell reminded Lilly of the first time Tateh took her to Fat Gussie's.

"Taste, bubeleh," her father had said, blowing on the knish, touching it to his lips to make sure it wasn't too hot for her and then kneeling down on the pavement to hold the knish close to her mouth. As she took a bite, she delighted in the moist, almost creamy texture of the cabbage inside the strudel dough crust.

Now Lilly noticed a group of men on the opposite corner, holding beat-up metal tool boxes. They ignored the stench of chicken feathers and the trickle of dark red that ran under their feet across the pavement from the kosher slaughterhouse behind them.

"What are those men doing?" Lilly knew she sounded like a little sister asking all these questions, but she liked the feeling of having an older sibling.

"I guess they're waiting for the boss contractors to drive by and pick their men for day work," Miriam responded.

Two years older, Miriam Fuchs was Lilly Abramovitz's mentor; she had already completed two years at Hunter College. Lilly had just finished Girls' High School in Brooklyn. While Lilly wore barrel curls, a common style for high school girls, Miriam wore her black hair Lillian Gish style with short, partially side swept bangs, and wavy tresses. She had a streak of premature gray in the front that made her look wise.

An emaciated young woman with a kerchief covering her hair, runs in her stockings and three small children in tow hurried by. Miriam touched her arm and the woman paused mid-stride. "You don't have to keep on having babies," Miriam said. "You can't breast feed forever, and it doesn't protect you very well from getting pregnant. Your husband can wear one of these."

The young mother bit the inside of her cheek, contorting her face, as Miriam opened a round tin of "Merry Widow Perfectos" showing her the three rubbers inside. A funny brand name for prophylactics, Lilly thought, as it was the women whose husbands were *alive* who really needed them. But Mrs. Rachman, the social worker at the center, a schoolmarmish-looking woman who one wouldn't expect to be handing out condoms, told the girls to offer the women the Widows and the men the Sheiks with the picture of a Lawrence of

2

Arabia look-alike on the front. Lilly thought it was demeaning to think working class people would be more willing to use rubbers because of the pictures on the tin, but she didn't argue.

"My Chaim won't use anything," the young mother said with a gap-toothed smile, shaking her head as if to say, *Are you kidding?*

"Well, there's something *you* can use," Miriam told the woman. "You don't have to convince him to use it—you can do it yourself. If you go to the center they will give you one and show you how to use it." Miriam smiled knowingly as she bent over to pull out a diaphragm from the bag of materials Mrs. Rachman had given them.

The young mother looked at Miriam and Lilly's hands and not finding rings, said in Yiddish, "*You're telling me what to do with my husband? My husband studies the Talmud, so don't tell me what I should do. You're not even married. What do you know about anything?*"

The young woman's venom made Lilly's cheeks burn. It was true. She didn't know what it was like to live with a man—especially one who expected sex, wouldn't use birth control and read Jewish texts all day instead of working. But she felt sure she was never going to be stuck with someone like that. She was going to have a career and travel, not answer to a man.

Lilly looked at Miriam and realized she was unfazed. Miriam was self-sufficient, confident—she had a part-time job as a hat checker at the Broadway Dance Casino in Manhattan on Friday and Saturday nights, while Lilly was getting an allowance from her father and being taken to shows in the City.

Miriam stood with her head slightly tilted under her wide-brimmed hat fashionably turned up in the front, her eyes fixed on the young woman. She nodded as if to say, *I know you're angry because you feel helpless and you're just taking it out on us.* Lilly knew what she was thinking because she'd heard Miriam say it about other defensive wives.

Suddenly an unkempt, bow-legged man stopped right in front of Miriam and put his wrinkled face within two inches of her nose. He had a tiny gray beard like the tuft of hair that dangles from the throat of a goat. His breath and clothing reeked of stale tobacco. He said in Yiddish, "*What do you know? You little pishers. Are you crazy?*"

The young mother used the distraction to walk away. She walked past the rack of colorful cotton house dresses in front of Fritzi's Fashions, heading down the street without a glance. She ignored the apricots, giant prunes, dates and walnuts displayed neatly in front of the nut and dried fruit store, and tugged the arms of her children when they reached out to touch them. "Hurry up, don't touch," Lilly heard her admonishing the children. Not much older than Miriam, this mother had three children. A wave of sadness washed over Lilly.

This emaciated woman was already poor and the more children she had, Lilly thought, the worse it would get. She probably had to use chicken necks and backs to make chicken soup for Shabbos dinner, while Mama used a whole soup chicken. The succulent meat fell off the bone and Mama threw the neck and back in the garbage with the rest of the bones. Lilly wanted to run after her and ask her address so she could bring her one of her Mama's challahs.

Miriam was still occupied by the hunched old man. *"A child's wisdom is also wisdom,"* Miriam said in Yiddish.

"A lie you must not tell; the truth you don't have to tell," the old man snorted with a smirk in his eyes. He waddled away with his arms held away from his body like Charlie Chaplin.

Miriam shrugged and mimicked Mrs. Rachman's tone as she said to Lilly, "Not everyone will want to be educated." Then she elbowed her and said, "Lilly, look, isn't that your father in front of the fish store?"

Indeed, there he was, Herschel Abramovitz, standing across the street with carp and whitefish wrapped in butcher paper for Mama's Friday night gefilte fish. Tateh's eyes were closed and he smiled, clearly enjoying the warmth of the spattered sunlight peeking through the clouds.

Miriam squinted, studying Herschel across the street. "Your father's so handsome—so American," she said. "He doesn't look like some immigrant straight off the boat."

Lilly was taken aback—he was her father, not some potential suitor for Miriam to gawk at! But then she realized Miriam was comparing him to her own father. Abraham Kaplan had never learned to speak English fluently. He had worked as a house painter, but chronic asthma had forced him to stop, so the family was on public relief. When Lilly visited the house, he sat in his paint encrusted

4

overalls, elbows on the kitchen table, a creased fan above his brow, reading the *Forward* and dunking *mandelbrot* in his tea. Tateh, on the other hand, wore a suit and tie and his dark brown hair was parted almost down the middle, just a little to the left of center, although it wasn't visible under his fedora. Clean shaven except for a mustache with a small handlebar, he had a prominent dimple in his chin. He walked with his shoulders pulled back and his chest out.

As Tateh stood in the sun in front of Epstein's fish store across Pitkin Avenue, he hummed his favorite tune:

> Life is just a bowl of cherries.
> Don't take it serious; it's too mysterious.
> You work, you save, you worry so,
> But you can't take your dough when you
> go, go, go.

Lilly knew he would eventually spot her, and as he turned with his package of fish, he saw them. His face turned red and his body stiffened. He was at once horrified and not surprised at the scene. There she was, his daughter, making a fool out of him in public. During their frequent arguments at home in the months since Lilly volunteered at the contraception center, he said this was the rent he paid for his financial success.

Tateh crossed Pitkin Avenue to greet them. "*Oy veh!*" he mumbled to himself as he darted between horse drawn carts, trolleys and cars.

Miriam laughed as she watched him dodge the vehicles and the horse droppings like a child playing hopscotch. She hummed: "It don't mean a thing if you ain't got that swing." But Lilly didn't think it was funny.

"Hi Tateh." Lilly smiled nervously, knowing full well her father was not going to be happy.

"Good morning Mr. Abramovitz," Miriam greeted him respectfully. Lilly stood silently biting her lip.

Tateh put his arms around Lilly hugging her close to him. She could feel his heart pumping and smell his Pinauld Lilac After-Shave. But as he released her, he shook his head in chagrin. "Oy, you're killing me with all this talk on the street. It's one thing to talk about it at home, but on the street? You think this is good? What if Zayde Shmuel had ever heard you ranting on the street like a *shiksa*?"

Miriam held her hand over her mouth trying to stifle a laugh; Lilly felt embarrassed and exposed as if Miriam had seen her underwear hanging on the clothesline.

"Margaret Sanger is a *shiksa*!" Lilly said.

When she was a young woman, Mama had helped Margaret Sanger open her first birth control clinic on Amboy Street. She understood that having so many children kept immigrant families poor and caused women to die young.

Lilly knew Tateh agreed with everything in the pamphlets. He was just ashamed of her talking about sex with strangers on the street— it was a *shanda*.

"Who are you to tell married people how many children they should or shouldn't have?" Tateh asked.

"What about Grandma? If she used birth control she'd still be here," Lilly said, her hand on her hip.

"*An example is no proof*," Tateh snorted in Yiddish.

"I'm not telling people how many children to have; I'm just helping women decide how many children they *want* to have." For Lilly it was as simple as the difference between kosher and *traif*.

"*Bubeleh*," he said with his hand over his mouth so that Miriam wouldn't hear, "a man works all day and what he does when he comes home is none of your business."

Fat Gussie, wearing a stained apron that barely tied around her hefty breasts and considerable belly, was sweeping the street in front of her store and stopped to watch the interchange. With a pouting lower lip and her chubby fingers splayed around the broom stick she glared.

Tateh's face lost its color. He bit his lip. Miriam, and now Gussie, overheard them and they were not family.

"That's the whole point," Lilly said. "They can still have sex," she said in a whisper. "It just doesn't have to lead to more children."

Tateh put one hand in his pocket, shifted his weight from one foot to the other and shook his head incredulously.

"You always say I should fight for what I believe in," Lilly said scowling.

"*A good name,*" he said in Yiddish with one eyebrow raised, "*is better than a precious stone.*"

6

"So you agree with me, but you're embarrassed that people will see Herschel Abramovitz's daughter on the street talking to women about sex?"

As soon as the words were out, Lilly felt guilty for publicly admonishing her father. She put her arms around him and kissed his cheek, but he didn't kiss her back. He shook his head, shoulders rounded, turned and walked away without saying goodbye.

Watching him go, a tear meandered down her face. What she was doing was important—why couldn't he see that?

"You know Wollstonecraft, long before Emma Goldman, said that marriage is another form of slavery," Miriam said. Lilly was surprised, but then realized she was trying to change the subject because Lilly was upset. "The man owns you, you even take his name like the slaves took the name of their masters," Miriam said.

"But my parents aren't like that," Lilly said. She knew their marriage was strong.

"Your mother is lucky, she seems to love your father and he's nice to her. But she couldn't support herself without him. I don't want to depend on a man that way. I want to have a career and only marry a man because I love him. Or maybe I'll be like Emma Goldman and never marry at all."

"What about your parents?" Lilly asked.

"Mama is stuck with my father; she never loved him," Miriam said. "They were matched in Kishniev, but she can't leave him." She rubbed her eye and her eyeliner smudged. "Especially now, when he can't take care of himself." She looked away for a moment and the energy seemed to seep out of her. "At least she can do piece work. But it's not about love. It's about obligation. I don't think they've had sex for years—who would want to have sex with him?" She made a face. Then she smiled and said in Yiddish, *"The clothes make the man."* They both laughed. "By the way," she continued, "how did your father get so rich?"

Lilly was embarrassed and taken aback by the directness of Miriam's question. She had been reluctant to invite Miriam to her house at first because she didn't want her to think her father was a rich gangster like Meyer Lansky.

"He owns places," Lilly said softly, hoping Miriam couldn't hear her. But she did. Lilly felt the muscles in the sides of her neck tighten.

"When did he get here? My parents got here in 1903, after the pogrom."

Every Jew knew about the Kishniev pogrom. A Christian child was murdered and the newspapers claimed it was a ritual killing by the Jews. More than a hundred Jews were slaughtered and many times that were injured. The mobs burned their houses and looted their businesses. Miriam's parents were smart to leave because no Jew could be safe there again.

"He was sent away by his parents when he was 15," Lilly said, "so he could escape service in the Russian army. My mother says he still feels like a tree that was torn from its roots."

Miriam pulled a tube from her bag and refreshed her lipstick. She was practiced at it; she didn't need a mirror.

"So how did he get so rich?" Miriam asked. "Do you think he felt guilty making so much money when his poor parents were still in the old country?"

There was a commotion as working men lined up in front of Gussie's to buy knishes for lunch and stood around eating them. Lilly was relieved when a young man with curly hair and a tan cap looked at her and asked, "Do you have any Trojans?" He munched on his knish out of a brown paper bag. There were dark spots where the grease had dripped. He smiled and bits of potato peeked out of his teeth. "Rubbers cost a fortune in the drug store, so I'd love to have a few." He had deep dimples and big blue eyes.

Lilly was flattered that he directed the question to her rather than Miriam. Lilly felt that boys looked past her as if she were invisible when Miriam was around—except for Howie, the City College boy Lilly had met at the settlement house. Lilly's face felt hot. Looking down at the bag, she said, "We don't have Trojans, but we have Sheiks. The social worker at the center says they're just as good and a lot cheaper. She says it's just a capitalist marketing ploy to sell Trojans in pharmacies and charge more."

He licked his fingers and wiped them on his workpants before taking the tin with the picture of an Arab on horseback that Lilly offered. His nails were bitten and he had a crooked knuckle. Lilly

8

imagined he broke it at work and never went to the doctor to have it set because he didn't want to take time off from work. "It's tough to dole out money for rubbers. Who's got extra money for that? So thanks," he said taking the tin.

When the young man walked away, Lilly returned to the conversation with Miriam. "A lot of the boys never came back from the Czar's army," she said.

Miriam still didn't look convinced, so Lilly kept trying.

"My mother said some parents cut off their sons' index fingers so they couldn't serve—you can't shoot a gun without one. Bubby and Zayde Itzhak couldn't bring themselves to do that. Tateh sends them money, but he doesn't really know how they are. Mama says it's a thorn in his heart."

"So he got rich like the German Jews on the Upper East Side," Miriam scoffed. Lilly usually admired Miriam for her nerve, but she didn't appreciate her pushy questions.

"No, not that rich," Lilly whispered. But then she thought about how many German Jews lost their money in the crash and smiled to herself. Tateh had stayed out of the stock market; he kept his money under the mattress.

2

Like most Jews in Brownsville, Herschel Abramovitz was sympathetic to the Bolshevik Revolution. His parents had sent him away to protect him from having to serve in the Russian army for 25 years under the Czar's Cantonist Decrees.

Tateh had told Lilly the story of leaving Russia many times. Sometimes it was before she went to bed, instead of Grimm's fairy tales; other times it was while he was weeding the garden.

"Tateh, how did you get here?" Lilly asked.

"It was a long journey," he always replied. "My mother packed a bag with bread, cheese and apples for the trip to the German border."

Although Lilly had heard the story many times, her eyes always teared as she imagined the anguish Bubby must have felt saying goodbye to her 15-year-old only son knowing she would never see him again.

"What did your father give you?" Lilly asked.

"He gave me 70 rubles to pay for bribes, the train and the ship," he continued. "My berth was an iron bunk with a mattress of straw and no pillow."

"That must have been uncomfortable," Lilly offered.

"That wasn't even the worst of it. The floors were wood and sprinkled with sand to absorb vomit. There were only two washrooms and the men and women shared. There was a small sink."

"How long did it take?"

"It took 12 days and each day the filth got worse. The ship docked at the East River pier and the first and second class passengers got off. But my group wasn't allowed. We were taken to Ellis Island for a medical inspection." He smirked and added, "They assumed if you had enough money to buy a first or second class ticket you didn't have consumption."

Tateh supported the communists' triumph in Russia, but used Marx as a primer on capitalism in Brownsville: he bought low and sold high; he reinvested his profits to build tenements; and he extracted surplus value by becoming a landlord. Marx didn't turn Herschel into a revolutionary, but rather a more efficient capitalist. He had bought two pieces of land on the north side of Pitkin Avenue for $50 each because he suspected the Williamsburg Bridge, when it was completed, would transform property values and he was right. They could afford to leave Brownsville.

The new house was a brick and stone Queen Anne on William Street in Brooklyn Heights with bay windows and gables on the outside and fireplaces in the living and dining rooms. The first time Mama saw it, she gasped at the architectural details: chestnut floors, multi-tiered molding, and raised panel wainscoting beneath the chair rails in the dining room. She was delighted by the crystal knob at the bottom of the staircase railing and the original Tiffany stained glass chandelier with pink flowers and green leaves. Lilly thought it was too precious, but despite her communist sympathies, Mama appreciated the finer things in life.

One morning as drowsy sun seeped through the window and steam hissed from the radiator, Mama put on her reading glasses and spread out the pages of the *Brooklyn Eagle*, March 1, 1933. Her right arm was covered with a greenish- tinged white cloud from her fingers to her elbow. It had been seared on her skin in the fire that ravaged the factory she had worked in as a girl. She sat in her bathrobe, fresh from her usual cold shower (she says it reminds her of who she is) and read out loud: "Rivera is the most talked about artist on this side of the Atlantic."

Tateh came in from the backyard. Before breakfast, no matter what time of year, he liked to take his glass of tea and sit in his garden. He loved the lobed leaves of the fig tree and the bronze fruit that dropped into the garden all summer long; he carefully wrapped the tree in burlap each winter just as the Italian bootlegger who had previously owned the house had instructed.

"Rivera's political ideas are more revolutionary than his artistic ones," Tateh said as he sat down next to Mama, rubbing his new brown cardigan sweater against her arm. "What's so revolutionary? His murals are just big paintings with pictures all over the place. What's the big deal?" He pointed to the two Chagalls hanging on the wall: "The Green Violinist" and "Paris Through the Window." Tateh had bought the paintings at the Reinhardt Gallery when Lilly was a little girl. He said, "Those are revolutionary paintings!"

He loved Chagall's painting because Tateh remembered when Chagall was Moishe Segal, one of nine children, son of a herring

11

merchant. They went to the same school and Tateh was in the same class as Chagall/Segal's brother Itzhak. Tateh said the figure of the violinist with a green face and purple coat dancing in a rustic village of wooden houses reminded him of his childhood in Belarus.

"I can still smell the cow dung in the pasture and see the steam rising from a new bucket of milk. You had to use two hands like this," he gestured with his thumb and forefinger as if he was grasping two teats, "and you squeeze down." Tateh took a deep breath and smiled.

Lilly loved the Chagall paintings as much as Tateh did. They were poetic. They affirmed man's potential to soar above everyday reality—but she still wanted to see Diego Rivera's show. He had given a talk at the John Reed Club before Lilly and Howie started going to lectures there and many members were still arguing about it. Some people thought he shouldn't have been invited to a Communist club because he painted murals for the San Francisco Stock Exchange. But Lilly didn't care. She thought he was true to his principles because he always painted what he believed, no matter who paid him for it.

"Tateh," Lilly said, "Chagall idealizes village life, while everything I've read about Rivera says he focuses on the hardships of everyday life in Mexico—the exploitation of the peasants."

"Maybe the subject is revolution, but it's not revolutionary art," Tateh insisted with furrowed brows, tapping his fingers on the table.

"Hershey, you're wrong," Mama chimed in, agreeing with Lilly. "The *Tribune* reviewer said it's not just the subject, it's the technique."

She took off her glasses and looked Tateh directly in the eyes. "Rivera insisted that the admission fee for the first two days go for emergency unemployment relief. That's enough reason to go." Tateh's success had changed her lifestyle, but not her thinking. "So let's go to the city and see the exhibit."

Little Sol came running into the dining room at the mention of the City. Lilly and her younger sister Gertie called him "Little Sol," because he was five years younger than Gertie and the sisters had treated him like a plaything when he was born. Now he was ten years old and almost as tall as Gertie, but they still referred to him as "Little Sol."

"I want to go to the top of the Empire State Building!" He had a poster of it on the wall of his bedroom and he'd been pleading with Tateh to take him to see it for months.

"Okay, okay. We can all go and we'll do both," Tateh said.

*   *   *

Surfacing from the dark subway to the bright morning light, Tateh, Mama, Lilly, Gertie and Sol stood at Herald Square, transfixed by the sight of the limestone giant—it overshadowed every other structure in the area. The reflection of sunlight off the building was dazzling. Tateh, Mama, Gertie and Sol couldn't get their eyes off the tower. Lilly had seen it in all its stages of progress on her way up to City College to see Howie and his friends.

"God in Heaven, look at that," Tateh said, his hands on his cheeks.

Sol's rubicund face was aglow.

People pushed past as they hurried across the street to join the line in front of Macy's—waiting to rush in when the doors opened at 10 A.M. Trolleys clanged and cars beeped their horns.

Tateh stood with his chest out and chin held high: a family trip to the city was a big event. Gertie wore a wool jacket that covered the top of the navy skirt that Mama had sewn for her—a little longer in the back than front with pleats below the knee.

Gertie had beautiful green eyes, but the pupil of her left eye was smaller than the right. Although she was able to read and function normally, her depth perception was impaired.

Mama smiled at Gertie who wore a new outfit of Mama's making. She had been a dressmaker before Lilly was born. She no longer had to sit at a sewing machine all day, but in the evenings sometimes the children could still hear the treadle banging against the wooden floor when she was mending Solly's pants or making Gertie or Lilly a skirt from a pattern in *Good Housekeeping*.

Sol was dressed up in his good slacks and new brown jacket, and Lilly was wearing her usual combination—a black skirt and sweater.

Sol skipped ahead and Tateh ran after him, while Mama, Gertie and Lilly walked slowly from Broadway to Fifth Avenue looking in every window, enjoying the winter sunshine. When they got to Fifth Avenue, they stopped to look in the windows at B. Altman's.

"For heaven's sake, the store looks more like a palace," Gertie said, breathless.

"Fifth Avenue used to be like Park." Mama pointed toward the blocks north of 34th Street. "And they didn't want a retail store here, so Altman built a store that didn't look like a store so they wouldn't give him trouble."

Sol appeared at Mama's side and pulled at her coat sleeve trying to get her to stop talking and move on.

"Vanderbilt's mansion's on 51st," Tateh said, "and he didn't want some Jew from the Lower East Side building a store here."

Looking up Fifth Avenue, Gertie asked, "Why are so many of those mansions boarded up?"

Lilly thought it was pretty obvious. The President just closed all the banks.

"The crash, they lost their money," Tateh said. He took Mama's hand and added in Yiddish, *From fortune to misfortune is a short step; from misfortune to fortune is a long way.*

Lilly remembered Miriam's questions about how her father got rich—comparing him to the German Jews on the Upper East Side. The way Tateh responded to Gertie made her realize how lucky he felt.

"They made their money by exploiting working people and now their beloved capitalism has destroyed them. Good," Mama said, nodding her head.

Lilly put her arm on Mama's shoulder and kissed her cheek. She was such a mixed package, her mother. She belonged to the Brownsville Unemployed Council on Stone Avenue and had worked on two campaigns for Socialist and American Labor Party state assembly candidates, but she voted for Roosevelt. A few years before she had helped organize an all-women's meat strike because kosher butchers' prices were much too high. But she looked like Greta Garbo with her silver fox collar and moss green felt hat tilted to one side exposing her finger waves and pearl earrings. Her bitterness at capitalists had been burned into her consciousness. Before she married Herschel, she had worked at a shirtwaist factory. The story was one of the family's grim tales. Yetta, the bookkeeper on the 8th floor, was Mama's best friend and she called up to the 10th floor to warn everyone. When Mama

14

picked up the phone Yetta screamed: "Get out! Fire! Get out!" Mama got out, but Yetta and 144 others died that March day of 1911 at the Triangle Shirtwaist factory.

The sun receded behind a cloud as the family made their way through the masses waiting to enter the cavernous three-story marble lobby of the Empire State Building. Sol, Gertie and Tateh gasped at the grand space. Mama was silent as she looked around and Lilly imagined they were both thinking the same thing: *Capitalists are willing to spend millions on a stupid lobby, but they lock fire doors to make sure their workers don't take unauthorized breaks to go to the bathroom.*

They walked to one of the 73 elevators—an express to the 86th floor observatory. People were pushing, so Tateh took Sol's hand and Mama wedged herself in a corner of the elevator. Gertie and Lilly faced each other, sandwiched between two obese women. Lilly felt the pressure of large breasts on her back and Gertie's flat chest in front. She reached out to find one of her mother's cold sweaty hands. Mama's face was white and her forehead was dripping with sweat. She had had attacks before on crowded elevators. When the elevator door opened and they were set free, the color returned to Mama's face and she smiled as they looked out the large windows at the East River sparkling in the sunlight. The bridges to Brooklyn looked like constructs from Sol's Erector Set, and then, just a little to the right, stood Lady Liberty in New York Harbor.

"There's Ellis Island," Tateh said pointing.

"First stop in the golden country." Mama leaned over and kissed him on the cheek. The terror had receded.

"What's this building for?" Sol asked.

"Offices," Tateh answered. "They rent out the office space. But their timing wasn't very good. Most of it's empty."

When they left the Empire State Building, they continued walking up Fifth Avenue to 40th Street passing the Public Library where Sol ran off up the steps toward the marble lions. They headed over to Sixth Avenue to see the new Radio City Music Hall—the first part of the planned "Rockefeller Center." They had been reading about it for almost two years—6,000 seats and the largest pipe organ anywhere. They walked into the ornate rococo Grand Foyer to see the three-story high mirrors, miles of red and orange carpeting, huge glass cylinder chandeliers and the giant red and yellow "Fountain of Youth"

15

mural. Lilly thought it was obscene. In the middle of the Depression, with people all over the United States living in tent camps and shack towns, the Rockefellers had spent more money on this monstrosity than it would cost to solve the national housing crisis.

"The Rockefellers seem to be alive and well," Lilly muttered as they left the Music Hall.

"That's for sure," Mama smirked.

"Even Rockefeller is having hard times," Tateh chided. "He bought all this land to build a new Metropolitan Opera and they decided not to do it. So Rockefeller has troubles with tenants, too." He laughed. "They say he lost half his fortune in the crash," he said more seriously.

"Who cares?" Lilly groaned. "I should feel sorry for Rockefeller?"

Mama elbowed her as if to say, *Don't be rude to your father.* But Lilly knew she agreed with her.

When they finally got to the Museum of Modern Art, Lilly stood swooning in front of Rivera's "May Day in Moscow." The movement of the people seemed rhythmic and elastic like a group of people doing a synchronized dance.

"I don't get it," Gertie said, tilting her head a bit as if she wanted to make sure there wasn't something in the painting she wasn't seeing. "And what does this one have to do with Communism?" Gertie asked casually pointing to "Flower Festival: Feast of Santa Anita,"— which depicted a flower festival held on Good Friday.

Lilly knew that Gertie was more interested in Frida Kahlo than Diego. Lilly thought she identified with Frida because she too was damaged—badly injured in a bus accident. Gertie had a print of Frida's "Self Portrait in a Velvet Dress" hanging on her side of their bedroom.

"It's a glorification of the common people," Mama said fingering the pearl necklace that Tateh had bought her for her last birthday.

"But they're just peasants having fun," Gertie said.

"What do you know, you're half blind," Lilly blurted.

"Lilly, don't you dare speak to your sister like that." Mama glared at Lilly, her face burning.

"I'm just asking a question, you don't have to get nasty. And it's a religious holiday—not very communist is it?" Gertie said.

"That's right," Mama said sternly. "Lilly, it's good for Gertie to think about what she's seeing."

Gertie wasn't usually confrontational, but with Mama clearly on her side she put her hands on her hips and said, "Cezanne painted peasants playing cards. So don't tell me painting peasants *has* to be revolutionary."

Mama took Gertie's hand and walked over to "Indian Warrior." Lilly was pricked by her harsh glance as she looked back at her. Mama pointed to the painting and said to Gertie, "This one's about Mexican history—the Aztec warrior wearing the costume is stabbing the conquistador in the throat with a stone knife," she said.

Watching Mama patiently explaining to Gertie why Diego's work was revolutionary made Lilly angry. What kind of a communist was Mama anyway? With her fancy pearls? But as she watched Gertie take in the painting, when her head tilted to one side, Lilly was filled with remorse. She was ashamed of herself for saying Gertie was half blind. She remembered when Gertie came home from the emergency room with her eye bandaged and stumbled over the coffee table in the living room because she wasn't used to seeing with one eye. For months, every time Lilly lay in the bathtub she covered one eye to experience Gertie's way of seeing.

She remembered seeing Gertie's eye when Mama took the bandage off. The area around her eye was dark purple and her lid was swollen closed. Mama had cried, but Lilly was relieved. She had been afraid to see how the eye was going to look. She imagined an empty socket or a white glaze. In a few days the swelling had gone down: Gertie opened her eye and it was completely bloodshot. Lilly tried not to look at it. After two weeks the white of her eye was visible again, although bloodshot, but the iris looked different—a lighter shade of green. And when Gertie looked at you—it was blank.

Tateh must have noticed Lilly's drooped shoulders. He put his arms around her, kissed the top of her forehead and said, "You have to be careful not to let ideas become more important than people."

*   *   *

When she fell asleep that night, Lilly dreamed that she and Gertie were sitting on the stoop in Brownsville. *It was a warm, sunny day and a group of Irish boys from the local Catholic school were laughing and jostling each other as they walked down the street. As they got closer to the sisters, one of them, a tall skinny boy with curly black hair, pointed to them and said, "Look at the two little Jewish girls." Lilly's back stiffened and she moved closer to Gertie. His friend, a short redhead with freckles, wearing knickers, yelled, "The Jews killed Christ" and threw a bottle toward the girls. They all laughed and yelled, "Dirty Jews" as they ran away. The bottle hit the top edge of the step just beneath the girls. Lilly closed her eyes and tasted root beer as the glass shards smashed into their faces with the force of a breaking wave. Gertie screamed. Lilly thought it was from shock. There was soda all over. Lilly was about to pick the pieces of glass off her skirt and blouse when she looked at Gertie. Blood splattered on her white sweater; it was flowing down her cheek. She held her eye and shrieked, "Mama!"*

Lilly woke up startled—as she always did when she had this dream.

*   *   *

Two months later, Lilly walked into the dining room where Tateh sat at the table reading the *Herald Tribune*. "It's so ridiculous," he said, taking off his reading glasses, but still holding the paper in one hand and his glass of tea in the other.

Lilly sat across from him with the silver urn-shaped samovar in the center of the table between them. "What do you mean, Tateh?" Lilly asked, rubbing her sleepy eyes.

He lisped a little because he had a sugar cube between his teeth as he sipped his tea, but he summarized the story. "Rivera decided to change the design the Rockefellers had approved and put Lenin's face in it and Nelson Rockefeller asked him to take it out. Rivera refused to compromise and was dismissed. Now he's saying the cancellation of the mural is 'cultural vandalism.'"

The sleepiness drained out of Lilly like water from a cracked pitcher. "How can they do that?"

"It's a commissioned work—they already agreed on it. They're paying Diego to do it. He can't do whatever he wants," Tateh said.

"He's a man of principle; he won't give in to Rockefeller or Stalin." Lilly stiffened up in her chair. This was precisely why she'd disagreed with the people at the John Reed Club who had criticized

Diego. He was willing to work for capitalists and take their money, but he refused to compromise about what he painted.

"Rubbish! He's a communist who makes a fortune selling his art to capitalists. What's the principle?" He tapped his glass with his fingers.

"Talk about principles! You extol Marx and own tenements."

Last year when Lilly had joined Tateh on his rent collection rounds, she stood next to him in the hallway with a metal cash box as he knocked on each door. Nausea overcame her as the combined stench of feces emanating from the communal bathroom and *Shabbos* chicken soup wafted from the apartments. She couldn't forget the stench for days afterward.

"It stinks in here," Tateh had said. "It costs me a fortune to have plumbers in here every other day because they stuff the toilet. They don't care. Four families share the bathroom and no one takes responsibility for cleaning the toilet or the floor. The cleaning lady comes once a week, but in-between they won't touch it."

"You own it and make a profit, isn't it your responsibility?"

"I own it, but they live here and they don't have to live like animals."

Mrs. Cohen, a short buxom woman with a mustache and curly hairs on her chin had answered after Tateh banged on her door for five minutes and called out her name. Who else would be knocking on her door on the 30th of the month just before Shabbos? She finally opened the door. She stood before them dressed in a pink flowered *shmata*. "Mr. Abramovitz, take pity on us; my Moishe lost his job and my little one is sick," she said.

"Mrs. Cohen, I'm so sorry for your troubles. But I can only wait another week. After all I have my own bills to pay."

"You're a good man Mr. Abramovitz. I understand."

Tateh had turned to walk down the steps and whispered to Lilly, "She's a nice woman." He added in Yiddish, "*Gold glitters even in the mud.*" Lilly had stayed silent, but she felt her heart break for Mrs. Cohen.

Now he was sitting in the dining room criticizing Diego for being a hypocrite.

"Your tenants lose their jobs and you evict them—a real man of the people," Lilly shouted. She couldn't hide the contempt in her voice.

19

Mama walked into the dining room wiping her hands on a towel. "What's going on?" she said. She took Tateh's hand. "That's enough. He does his best," she said to Lilly, "but he has to pay the mortgage on the property or he'll lose it." For emphasis, she added in Yiddish, *"She who keeps quiet is half a fool; she who speaks is a whole fool."*

Why was Mama defending him? She was a communist. She didn't believe in private property owners extracting profit from their tenants. Lilly got up from the table and retreated to the room she shared with Gertie. There were two single beds in the room separated by a small table with an RCA Victor Victrola record player that Tateh had bought Lilly for her 16th birthday as soon as it was in the stores. She put on "Minnie the Moocher" and sat on her bed Indian style, twirling the ends of her hair. It soothed her like sucking her thumb or lying on her mother's lap once did. Angry tears rolled down her face.

Mama knocked on the door.

"Come in," Lilly said grudgingly.

She ignored Lilly's unmade bed and the newspapers strewn all over it and kissed her hair. "Your father loves you. Why do you make such a big deal about everything with him?"

"Mama, I don't understand you. How do you live with him? He's a landlord!"

Mama sat next to Lilly, put her arms around her, and pulled her close. Lilly could smell her Jean Nate bath oil. Lilly's face rested on top of her mother's breast. It was warm and soft.

"Shh…It's not so simple," Mama said. "Your father is a good man and he has to make a living. He loves us and wants to take care of us. He's not a factory owner making people work until they drop. He's not Rockefeller. What would it solve if he didn't collect rent and couldn't pay the mortgage? Would other people live better? "

"But Mama, look how we live compared to so many other people—the jewelry you wear and your fur coat. Don't you feel guilty? What about all those poor people?"

"No, Lilly, I don't feel guilty. We do what we can. You know when I first met your father, he had nothing—no family, no money, *bupkis*. He saved every penny he made in the factory and invested in property. He didn't hurt anyone. And he gives charity for the poor every Friday night in synagogue."

20

Mama got up from the bed and put her hand out for Lilly to take. Lilly took her mother's hand and stood up. She was already a few inches taller than Mama.

Mama put her hand on Lilly's shoulder as she opened the door. Lilly could hear Westbrook Van Voorhis' "Voice of Doom" on the radio. "So what's on 'The March of Time'?" Lilly asked as they walked into the kitchen.

"Al Capone went to prison," Sol reported pumping his fist.

Tateh looked up at Lilly tentatively. "So?" he said. He wrinkled his eyebrows.

"So I still love you even though you're a capitalist." She walked over to the kitchen table and kissed him on the top of his head.

*   *   *

Later that night, when Lilly's anger at Tateh had fully receded like the low tide, Gertie and Lilly withdrew to the room they shared.

They lay on their twin beds on their green and yellow quilts that matched the cotton curtains Mama had sewn for them. They were pinch pleated with bouquets of yellow roses and green leaves. Gertie was reading Alfred Adler's *Neurotic Character*. She was always reading psychology books, as if there was something she was trying to figure out about herself and she wouldn't be satisfied until she found it. Lilly was engrossed in Emma Goldman's autobiography and was up to the part about Goldman and Alexander Berkman in March 1921 trying unsuccessfully to mediate between the Kronstadt sailors and the Communist government. Imagine, Lilly smiled, two lovers trying to stop a massacre, united in their willingness to stand up for the sailors. She sighed, picturing herself and Howie with bullhorns shouting to the Soviet troops, "The sailors are peaceful!"

Gertie put her book down. "You know what I really admire about Alfred Adler? He had rickets as a kid and didn't walk until he was almost four. Can you imagine how horrible that must have made him feel about himself? And at five he developed pneumonia and wasn't expected to survive."

More tales of the sick and maimed, Lilly thought. Next to her Kahlo, Gertie had a depressing Van Gogh print hanging, "Self Portrait with a Bandaged Ear." Gertie said he must have been looking in the mirror while he painted it.

21

"And Lilly, he talks about the importance of birth order on psychological make-up. He thinks the firstborn child is loved and nurtured by the family until the arrival of a second child. The second child makes the first born feel dethroned, no longer the center of attention and…"

"Wait a minute," Lilly interrupted, realizing that this was going in an entirely different direction than she'd expected. She threw her pillow at Gertie. "I didn't feel dethroned when you were born. I was excited. I wanted to hold you."

"Also," Gertie continued, ignoring Lilly, "he says the older child feels excessive responsibility for the younger ones."

"That's ridiculous, I never felt responsible for you and Solly. I helped Mama take care of you, but I was just helping." Lilly felt a pang of guilt. She remembered the two of them sitting on the stoop that day, the soda bottle crashing. Remorse washed over her. *Maybe I didn't feel responsible enough for her; I should have protected her.*

"And the loss of the pampered position makes the older child neurotic." Gertie folded her arms across her chest and smiled.

"I'm not neurotic." Lilly felt her lower lip curling into a pout.

"Youngest children, Adler says, tend to be overindulged, especially if they're a different gender than the older siblings. It leads to poor social empathy. See I always tell Mama she's pampering Sol."

It was too soon, Lilly silently retorted, to tell about Sol's social empathy.

"But," Gertie continued, "it's the middle child, who experienced neither dethronement nor overindulgence, who's most likely to develop into a successful individual."

"Well now, I certainly understand why you like Adler," Lilly joked and threw her other pillow at her sister. Gertie tossed it back.

"I think we already have proof that he's right!" she said grinning.

3

Lilly and Miriam walked from the subway to the uptown City College campus, as they did once or twice a week when they visited Lilly's boyfriend Howie Freedman and his friends. Lilly and Miriam had both met him at the settlement house where he tutored non-English speaking children to supplement his widowed mother's salary as a sewing machine operator.

The door of Ender's delicatessen on Amsterdam Avenue and 140th Street was open on this bright October day and Lilly smelled Jewish ambrosia: franks sweating on the grill next to potato knishes; the briny smell of barrels of sauerkraut; and the smoke and pepper aroma of steaming hot pastrami. Miriam tugged Lilly's arm trying to get her to move on, but Lilly couldn't resist the temptation of a roast beef sandwich and a Dr. Brown's cream soda. Mr. Ender cooked the roast beef exactly the way she liked it, medium rare. Lilly ordered it sliced paper thin with a half-sour pickle.

Mr. Ender turned to Miriam and said, "And you pretty girl, what would you like?"

"Nothing for me, thank you," Miriam replied.

While they waited at the counter for Lilly's sandwich, Miriam asked, "What's wrong with you? Why don't you bring a sandwich from home like everyone else?"

"I don't want to stink from canned sardines and onions all day, like you," Lilly replied, sticking her tongue out at Miriam with a smile.

Miriam smiled back, rolling her eyes. Then her face grew more serious and she said, "You're like Daisy Buchanan. Your voice is full of money. But at least she didn't claim to be a communist."

Stabbed in the heart, Lilly stared at Miriam and turned to leave the delicatessen. She lagged a few steps behind Miriam with her sandwich and soda as they crossed the street to Shepard Hall, the Gothic style main building of City College, and then walked downstairs to the immense cafeteria.

Lilly had wanted to go to City College with Howie, but it was an all-male campus. Miriam went to Hunter College. She said it was ridiculous for Lilly to pay tuition at a private university when she could go to Hunter for free. But Lilly wanted to go to a co-ed school and she didn't want to commute from Brooklyn to the Bronx three or four times a week. Downtown City was closer, on East 23rd Street, but it was a business school. She thought of going to Brooklyn College which had just opened on Court Street a few blocks from her house, but Tateh said Brooklyn was too new—it didn't have the facilities or the variety of course offerings of the other colleges. Lilly became excited about NYU because Howie and a few of the boys she knew from uptown City had been auditing Sidney Hook's classes on Marxism and sometimes she joined them. Tateh said, "What's money for? Go to NYU. You get what you pay for."

Lilly loved walking through the cobblestone street of the Mews between Fifth Avenue and University Place lined by quaint artists' studios that had been converted from stables. Occasionally she saw Gertrude Vanderbilt Whitney or one of the other artists in their paint or clay splattered overalls taking a cigarette break. Walking past their studios and occasionally stopping to chat with one of the artists made Lilly feel like she was at the center of Bohemian life. But she still enjoyed taking the train up to City to visit Howie.

Lilly and Miriam walked over to the boys at their usual spot in the cafeteria.

"Hi, Miriam," Mooch said, "how's life at Hunter?"

"Not bad."

"Mooch's" real name was Joey Rosen, but the boys at City called him Mooch because he was always bumming cigarettes from the other boys. It wasn't that he couldn't afford them, he was just cheap. His father worked for the Hunter coal company on Flatbush Avenue and people needed fuel no matter how bad things were. Skinny but electric he was, as Tateh said when he met him once: "twenty pounds of life in a ten pound bag."

Lilly was distracted by a plump cockroach making its way from the stained wall to the low ceiling.

"Who's going to be the new President of Hunter?" Mooch asked.

"Not a woman," Miriam said. "That's all that's certain,"

Lilly smirked and nodded her head, trying to ignore the roach.

Tapping his foot nervously and turning to Lilly, he said, "So what's in the bag, Lilly? Are you collecting rent for your father?"

All the boys laughed.

24

Miriam was right. The boys always made fun of her capitalist father, and it hurt every time. Howie put his arm around Lilly's shoulder and pressed her close to him. She felt protected the way she did when she was a little girl and Tateh picked her up and carried her across the trolley tracks or when they walked through a bad neighborhood.

"Leave her alone," Howie said leaning his chin on the top of her hair, "Lilly has nothing to be ashamed of." He smelled of peanut butter. Howie always packed peanut butter and jelly.

"Come on Lilly, what's in the bag? Is it from the deli?" Butcher asked, his cheeks red with anticipation. Arnie Glantz was called "Butcher," because before and after school he stood in a shop among the aproned butchers, slapping thick chops on heavy sheets of brown paper with blood dripping onto the saw dust floor. Tall and stocky with rebellious hair that refused to stay in place no matter how much pomade he put on it, he was a powerful handball and paddle tennis player. But he didn't have much time to play since his father had lost his job driving a wagon for a fruit and vegetable distributor and the family counted on the money and meat that Butcher brought home. Kosher salami was his standard sandwich—probably because he got it free. But it made him smell of garlic.

"Did you listen to the Yankees murdering the Senators?" Mooch asked Butcher. He took a bite of the deli sandwich and licked some mustard off his finger.

"I didn't have time to listen to the game," Butcher said, "but I heard there was a brawl between Ben Chapman and Buddy Meyer."

"Chapman spiked Meyer sliding into second and Meyer went nuts," Mooch said.

He was finished with the roast beef and struggled with the egg salad that kept falling out of the pumpernickel bread. Specks of green olives and bits of pimento fell on his shirt.

"The Senators were already getting killed and I guess he felt enough was enough. All the fans got into the brawl. They came running on to the field. It was great."

"What's so great about it?" Lilly asked.

"Yeah," Miriam seconded her, "you're supposed to be a Marxist and you're gloating over the working class fans beating each other up over some stupid play."

Mooch was briefly quiet, folded his mouth as if deep in thought and then, completely ignoring Miriam, said, "Mel Ott is going to get the pennant for the Giants, mark my word."

"It's true, Mel Ott is good," Howie said. "But, come on Mooch, the Giants were in 6th place last year. They lost ten more games than they won. Anyway, Lefty O'Doul is batting .368 for the Dodgers. So much for Mel Ott." He smiled triumphantly and bent down to tie his shoe lace.

"Howie, you're such a schmuck…It's as plain as the nose on your face," Mooch laughed, pushing Howie playfully as he tied his lace. "You saw what the Giants did to the Dodgers a couple of weeks ago."

Lilly remembered the game at the Polo Grounds when Mel Ott hit a home run into the right field bleachers near where she, Mooch and Howie were sitting and the Giants crushed the Dodgers 8-2. Being a Dodger fan like Howie, Lilly wanted to forget it.

Just then a dark haired, Italian-looking girl with large breasts passed by and Mooch stopped chewing and gaped at her.

"*If you're going to eat pork, let it be good and fat,*" Mooch said under his breath in Yiddish. The boys laughed and Miriam and Lilly rolled their eyes.

"My mother's worried that I have a crush on that Italian girl who lives in our building," Mooch said.

"Well, do you?" Lilly asked.

"Kind of…," his eyes glistened as if he was imagining how she looked.

"What do you need an Italian girl for?" Miriam brushed her hair back with her hand. She wasn't interested in Mooch romantically, but he was a good dancer and the two of them often went dancing at speakeasies or community center dances and the idea of his preferring *shiksas* offended her. "Jewish girls aren't good enough for you?"

"Italian girls aren't smart mouths like you," Mooch teased. "They're sweet."

"It's bad enough to marry a *shiksa*," Butcher said, "but if you get involved with an Italian girl you can end up in cement. No *shiksas* for me."

"Not every Italian is in the mob, you know," Howie said. "And there are plenty of Jews in the mob too like Meyer Lansky and Arnold

Rothstein. Anyway, I'm not interested in *shiksas*," Howie leaned over and kissed Lilly on the cheek, "I've got my nice Jewish girl."

"You're such a wimp," Mooch said punching Howie in the arm.

"No he isn't," Lilly said, putting her hand on Howie's shoulder.

After lunch they all walked down the hall past the large dirty windows that filtered out the light to one of the dozen alcoves fitted with benches surrounding long walnut tables. Each poorly lit alcove was colonized by a different crowd, a kaleidoscope of groups: the Catholic Newman Society, the athletes, the few blacks that were at the college, the Orthodox Jews, the Zionists and the Jewish Science group who believed in divine intervention through prayer therapy. But the only alcoves that Lilly ever frequented were Alcove Nos. 1 and 2. Alcove 1 was the home of an array of leftists: anarchists, Trotskyists, supporters of Norman Thomas and "mobile Marxists" who were leftists who could not bring themselves to join any group. Alcove No. 2 was the habitat of the Stalinists, most of whom belonged to the Communist Party.

With lunch over, discussions of classes, baseball and *shiksas* gave way to politics. The Stalinists from Alcove 2, like Butcher, were visiting Alcove 1 and arguing as they always did. The disagreements were inescapable: Who was Lenin's choice for successor? Did he intend for Stalin to take over? What made more sense—Trotsky's theory of "permanent revolution" or Stalin's idea of "socialism in one country"?

"It's impossible to build socialism in Russia. There are so few workers and the peasants don't want it," said Howie, explaining the Trotskyist position as he settled on the bench.

His large brown eyes sparkled as he articulated each idea so clearly, yet simply, and then wove them into a complicated argument. He was a good writer as well—he had won the *New York Times* National Oratorical Contest for the best written oration on the Constitution when he was a senior at Thomas Jefferson High School, and at City he was a regular contributor to *The Campus*, the college weekly. He had his own column, "Gargoyles." It was named after the animal sculptures that decorated the front of Shepard Hall, but Howie used the column to discuss all the grotesque events going on in the world.

"That's ridiculous," Butcher said, towing the Stalinist line of the Alcove 2 boys. His stained shirt never stayed tucked in and Lilly imagined that the discoloration was from carrying animal carcasses to and from the icebox.

"You have to bring the peasants into the revolution," Mooch said dragging on a cigarette Butcher gave him. He disagreed with him, but was willing to bum a cigarette anyway. "You can't just sit around and wait for the workers in the West to make a revolution."

"Stalin's not going to bring them into the revolution. He's going to starve them out," Howie said. Howie loved Mooch, but he didn't think he really understood the situation. "That's what the seizures of grain were all about. He's stealing their land and murdering them." He rolled out the facts and layered them as calmly as Mama making rugelach.

In the middle of the discussion Manny Gutman peeked into Alcove 1 and, seeing Butcher was there visiting from Alcove 2, put his textbooks on the table and sat down on the bench. He looked Irish with porcelain skin and thick wavy hair the color of red maple leaves in autumn. Lilly had first met him a year before when she joined NYU professor Sidney Hook, Miriam and many of the City College boys as volunteers for the Communist Party's William Z. Foster/ James Ford 1932 Presidential campaign which proposed an end to capitalism and the creation of a workers' state. They had all gone to Foster's speech at NYU that Sidney had arranged.

Occasionally Howie and Lilly also ran into Manny and Butcher at John Reed Club meetings. The Club was named after the journalist who reported on the Bolshevik Revolution and was a meeting place for leftist and Marxist artists and intellectuals. Socialists, Stalinists and Trotskyists attended lectures and panel discussions, arguing endlessly.

The youngest son of an unemployed metal spinner who lived in East Harlem, Manny worked part-time at the City College Bookstore to pay for his books and trolley fare. Lilly had never seen Manny with a girl and wondered if he had a girlfriend.

Manny was wearing a short sleeve shirt and Lilly noticed his broad shoulders and the way his muscles made the sleeves tight. His arms were tanned, but a slice of white skin with freckles peeked out at the edge of the sleeve.

28

"Remember," Butcher said to Howie, "Marx said the peasants were rural idiots."

"Are you trying to justify Stalin murdering them? I don't care what Marx said—he was dead long before the Bolshevik Revolution. The revolution happened in a peasant society, not a proletarian one like Marx thought," Howie said.

"It's not that the peasants are idiots," Manny said, banging his fist on the table, trying to clarify Butcher's point. "It's that they're individualistic and resist collectivizing." His veins popped out of his neck and his hair was falling into his denim blue eyes. Lilly had the impulse to brush it away.

"Yes, that's exactly why Stalin is stealing their grain," Howie said with a wry smile.

"Don't you get it? The workers are starving in the cities. The peasants can't just hoard their grain," Manny yelled. His exasperation with Howie's criticism of Stalin spewed out like blood from a chicken.

"So you are justifying Stalin murdering them!?" Howie asked with eyes glaring.

"Sidney Hook says Stalin is putting the needs of the state above the hope for international revolution," Lilly added calmly. "You can't have a proletarian revolution without a proletariat."

Manny rolled his eyes. "Hook's a Trotskyist!"

Howie took Lilly's hand and agreed, "Yes!"

Butcher blurted out, "Look what Azaña's doing in Spain." It was just like him, Lilly thought, to say something that had no relationship to the prior conversation—either about baseball or revolution. Manuel Azaña took part in the liberal revolution that overthrew the monarchy and became Prime Minister in 1931. Butcher's ideas were intelligent, but lined up in no particular order or connection to each other.

"Butch," Manny said patiently, striking a match to light a cigarette, "we're not talking about Spain—we're talking about Russia." Lilly was surprised he was protective of Butcher though he was so zealous about Stalin. She felt herself let go of Howie's hand and turn to face Manny who inhaled deeply as if he were trying to control himself.

As he exhaled, he picked a couple of pieces of tobacco from his tongue. Lilly noticed the hairs on the back of his hand were the same color as the curly hairs that peeked out of the open collar of his shirt. She wondered what the rest of him looked like.

4

"This is incredible," Lilly said, imagining this was what it would be like to enter a grand house in Florence or Paris. The sidewalk in front of the entrance of the Whitney Museum which had recently opened on West 8th Street was patterned with masonry fragments that looked like terrazzo. She had passed it many times going to and from classes, but had never gone in.

"Do you know Gertrude Whitney offered her whole collection to the Met and they refused it?" Howie said scratching his head.

"Why?" She put her arm under his.

"I don't know. It's an all American collection and maybe they're snobs," he said. "It's crazy—she's been collecting for years. It's probably the best collection of American contemporary art in the country."

Howie opened the molded glass inner door which was divided into sections containing bas-relief sculptures of human figures and animals.

They entered an empty courtyard with the wintry remains of a manicured garden. A cloud muted the sunlight as the clean, crisp water whooshed gently over a basin supported by three figures forming a tripod-like pedestal in the center of the courtyard. Howie put his arm on Lilly's shoulder, pulling her toward him. She felt his warmth and was happy to snuggle against him on this chilly December day. He whispered, "Lilly, when we get married we'll have a fountain in our garden." She laughed. He smelled woody like moss after rain. He took her in his arms, bathing her in his gentleness. He kissed her, sliding his tongue into her mouth. As they stood kissing, the cloud moved on and they felt the warmth of the morning sun, and with a shock Lilly realized it was Manny's lips that she wanted on hers. *What did that mean?* She loved Howie, she had no doubt. But kissing him was as familiar as a beaten path.

They were both startled when they heard a cough—a professorial man wearing a three piece suit and his gray-haired wife were staring at them. He had bluish veins protruding from his temples, a wrinkled forehead and eyes sunk deep in their sockets. His wife held her purse tightly with gnarled arthritic fingers. Lilly wondered how she could ever get her wedding ring off. Perhaps she would have to wear it until death did them part. Did it cut off her circulation? Lilly imagined her once rosy cheeks and her fingers once straight and eager to touch. What happened to her? To them?

"They're jealous," Howie whispered as he guided Lilly to the door to the galleries. He turned and smiled at her, his dimples long and narrow on each side of his face.

"I want to go to Hopper's studio," he said. "It's just around the corner and I heard Gertrude Whitney buys his paintings as soon as they're dry. But I'm guessing you don't like them. You like paintings about people and every-day life." He took her hand and said, "Like this one," and led her to a painting called "Bread Line—No One has Starved" by Reginald Marsh.

Lilly laughed, loving the fact that Howie knew her so well. "It's true," she said, "Hopper's paintings are all about isolation and solitude—empty stores on Sunday morning or an empty old house."

Howie pulled her closer to him and whispered in her ear, "I know. Let's skip it."

He was the first boy she'd felt completely comfortable with—she could talk to him about anything. It was just like talking to Miriam.

When they left the museum they walked toward Washington Square Park and Lilly pointed to Hopper's studio—one of the brownstones on the north side of the park. It was a cold, but sunny day as they walked through the park past lovers hugging, old men reading newspapers, students underlining passages in their assigned readings and homeless people in soiled clothes huddled next to their only belongings.

At MacDougal Street they stopped at a cafe for coffee. Men of all ages sat at small tables drinking espresso, smoking cigarettes, talking Italian, laughing and gesticulating with their yellowed fingers as young girls passed by.

"What's the story with all these men sitting here during the day?" Lilly asked in a whisper, as they sat down at a table.

"They don't have work, I guess," Howie said. "And some of them are in the mob. That's why it's the safest neighborhood in New York."

"But why aren't there any women with them?" Lilly asked.

Across the street big breasted women wearing house dresses hung out of windows watching the children playing on the street below. Occasionally one of them would shout in Italian at a child who was chasing after a ball on the street in front of the cafe.

"These guys are probably married to the women in the windows. It's Italian culture," Howie whispered. "The men hang out together and the women cook and take care of the kids."

"It's a good thing I'm not Italian," she said with her hand over her mouth to muffle her voice.

Howie laughed, "Yes, Lilly, it certainly is." He leaned over the table and put his hand on top of hers.

*   *   *

A few weeks later, on a Sunday night in January, Howie called Lilly. "I have a terrible cold," he said. He was coughing and his voice sounded like he was holding his nose. "I can't go to the John Reed meeting tonight. I have to go to bed. I'll call you tomorrow."

"Okay, feel better. Have some tea with honey."

"Are you going to go?"

"I don't know. Maybe." She felt uncomfortable going to the meeting alone. There weren't many women there and none of them came by themselves.

"Why don't you go with Miriam?" Howie offered, sensing her discomfort. "It should be good. It's a panel discussion on 'Bourgeois and Proletarian Types in World Literature.'"

"What's that mean? Types of characters or what?"

"I don't know, that's why you should go," he laughed and then coughed.

Miriam agreed to meet Lilly at the Club. It wasn't far from Washington Square—Sixth Avenue between West 9th and 10th.

It was cold and damp as Lilly walked up Sixth Avenue from the subway on Waverly Place. When she reached the building, Miriam was standing in front waiting for her. There were young men with caps and beat up leather jackets standing around the entrance in small groups. Some were speaking Russian, while others spoke English peppered with Yiddish. As the girls passed them to go inside, three men argued about whether Arab attacks on Jewish settlers in Palestine were justified. A short man with a beard shook his head and said in Yiddish,

"For the disease of stubbornness there is no cure." His friend replied, *"You can't pee on my back and tell me that it's rain!"*

The staircase was poorly lit and the dusty steps were scattered with cigarette butts and scraps of paper.

"This place is disgusting," Miriam said.

"Yes," Lilly agreed, "if I dropped anything on the floor, I wouldn't want to pick it up."

When they walked into the main room, a few men leaned against the wall reading *The New Masses*, while others stood around talking. There were piles of coats on old kitchen chairs. Lilly noticed Manny standing on the other side of the room—he was wearing a red flannel shirt and had a black eye that looked like the inside of a purple plum. She wondered what had happened to him.

"It looks like somebody beat Manny up," she said to Miriam.

"Mmm," Miriam replied skeptically. Neither of them thought that was a real possibility.

Lilly heard the panel members discussing Monsieur Jourdain, the protagonist of the play "Le Bourgeois Gentilhomme" by Molière. But she could not concentrate because she spent the whole time wondering if Manny got beat up. She imagined he walked into a telephone pole because he wasn't paying attention to where he was going, or maybe he bent over to pick something up in his house and smacked his face.

When the meeting ended, Manny came over and greeted them.

"What happened to you? To your eye," Lilly asked.

"I was beaten up by the police last night." He put his hand on his swollen cheek. "We organized a demonstration for workers in Harlem and the bastard cops beat the shit out of us."

"That's terrible," she said, feeling a surge of excitement. "What was it about?"

"It was to get rent and food money for Negroes who are out of work," he said. The vein in his neck bulged. "They can't get the relief money they're owed. It's racist."

Lilly imagined Manny walking across 125th Street with a crowd of Negro men, women and children behind him carrying signs saying "Justice for Negro workers."

"The unemployment rate for Negro men," Manny explained shaking his head, "is twice that of whites. With things so bad, Negro

34

janitors or elevator operators get fired and replaced by whites. And the real kick in the head is that when they go for unemployment benefits they get turned away."

"That's terrible, but bravo for helping the cause!" Miriam turned to Lilly with a wink. "I've got to go. You'll see her home safe, won't you?"

Manny nodded as Miriam disappeared.

Just as Manny and Lilly walked out of the building together, it started to rain. "Ugh, I'm like a goat," she said, "I hate to get wet."

Manny opened his umbrella and brushed against her breast with his hand as he lifted it over her head. She wasn't sure if it was purposeful or not; part of her hoped it was, but she reflexively moved her purse so that it separated them. She could smell the Vitalis in his hair and she felt clammy and tingly.

"It was really scary last night," he said. "I felt like the cops wanted to kill us."

"Really?" she gasped. She was shocked, but touched that he told her he was frightened. She felt a tic in her eye and wondered if he could see her lower lid fluttering.

"Yeah, they hate the Negroes and anyone who wants to help them... Where's Howie tonight?"

"He's sick." Lilly was sorry he'd changed the subject—especially to Howie.

"I'm sorry to hear that. I wonder what he'd have to say about the meeting. He has some strange ideas. It's crazy to think Stalin had anything to do with the famine in the Ukraine."

"Do you ever enjoy walking in the rain?" Lilly asked, with a hint of flirtation in her voice.

"Not really... You know Stalin just wants to collectivize the peasants, he doesn't want to kill them," Manny replied.

Why can't he give it up for a while, she wondered, *and think about something else?* She sighed and followed his lead back to the famine. "Sidney Hook says Stalin is lying about the famine," she said. "He's crushing the peasants. That's why he won't let any foreigners go to Ukraine."

"What's all this about 'Sidney says this' or 'Sidney says that'? I stopped listening to him a long time ago. He's become a fucking Trotskyist or something."

A gust of wind blew the umbrella and Lilly felt Manny's forearm muscles contract as they both held on.

"What do you mean?" She realized she'd stepped on a land mine.

"He's not a communist. He's a middle-class reformer like Dewey—a pragmatist, not a revolutionary." His posture stiffened.

She didn't want to fight with him. But she agreed with Sidney's criticism of Stalin and the dogmatism of the American Communist Party. Hook taught the only course on Marxism in the city. A slight man, only 5' 3 or 4 with wild eyebrows and a mustache, he had a high forehead with the kind of wild but sparse curly hair that is common among young Jewish men who are becoming bald. Sometimes he gesticulated wildly, told jokes and contorted his face to make a point more dramatic. Other times, to emphasize how awful he thought something was, he put his hands in his pockets and walked around the front of the classroom with stooped shoulders. The combination of his animated style and intellectual clarity made his lectures awe-inspiring. Lilly loved his lectures. His class was filled to standing room only with NYU students and auditors from all over the city.

Lilly felt guilty that she wanted Manny's lips on her neck and his hands under her blouse—and angry that he was thinking about Stalin and Ukraine and how much he didn't like Sidney. Talking to him felt like trying to open your umbrella when the wind is blowing in your face.

Touch me. Why don't you forget about Stalin for a while and touch me? But a door had slammed between them. She tried to pull it open, but it was heavy. "How are your parents doing?"

"My father's still out of work," he said. "He sits around and drinks *schnapps* all day. Then my mother says he should stop drinking and he yells at her."

That didn't work either. By the time they arrived at the subway, she'd given up trying to change Manny's sour mood. *Of course he didn't kiss me,* she thought, *I'm Howie's girlfriend.* He said goodbye and headed for the uptown side while she climbed the steps for the downtown train. Hiding her disappointment, she smiled and yelled goodnight over her shoulder.

Later, lying in bed alone she stroked herself slowly, thinking about Manny's bulging forearm under the umbrella. As soon as she

36

realized what she was doing, she flushed with guilt. She sighed loudly and whispered to the darkness, "Oh no."

"Why are you smiling and talking to yourself?" Gertie asked from the other bed. Lilly thought she was asleep.

"It's nothing," Lilly said, feeling exposed. She could feel the heat in her cheeks.

"Oh come on, what's going on with you?"

"I've got a crush on Manny. I can't help it! I feel guilty, but I can't help it."

Lilly could hear Gertie turn toward her as the bed creaked under her weight. "Manny Gutman? Stalinist Manny?"

"Yes."

"He's not funny like Howie," she said matter-of-factly.

She was exactly right. Manny wasn't funny like Howie. He was all politics all the time. Lilly felt relieved. "Yes, you're right. He's serious," she said with a shrug.

5

At the end of the spring semester of 1934, Sidney Hook invited a few of his students to visit him at Yaddo, the idyllic, 400-acre artists' community in Saratoga Springs, New York. He was going to be teaching about Marxism to artists and writers who were invited there for the summer. It would be a chance of a lifetime, he told Lilly, to meet some of the most interesting intellectuals in the country. She felt as if Moses had invited her to join him on Mount Sinai.

Sidney went without his wife; Miriam warned Lilly not to go. She predicted Sidney was going to tell Lilly about his marital problems and make a pass at her. Miriam said the rules at Yaddo were very strict and families were supposed to be left behind, which encouraged lots of sex. Lilly was worried. She didn't want Moses to be like all the other guys. She wanted him to be above all that. But just in case, she decided to bring Miriam with her.

When they arrived in late July, Yaddo was glorious with pine groves, vast lawns, rose gardens, a lake with ducks and a white marble fountain. The estate was originally owned by a rich banker, Spencer Trasks, before it was turned into a retreat where artists and writers could pursue their creative work free of cost without the usual interruptions of daily life or any thought of the Depression. There were more than 20 people staying in the main house. The regimen at Yaddo was conducive to any creative art that required solitude. Quiet hours—from 9:00 a.m. to 4:00 p.m. each day—prohibited visiting or loud conversation anywhere on the premises. Notices on the wall explained that deviations from this rule would end in enforced departures. But after quiet hours, there were poetry readings or musical performances and then conversations, often fueled by liquor, lasting well into the night.

During Lilly's first night, Marc Blitzstein played excerpts from "The Cradle Will Rock," his the revolutionary opera that was his work-in-progress. He was a lean, good-looking man with a mustache and flashing gray eyes. He sang all of the parts in a cracked voice that sounded like he was being choked. After the performance, Diana Trilling, or "Di" as Sidney called her, went to bed. Lionel Trilling and Sidney stayed up drinking red wine on the terrace. Miriam had gone off to talk to the poet Lola Ridge. Lilly was tired, but lingered on a rocking chair a few feet from them. She was determined not to miss an opportunity to eavesdrop on their conversation. To her delight they talked as if they forgot she was there.

"Blitzstein's such a fairy," Sidney said. "I don't know why Eva puts up with him."

Lilly was aghast. She tried not to betray her shock—she knew Blitzstein was married to the novelist Eva Goldbeck. Did she know, she wondered, that he was a fairy? Why would she have married him if she knew that?

"Who knows what's going on with other people," Lionel said, taking a generous sip of wine.

"So how's it going," Sidney asked, changing his tone to a more empathic one, "with the research on Matthew Arnold, Li?"

Trilling was slow to answer. He was a handsome man, about 30 years old like Sidney, with wavy brown hair and sad hazel eyes. He winced as if in pain and his brows almost touched. He said, "It's not going..."

"So what's the story? It's your dissertation for God's sake. What's going on?"

"Diana says it's about my mother. She goes to a Freudian five times a week and lies on a couch," Lionel said nonchalantly.

Lilly's jaw dropped and she stifled a gasp. Five times a week?

"He told her my problem is my mother. She was English, you know." He stopped and took another sip of wine. He looked at the full moon and swished the wine around in his glass.

"My mother loved English literature and especially Matthew Arnold." He nodded as if he was agreeing with himself.

"So you had a Jewish mother, what else is new?" Sidney smirked and emptied his wineglass in one prolonged gulp. Then he took the bottle and refilled Lionel's goblet, Lilly's and his own. Lilly was trying to pace herself, but he kept refilling the glasses.

"She wasn't your usual Jewish mother, she was an intellectual. She introduced me to literary criticism and read English literature incessantly. She talked about it constantly." He cleared his throat. Lilly thought she saw a tear in his eye. She imagined her mother sitting at the kitchen table reading the newspaper and commenting on every article.

"She always said I was going to get my doctorate at Oxford."

"So, you're not finishing your dissertation at Columbia because you feel you're disappointing your late mother?" Sidney asked in a gentle voice.

Lilly was impressed by Sidney's sensitivity toward Lionel; he was a good friend. She'd never seen him in a personal context before.

"Wouldn't she be more disappointed," Sidney continued, "if you didn't finish your dissertation?"

Trilling didn't answer. He slumped in his chair and stared at his glass. Lilly felt sorry for him; he was never going to be what his mother imagined. It made her think about Tateh's face when he saw her handing out birth control information on Pitkin Avenue with Miriam. Maybe she was never going to be what he imagined either.

"You're right out of Freud." Sidney laughed. Lilly thought he was being harsh now. Poor Li was bereft.

"That's what Diana thinks...." He put his hands over his eyes, as if he didn't want to see how paralyzed he was. "I think I'm going to turn in."

Lionel stumbled as he rose from the chair and spilled some wine on the table. "Oh sorry," he said as he straightened the chair and surveyed the red kidney-shaped spot. He stood still for a moment to steady himself and then walked toward the exit.

When Lionel was out of sight, Sidney turned to Lilly and said, "He's depressed, poor guy. He needs to finish the damned dissertation and forget about pleasing his mother. It's sad how a grown man can be so entangled with his mother. I guess women stay entangled with their fathers too."

Lilly stayed quiet. Her feelings about Tateh were certainly tangled.

"So what's with you and Howie?" Sidney asked, lighting a cigarette then picking up his glass. Lilly had introduced Sidney to Howie a few times when he sat in on Sidney's lectures with her, but she was surprised that he had remembered his name.

"We're close," Lilly said. "But I've never been with anyone else so I have nothing to compare it to."

"Take your time. I'd never been with anyone before I married Carrie," he said, emptying the goblet and filling it up again.

He looked up at the stars as if he might glean his future. The night was black. There were no street lights here, just the waxing crescent moon low in the sky, its pale glow suggesting what was hidden. Sidney sat silently puffing on his cigarette, when Miriam came and sat down. She was wearing a pistachio and yellow print dress. Her black hair was pulled back with a part in the middle and her arched eyebrows emphasized her large brown eyes. She was stunning. *Wallis Simpson without the jewels.*

"It's nice to meet you, Sidney," she said, her voice low and sultry.

She looked perfect. Lilly hated her. She had felt this way about Miriam before. She remembered a night she and Howie were at Mario's—a speakeasy on the two lower floors of a brownstone in the West 40's during Prohibition. When they knocked, the owner looked at them through a peephole in the locked front door. They weren't afraid the New York police were going to raid the place, but they were concerned about going blind or dying from wood alcohol. The *Eagle* published gruesome stories every day. Howie said you always had to order by brand at a speakeasy, like Dewar's on the rocks. If you ordered generically you could get creosote in your drink.

That night the band had been playing "I Got Rhythm" when they walked in to the club. A lot of their friends were already on the dance floor—Butcher and his girlfriend Fritzi were fox-trotting. She snuggled on his shoulder, her abundant coarse hair tickling his face as she waddled her substantial behind. Howie grabbed Lilly's hand and pulled her to the dance floor, leading her around the room holding her tightly against his chest with his hand on the crevice in her lower back. She felt the blood pulsing under his skin and the pressure of his erection against her. She kissed his neck, her lips scraping against a few whiskers that he'd missed while shaving." Just at that moment they crashed into Mooch and Miriam. She was wearing a low cut dress and dark Chinese red lipstick with matching nail polish, while Lilly was wearing a black dress with long sleeves and a round collar. Miriam was riveting. Mooch could barely take his eyes off her breasts long enough to say hello to Lilly and Howie. *Miriam wears her sexual desire as a badge*, Lilly had thought.

Sidney smiled at Miriam. "The pleasure's all mine." His eyes locked on hers as he shook her hand. Lilly thought he fell in love with her as soon as he saw her; his eyes lit up and his body relaxed. *He has always treated me*, Lilly thought, *as a student he was mentoring, not as a woman.*

Miriam and Sidney were flirting. Lilly couldn't believe it. He was a married man and she was her best friend. And she'd warned Lilly about this very thing happening. *How could this be possible?*

"So Sidney, do you think you will have the same teaching assistant in the fall?" Lilly asked.

"No, I don't think so," he said without taking his eyes off Miriam.

"I really like that guy Robert—he was very good in the recitation sections," Lilly said, biting her lip.

Sidney didn't answer. He poured some wine in Miriam's glass and their hands touched before he refilled his own.

Lilly gave up trying to pry them apart and said, "Goodnight, I'll see you in the morning." They continued looking into each other's eyes and barely mumbled, "Goodnight." Lilly could hear them laughing as she walked to the room she was sharing with Miriam in the mansion. The vast carpeted central hall had a huge Russian sleigh on display. She hugged herself, feeling a chill as she mounted the grand staircase to Siberia. *You bitch,* she thought, *you warn me about Sidney and then sleep with him yourself!*

She tossed and turned all night. She dreamed that her parents were in a train crash. She ran to the crash site to try to find them. She was digging through rubble and screaming; she reached her mother but she was dead, but she kept digging and she found Tateh. He was barely alive, but she dug him out and was able to get him safely away from the crash site.

The next morning Miriam was not in the twin bed next to hers when Lilly woke up. She couldn't believe it. *She slept with Sidney.* Walking to breakfast which was served promptly at 8, Lilly wondered if Miriam would be there with Sidney. Indeed, there they were drinking coffee and eating scrambled eggs with Di and Li and two men Lilly didn't know. Sidney was wearing a fresh short sleeve shirt and Bermuda shorts, while Miriam was still wearing the pistachio and yellow dress. She wore no make-up and her hair looked a bit disheveled. She looked up and gave Lilly a plastic smile when she walked over to the table, but didn't say anything. As Lilly sat down,

Miriam put her hand on top of Sidney's as if she were claiming territory.

Lilly made a fist digging her nails into the palm of her hand.

Sidney smiled and said, "Lilly, you already know the Trillings. I'd like to introduce you to this young man who works on the ferry and who's going to be a writer some day, John Cheever. And this is Aaron Copland who is writing great music for the masses."

Lilly greeted each of them. John was about Lilly's age, while Aaron looked like he was in his early 30's. Lilly was speechless. She couldn't look at Miriam. How could she have slept with Moses?

Lionel said, "What a nice cast of characters we are," and with a twinkle in his eye kissed Di on the cheek. Lilly wondered what they thought about Sidney sleeping with Miriam. *Did they have sex with other people?*

Aaron and John were making small talk with each other and Miriam was taking hash browns off Sidney's plate. Lilly sat in a catatonic stupor. When Sidney offered to pour her some coffee, he woke her up.

Sidney began holding court—criticizing the *New Masses* for being a Stalinist magazine because it wouldn't print any dissenting views by Trotsky or anyone else. With his high forehead, bushy eyebrows, frizzy Jewish hair and mustache, he looked like Groucho Marx without the cigar. Miriam brushed a fly off Groucho's shirt as he talked.

Di scratched her head and added, "Granville Hicks is a Stalinist so what do you expect. If the editor is in the Party, he calls the shots." Her wavy hair, parted in the middle and thoughtful dark eyes reminded Lilly of Clara Bow—she had heard she was born in Brooklyn. "You know," Diana continued, "my analyst is a Stalinist. I overheard his wife talking to one of her Stalinist friends."

"I thought you're not supposed to know anything personal about your psychoanalyst." Lilly said.

"I have to walk through his house to get to his office," Di explained to Lilly.

"Come on, Di," Sidney said with a sly grin, "your psychoanalyst is a Stalinist?"

They all laughed.

"Yes," she said good-naturedly, "I swear, at least his wife is. I heard her having coffee with a friend and talking about 'the upstarts' at *Partisan Review* because they're publishing writers who aren't in the Party."

After breakfast, when everyone left the table except for Miriam, Sidney and Lilly, the flames had gone out, but the smoke was still thick. Lilly asked Sidney, "Do the Trillings have children?"

"No," he contorted his face, "they think that's too conventional."

"Oh, what does Di do? Is she getting a doctorate as well?" Lilly asked.

"No, she isn't. She was invited here because she's supposedly writing a play, "The Young Wives Tale." But that's a joke. The rules are that you have to be working on something to be invited as a summer resident. Her job is really the care, feeding and analysis of Lionel."

"Strange," Lilly said, "don't you think?"

Miriam nodded.

"Why?" Sidney asked.

"She's such a bright woman. And if having children is too conventional, isn't supporting your husband to finish his dissertation without having a career of your own?"

"You better stop reading Emma Goldman," he laughed.

"No, keep reading," Miriam elbowed Sidney and smiled at Lilly.

"Okay, don't gang up on me," Sidney quipped. Then his demeanor changed. He looked at his hands and mumbled. "I've been beaten up enough." He got up from the table and said, "I have to go and work."

Miriam and Lilly were left to themselves.

"How could you have slept with him?" Lilly hissed.

"It was very nice. It's not a big deal. Lola said everybody here is sleeping with each other. What's your problem?" Miriam said. But she did not look at her.

"You warned me he was going to make a pass at me and came along so that wouldn't happen and then you go and sleep with him. What *chutzpa*. Not just that, he's married."

"You heard what he said. He feels beaten up. That marriage is over."

"It doesn't matter," Lilly insisted.

*   *   *

In September of 1934, when Lilly returned to NYU, she and Sidney were having coffee at Stewart's Cafeteria in Sheridan Square. The large smoke-filled room was open all night and always filled with NYU faculty and students, actors, and leftists of all stripes who loved the incessant talk and the meals you could get for under a dollar. Sidney told Lilly that he and his wife Carrie were having problems because he was critical of the Communist Party.

"My parents have been married more than twenty years and they have political differences." *And*, she thought to herself, *Tateh would never cheat on my mother, like you did with Miriam!*

Sidney made a face to indicate that she didn't understand the seriousness of the matter. He looked over his shoulder to make sure no one was listening. There were two young men flirting with four boys sitting at a table nearby. Stewart's was a favorite hangout for homosexuals. A few of them always sat at the large window and watched the boys go by on Christopher Street.

They were involved in a spirited conversation about God's view of fairies with the boys at the table. Lilly was surprised they worried about that. She never thought about God's view of anything! She wasn't even sure she believed in God. *What about their parents?*

When Sidney was satisfied that the fairies weren't listening, he continued. "Party people see me as dangerous. I get threatening letters telling me that I better drop my attachment to John Dewey because he's a liberal, not a revolutionary." He pulled a letter out of his jacket pocket and unfolded it. "I just got this the other day from Earl Browder." He moved his finger down the page to someplace in the middle and read it out loud in a lowered voice, "'Hook, you're going to be sorry if you keep pushing Dewey and this social reformist bullshit.'" He shook his head, looked at Lilly directly and said, "That's what Carrie thinks too—the most horrid thing she can think to say to me is: 'You're a social reformer.' It's a curse, much worse than just being a schmuck."

"My mother is a communist and my father is a real estate developer and they argue about it, but it doesn't make them stop loving each other."

"Being a communist sympathizer is one thing, being in the Party is something quite different. Carrie's a Stalinist—there's no room for disagreement. She's married to the Party. It's like being a nun—you're married to Jesus. There's no room for another husband."

Just then William Phillips, publisher of *Partisan Review,* and his wife walked in hand-in-hand. Lilly recognized them from the night John Strachey gave a talk on "Literature and Fascism" at the John Reed Club to raise money to fund the first edition of *PR.*

They stopped to choose their food plates and then walked over to the table. William shook Sidney's hand and then turned to Lilly and said, "Hello, I'm William Phillips and this is Edna, my alter-Iago." Edna gave him a mock hit on his arm and they all laughed. She rolled her eyes, but smiled warmly at Lilly and walked over to Sidney and kissed him on his cheek.

As they sat down, Lilly's temples pulsated and her right eyelid twitched. King David was about to join them.

"We just had dinner with Edmund Wilson the other night," William continued. He turned to Edna and asked: "Do you think this cottage cheese is fresh?"

She smiled, "Yes, honey it's fine. Don't worry."

"Edmund Wilson?" Lilly had just read Wilson's book *Axel's Castle* for a class on literary criticism at NYU. She was torn between being impressed that they knew Edmund Wilson personally and surprised that William seemed paranoid about food and needed his wife's reassurance.

"Yes, of course, Edmund Wilson. What do you think of him?" William asked. He pushed the dish with the uneaten cottage cheese aside and leaned forward, putting his elbow on the table and his hand under his chin.

"I loved his criticism of T. S. Eliot," Lilly said. But she felt that sounded simplistic and she needed something more substantive, so she added, "and his lucid explanation of why the writer has to be involved with society and not just involved in some narrow aesthetic."

Sidney smiled. William shifted in his chair and then put both elbows on the table. Lilly thought that was a sign of engagement.

"And tell me, Lilly, what do you know about my co-editor Phil Rahv?"

"I know he's not a mechanical Marxist," Lilly offered. She looked at Edna who nodded her approval. She had smiling eyes and a comfortable disposition—a woman who was comfortable in her own skin.

"Yes…" William seemed to be prodding for something more. Sidney was rubbing his eyes. Lilly wondered if he was bored. She wanted him to be engaged and rooting for her.

"He believes bourgeois literature isn't homogeneous and shouldn't all be thrown in the garbage," Lilly said. She smiled to herself, remembering the lecture on "Bourgeois and Proletarian Types in World Literature" that she'd attended at the John Reed Club the night she began having conflicting feelings for Manny.

"What kind of bourgeois literature do you like?" William asked.

He's testing me. She was nervous; she felt Sidney watching her, waiting to see if she would dive in the water.

"All kinds," she smiled, feeling the anxiety blow away like sand. "I like Blake and Browning, Huxley and Virginia Woolf," Lilly said finding her tempo. "I like Charlotte Perkins Gilman and she's not a Marxist. *The Yellow Wallpaper* is about the oppression of women, but it's not a critique of capitalism."

William smiled, playing with his napkin, and challenged further. "But what about her other writing—*Women and Economics* for example? She's not talking about the revolution, but she certainly understands the underlying importance of the economic relationship of the sexes."

Lilly was silent for a moment, taking care to organize her thoughts. Sidney smiled at her and nodded as if to say, *Go ahead, you know what you're talking about.*

She momentarily flashed on Tateh watching her swim without a tube for the first time.

"Well, I think you're right that between writing *The Yellow Wallpaper* and *Women and Economics* Gilman evolved into more of a theoretician. But she sees the solution to gender inequality as the overthrow of patriarchy, not capitalism. That's a big difference between Gilman and Emma Goldman." She knew she was hitting her stride now, but she tried not to smile.

William laughed appreciatively.

Edna sat back in her chair smiling at Sidney and said, "Well, Sidney you told us she was a smart girl."

It suddenly dawned on Lilly that this meeting was not accidental, but orchestrated by Sidney and Edna. *He could have set it up for Miriam, but he didn't.* Part of her hoped she would be jealous. He kept them in different rooms: Miriam was in the bedroom and Lilly in the salon.

Sidney and Edna seemed to be close friends. Sidney later told Lilly they had met because she and his wife, Carrie, belonged to the left-leaning local chapter of the American Federation of Teachers. He said Edna and William had agreed not to have children because they wanted to devote their lives to being intellectuals.

Lilly couldn't understand such a decision. What did having children have to do with being an intellectual? She couldn't imagine not having children.

William said, "You're a smart girl, Lilly. Would you like to work for *Partisan Review*? We can't pay you, of course. But would you like to be a volunteer?"

Lilly gasped with delight and looked over at Sidney whose intense brown eyes were beaming behind his Trotsky glasses.

"I would love to help you with *PR*. I can't imagine anything more exciting," she said.

Just then, Miriam walked into the cafeteria. She had a big smile and walked directly to the table. She stopped behind Sidney and put her hands on his shoulders. He smiled and reached up to touch her. William's face showed no reaction, but Edna's eyes opened wide. Lilly knew she was a friend of Carrie's, so she wondered how she felt about Miriam's flagrant show of intimacy with Sidney.

Sidney introduced William and Edna to Miriam. Edna looked at Miriam, sizing her up. Lilly wondered if Edna knew Sidney was sleeping with her. Then Sidney announced to Miriam, "Lilly's going to work for *Partisan Review*." Sidney, Edna and William were smiling, but Miriam was not. Her cheeks were red and her eyes were squinted. "Good," William said, pulling his chair out and standing up. He put his hand out to shake Lilly's. "Can you come to the loft on Monday so we can work out your schedule?"

"Of course," she smiled though William's tight grip hurt a bit. Finally, she thought, she would be at the center of things.

6

One month after Lilly began working at *Partisan Review,* she and Howie walked into the City College cafeteria. The boys of Alcoves 1 and 2 were having an animated discussion about the massacre of the Asturian miners in response to their strike. Howie chimed in immediately. "Franco and the Fascists murdered 3,000 of them," he said, shaking his head in disbelief.

"The bastards—now they're going to torture the rest of them in prison. I can't bear going to school and acting like the world isn't falling apart," Manny said. Lilly noticed the tears welling in his eyes and wanted to put her arms around him, but contained herself.

Suddenly, Sean Carey, one of the boys from the Catholic Newman Society alcove burst in—a City basketball player who wore a "CCNY Lavender" T-shirt and a large silver cross.

"What's wrong with all you commies?" Sean's voice was breaking, he was almost crying. "Those miners killed over 40 priests and burned down churches that were 500 years-old. They're all Jews and Bolsheviks and they're going to hell and so are you!"

Butcher, Howie and the others were trying not to laugh. Mooch tapped his foot, covering his mouth with his hand. But Lilly didn't think it was funny. She looked at Manny and he wasn't laughing, but she realized it wasn't because he sympathized with Sean. *He was probably thinking the priests deserved it.* Lilly said, "I'm so sorry Sean...But you have to understand what the Catholic Church has been doing in Spain..."

"Don't give me that commie line, please. I don't feel sorry for those anarchists. They got what they deserved." Then he turned and walked down the hall to the Catholic alcove where his Irish friends greeted him with pats on the back for telling off the commie bastards.

Howie came over to Lilly and put his arms around her. She looked to see if Manny was watching them—hoping he had his eyes fixated on her. But he wasn't. He was rubbing his eyes and probably thinking about wanting to kill the Fascists in Spain. Howie kissed Lilly's hair softly. "That was so sweet, Lilly. But you're crazy trying to comfort him when the guy's a *shaigitz* Neanderthal. Irish Catholics are the worst—they support the Church no matter what it does."

                              *   *   *

Between school and working at *PR,* Lilly had not visited City
College for two months. The last time she had been there, before
Christmas vacation, she and Manny had an argument about Sidney.

"Tell me," he had said narrowing his eyes, "what is really going
on between you and Sidney Hook?"

"Nothing is going on between us. He's tried to help me, that's
all. To introduce me to some interesting people."

"Come on Lilly," he had pressed, "the guy is a Trotskyist
traitor. What's the story with you?" Manny was smirking as if he was
sure it wasn't Sidney's ideas that attracted her. His eyes twinkled and
she noticed his long eyelashes.

"Manny, I know this is hard for you to understand," she'd said.
"But it's possible to disagree with Stalin's policies without being a
Trotskyist traitor…I'm so sick of hearing 'Trotskyist traitor' as an
epithet any time someone criticizes the Party or Stalin."

"Now is not the time for dissent. The situation in Spain is
desperate." His jaw was clenched, the muscles in his neck tight.

"Manny, why can't people have different approaches to the
problem?"

He had frowned and lapsed into silence.

Now she and Howie were going to a show in midtown and since
she hadn't been there in a while, she decided to meet him at the
cafeteria before heading downtown to the theatre. When she arrived,
Howie had not yet arrived. She hoped to see Manny, but she was also
afraid to see him. Just as she walked into the cafeteria, Butcher came
running in tugging Fritzi's arm yelling "Azaña's acquitted!" He was
waving the *New York Times* in front of Lilly's face so closely she could
read the date: December 19, 1934.

Earlier in the year there had been violent anti-government
demonstrations in Barcelona and Asturias and the center-rightist
government had accused former Prime Minister Manuel Azaña, leader
of the Radical Socialists of encouraging them. He had been arrested
and interned on a ship in Barcelona Harbor, but there was not enough
evidence to convict him. When he was Prime Minister, the Stalinists
criticized him for not being left enough, but now that the rightists
arrested him on trumped-up charges he was a hero.

The boys from Alcoves 1 and 2 all started to shout and pump their fists in delight. Manny was yelling, "Bravo, Azaña." He ran over to Lilly with a warm smile, put his arms around her and kissed her on the cheek. Shocked that he was so demonstrative, Lilly stiffened but noticed he smelled like new leather.

The crisis in Spain was the only thing the boys agreed upon. Anti-fascism was a cause about which socialists, communists, even anarchists concurred, but the Trotskyists in Alcove 1 were critical of Stalin for not showing more support for Azaña. They believed Stalin was doing a balancing act in Spain: he wanted to get credit for supporting the Republicans, but he didn't want Spain to turn into an alternative model to Soviet Communism.

"Stalin has ditched the proletariat of Spain," Mooch said loudly enough for the Alcove 2 boys to hear.

Alcove 2 celebrated Azaña's victories, but never criticized Stalin. "He completely supports the Popular Front; you don't know what you're talking about," Arnie said adding, "And you keep complaining about what Stalin is doing to the poor peasants in the Soviet Union."

"So?" Mooch said tapping his foot. Lilly noticed he was eyeing an Italian-looking girl with an exposed décollage at the next alcove over.

"People in Moscow are starving," Arnie said, "because the peasants kill their animals rather than sell them to the state."

Fritzi smiled knowingly.

Manny didn't say anything; he sat with a cigarette dangling from his mouth. He looked quizzically at Fritzi and then his gaze went back to Arnie—Lilly wondered what he was thinking. Did he think Fritzi was a jerk, like she did, or was there something more in that look? She wondered if he was jealous of Fritzi because Arnie spent so much time with her. Manny and Arnie had been like Siamese twins—if they weren't at City, they went to lectures at the John Reed Club or watched ball games at Yankee Stadium. Communism and the Yankees—their two shared passions.

"Stalin's tried to force collectivization with huge taxes for farms with livestock so they slaughter the animals as a 'fuck you'," Mooch said. He often still dropped by the cafeteria because he couldn't find a job.

Lilly didn't get involved in the argument because she knew both Arnie and Mooch were stretching the truth. They were both parroting their pre-conceived ideas and not listening to each other. The *Herald Tribune* reported that there were abundant crops in the fields, but there was no means of transporting food to the cities. The horses and carts had disappeared, but there were no motor trucks and roads to transfer food. The emphasis on industrialization instead of infrastructure was at the heart of the problem.

"We don't talk to Trotskyist traitors," Fritzi shouted back to much applause. *There are the epithets again,* Lilly thought.

Manny wasn't clapping. He raised an eyebrow and screwed up his face.

Howie arrived just as the boys returned to their alcoves like bees returning to their respective hives. Kissing Lilly, he asked, "What's going on?"

"You missed the drama," Lilly said.

Manny gave a curt wave to Howie and Lilly as he walked off with Arnie and Fritzi. Disagreements about Stalin's support of Azaña and whether the peasants were the major hindrance toward building communism caused so much tension between the alcoves that the boys no longer visited each other's hives and usually didn't even stand together when they were having their sandwiches.

Lilly and Howie headed for the subway downtown to the theater, but she wondered what Manny was doing.

* * *

At the end of spring semester of 1935, just before graduation, Howie accepted a position as Assistant to the Director of the Teaching Project, which created art and writing classes for workers in community centers and neighborhood houses. In September, Lilly and Gertie visited the first class he taught at the Henry Street Settlement on the Lower East Side. Howie sat on the desk in the front of the class filled with men in loose-fitting overalls and a few neatly dressed women.

"I'm so glad to see you all. I know how difficult it is to get here after work," he smiled warmly.

A few of the men mumbled a response under their breath in Yiddish or Russian, while the women smiled back.

"I'd like all of you to take out a pencil and a piece of paper and write an answer to the question: 'Who am I?'"

The man directly in front of Lilly jerked his head, as if he was shocked by the question. There were no mumbles. Silence filled the room, as if no one had ever asked them that question. Lilly felt proud that Howie was her boyfriend.

He made $35 per week.

*   *   *

After Howie and most of his friends graduated, Lilly had no reason to visit City College and she did not see Manny. She was busy at *PR,* at school studying for classes, or hanging out in Stewart's cafeteria with Sidney and his graduate students. Her greedy ears took in each word, straining to hear every nuance of the endless arguments about Hegel, Marx, Stalin, Trotsky and Franco.

It was many months after their last meeting at City that Lilly got a call from Manny. His voice sounded different on the phone than in person. She didn't recognize it immediately. When he asked her to meet him at the Brooklyn Botanical Gardens, she was startled. She felt guilty about wanting to see him.

"There's something I want to talk to you about," he said.

Maybe he's been hiding his real feelings for me, she thought. *Maybe after all this time, he's going to ask me to leave Howie.* What would she do? She loved Howie, but was she "in love" with him? She felt she could fall in love with Manny.

They met at the Washington Avenue entrance of the Brooklyn Botanic Garden. Manny was wearing a red short-sleeve shirt that showed the contours of his chest. He didn't greet her with a kiss. He just smiled and said, "Hi." Lilly inhaled the bouquet of the Herb Garden that had been recently built by the Works Progress Administration. Walking through it, she could identify rosemary, the softer slightly musty odor of English lavender and the licorice smell of anise basil. To Lilly's surprise, Manny put his arm around her waist and rested his hand on her hip. Howie always walked with his arm on her shoulder making her feel weighted down. But Manny's hand moved weightlessly with her hip as they walked. She wondered if anyone she knew saw them walking that way. What if someone told Howie? She knew Howie would be distraught if he knew she was seeing Manny.

They had never discussed monogamy, but it was understood between them. Howie trusted her and, until now, she thought he could.

They walked to the Cherry Esplanade, a broad green field bordered by two allées of dazzling cherry trees. She started to skip along a path of pink petals and, to her delight, Manny joined her, laughing the whole length of the allée. *This is a whole new Manny*, Lilly thought. They sat down to catch their breath on a bench in the Japanese Garden overlooking the goldfish pond.

"My sister told me there's a California Post-surrealist exhibit at the Brooklyn Museum."

"Oh," he said.

"She's very excited about it because it's an exhibit of women artists."

Manny was quiet. *He's not interested,* she thought.

"So your sister's interested in art?" he said. He put his arm around her, pulled her toward him, and kissed her. She tasted tobacco on his tongue and felt wet and guilty. Churning with excitement, she expected him to ask if she would leave Howie for him and she imagined replying, "Yes, yes."

"This is so difficult for me. I wanted to say goodbye to you. I'm leaving," he said, pulling back from her.

Stabbed, she blurted out, "What? Where are you going?"

"I'm going to Spain. I can't stand by and let the Fascists take over. The revolution in Spain is the great hope for proletarian emancipation. I have to go and be a part of it."

"Now?" She was aghast.

"Yes, I've made the arrangements. I just wanted to see you and say goodbye." His eyebrows curved downward and his lower lip plumped up.

Her chin dropped.

They both stood up and hugged tightly. She felt the coarseness of his unshaven face and the smell of sweat. He wasn't a boy; he was a man choosing to go off to war. When they moved apart, Manny cleared his throat and recited Robert Louis Stevenson:

> "Armies march by tower and spire
> Of cities blazing, in the fire;
> Till as I gaze with staring eyes,

The armies fall, the luster dies."

Lilly imagined Manny on a truck full of men carrying rifles; running across a field with an army of workers and peasants; being confronted by Franco's tanks and Luftwaffe dive bombers.

"Let's hope it's Franco's luster that dies," she mumbled and kissed his cheek.

"Yes," he smiled and took her hand. He sat back down and gently pulled her down beside him. The afternoon sun withdrew behind a cloud and the branches of the trees shivered. They sat there for a long time—her head on his shoulder and his arm around her.

They were quiet most of the way home; their hands clasped in a tight grip. She held her breath at moments as if that would extend their time together. When they arrived at her house, Lilly looked around, worried for a moment that someone would see them. He held her tightly in his arms and kissed her deeply. Then he moved away, looked into her eyes and said, "Goodbye, Lilly."

She went into her room and lay on her cold bed thinking about the pressure of Manny's mouth on her lips, the way his tongue moved around hers, the feel of his hand on her hip. She thought about the way the cotton shirt accentuated his muscles and the hairs on her arm stood up. She undressed and stroked her breasts. Her nipples were hard as she circled her fingers around each one. Then down to her stomach and then down, down to where she was wet. Two men wanted her. She wasn't sure if she could stay with the perennial year after year and she wasn't sure if the annual was coming back.

*   *   *

Two months later Lilly walked into the house, as she had done every day since Manny had left, and looked through the pile of mail on the floor that the mailman dropped through the slot. Finally, a letter from Manny! She didn't open it immediately. She wanted to savor it, but felt the familiar pang about Howie.

"What's going on with you?" he had asked her the day after Manny left. "You seem like you're in a daze."

"Lilly, you seem so distracted," he said after Manny had been gone a week.

56

"I'm getting worried about you," Howie squinted after two weeks. "I know something's been bothering you and you won't tell me."

She had denied anything was wrong all these weeks. Now she went into her bedroom, took off her shoes and sat on the rug that separated Gertie's bed and hers. There was a light patter of rain on the window panes. She looked at the postmark. It was from France. She smelled the envelope and then rubbed it on her stomach and on each breast. She smelled it again and now it smelled of both of them. She put her finger at the edge and moved it along the top of the envelope. Then she took the letter in both hands and began to read the left-leaning penciled script. His handwriting was spare, no extra lines or curves.

October 13, 1936

Dear Lilly:

I'm sitting on my bed in the barracks thinking about you. About the day we sat at the goldfish pond and I kissed you and told you I was leaving. I hope that you remember and that you will write to me.

I sailed to Le Havre on the SS Paris and headed south across France. A group of us from New York crossed the Pyrenees on foot through the night. I guess it was a good time to do it before the snow, but I had a terrible toothache and spent the journey chewing aspirin. Some of the guys are comrades, some are Wobblies and some are here because they feel the Jews will be the first to suffer when Fascism comes. Some of the Jewish guys are religious and in New York I would never have talked to them. But here it's comforting when they speak Yiddish or say their prayers. Sometimes they ask me to make a *minyan*. In the old days I'd have refused to be a part of

such rubbish and now I'm happy to do it.
Who knows who among us will be here
tomorrow? Whether there'll be enough for a
minyan. The other day I even said the Sh'ma.
You'll laugh, but the words made me feel
calm inside. My mother would be so happy.

I'm in Albacete now –about 200 miles
southeast of Madrid. I'm training with the
Canadian Mackenzie Papineau Battalion.
They are expecting a siege of Madrid by the
Nationalist troops and they want to be
prepared.

Please write to me—I'm lonelier than I could
have possibly imagined.

Love,
Manny

Thunder burst and she jumped. Electricity ran through her. Her
hands shook. She hugged the paper to her chest as if that would keep
him safe. She felt proud of him for going to Spain to fight against
fascism, but frightened that he could die there.

     *   *   *

Soon after she got that first letter from Manny, Howie and Lilly
were alone in his mother's apartment, where they often went while she
was at work. They were lying naked on the couch in the living room
that was his bed. He took a drag on a Lucky Strike. Her head was
resting on his chest as she played with his curly hairs and enjoyed the
smell of his body and the smoke. Suddenly, seemingly out of the blue,
he said, "I saw a one bedroom apartment not far from here for $22 a
month. I'm making a decent salary. We could afford that. You can
finish school and then you'll get a job and we'll be able to afford a
baby in a year or two."

"What? Are you kidding?" She jumped up. Something
crumbled inside her. "How could you?" *How could he possibly*

imagine, she wondered, *that I want to get married? And have a baby? I'm not old enough to give up my dreams*, she thought. *I don't want grooves steering me through every day of my life. I want to be free to make turns and change direction, maybe do something no other woman had ever done, like Amelia Earhart. Or risk my life for the emancipation of the working class, like Manny.*

Howie got up from the couch. His hair was tousled and she noticed that it was thinning in the front. He took her face in his hands and turned it to look at him. His eyes welled up with tears and he demanded, "How could I what? For God's sake I'm proposing to you!" The veins in his temples bulged. He fumbled for his boxers on the table and almost fell, stepping into them.

She put on her slip. Like Adam and Eve in *Paradise Lost*, they both felt self-conscious and wanted to cover themselves.

"Yes, you're proposing to me. But what's wrong with you? The world is falling apart and you want to get married?" She was thinking about Manny, somewhere near Madrid, waiting for the siege of Fascist forces.

"What are you talking about?" He shook his head. "What does that have to do with getting married?"

It was like standing on one side of a wide street and she could see Howie in the distance on the other side, but she felt there was no crossing. He didn't understand her at all. "I'm not ready to get married." She tried to breathe calmly. "I understand that you want to move out of here. But Stalin is murdering all the original Bolsheviks and Franco is trying to destroy the Republic. How can I think about getting married and having a baby now? Don't you know me at all?!" Her voice had started to rise. She felt pressure in her forehead, as if her head were going to explode.

She wasn't sure if her revulsion to the idea of getting married had to do with her need for adventure or her holding out to see if Manny was going to come back to her. She couldn't say yes to Howie when she was fantasizing about the taste of Manny's kisses. *Maybe I should go to Spain and find him*, she thought. *Maybe I should join the Lincoln Brigade.*

He was silent for a few minutes and then he rubbed his eyes as if he were trying to see clearly before he spoke. "You're disappointed in me aren't you? You thought I was a revolutionary and I'm not. I

59

want to have breakfast with you every morning and lie next to you every night. I want to have a job I care about and make enough of a living to support us. I think the New Deal is great. I don't want to go to Spain or Russia."

She knew she wasn't being fair. She wasn't disappointed in him—it was the opposite problem. She knew he snored if he slept on his side; that he would always kiss her on the neck to indicate he wanted to have sex; and that he would always love her. But what would it feel like, she wondered, when Manny was inside her?

Howie went back to bed and she lay down next to him—alone next to each other. Back to back. After what seemed like hours, she heard him crying. She turned around and put her arm around his shoulder. He turned around to face her, taking her hand and kissing it.

"I'm sorry," she said kissing his tears. She loved him; she didn't want to hurt him. But she knew she couldn't marry him. She wasn't going to join the Lincoln Brigade, but she wasn't ready to get married.

"Yes, I know. Maybe I knew before I asked. I was just hoping."

*   *   *

A few days later, Miriam and Lilly were drinking espresso and eating Italian cheesecake at a tiny table in a cafe on MacDougal Street. The walls had posters from famous places in Italy, like the Uffizi Gallery and signed photos of the owner with his arm around fat Italian men in suits. Lilly imagined they were famous gangsters.

Although Miriam had been living with Sidney since Carrie left, in an apartment around the corner on Sullivan Street, Lilly didn't see her very often since she had graduated and started teaching high school English. Lilly felt uncomfortable asking her what was going on in her relationship with Sidney—as if she were prying into her professor's private life. Breaking the silence, Lilly looked down at the table, not at Miriam. "Howie proposed to me. He wants to get married and have a baby."

"Is he crazy?" Miriam scowled so her arched eyebrows almost touched. "Isn't it enough that you don't sleep with anyone else? He wants to get married? And have a baby yet?"

"Yes," Lilly said biting a hangnail. "He wants to tie me down. He wants me to give up my dreams. I thought we were like Emma

Goldman and Alexander Berkman, but he wants to be like Gloria Swanson and Laurence Olivier in *Perfect Understanding*."

Miriam laughed. Her lipstick accentuated her curved lips.

"I feel terrible about it. I love Howie—I don't want to hurt him."

Miriam sighed. "You're so bourgeois.

'Guilt is the cause of more disorders
than history's most obscene marauders...'

e.e. cummings can't be wrong," she said.

Lilly pursed her lips and showed her Manny's latest letter. It was crumpled by now—after so many readings. As Miriam read it silently, Lilly closed her eyes and sucked on a dainty cappuccino spoon.

November 15, 1936

Dear Lilly:

I miss you. I think about you at night when
I'm afraid of falling asleep and in the morning
when I'm afraid of waking up. Afraid that we
could be attacked any time. I wonder if I'll
ever see you again. We arrived in Madrid last
week with Soviet, German and British
comrades. I rode in a Russian tank which was
fun until the Fascists started lobbing grenades
at us. It's crazy here. I have headaches from
the constant bombardment.

I met an interesting Spanish guy—Ramon.
He's helping me with my Spanish. The
anarchists just arrived and the word is that the
head of their brigade was killed in the
fighting. Ramon says they'll probably blame
us. Sometimes I think the anarchists are worse
than the Fascists.

61

I haven't heard from Arnie or any of the City
College guys. They don't get what's going on
here. They live in a cocoon, insulated from
blood and gore. Safe from the Fascists that are
destroying this country village by village. I'll
write when I have more time. Please write
more if you can. I so look forward to your
letters. Can you send me a picture?

Love,
Manny

"It's funny," Miriam smiled, scratching her ear. "I always
thought Manny was a fairy. He seemed so attuned to Arnie and he
never made a pass at you or me."

"What, are you crazy? No way."

"No. I mean it." She couldn't quite get the last piece of
cheesecake on her fork so she finally gave up and used her finger to
push it on. "Think about it. He went to Spain right after he found out
that Arnie was engaged to Fritzi."

"No, believe me you're wrong," Lilly said. She knew Miriam
wouldn't judge her for cheating on Howie. She wouldn't even consider
it cheating: Lilly didn't sleep with Manny. She would probably laugh
about it, but Lilly didn't want her to laugh. She didn't want Miriam to
know anything about it. She made her own judgment: guilty. "He went
to Spain right after the siege of Madrid began, it had nothing to with
Arnie."

"Okay, believe what you want," Miriam said yawning. "But I
think he's running away from something. It's right out of Freud—he
thinks he's a fairy so he goes off to war to prove to himself that he's a
macho guy."

"You don't know what you're talking about."

She shrugged and changed the subject. "What do you think of
the Japanese Pessaries case? Some people see it as a great victory for
Sanger and birth control, but I'm not so sure."

"What do you mean?" Lilly asked.

"It makes contraceptives legal only if a doctor prescribes them."

62

"Isn't it better to be able to get a diaphragm from a doctor than not being able to get it at all?"

"It was the wrong case to bring. Sanger's changed," Miriam shook her head. "She's allowed the doctors and the eugenicists to take over the movement."

"It's a way to legalize birth control," Lilly said insistently. "It's a foot in the door."

"Did you ever hear of 'the displacement of goals'? That's what this is," she lectured. "The preservation of the organization becomes more important than the original goals."

"No, I never heard of that," Lilly said. "It's what's happened to the Party as well." Miriam didn't respond.

"Sidney is completely distracted by the Moscow trials," she said bouncing her foot. "He comes home and falls asleep." She looked up, as if the answer to her problems was on the ceiling.

It was true, Sidney was distracted. He was trying to mount an opposition to the trials. Although Trotsky had been in exile when the alleged crimes were committed, he was being charged in absentia with organizing and directing anti-Soviet terrorism through a secret alliance with Nazi Germany. Sidney, Edmund Wilson, Norman Thomas, John Dos Passos, and Franz Boaz created "The American Committee for the Defense of Leon Trotsky" soon after the Moscow Trials began.

"All he talks about is the trials and Trotsky." Miriam was building up steam. "He's outraged that writers like Upton Sinclair defend the trials."

"It's true, they say the enemy is Fascism," Lilly said, "and Russia is an ally that we can depend upon."

"I don't care. I can't stand it anymore," she said. "He spends every night at meetings trying to organize a leftist opposition to the trials. There's no room for me. There's three of us in bed—Sidney, me and Trotsky!"

Lilly laughed. She couldn't help herself. But she knew it wasn't funny.

"I'm not waiting around for him," Miriam said.

"What do you mean?"

"You know exactly what I mean, don't be cute."

"You're cheating on him?" Lilly felt angry at her for treating Sidney that way. She was afraid he was going to find out and be hurt—

especially since he was still dealing with the pain of his wife leaving him after he met Miriam.

Miriam smirked.

"What?" Lilly gasped. "I can't believe it. How can you do that to him?"

"I'm a free person. I can do whatever I want. You're not my mother."

Miriam keeps lighting matches and throwing them on newspapers, Lilly thought. It was just a matter of time before one of them caught fire and flared up.

7

"He knows I don't believe in monogamy," Miriam said, as she drank tea at Lilly's kitchen table three weeks after she first told Lilly she was having an affair. "He thought it would be different with him—that he would change me." She picked at a piece of Mama's chocolate babka as she talked.

Sidney had returned to the apartment he shared with Miriam and found her in bed with one of her professors from Hunter.

"So what did he say?" Lilly was trying to control her voice, but she was shaking inside. She wanted to yell at her. *How could you do this to him? Especially now, when he's involved in something so important, so historic. How can you be so selfish?*

"He wants me to move out," she said tapping her foot on the floor. Without looking at Lilly she asked, "Are you happy now?"

"What do you mean?" Lilly feigned ignorance, but Miriam was right: she was glad that Sidney wasn't going to be a schmuck and let her cheat on him.

"You know what I mean," she screwed up her face. "Don't act coy. You were angry at me for getting involved with your precious Sidney and you couldn't stand the fact that he loved me and not you."

"I didn't want to have a sexual relationship with him so it's not like you took him away from me." Lilly knew that wasn't entirely true even as she said it.

"Maybe you didn't want to have sex, but you didn't want me to have sex with him either," Miriam said, shoving babka in her mouth.

"That's not true." Lilly bit her hangnail. "Why would I care if you have sex with him? Other than he was married at the time."

"So that was your objection—you didn't want me to hurt his wife's feelings? The idiot Stalinist who wants a divorce because Sidney isn't devout enough for her? You're worried about her feelings? Come on, Lilly."

"Okay, okay." Lilly rubbed her eyes. "I might have been jealous of you having a romantic relationship with him."

"Well, I didn't like the fact that he has sex with me, but when he sees an opportunity for a great job he always thinks of you." Her sharp face was impassive.

"You're jealous of me?"

Miriam rolled her eyes impatiently. "You've got Howie and Manny and you spend more time with Sidney than I do. He's more interested in your future than he is in mine. He never has the time to read my poems or stories. 'Later' he always says. But later never comes. He's saving the world—or at least Trotsky." Her veneer had cracked. She sat with stooped shoulders, looking at the floor. Lilly was speechless for a moment.

"I'm sorry," Lilly said.

"It's not your fault. Why are you sorry?" Miriam finally looked her in the face.

"Because," Lilly said, "I was oblivious to how you feel. That's why I'm sorry." Sidney had asked her to be the secretary for the Trotsky Defense Committee. Of course she was flattered at being offered such an opportunity. And she had wondered why he hadn't offered it to Miriam. Maybe he knew Miriam didn't understand politics, she thought. She was obsessed with free love and literature, but she didn't care about the issues between the Stalinists and the Trotskyists. On the other hand, Lilly's experience working at *PR* had sensitized her to all the subtle, and not so subtle, divisions on the Left. Whatever the reason, Lilly had felt a twinge of pleasure that he'd chosen her rather than Miriam. Now she felt bad for it.

"So, what are you going to do?" Lilly asked.

"I'm going to take a leave of absence from teaching and go to Paris for a while," she said, putting her head on the table. "I've been reading *The Autobiography of Alice B. Toklas.* It's so brilliant—an autobiography written by another person." She smiled and her eyes sparkled. "Gertrude Stein went to Paris and found herself as a writer and as a woman. I want to be a writer. And I need to find out what I'm really about."

"Can you just pick up and go to Paris?" *First Manny goes to Spain*, she thought, *and now Miriam's going to Paris?*

Miriam didn't answer. She shrugged as if to say, *Why not? I can do whatever I like.*

"Gertrude Stein is a fat lesbian! You're not anything like her," Lilly said. *Besides, you do whatever you want in New York, why do you need to go to Paris to be liberated?*

66

"I don't want to be Gertrude Stein," she laughed. "But I want to go to Paris and meet interesting people and find out if I can be a writer."

"You don't have to go to Paris to find out if you can be a writer. After all, you write in English. Your chances of publishing your work are much better here in New York."

Miriam put her hand out and took Lilly's. "You'll be fine. But I have to go to Paris."

Lilly felt sad for Sidney, but worse for herself. Miriam was the only person to whom she could talk about Howie without fearing a negative judgment. She didn't know what her mother would say if she told her she didn't want to marry him: *Are you crazy? What's wrong with you? He's so perfect.* God knows what she'd say if Lilly told her about Manny. There was the part of her mother that was still a radical—she certainly supported the Lincoln Brigade. But another part of her felt grateful for the love and security Tateh offered and wanted Lilly to have that too. She knew Tateh would be upset too—he really liked and respected Howie and felt sure he would be a good husband. Miriam was the only person who could understand Lilly's dreams and she was leaving Lilly behind.

*   *   *

Lilly felt she had to keep her connection with the Defense Committee a secret from Manny. She assumed he would defend the Moscow trials. She remembered the time they walked to the subway together and Manny got angry and said Sidney wasn't a communist at all, "just a liberal like Dewey." In her letters, she didn't mention helping Sidney mount opposition to the show-trials or anything else about Trotsky. She thought if she spoke to him in person, she would be willing to risk the consequences of telling the truth. But it seemed cruel to bring up something incendiary when he was fighting another battle. She pressed the pen against the paper and started to write, "I have exciting news…". No, she crumpled the page and threw it in the garbage. *He should only know*, she thought, *how many letters I started and threw in the garbage.* Then she decided that telling him how she felt about him would be a good start. Then world politics, but nothing about Trotsky. Or about Dewey. Or about Stalin. A movie she saw or a book she read. That was good—anything but what was front and center on her mind.

December 11, 1936

Dear Manny:

I hope you're all right. I think about you all the time, wondering if you're safe. I imagine holding you tight, protecting you from all the terrifying things that are going on around you.

I was horrified at the French government's decision to stop selling arms and ammunition to the Republicans. They are trying to appease Hitler and it's going to boomerang. But in the meantime, I'm sure it's discouraging to you to be fighting Fascism next door to the French and have them abnegate all responsibility in the fight. But we shouldn't be surprised after all the countries that joined in the propaganda fest for Hitler at the summer Olympics! At least Jesse Owens gave the Aryans something to think about.

Miriam and I went to see *Modern Times* and it's absolutely brilliant. No one can talk about unemployment, poverty, and hunger like Chaplin. The scenes of him working on the assembly line are the best possible way to communicate the frustrating struggle of proletarian man against the dehumanizing effects of the machine.

I'm ashamed to admit it to you, but Miriam and I both loved *Gone with the Wind*. Everybody's reading it. It's a best-seller. My sister, Gertie, has read it five times—even my mother read it. It's a romantic novel that begins in 1861 the day before the Confederate men are called to war, Fort Sumter having been fired on already. It takes place at the "Tara" plantation, which is owned by a wealthy Irish immigrant family, the O'Haras. Scarlett O'Hara "was not beautiful, but she had an effect on men, especially when she took notice of them." The author doesn't deal with the moral issue of slavery (actually she kind of defends it) or the economics of it either, but every woman I know, Marxist or not, is reading it!

That idiot Edward abdicated today to marry that stupid Wallis Simpson woman. They're both Fascists. At least Albert—or whatever his new name will be—won't support Hitler.

I'm sending some books and warm socks in a separate package.

Love,
Lilly

She wondered if Manny would think her letter was mundane. Would he think she was terrible for loving the romance of Rhett and Scarlett—overlooking the book being an apologia for slavery? But, she felt she couldn't tell him that the other members of the Defense Committee asked Sidney to try to solicit John Dewey to endorse Trotsky's right to a fair hearing in response to the charges in Moscow. No, she couldn't tell him that. *Is it better for him to think my letter is unsophisticated,* she wondered, *or for him to think I'm a Trotskyist?* She decided to go with the mundane.

*   *   *

A few days later, over cherry cheesecake at Stewart's cafeteria, Sidney complained to Lilly that it was not easy to convince Dewey that the project made sense.

"Dewey's concerned that the Trotskyists are blurring the distinction between Trotsky's right to a fair hearing and his political program."

Dewey, Sidney said with cheesecake still in his mouth, had no sympathy with Trotsky's ideology and didn't want to be used as a tool to justify it.

"Albert Einstein," Sidney said putting down his fork, "has the same problem with endorsing the Committee—he's afraid it would be taken as an endorsement of Trotsky's ideas."

Lilly's stopped chewing her cake. Sidney had talked to Albert Einstein!

"Dewey asked me," Sidney continued, "if he should go to Mexico, but I didn't want to take that responsibility. It's funny. You know he was my dissertation advisor at Columbia. Anyway, Suzanne La Follette, who's a member of the committee, called Dewey and asked him to come to her apartment to read a letter that Trotsky sent to her. Can you believe it? She lives at the Chelsea hotel. Her father's William La Follette, the Congressman. And now Dewey's doing it—he's going."

"So what did Trotsky say in the letter that was so convincing?" Lilly asked.

"He said," Sidney laughed, "that Voltaire was willing to descend from his philosophical heights in order to redress a miscarriage of justice and Mr. Dewey should too."

"Trotsky's like a Jewish mother," Lilly said, smiling. "He knows just how to make people feel guilty."

"Exactly. After listening to the letter, Dewey felt challenged. And at the end of the meeting, Suzanne said it was obvious that Trotsky had succeeded in getting to him because she said that Dewey had said, 'This case ranks with the Dreyfus Affair and Sacco and Vanzetti.'"

"Well, it's true. In both cases, flimsy evidence was drummed up to prosecute innocent men." Lilly nodded.

"His kids and a lot of his friends don't want him to do it," Sidney said scrunching his face. "Even before he said he'd do it, the

Party already spread the word that he's senile. Who needs that? I didn't want to press him. I really admire the guy."

Lilly agreed. Dewey was going to interrupt his life, maybe even *risk* his life, to go to Mexico for a cause he believed in.

*   *   *

The lavender bubbles relaxed every muscle as Lilly sat in the bath and Gertie on the toilet seat applying their favorite facial—egg white. But once they dabbed it on our faces with cotton and it hardened, Lilly asked Gertie to leave her alone in the bathroom. She reached over and took the letter out of the pocket of her skirt that she'd left on the toilet seat. Her wet fingers made the onion skin paper transparent. She felt the pull of the dried albumen on her face and a little ashamed to be reading Manny's letter in such luxury.

January 5, 1937

Dear Lilly:

We didn't have a very happy New Year.
There was house to house fighting around the
slaughterhouse near the university campus.
They broke into homes and opened fire on
whole families. Snipers shot children on the
street scurrying to get back home from the
store. They lay on the street in pools of blood
with fresh bread in their hands.

The Nationalists tried to cut off the Madrid-
La Coruna Road but we gave them a run for
their money and they suffered heavy losses.
Ramon says Franco couldn't take Madrid by
storm so now he's trying to isolate us. I hear
American companies like Ford are supplying
some of the tanks and equipment for the
Fascists. It's depressing. The working class
has to raise its voice against Fascism. I hope

71

the *Daily Worker* is reporting what's really
going on here.

Mussolini is supplying the Nationalists with
men and equipment. And Hitler wants Franco
to take over Madrid and put an end to this
quickly.

I told my mother I was coming to Spain to
work in a factory. When I write to her I tell
her I'm far from the fighting. I hope she
doesn't end up seeing my picture in the
Forward. How's your family? Is your sister
still interested in art?

Please write.

Best,
Manny

Lilly realized their letters must have crossed in the mail. His
letter felt distant to her. She was frightened and ashamed. She didn't
want to end up seeing his face in the *Forward* either. Going to her
classes at NYU and to the movies with Howie seemed so pedestrian
when the world was falling apart. She wanted to do something that
mattered.

          *   *   *

Sidney and Lilly sipped coffee and shared a cheese Danish at
Stewart's cafeteria late one afternoon.

"Lilly, I have something to talk to you about."

It sounded serious. Lilly felt a tic in her eye lid. Sidney's
usually animated style was gone. She wondered if this was about
Miriam—if he finally wanted to talk to her about what had happened.
He seemed almost lifeless; the skin under his jaw sagged a bit. He had
dark bags under his eyes.

He took a breath and said, "I have an important question to ask
you. Dewey and the Commission are going to Mexico City for the

proceedings." He stopped, looked directly in Lilly's eyes and continued, "Dewey has his own personal secretary, but he needs more than one person to help sort out all the documents for the Commission. It's just clerical work, but I think it would be an incredible opportunity for you, a once in a lifetime experience. Since *Partisan Review* stopped publishing last semester and you're not doing that anymore, I thought you might be interested in this. You'll only be gone a couple of weeks and you'll get to know John, one of the most brilliant thinkers of our time, and you'll meet Trotsky and experience an historic event. And imagine how this will look on your curriculum vitae!"

Lilly was stunned. "I can't believe you're offering me this!" She popped up from her seat so fast her coffee launched toward Sidney. He jumped up to avoid the waterfall and though he didn't manage to miss all of it, he started to laugh. Lilly walked to his side of the table. "I love you Sidney!" she blurted out and kissed his cheek. She smelled stale tobacco on his shirt.

"So does that mean you want to go?" he asked, using a napkin to blot at the coffee stains that looked like chest wounds on his red shirt.

"Are you kidding? I can't imagine anything more exciting. Yes, I certainly do want to go."

When she left Sidney, she felt like skipping. The winter air was crisp; the reflection of the afternoon sun made the small mounds of leftover snow on the street glisten; the clouds in the sky looked like ocean surf. On the subway, the man next to her smelled like fresh cut wood. He held the *Forward* with his calloused carpenter hands. She craned her neck to check the front page. *No pictures of Manny*, she thought, *thank heavens*. Then her thoughts turned to Howie. He was never going to be on the front page and he didn't want to be. But, she thought to herself, she was going to have a major adventure. Not as dangerous as what Manny was doing, but the Dewey Commission Report *would* be on the front page for sure.

When she got off the train, the weather had changed. The sun had receded behind dark clouds and it looked like rain. There was a sudden onslaught of wind and the clap of thunder.

"It's a once in a lifetime experience. I'll be part of a seminal moment in history," she said when she called Howie to tell him the news. She was grateful no one was in the kitchen because she knew

Tateh and Mama were not going to be happy about her going to Mexico. But she thought Howie would be excited for her. "Just think of what it would mean if the Commission decides Trotsky's innocent and that it's all a frame-up by Stalin."

"I know that this is a turning point, it will expose Stalin for the murderer he is." His voice cracked. "But I'm frightened for you. Stalin is not going to take this lying down." He paused. "I love you Lilly and I don't want you to do this. Please don't do it."

She was surprised at his reaction. "I'll be back. Don't worry. I love you and I'll be back. It's only a couple of weeks. I have to do this. Please understand." She felt the tic in her eye.

"No, I don't understand," he yelled into the phone. "Stalin is going to try to kill Trotsky. He's furious about the Dewey committee. Why put yourself in the middle of this?"

"I'm sorry, I have to go." She hung up crying and angry. *Why can't you just be happy for me?*

*   *   *

The next afternoon Lilly sat at the kitchen table with the red and white checked oil cloth reading Manny's letter. Mama had made chicken soup and put the mixture for the matzo balls in the icebox. She went out and Lilly was supposed to roll the mixture between her palms to make balls, add them to the hot soup, and then sit and wait in the kitchen to make sure the soup didn't boil over when the matzo balls expanded to two or three times their original size. But she couldn't do anything until she read the letter.

February 13, 1937

Dear Lilly:

Sorry I haven't had time to write. The Fascists tried to cut off the city by crossing the Jarama River to the south east and severing our communications with Valencia. The Fascists wipe out whole villages—women and children are bombed in their sleep and going to the market.

Lilly stopped reading. She put her head down on the table—feeling nauseous from smelling chicken soup while reading about women and children being bombed while they slept. After a few deep, slow breaths, she went back to the letter:

> Franco sent men from the Army of Africa and we've been trying to block their advance. I ran across fields as they fired on us and men dropped all around me—screaming in pain. Our guys have been really hurt. I don't want to tell you what I've seen. The Nationalists moved in mobile columns and took the Brits by surprise. The British had to retreat to Suicide Hill where they were surrounded. They lost three quarters of their men. Blood and carnage is everywhere. You walk through a field of sunflowers and stumble on body parts.

Starting to heave, she put the letter down and ran to the toilet. She bent over the toilet and put her hand on her forehead as Mama did when she was a little girl, but there were only dry heaves. After a few minutes, she put down the toilet seat and sat on the marble floor holding her face in her hands. When her stomach felt settled she got up and returned to the kitchen table to finish the letter. She felt obligated to read it. *If he could bear to experience it*, she thought, *I can at least read it:*

> Lots of boys are in the hospitals and rest places and time drags on for them with nothing to do. Ramon and I try to visit whenever we can and read to them. The place stinks from ether because they're doing so much amputation. The other day I saw a bald man with no legs sitting on his bed sucking his thumb.

She ran to the bathroom. Dry heaves again, but she couldn't get the image of the bald man out of her mind. She decided to take a bath and started to run the water. Then she went back to the kitchen to get the letter. She sat at the edge of the tub with the water running reading the letter:

> I told Ramon about you. We were both wondering if the Friends of the Lincoln Brigade can send us books. Most of us are trying to learn Spanish. I'm improving because of practicing with Ramon. His English has improved dramatically as well. Second hand Spanish grammar texts would be great. Old copies of the New Masses would be mighty useful too.

> The book by T. A. Jackson on Dialectical Materialism has never appeared in this part of the world. Ramon and I are both eager to read it. Can you send a copy? He was brought up by a Communist. His mother (can you believe it?) was in the Republican people's militia and she led an attack on Francoist machine gun positions in the central plaza in Barcelona. They wiped out Franco's men. He says it was a ferocious onslaught with handmade grenades and rifles. She wasn't hurt, but a lot of people died. After that, she was being hunted down by Franco's men so she went to Mexico.

> Old and especially new Daily Workers are a special delight. But reading about the Party Builders Conference and seeing the remarks making fun of the delegates is the kind of news that is depressing. The Daily Worker

writers ought to come here and get a taste of
the war.

Our commander was wounded badly. Ramon
tried to save him—he carried him a mile on
his back to the medics' tent. But the poor guy
didn't make it. He was an economics
professor at Berkeley and moved to the Soviet
Union before he came here. It's ridiculous—
he was the commander because he was in
ROTC at college. That says a lot about the
rest of us!

It's cold here. Can you get us some wool
socks? A lot of the guys don't have any more.
How's your family? Have you seen any of the
City boys?

Best,
Manny

She put the letter down and climbed into the warmth of the bath
feeling heartbroken to be warm while Manny was freezing and needed
wool socks. And this Ramon. "Ramon says…" "Ramon thinks…"
What did he mean to Manny? He seemed to be the new incarnation of
Arnie, except Ramon was a war hero to boot. *Even his mother was in
the people's militia for god's sake!* Then she felt a jolt of guilt. *What is
wrong with me? I'm feeling jealous when all these people are fighting
and dying.*

Disgusted with herself, she got out of the bath and went back to
the kitchen to take the matzo ball mix out of the ice box. She took a
dollop of the gritty mix in her fingers, rolled it around between the
palms of her hands and dropped the ball into the soup. She repeated
rolling the balls until the dish of matzo ball mix was emptied then
washed her hands and went back to the kitchen table.

She felt sorry for herself; Manny's letter was horrific, yet he
seemed distant. Was it because of Ramon? Or was it because he was in
Spain—in the middle of a war? And she couldn't tell him that she

didn't read the *Daily Worker*, never mind that she was going to Mexico City with Dewey. The attitude of the Communist Party toward the Commission was uncompromising hostility. She knew Manny would defend the Moscow trials. She heard the chicken soup boiling over from the expansion of the matzo balls and jumped up to lower the flame and wipe up the mess on the stove. She wasn't sure how her parents were going to react when she told them she was leaving.

Finally, she could no longer stall. She asked her parents to sit at the dining room table. They sat down and held hands, not knowing if this was going to be good news or bad. Gertie and Sol saw that something important was happening so they came and joined them. Sol tore himself away from listening to the near death of Ruby, Amos' fiancé on the "Amos and Andy" show. Tateh looked tired. Lilly could see the creases in his forehead and the crow's feet around his eyes. In the few moments of silence, Mama decided it was going to be bad news. She let go of Tateh's hand and folded her hands on *The Joy of Cooking*, which was sitting on the table. She grimaced; her worried eyes avoided Lilly's.

"I've been asked to be a secretary for the Dewey Commission and go to Mexico City for the proceedings." She held her breath as if managing her airflow would control their response.

"Oh my God, you're going to the Blue House," Gertie screeched with glee. She knew that Trotsky and his wife Natalia were living at Frida Kahlo's house since Diego Rivera had persuaded President Uzaro Cardenas to grant asylum to them.

"Shh," Mama told her. "What are you saying Lilly? You want to go to Mexico?"

"Of course, what do you think she's saying?" Tateh blurted out. Mama winced.

"*Every day brings forth its own sorrows.*" Tateh had a nose for trouble.

"Tateh it's not a sorrow, it's a good thing. She's going to be with Frida and Diego," Gertie gushed.

"It's not about Frida and Diego, for God's sake," Mama said with tears in her eyes. "How can you just take off and go to Mexico of all places?"

"It's crazy. There's no way you're going to Mexico," Tateh said shaking his head.

Lilly tried to calm them. "I'm going with John Dewey, his secretary and the rest of the Commission. I'll only be gone a couple of weeks and then we'll come back and start working on the report of the proceedings."

Tateh was still shaking his head. He said, "This is dangerous business. I don't want you to go and I'm furious at Sidney Hook for suggesting it. Let him go. He's such a big deal, let him go."

"Sidney's not on the Commission. He can't go. And I'm going as Dewey's assistant. This is a chance of a lifetime for me. After this I'll be able to get into any graduate school I want to with a letter of recommendation from John Dewey."

"How will you travel?" Mama asked.

"We'll be taking a train that will take about 5 or 6 days and we will be working the whole trip."

"What about security?" Tateh asked.

"The train's perfectly safe and when we get to Mexico City we will have all kinds of security—Trotsky's security agents."

"I don't like it," Tateh said. He inhaled, his chest expanding as if he needed to make room for all the pain he was expecting, then sighed.

"Hershey, it's about Trotsky," Mama's arms were folded on her chest and she rocked back and forth in her chair. Then she stopped rocking, unfolded her arms and sat straight up. "Lilly's going to be present at an historic moment." She nodded her head as she made up her mind. "She's standing up against Stalin." She put her hand on Tateh's arm.

"That's the whole problem," he yelled, "Ida, *don't you understand,* the verdict against Trotsky is a death sentence?" He pulled Mama's hand off his arm. "Don't you think Stalin wants to kill Trotsky? You want her to go to Mexico and spit in Stalin's face?"

Sol got up from the table and walked over to Tateh, leaned over and put his arms around him. He whispered, "Tateh, don't be frightened." Then he straightened up and said, "She's doing the right thing. Stalin can't kill Trotsky. And she's going with John Dewey; Stalin's not going to kill John Dewey."

"That's right," Mama patted Sol's arm to show her affirmation. "She's standing up for the truth."

"The truth has many faces." Tateh's hands covered his eyes.

"I've never seen Tateh cry before," Gertie said as she sat on the toilet with the door open talking to Lilly. Lilly was taking off her clothes and putting on her nightgown. The shadows of the tulip-shaped fixture in their bedroom danced on the ceiling.

"He cried the day of your accident and he cried at Sol's *bris*," Lilly said as she slipped her cotton nightgown over her head.

Gertie flushed the toilet. "But it's pretty rare. He must be frightened for you."

"I know. But I have to go and I'll be perfectly safe with John Dewey," Lilly said. She thought about Manny. *How can you compare the danger of going with Dewey to what he's facing in Spain?*

Gertie came back into the bedroom and pulled back the duvet to get into bed and Lilly went into the bathroom to brush her teeth.

"Of course you're going; it's so exciting. I can't believe you're going to meet Diego and Frida and Trotsky. How lucky can you be? You can't pass it up." Then her tone of voice changed. "But do you *really* think there's no reason to be worried?"

Lilly stopped brushing and answered with her mouth full of toothpaste. "I'm sure there's nothing to worry about. Really." She felt a twinge in her stomach. What kind of security *would* there be at the inquiry proceedings, she wondered. What if Stalin decided the best way to stop the Dewey Commission was to kill Trotsky while the Commission was in Mexico? *No, no,* she reassured herself. *The place will be crawling with Trotsky's security guards*. She didn't say anything to Gertie. She put it out of her mind the way Tateh put smelly garbage in the can outside the house and went to sleep.

8

"You're a son of a bitch," Jack Dewey said. "And if anything happens to my father I'll kill you."

Sidney's face was flushed and his mouth was open but nothing came out. Lilly thought he was afraid Jack was going to punch him. Sidney was the kind of man who learned early to give up his stick ball bat when a bigger kid demanded it. He could not win with his fists. By the time he muttered: "But…" Jack had already walked out of Stewart's Cafeteria. Sidney had told Lilly that Dewey's children were vociferously opposed to his going to Mexico to serve as Chairman of the Commission of Inquiry into the Charges Made Against Leon Trotsky. They believed it would involve too much of a time commitment in light of his work on *Logic,* the culmination of all his philosophical thought. More important, they feared for his life! Jack's rage at Sidney frightened Lilly about going with Dewey. She wondered if Howie and Tateh were right about the danger, but she had already committed herself and she was not going to back down.

Returning home that day, Lilly wished she could talk to Miriam. She would understand how important it was to go to Mexico with Dewey. Missing her, she sat at her desk to write.

February 20, 1937

Dear Miriam:

I have very exciting news. Have you heard
that John Dewey has been named as
Chairman of the Commission of Inquiry into
the Charges Made Against Leon Trotsky in
the Moscow Trials? Of course, Sidney is in on
this and he has arranged for ME to be one of
Dewey's assistants and go to Mexico with
him!! I'm dying to go, but Tateh and Howie
keep telling me it's dangerous because Stalin
is probably trying to stop the inquiry and kill
Trotsky. Dewey's son came to the cafeteria

today day and threatened Sidney. It was pretty
scary. I'm frightened, but I figure Stalin won't
be after me! And I'm sure the security will be
very tight.

I have been getting letters from Manny about
how horrible things are in Spain. I can hardly
bear to read them.

How are things in Paris? Are you writing?
Have you met Gertrude Stein?

Love,
Lilly

*   *   *

On April 2, 1937, John Dewey, Kate Duffy, his personal
secretary, and Lilly departed from New York to Chicago where they
boarded the Missouri Pacific "Sunshine Special" from Chicago to El
Paso. Dewey was 78 years old, as old as Zayde Shmuel, Lilly thought,
and yet from a different planet. Having met his son Jack, Lilly
wondered if Dewey was a grandfather: it was hard to imagine him
telling stories about his childhood the way Zayde did on Friday nights.
Dewey was a gentile so there were no Shabbos dinners, she realized,
but maybe they had family dinner on Sundays.

He had sparse white hair parted almost in the middle and a
Charlie Chaplin mustache that had a few brown strands left in it. He
was a tall man with large ears that stuck out a bit and he was always
dressed in a three piece suit and a tie. Lilly wondered if his
grandchildren pierced his Spartan armor by tickling him or making fun
of his ears. She and Gertie always made fun of Zayde Shmuel because
he had hair on his ears.

Kate was Irish—a slight, doleful 50-ish woman with a smoker's
rasp—the kind of woman who has a black mark smudged across her
forehead on Ash Wednesday. Her short brown hair framed her face
with hard curls, but the crown was flat to accommodate her hat. She
was crisp like a stalk of celery. The large gold cross around her neck
had the figure of the crucified Christ with a crown of thorns on his

head. Lilly wasn't sure if all Catholics were that morbid because she hardly knew any. She'd never looked closely at a cross before. During the day, the three of them shared a private compartment that seated six. It was small, but Dewey sat on one side and Kate and Lilly shared the banquette on the other.

Kate was the quietest thing, almost invisible, and yet vital for Dewey's functioning. Lilly wondered if she had any life other than serving Dewey. When he spoke, her eyes glazed over in ecstasy. *Was she a supplicant devoted to Dewey,* Lilly wondered, *or was she in love with him? Maybe she had given up on ever having him and decided to accept the crumbs.*

Dewey had a private room and Kate while Lilly shared a small sleeper with bunk beds.

"You don't want to bother climbing up and down. I'll take the upper one," Kate said.

"Don't be silly," Lilly told her, "I'm happy to take the top berth."

"No, no, I insist," she said, crossing her arms over her chest.

Lilly had shared her room with her sister Gertie for most of life, but this was different—Gertie and Lilly were used to each other. They never closed the bathroom door. They were used to conversing from the bathtub or the toilet. But Kate was a much older woman and a stranger. She was prim and proper, glistening clean like a scrubbed porcelain sink.

Listening to Kate say her prayers each night before she went to sleep felt creepy to Lilly. She'd never heard a prayer to Jesus Christ. When she and Gertie were children, Tateh always came into their bedroom and said the *Sh'ma* with them : "Hear O Israel, the Eternal One is our God, the Eternal God is One." She'd never thought about it before. But now she realized that if you believe Jesus Christ is your God then you don't believe God is One. That was strange to her.

Kate woke up in the middle of each night to go to the bathroom. She sat up in her pink cotton night gown and Lilly could hear her contorting herself in the tiny space to pull on a robe before climbing down the ladder. Once on the ground, she carefully covered her sagging breasts.

She whispered, "I'm sorry to bother you" and headed down the narrow passageway to the ladies' room. Ten minutes later she returned, climbing up the steps into bed before she removed her robe.

The physical proximity to Professor Dewey was even more uncomfortable. One early morning Lilly met him in front of the bathroom, standing in his terry cloth bathrobe, waiting his turn. She'd never seen him wearing anything but a three piece suit. White curly hair peeked out of the neckline and since he was a tall man the robe didn't reach his knees. He had hair on his legs between his knees and mid-calves, but his legs were naked below that as if he had shaven the bottom half. Lilly assumed over 50 years of wearing high socks had rubbed off the hair. He smiled politely at her and went back to reading his *New York Times*—too embarrassed to strike up a conversation in his compromised position.

The train had mahogany walls and plush crimson carpet. It felt like an austere men's club—she imagined the New York Bar Association or the Harvard Club looking like that, although she'd never been to either. Those were places that were probably off-limits to Jews. She imagined portraits of Protestant men who looked like Dewey sitting rigidly with their chins high. No portraits of women, flowery slip covers or stuffed pillows.

The long passageways of the dining car were broken up by beige divans and tables placed crosswise. Mirrors gave the feeling of width to the narrow car. There were banquettes for three facing the windows and a speedometer was built into the center banquette to impress the passengers with the speed of the train.

During meals and breaks there were conversations, but always of a serious nature. Four other Commission members were also on the train, but Dewey had little interaction with them during the journey, preferring to read briefing material alone. Dewey was not a casual man and Kate was not chatty in his presence. But the second night, after she had said her bed-time prayer, Kate told Lilly about herself.

"It's funny, you know you're the first Jewish person I've ever really talked to. In my neighborhood everyone's Irish or Polish."

"Where's that?" Lilly asked

"Greenpoint," she answered, and then continued, "I've met Jewish people, Sidney Hook and some of Professor Dewey's students are Jewish, I think, but I've never really talked to a Jew."

84

"That's so funny because I can say the same thing. I had gentile professors and some of the students in my classes at NYU weren't Jewish, but basically all my friends are Jewish."

Kate stuck her head out over the edge of her berth and looked down at Lilly. Grasping the top of her nightgown, with a net over her hair, she hesitated a moment as if she were still deciding whether or not she should ask her this question. Finally she blurted, "So tell me something I've always wondered about. Please don't be offended. I really want to understand this. Why did the Jews kill Christ?"

Lilly giggled nervously, but she didn't think it was funny. She was aghast: she couldn't believe Kate was actually saying this to her. Then she realized Kate was brought up in Greenpoint and was probably taught by nuns in a Catholic school. Although Greenpoint was in Brooklyn, as far as Lilly was concerned, it could have easily been in Minnesota—there were no Jews in Greenpoint, only Irish, German and Polish immigrants. Her family never went there to shop or visit anyone. She heard of the Greenpoint Savings Bank, but that was the extent of her knowledge.

"Sorry, it's just that it's not true." Lilly was glad to hear her voice was calm. "And that lie has been used as the excuse to murder Jews for centuries. Pontius Pilate and the Romans crucified Christ. If the Jews were going to kill him they would have stoned him to death— Jews didn't crucify people on crosses."

"Wow," Kate said. Lilly imagined Kate's mouth open in shock.

"Look, there might have been some Jews that helped the Romans. Sure." Lilly was trying to give a balanced analysis. "But to blame the whole Jewish people for the death of Christ is just crazy."

"Lilly, I'm so glad we had this conversation," she said in a whisper as if she were afraid a priest or nun might overhear. "I've never heard it from that perspective before."

"Good night, Kate." Lilly wondered whether Kate took in what she said. *Does she know Jesus was Jewish?* She thought of Tateh, and smiled pondering what Yiddish phrase he would say at a moment like this. Probably, "*Scratch a gentile, find an anti-Semite.*"

"Good night, Lilly," Kate said as she pulled the covers over her. A few minutes later she was snoring.

During the two days from Chicago to El Paso, Kate and Lilly went through reams of material and put them into files and labeled them for easy retrieval. Porter Lawrence (they didn't know if Lawrence was his first or last name), a jocular man with a wide, flat nose brought them fresh water in insulated silver carafes every couple of hours. He was careful not to interrupt them, removing the empty carafe and setting down the fresh one without a word—only a slight nod of his head as if to say *done*. Porter Lawrence's woolly hair was cut close to the scalp, exaggerating his large ears, and he had several razor bumps on his neck just above the collar of his crisp uniform. His skin was coffee with a dash of cream in it, but his palms and lower lip were pink like a newborn baby's skin. Lilly was surprised that his smiling eyes were not black or brown, as she expected, but hazel. She imagined his grandparents had been slaves and that he had some white blood.

Professor Dewey read through all of Trotsky's writing as well as the transcripts of the Moscow Trials and took copious notes in a composition book with a black marble cover, but he always made a point of saying "thank you" when Porter Lawrence put down a fresh water carafe or replaced his dirty ash tray with a fresh one.

"You're very welcome, sir," Porter Lawrence always replied.

While the three of them were at breakfast, Porter Lawrence "made up" the berths—the upper berth, where Kate slept, was closed and the lower berth was converted to day time use with a table between facing couches. When they were at dinner, he "made down" the sleeping berths. Once or twice Lilly forgot something and returned while he was in the midst of it. Since Mama, Gertie and Lilly always changed the sheets at home, she thought it was strange to see a man putting sheets on beds and tucking in the salmon colored blankets. He unfolded the sheets so deliberately, she assumed he always put them on and removed them in exactly the same way. Watching a Negro man doing this kind of domestic chore made her shudder. This was not the part of Scarlett's life she and Gertie had fantasized about—only the Rhett Butler part.

The only person she knew who had Negro friends was Manny. He lived close to Harlem and unemployed Negro workers used the Harlem Communist Party headquarters as a social and educational center. But she didn't know any Negroes. There were many in New York, but they were invisible to her—part of the scenery. They weren't in any of her classes in elementary or high school or even at NYU.

Dewey scratched his head or his nose every once in a while or lit a cigarette, but Dewey, Kate and Lilly were silent through most of the trip. Looking out the window on Friday as the sun turned red and dipped into the plains, Lilly thought about her family having Shabbos in Brooklyn: the table was set by now with a white tablecloth and the beige dishes with golden rims. Mama's challah was on the silver plate and the crystal goblets were all put in place. She imagined Solly looking for his yarmulke and yelling for Mama to help him find it; Gertie putting on her pink and green dress with the open collar; the smell of roast chicken with lots of garlic exuding from the kitchen; and Tateh saying Kiddush over the wine.

Kate said a prayer and crossed herself before each meal.

Dewey did not partake in the prayer. He just sat there with his eyes down and hands folded politely on his lap until she was finished. Lilly had no idea what to do so she followed his lead. Part of her felt like Margaret Mead observing a coming of age ritual in Samoa, but another part felt like she was doing something she shouldn't. Jews aren't supposed to enter a church or interact with people engaged in idolatry. She wondered if she was doing that. No, she decided—she was just sitting at the table with someone engaged in idolatry. She wasn't saying the prayer.

At lunch on Saturday, Dewey was sipping coffee and smoking a cigarette. He took off his rimless glasses as if his spectacles interfered with his ability to reason and said, "The Russian situation as it's illustrated in the purges and frame-ups exemplifies the complete breakdown of revolutionary Marxism." He put his cup down and loosened his tie. His fingers drummed the table waiting for a response—Lilly's response.

What an overstatement! Lilly was about to say, "How can you say that?" when a stout man having lunch across the car put two fingers in his mouth and whistled for the porter as if he were calling his dog. Lilly was furious and could feel the heat in her face. She wanted to yell at the man, "Who do you think you are? Slavery is over."

Lilly looked at Professor Dewey—his eyes opened wide and his bushy eyebrows rose as if he'd seen a ghost. He too was outraged. Lilly smiled to herself thinking he wasn't just a pompous ass.

"Are you saying," Lilly asked when she gained her composure, "that all communism, including Trotsky's, is broken?"

Kate was quiet; she had told Lilly she never discussed politics with him. Lilly wondered if it was because of her intellectual insecurity or Dewey's lack of respect for her opinion. She always seemed up on the balls of her feet when she spoke to him—anxious to please. Pulling her handkerchief from the sleeve of her white cotton blouse that was buttoned up to the neck, Kate blew her nose. Then she put her handkerchief-covered forefinger up each nostril, rotating her finger to reach every nook and cranny.

"Yes, the great lesson for American radicals and communists who sympathize with the USSR is that they have to reconsider how to bring about social change." Dewey removed his glasses and rubbed his eyes with his thumb and forefinger. He had dark pouches under his eyes. "I believe in a democratic approach to social change. I don't think Trotsky represents that any more than Stalin." Dewey leaned forward and lowered his voice. "Just because I think Trotsky has the right to defend himself against Stalin doesn't mean I agree with his methods."

"But Trotsky's methods," Lilly shook her head, "are not the same as Stalin's."

Kate raised her pencil thin eyebrows and straightened her blouse. Lilly wondered what she was thinking: did she agree with her? But she didn't want to put Kate on the spot so she didn't ask her.

Dewey tapped his foot on the floor. "Come on Lilly," he smiled wryly, "when violence is used as a means of getting economic or social reform, the new government has to be kept in power by coercion. Violence breeds violence."

"Do you think slavery would have ended if there wasn't a Civil War? Sometimes violence is necessary."

He sighed, lit a cigarette and then squinted at Lilly as if he was trying to read small print. "How do you explain Trotsky's response to the Kronstadt Rebellion? He was just as ruthless as Stalin. Suppression of opposition, even within the Party, is the major method of maintaining power." The vein in his neck protruded. "This is why this whole thing is such an object lesson for American democracy. The dictatorship of the proletariat has led, and I believe, will always lead to a dictatorship *over* the proletariat."

Kate sneezed and Dewey said "God bless you."

"And in every country," he continued, "where there is an attempt to create a communist government, the same thing will happen.

88

But enough of this, let's get back to work," he said as he folded his napkin and stood up.

Lilly didn't agree with him. Trotsky was different. She knew about his role in putting down the Kronstadt Rebellion. The sailors and workers who wanted a return to the ideals of the Bolshevik Revolution were crushed by the Red Army in 1921, led by Trotsky. But she thought the reality was more complicated.

She looked up at Dewey towering above her, feeling a crick in her neck. Dewey smirked as he looked down at her still sitting at the table.

"Trotsky wouldn't be having show trials," she said, "in order to execute any one he imagined might oppose him." She folded her napkin and stood up, the top of her head almost reaching the bottom of his chin.

Dewey made a face as if he had bitten into a lemon. "Touché," he said and turned to leave the dining car.

For the moment at least, the conversation was over.

*   *   *

After two nights on the train from Chicago they reached El Paso where they had to change to the Texas-Mexican railroad. Constructed in red brick, Union Depot featured a six story bell tower topped with a tall spire that Pancho Villa used as a lookout position during an attack on Ciudad Juarez just over the border. Emerging from the train they were greeted by sunlight streaming through the large semi-circular windows which ringed the upper level of the Depot. The windows were divided into three compartments and reminded Lilly of the ones she and Howie had seen in pictures of the Roman baths at the Metropolitan Museum. She wished Howie was standing there next to her smiling, taking in every detail, the way he always did.

Once on the train, they were given a private compartment similar in size to the one they had just exited. The train passed a Mexican village composed of flimsy structures made of corn stalks or bamboo with thatched roofs that looked like a strong wind could blow them down; more substantial adobe tile-roofed houses; and some large Spanish-looking houses made of brick or stone that were surrounded by outer walls built flush with the street. Lilly guessed that the people who lived in the flimsy houses worked in the fields owned by the people in the Spanish-looking houses.

A tall colored man wearing a Pullman uniform with shiny buttons introduced himself.

"Good evening. I'm Porter Johnson." He bowed slightly.

Now it was clear, "Porter" was a title like Mr. and it was followed by the last name. Porter Johnson was darker than Porter Lawrence—he had shiny black skin like patent leather. A chubby man with no distinguishable chin, his chin and neck melted into each other like a gullet.

"If you would like your shoes polished or jacket brushed," Porter Johnson said, "please be kind enough to place them outside the door in the evening and I will return them in the morning. If there is anything I can do for you, please ring for me." He smiled as he put a carafe of water and a few menus on the table. Lilly noticed, as he withdrew out the door without turning his back to them, that he had small hands and manicured nails. He was more formal than Porter Lawrence—extremely polite, but there was no smile in his eyes. Professor Dewey, Kate and Lilly all said "thank you" in concert.

Lilly felt a hunger pang and wished she could order a bagel with lox and cream cheese or stand at the counter next to Howie at Nathan's in Coney Island eating a frankfurter with mustard and sauerkraut. She didn't mind eating food that wasn't kosher, but the train menu was filled with dishes that mixed meat and cheese. The combination made her queasy.

"Is something wrong, Lilly?" Kate asked noticing Lilly's discomfort with the menu.

"No, I'm just trying to decide what to eat," Lilly said casually.

She was quiet as if she was considering the problem. Then she smiled, "Why don't you try the pork tacos? They come with black beans and avocado and sour cream. That's what I'm going to have."

Lilly felt a wave of nausea rising up at the idea of pork with sour cream. Once it passed, she wrinkled her nose and said, "No, no, I don't think that works for me."

Kate's face dropped and her eyes opened wide. She paused for a moment, but then must have decided to take the risk. "Are there things Jews can't eat?"

90

Lilly smiled. "Jews aren't supposed to eat pork or mix meat and cheese; it isn't kosher. That's what our dietary laws are called. But it's not that. I'm not religious. It just makes me queasy."

Kate pouted sympathetically. "I'm sorry." She put her hand on her chin. "What about the mole?"

Lilly didn't want to tell her that the idea of chicken with a chocolate sauce called "mole" sounded disgusting. Chocolate belonged in egg creams. *Doesn't she know that,* Lilly wondered, *she's from Brooklyn.* For the first time, Lilly realized Brooklyn wasn't just a place that you could leave. It was a culture with tastes and smells and language that was inside her and traveled with her. Not only that, there were different Brooklyns—and Lilly's in no way resembled Kate's.

"I really just want plain roast chicken," Lilly said in a controlled voice.

Gazing through the window, they passed through the city of Chihuahua with its dominating Baroque cathedral and headed south paralleling the Sierra Madre Oriental. All three of them looked up from the Moscow trial proceedings and Trotsky writings to gaze at the snow-capped Pico de Orizaba in the distance—the highest peak in Mexico.

Kate pressed her nose against the window and bubbled over like a glass of seltzer. "Isn't that amazing?" She was transfigured, vibrant. Dewey nodded and smiled. Lilly had never seen real mountains before this trip and she felt sure that Kate hadn't either. Mama took Gertie and Lilly to a bungalow colony in the Catskills every summer when they were little and Tateh joined them on weekends. But that was nothing like this. She'd never even seen the Adirondacks. Howie would be so excited, she thought, he loved to go hiking at Bear Mountain or in the Catskills. Manny crossed the Pyrenees by foot, but they could not be any grander than this. These mountains had been there for millions of years, she thought, and no matter what happened to Franco or Trotsky, they would still be there.

Dewey read ferociously—reading and re-reading every document. A lion with deep creases in his face, he occasionally looked up from the documents and growled to no one in particular, "No wonder the Party was trying so hard to prevent this hearing," or "They were afraid it would be a clear indictment of Stalin."

Lilly glanced out the window and noticed men in the fields taking a lunch break. She wondered if they lived in those flimsy huts the train had passed moments ago. They sat in the sun on small colorful blankets, shaded only by their Zapata-style sombreros, dressed in white cloth pants, collarless shirts and cotton jackets. Not too far from where they sat, a yellow bird with a curved bill sat on the branch of a dead peach tree, watching, waiting for crumbs.

When they broke for lunch, Lilly thought about those men sitting on the ground eating their lunch with their hands while she sat in the dining car eating with silver.

Dewey said, "The vicious element in all this is that the end justifies the means. The idea is ingrained in the communists."

Lilly glanced at Kate and noticed two black hairs above her lip and a few more on her chin. She thought of Mama sitting on her bedroom chair facing the mirror and plucking hairs and then rubbing a pumice stone on her face in soft circular motions.

"It's precisely because of the importance of social and economic equality," Dewey said, "that we must use democratic means to attain it. The Russian debacle shows that you can't get away from honest democratic methods without getting into trouble."

"But sometimes democratic methods don't work. They don't lead to greater equality," Lilly insisted.

The train stopped and a group of reptile-skinned men walking next to mules weighted down with bulging saddle bags met the train and put their goods on one of the cars in the back. A girl no more than 13 or 14 years old was sitting on a blanket close to the tracks nursing her baby.

Kate noticed the young mother. She stood up, looked out the window and crossed herself exclaiming, "Can you imagine? Look at that child nursing her baby right out in the open?"

Before Lilly could respond to Kate, Dewey said, "Lilly, the essence of fascism is no sweeter if we call it by any other name." He didn't say it, but his tone implied, *And that's that*.

By the time the train arrived in Mexico City, Dewey had decided that the accused, the old Bolshevik elite in Moscow, had acted like obedient goats and simply bleated out everything they had been ordered to say.

9

Leaving the Buenavista railroad station, they were assaulted by the blinding sun. It was April, but it felt like July. Before Lilly could get her bearings, two children clamored with their grimy hands extended, begging for change. Their skinny brown bodies were caked with mud and their shorts were torn. Kate started to search her purse, but Dewey put his hand on her arm and whispered, "No, if you give them anything, we'll have a trail of them in no time." Dewey waved them away and they turned their attention to other passengers leaving the station. Kate gave Lilly a guilty look and Lilly gave her a reassuring smile as if to say: "It isn't your fault." But Lilly also felt ashamed turning the children away empty handed and wondered why Dewey didn't. After all, she thought, he'd spent his life writing about the importance of education. Clearly these children were not going to school—they looked like they were starving. Outrage quickly rose to the surface—she wanted to yell at Dewey, *What's the point of school reform if the class structure remains?*

"So much for the idea that education is based on experience," Dewey said under his breath, wrinkling his chin.

"Yes," Lilly said, exhaling in relief that he was not the insensitive jerk she thought he was. But then she thought for a moment and said, "They're learning about inequality from experience, that's for sure. They're just not learning how to read and write."

"If they can't read and write," he said emphatically, "they won't be able to change their lives. Period." He picked up his briefcase and suitcase and walked into the traffic circle to find a taxi.

While Dewey looked for a taxi, Lilly and Kate stood looking at all the people milling around—throngs of passengers hugging their spouses and children; men shouting and waving for taxis; old Indian women and children begging.

"Who is that?" Lilly asked pointing to the statue at the center of the circle.

"I have no idea," Kate shrugged.

Lilly walked toward the statue. Her heart pounded as she worked her way through the crowd of differing shades of brown people speaking rapid-fire Spanish. She smiled to herself imagining her arms stretched out and yelling, *I'm in Mexico.* It couldn't have seemed more exotic for a young woman who had never travelled outside of New York State until she got on the train with Dewey. She approached the statue and looked at the inscription. Her head jerked back as if she'd been slapped. She quickly turned around, working her way back through the crowd to Kate.

"It's Christopher Columbus," she said, shaking her head, "I thought it would be Pancho Villa or Zapata."

Kate looked at her blankly.

"Christopher Columbus started the Spanish conquest of Mexico," Lilly said. "Why the hell did they build *him* a statue for?"

Now Kate looked shocked. Lilly wasn't sure if it was because she said "hell" or because she was talking about imperialism. But she didn't care. She stood shaking her head back and forth. She wondered, *How could they not realize?* Dewey was standing next to a taxi with the back door open waving. Lilly and Kate got in the back seat and Dewey sat in the front next to the driver.

The taxi smelled like sweaty feet. Lilly stuck her head out the window, excited to take in the sights of Mexico City—but she was greeted with a burst of hot dusty air. They drove along the broad Paseo de Reforma: there were tall buildings covering city blocks and limousines parked in front of hotels. The driver honked at an old man with a loaded burro that smelled of manure as he pointed to a large plaza with palm trees at the corners and said in heavily accented English, "See, is Zócalo."

"That's the central plaza," Dewey explained to Lilly and Kate.

Lilly knew that the National Palace on the Zócalo housed some of Diego Rivera's most famous murals, but she hesitated to say anything because Dewey seemed in charge. Barefoot children played with an old wooden crate while an Indian woman shielded herself from the sun with a tattered blanket. Lilly wondered whether she had any knowledge of birth control or if she was going to keep on having babies destined for poverty—she had the impulse to stop the taxi and talk to the woman. But she sighed, realizing that even if she acted out the impulse, she didn't have the language ability to communicate with the woman. Then she turned her attention to a tall man with sombreros piled on his head walking around the plaza selling hats.

"*Catedral Metropolitana de la Asunción de María*," said the driver. "Very old." He had a dark thick neck like a tree trunk with a scar just below his ear.

"It's the largest cathedral in the Americas," Dewey said. Turning to speak directly to Kate, he added, "The seat of the Roman Catholic Archdiocese of Mexico."

Lilly took a deep breath. She wondered, *How many Aztecs died building it? How many generations of Aztecs?*

"Yes," Kate smiled and sighed longingly as if someone had told her a romantic tale.

Lilly wanted to say something contemptuous to Kate. She wanted to ask, *What's wrong with you? Don't you know how much money the Church stole from the peasants of Mexico?* But she controlled herself. Lilly felt excluded from the special bond between Dewey and Kate. Dewey wasn't Catholic; he said he didn't believe in revealed truth of any kind: Marx or God. Nevertheless, he knew Kate well enough to know that seeing and knowing about the cathedral would be meaningful to her. Unlike Dewey, Lilly could not countenance Kate's pleasure at seeing this grandiose symbol of the Spanish conquest and Catholic wealth and power in the midst of so much poverty. *Don't you know*, she wanted to say, *it was Cortes who brought the Catholic Church to Mexico?* She wanted to yell at her, *Can't you see how disgusting this is?* Instead she asked Dewey how the Church fared after the Mexican Revolution.

"Actually," Dewey said, "that's a good question. Some of the first laws of the new Mexican Republic were anti-Church restrictions. In 1917, all Church properties were nationalized, many churches were closed and monasteries abolished—right out of the Russian Revolution handbook."

"Oh," Lilly said smiling in surprise. "I didn't know that."

Lilly looked over at Kate whose teary eyes looked down at her hands. Lilly couldn't understand Kate's reaction. Then it struck her that Kate saw the world through a Catholic prism that filtered out the poverty that surrounded the opulence of the Church. Lilly wondered if she also saw the world through a prism—a Jewish prism, a New York prism, or maybe a communist prism?

Her attention turned to two toothless men in dirty overalls and wide-brimmed hats leaning against the cracked adobe wall of a church

95

as if God would protect them from the sun, while a few feet away a barefoot man covered with an old suit jacket slept on a pile of paving stones.

Lamp posts and building walls were plastered with advertisements and posters with Trotsky's picture crossed out. Noticing them, Lilly's forehead was sweaty and her heart beat rapidly.

"What does that mean?" Dewey asked the driver pointing to one of the posters.

"Out Trotsky the Assassin," the driver responded.

"Oh," Dewey said, pulling out a pack of Luckies from his jacket pocket.

Kate's fearful eyes opened wide. Lilly grabbed her hand with her sweaty palms.

As they came close to the Plaza de Santo Domingo, there were crowds of people jumping up and down and pumping their arms in the air in support of speakers yelling angrily in Spanish. The only word Lilly recognized was "Trotsky," but she could feel the energy of the crowd like a giant wave gathering strength, about to break violently.

"What are they yelling?" Dewey asked the driver.

"They think government for Trotsky," the driver said, "and want him out."

"It's the Stalinists behind this," Lilly said, her heart pounding.

Kate pressed Lilly's hand so hard it hurt. "Ouch," Lilly blurted.

"Sorry," Kate said putting her hand on her heart, "I didn't mean to hurt you."

"Communist newspapers say Trotsky against Cardenas government," the driver explained, "and he friend with Fascists. Demonstrations for him to get out ever since he arrived."

"That's horrible," Kate put her hand over her mouth.

"It's frightening," Lilly agreed. She remembered her father turning to her mother and yelling, "Don't you think Stalin wants to kill Trotsky?"

Dewey said, "I knew there was a problem…but…"

Lilly imagined he was hesitating because the question hanging in the air was, *Why didn't you tell us?* She didn't feel she had the right to ask it. Who was she to call John Dewey's behavior into question? But this was much scarier than she had imagined. She felt a weight on her chest and her head was pounding.

96

"That's why hearings could not be public in Mexico City," the driver continued. "Moved it to *Casa Azul* where Trotsky and wife are living. More secure—about twenty minutes from here."

Lilly hadn't bargained for this at all. But after a few moments she consoled herself with the thought, *This is why we're here: the trial is going to exonerate Trotsky.* She nodded silently, trying to convince herself the mission was worth the risk.

Kate's chin dropped. She looked at Lilly with desperation. *Tateh warned me*, Lilly thought to herself, *he understood all this.* But she'd put it out of her mind, acted as if he was being overprotective. Then she thought about Howie—he begged her not to leave and she turned her back on him. Now she imagined his arms around her, holding her tightly and his voice whispering in her ear, "You'll be all right, Lilly. I promise, you'll be okay."

Dewey was quiet. Beads of sweat dripped down his neck dampening his tight shirt collar. He tapped the cigarette pack on his arm until a cigarette peeked out, then searched for a match and lit the cigarette, inhaling deeply. Lilly wondered what he was thinking. Was he thinking about his son Jack? She remembered the day Jack threatened Sidney at Stewart's cafeteria. Or maybe Dewey was feeling sorry that he had brought Lilly and Kate into a dangerous situation. Finally, like Tateh trying to distract Gertie, Sol and Lilly when they were frightened, Dewey said, "I have a great idea. Why don't we drive to San Angel and see the house where Diego and Frida live?"

"Yes, yes, let's do that," Kate and Lilly answered in chorus like two little girls happy to go to the circus.

Dewey smiled and asked the driver to go to San Angel. The house consisted of two spare, rectilinear structures, one white and one blue, each having a studio and living quarters. When Diego was in the news during the Rockefeller Center dispute, Lilly had read that the house was an ultra-modern functionalist house that the famous Communist architect Juan O'Gorman designed for them, but she was surprised to see that Frida's side was much smaller and joined to Diego's by a footbridge.

"Why do you think they live this way?" Lilly asked. She couldn't imagine her parents living that way.

"It's bizarre," Kate agreed.

"It's so separate and unequal. It's weird," Lilly said. She felt outraged at Diego Rivera.

"I'm not surprised," Dewey shrugged. "I met him at a dinner in his honor when he was in New York—Diego is an egomaniac."

"But why would Frida go along with it?" Lilly asked no one in particular. Her mother would never tolerate being treated that way; she herself would never tolerate being treated that way. She remembered the day in the Museum of Modern Art that she'd been nasty to Gertie for daring to question Diego's work. Now she felt another pang of guilt, not just for saying Gertie was half-blind, which was bad enough, but also because she was starting to feel that Diego wasn't entirely worth defending.

"I'm sure she goes along with a lot more than that," Dewey said and he and the driver both laughed a male snicker.

Lilly was surprised to hear Dewey allude to Diego's sexual indiscretions. It was hard for her to imagine Dewey as a sexual person; he seemed so controlled and distant.

At the end of the excursion to view Frida and Diego's house the driver dropped Kate and Lilly at the Gran Hotel de la Ciudad de Mexico where they would be staying. Dewey continued on to the home of Mrs. Robert Latham George on Avenida Amberes where he and a few other members of the Commission had been invited to stay. Mrs. George was the mother of Adelaide Walker—she and her husband, Charles, were in charge of public relations for the Commission and the house was to serve as the headquarters as well as sleeping quarters for the Commission.

"I'll pick you up at 8:30 tomorrow morning," Dewey said when Kate and Lilly exited the taxi.

Lilly felt like she had been released from jail for good behavior. After so many days with Dewey, she was about to be free.

A short, squat young bellhop in a blue uniform greeted them in English and took their luggage. He led them into the hotel lobby.

"Oh my God," Kate gushed, looking around at the beautiful Tiffany stained-glass ceiling and ornate wrought iron balconies which gave it a cathedral-like quality. "This is the most beautiful place I've ever seen."

Lilly was quiet. It was a luxurious hotel, she agreed, but surrounded by poverty like the Cathedral.

After checking in, they followed the bellhop into the elegant wrought-iron elevator and stepped off onto a plush carpeted hallway. He said in English, "This is the first room. Who will be staying here?" Lilly smiled, delighted that they were going to have separate rooms. She had developed a fondness for Kate, but it was a strain to share a room and constantly translate her thoughts into a language Kate could understand. Her experience with Kate had taught Lilly how much she took for granted—her Yiddish expressions, the kinds of foods that were familiar to her and her feelings about social inequality.

"You take it," Kate said, being the good Catholic girl she was.

"No, you take it," Lilly insisted. "I'll take the next one."

The bellhop took her bags into the room and Kate whispered to Lilly, "Do I tip him? How much?"

Lilly had no idea; she'd never been in a hotel before either. She shrugged. Planning to ask Dewey the next day, when the bellhop came out of Kate's room Lilly said, "We don't have any pesos, would it be all right if we catch up with you tomorrow?"

"Certainly," he said, picking up Lilly's bags and leading her to a room down the hall. The room had a plush red-orange carpet and velvet drapes framed the French doors leading to a small patio. When the bellhop left, Lilly giggled to herself, happy to be alone—and in Mexico City. On top of the engraved wood chest of drawers was a large green and yellow painted vase filled with varieties of dahlias in reds, purples and orange. Lilly threw herself down on the large bed to enjoy the afternoon light streaming through the open doors to the patio. The ceiling fan created a pleasant breeze and she lay there for a few minutes listening to the laughing Spanish voices and traffic on the street. She got up and walked into the bathroom to run a bath. She felt sweaty and smelly.

The walls and floor were marble and the bathtub was the largest she'd ever seen. Sitting on a glass shelf, there was a ceramic Tree of Life with the Virgin and child riding a goat. She giggled to herself, wondering if Kate had one of those in her room too. *She probably likes it*, she thought. Next to the tree were small bottles of bath oil, moisturizing cream, shampoo and an array of soaps for the face and bath. On another shelf was an Adam and Eve candlestick in bright blue, red, orange and green with candles inserted and a box of matches next to it. When Lilly sank into the bubbles of the lavender-sage bath with the lights out and watched the flicker of the candles, she felt every muscle relax—the fear and tension that had built up since arriving in Mexico City drained out of her.

When she got out of the bath, Lilly sat on the grand bed in the luxurious terry cloth robe provided by the hotel, her hair wrapped in a plush towel. A ripple of shame ran through her as she took in the sumptuous surroundings. *What kind of communist*, she wondered, *am I?* But she was overtaken by a wave of excitement. She dialed the hotel operator who answered in Spanish.

"I'd like to make a call to the United States," Lilly said. "To New York."

"Yes, of course," the operator answered in heavily accented English. "What is the number?"

Lilly stammered, stunned by the question. Who was she calling? Howie or her parents? She decided to call Howie first.

When she heard his voice say "Hello," she felt the excitement rushing through her.

"Howie, Howie, I'm here. I'm in Mexico City."

"Oh Lilly," Howie said in a voice that sounded at once relieved and longing.

"I'm so happy," she told him with tears rolling down her cheeks. "It's very beautiful, another world." She didn't want to tell him how scared she had been when she saw the posters and demonstration against Trotsky.

"How was the trip on the train?"

"It was wonderful. The countryside is magnificent. I wished you were with me so you could see it. But there's so much poverty here."

"Did you see Trotsky yet? How is it being with Dewey?"

"I haven't seen Trotsky yet. Tomorrow. Dewey is fine. He's kind of formal, but nice. Very smart. This call is probably costing a fortune. I have to go. I'll write to you every day. I promise. And I'll be home soon and tell you every detail. I love you."

"Wait, wait, I heard there are demonstrations against Trotsky and they had to change the venue."

"Yes, it's going to be in Coyoacán," Lilly said in a voice as upbeat as she could manage. She didn't want to tell him the city was plastered with posters calling for the deportation of Trotsky or how upsetting the demonstration was. "At Frida Kahlo's house. That's

100

where he's staying. Don't worry. I'm okay. Everything will be fine. I have to go."

"I love you Lilly. Stay safe and come home soon."

When she got off the phone with Howie, Lilly sat for a few moments thinking about him. She thought about his smile and the way his eyes always reflected the light. There was a weight in her chest and tears rolled down her cheeks. She missed him and her family too, but not enough to wish she was back in Brooklyn with them. She had intended to ring the operator again and call her parents to tell them she arrived safely. But after speaking to Howie, she realized the newspapers in New York were full of news about the demonstrations and change of venue.

She knew her parents would be frightened if she called and they would want her to come home. She decided to send them a telegram to say she arrived safely rather than call them. She called the operator and dictated a telegram: "Arrived safely in Mexico City. Very exciting. Love you, Lilly."

Hanging up the phone, she felt lonely. She'd never been alone before—she'd always had her family in the next room or Howie a phone call away. She realized this was a new feeling; it struck her that this was the first time in her life that she was lonely. She decided to get dressed and take a walk around the city to get something to eat.

Walking out of the hotel in the early evening, Lilly was greeted by the light blue sky with pockets of dark blue clouds and streaks of pink across it. The air was cool and the street was crowded with Indian women selling blankets and embroidered blouses, well-heeled tourists looking for restaurants, children begging for change and Mexicans going home from work. She took a deep breath and noticed the Indian women had a scent that she couldn't identify—musk maybe, she thought. A short, dark-skinned man in overalls looked directly at Lilly's breasts and muttered something in Spanish. She gave him a searing look and walked on. One block later, a man without shoes was sitting against a wall drinking a bottle of tequila. He looked at Lilly with a smile and wiggled his extended tongue at her. She felt frightened and decided to head back to the hotel where she felt safe to have dinner.

The next day four cars filled with Commission members and staff arrived at the hotel. Dewey was in the lead car and got out to greet

Kate and Lilly and usher them into his car. Then the convoy headed for Coyoacán.

"It means 'place of the coyotes' in the Aztec language," he told them.

It had rained for several days so the streets were rutted with puddles and mud. Braying donkeys with long ears and brown and white cows with bells around their necks sniffed whatever was on the road slowing the cars down. Lilly was content to look at the small pastel-colored adobe houses with chickens and dogs caked in mud rummaging for their breakfast. The street was covered with droppings in all shapes and colors—watery yellow chicken droppings and large black mounds from the donkeys and cows. Although the car windows were open, the smell was barely noticeable because of the clear, crisp air and the bright sunshine. As they drove down Calle Londres toward #127, they could see the twin snow-capped volcanic peaks in the distance.

It was almost nine when the fleet of cars arrived at the house. A phalanx of Mexican policemen stood in front of a twenty-foot wall that obscured the house. When they started to get out of their cars, the policemen motioned them to move close to the wall. John Dewey turned to Kate and Lilly and said: "Don't be frightened, they have tight security." Lilly's head was pulsating and when she looked over at Kate she thought that Kate looked like she was about to be executed.

Half the guards searched them, while the others stood watch with their machine guns held high. One of the police put his hands on Dewey's ankle and worked his hands all the way up to his crotch. Red-faced, Dewey kept nodding as if he was trying to convince himself this was not a big deal. The policeman who searched Lilly was a short, thin man who smelled from sweat and tobacco. He asked her to open her purse. Lilly blushed realizing she had put a Kotex in her purse because she was expecting her period. He tried to control his smirk as he worked his way through its contents with his beefy hand and found the pad. Snickering, he looked up at her face to see her reaction. She closed her eyes and held her breath. He laughed, removed his hand and returned the purse. The way he looked at her made her feel dirty. She turned to Kate who was holding onto the silver cross that hung around her neck until a stocky pock-marked policeman returned her purse.

Once they got past the entrance, they entered the garden patio. Magenta bougainvillea draped over the tall fence guarding the southern wall of the *Casa Azul* patio. The barely visible woody trunks were twisted and the stems had sharp thorns. Burro-tail succulents spilled over the other walls. The garden overflowed with blooming jacaranda trees filled with clusters of fragrant purple flowers that contrasted brilliantly with a magnolia shaped like a pyramid with large, showy white flowers. Fig and palm trees, red hibiscus and yellow wisteria grew in huge pots interspersed with stone benches and pre-Columbian sculptures shaped from volcanic stone. Two red birds bathed in a pedestal bowl with the face of a parrot on one side and a human on the other.

Lilly had never seen such a garden. She had spent many afternoons in the Brooklyn Botanic Garden with Miriam or Howie—and once with Manny. Lilly wondered what Manny was seeing in Spain. Not gardens, but homes and farms burned to the ground; bodies blown apart. She imagined women and children hit with shrapnel on their way home from the grocery lying in the street and members of the Lincoln Brigade lying in the hospital with spells of typhus. A wave of nausea passed through her, but then she looked up at the house.

They called it *Casa Azul*—cobalt blue on the outside with a dark red door and window frames. Diego Rivera, a whale over six feet tall and probably 300 pounds stood on his pillar-like legs holding a machine gun at the entrance to the house, with two other gun-toting Mexicans. Lilly's eyes opened wide. She knew they weren't going to shoot her, but they looked like they were expecting an armed attack. Kate grabbed her hand quaking with fright. Dewey greeted Diego and introduced him to each of the members of the Commission while Lilly and Kate walked into the house, eager to get as far away from the entrance as possible.

Inside, the thick adobe walls were painted blue, with green painted wood and metal work and yellow stained wood floors. The kitchen had a high ceiling and the walls were covered by bright yellow and blue ceramic tiles. One wall in the dining room was lined with retablos. Lilly thought that was strange because she had read that Frida's father was Jewish. Jews honoring patron saints? Maybe Diego collected them as folk art. She recognized paintings by Paul Klee, Diego and of course Frida's self-portraits throughout the house. She wished Gertie was there with her. It wasn't a museum; it was where Frida and Diego and now Lev Trotsky and his wife actually lived.

The hearings were scheduled to begin at 10 A.M. in the long dining salon on the south side of the single story U-shaped house. Bright klieg lights made the room look like a movie set. Dewey greeted several people who were standing and talking in the front of the room and then turned and introduced Kate and Lilly. There was the court reporter, Albert Glotzer, who nodded and smiled. Then there were the two legal advisers—Trotsky's attorney, Albert Goldman, and the commission's attorney, John Finnerty. Finnerty was a tall, thin, red-brown Irishman, dressed in a red-brown suit, with handsome tie and flowing silk kerchief. He looked like the kind of man who wants to know where one gets a Turkish bath and a masseur. Finnerty took Kate's hand and kissed it saying, "How do you do?" Kate's cheeks turned red. Then he turned to Lilly and did the same. No one had ever kissed Lilly's hand either. Lilly felt a sisterly connection with Kate, just as she had at the hotel when neither of them knew what to tip the bellhop. She had to quell the impulse to giggle.

Goldman nodded to Kate and Lilly. From his name, Lilly knew Goldman was Jewish, but he wasn't like the Jews she knew in New York. He had a sharp nose, a Midwestern accent and didn't gesture with his hands when he spoke. After greeting everyone, the five members of the commission sat at a wooden table at the head of the room and Dewey sat in the center while the court reporter sat at a separate table to the left.

Kate and Lilly stood looking around for a few minutes, as if they had walked onto a movie set and wanted to stare at all the actors for a few minutes before finding a place to sit in the audience. History was being made and they were witnessing it close up. The humiliation of being searched receded. If being searched was the price of admission, Lilly thought, it was worth it.

Across from the lawyers, on the commission's right, sat Lev Davidovich Bronstein—Trotsky. Lilly felt a fast drum beat in her chest: she was standing in front of Lev Trotsky. Fifty-eight years old, dressed in a three-piece gray business suit and a red tie, he looked more like an aging businessman than a revolutionary. He had thick lips, a white mustache and goatee that only partially covered his protruding chin. His piercing eyes glared through his famous rimless glasses.

Next to Trotsky sat his wife Natalia—a slight, melancholy, oval-faced woman in her mid-fifties with wavy grayish-brown hair.

Although Lilly had read that she had lived in Paris for several years, she was not a Schiaparelli woman. No simple suits with bold color accents, but rather a prim black and white print dress with short puffy sleeves. Lilly noticed her putting her hand on Lev's ink stained fingers and whispering "*Lvionochek.*" She knew that meant "My little lion" in Russian because Zayde used it as a term of affection for Solly. She wished Gertie was there so they could giggle together.

Jan Frankel, Trotsky's first secretary, sat next to him. With dark hair, an intense gaze and rumpled clothing, he looked like one of the homeless people who slept in Prospect Park.

Jean Van Heijenoort (Van), who was Trotsky's second secretary, sat next to Natalia. He was a tall, fair-haired man with a pompadour, dreamy eyes and a noble nose. In the first few minutes that Lilly noticed him, she was impressed that he spoke Russian to Trotsky, Spanish to the Mexican journalists, French to Natalia, and English to the members of the Dewey Commission.

Noticing that Kate and Lilly were standing aimlessly, Dewey walked over to them, guided them to where Van was sitting and said, "I'd like you to meet my assistants. This is Kate Duffy." Van nodded and smiled.

"And this is Lilly Abramovitz."

"It is nice to meet you," Van said in French-accented English. He looked Lilly directly in the eyes and held her gaze. Lilly felt the tic in her eye betraying her. He put out his hand to shake hers and she wondered if he could see her eyelid fluttering.

"It's a pleasure to meet you as well," Lilly said extending her hand limply. He gripped her hand solidly and she immediately realized this ritual called for a more robust grip. Shaking hands was as unfamiliar as pork and sour cream. She was both flattered and embarrassed at the difference in the way Van greeted Kate and her. She wondered if Kate felt jealous of her the way she used to feel about Miriam.

Once the proceedings began, Kate and Lilly sat in the onlookers' section taking notes. Lilly watched Van play with the gold pinky ring on his left hand while he listened to Dewey open the hearings with a condemnation of the nations that had denied asylum to Trotsky and thanked Mexico for its courage in offering him political asylum.

Diego Rivera looked like a frog-faced Buddha, with his thoughtful bulging eyes and huge belly. His double chin sagged like a wash line with wet clothes. There were 40 seats in the onlookers section, half filled with members of Mexican workers' organizations and the other half crammed with Mexican and American journalists. Seeing him surrounded by representatives of workers' organizations reminded Lilly of one of his murals she'd seen at the Museum of Modern Art—"Electric Power." The slim upper portion of the picture was a view over the Hudson River to the skyline of Manhattan and the rest of the painting was underground—three small chambers each with a worker holding an electric power tool. She felt another surge of remorse for her outburst at Gertie.

Frida Kahlo sat next to Rivera. She seemed small and fragile in the shadow of Diego's corpulence. Her big eyes, crowned by thick eyebrows that looked like a bird in flight, stared intently at whoever was speaking. Her black hair was parted in the middle like Delores Del Rio's. She wore an Indian-style outfit –a long ruffled skirt with ribbon appliqués and hand embroidery and a colorful *huipil*. It was a red fabric with vertical blue stripes on the *huipil* and horizontal on the skirt. A large jade necklace fell perfectly on her blouse and huge rings adorned every finger. *Gertie would be so excited to see her*, Lilly thought. She wished her sister was next to her, sitting close enough to touch Frida.

When Lilly went into the kitchen for a cold drink on the first day, Carlos, the only one of the kitchen staff who spoke English, insisted she try *tejuino* with a big scoop of lemon sherbet. Adamant that she taste it before he told her what it was made out of, he handed it to her with his thick fingers. He was right. She would never have tried it if she knew it was made out of rotted corn. But it was delicious. As she spooned the sherbet, he told her that John Finnerty was troubled by the altitude and was living on tomato juice. She laughed to herself, realizing she had imagined Finnerty as the type of man who would live on Irish whiskey rather than tomato juice.

Carlos was barrel-chested with a squat neck, a little shorter than Lilly, about 5'2," with a round face and straight black hair. He was like a Beagle, a loyal family companion, but there was no way to leash his nose for scandal or his delight in sharing it.

"You know, I worked for Frida's family since she was *niña*," Carlos confided in heavily accented English. "When she was 18 the bus from school was hit by streetcar. She hurt very bad. They thought she die. That's why she limp."

Lilly knew from Gertie that Frida had been impaled on a metal bar, fracturing her spine. That's why so many of her self-portraits portray her as bleeding and weeping.

"Never dressed this way before Diego," he said lowering his voice. "She wear men's clothing, covered scars, but Diego come back from Europe and wanted Mexican."

"You mean traditional?" Lilly asked.

"Yes, yes. Funny that Frida wear Tehuantepec clothes because they *muy caras*, made out of expensive fabrics, and Frida and Diego supposed to be communists," he chuckled at the irony.

"I love the way Frida dresses," Lilly said.

"It's from Oaxaca—Tehuantepec. The women there dress just right for Frida."

It was true, Lilly thought, the bright colors emphasized Frida's black eyes; the *huipil* suited her small shoulders and the long skirt covered her scarred leg. "Here, taste this," Carlos said.

"What is it?"

"I'll tell you after you taste," he insisted. "Taste first."

Lilly tasted the burrito he held out for her. "Mm. That's delicious. What is it?"

"Goat burrito."

Lilly almost spit it out. Carlos laughed.

"Goat?" Her revulsion to eating goat wasn't based on it not being kosher. She didn't know if it was kosher—and she had been eating all kinds of things that weren't kosher. She just wasn't used to thinking of goat as a food. She imagined the look on Howie's face. "You ate what?!"

At that moment Van walked into the kitchen and said something to Carlos in Spanish. Then he turned to Lilly and asked, "Do you like Mexican food?"

His smiling eyes said, *what's going on here?* Lilly imagined he heard Carlos laughing at her. Out of the corner of her eye she saw Carlos smirking, waiting to see what she was going to say about the goat burrito.

"Oh yes," Lilly said. She noticed the contour of Van's lips. "I just have to get used to some of the ingredients."

When Lilly and Van returned to the hearings, the tone of the proceedings had turned somber. They separated to go to their seats. Goldman asked Trotsky about the fate of his children.

"My two daughters are dead." He removed his glasses and pulled out his handkerchief to wipe the tears from his eyes. Natalia put her hand on his arm. Lev coughed in an attempt to regain his composure. "One was sick and the other…," he coughed again, "killed herself because Stalin took her Soviet citizenship."

Tears welled up inside Lilly at the thought of his daughter committing suicide.

"And your sons?" Goldman asked.

"Arrested." Lev put his arm around Natalia whose face had a ghostly pallor and who had started whimpering. Lilly assumed the sons were the children they had together.

"Under Soviet law," Goldman asked, "are the children of an alleged traitor guilty of something?"

"No," Lev smiled through his tears. "But in practice yes."

"Excuse me Mr. Trotsky," Dewey interrupted, "but can this be documented?"

"It's the witness' opinion," Goldman replied, "so it doesn't require documentation."

"This is not an opinion," Lev yelled, banging the table with his fist.

Even-keeled to the point of opaqueness, Goldman wasn't the kind of man who was used to being screamed at: he was speechless, his mouth agape. He was just giving Dewey the rules of evidence.

Suzanne La Follette sat mesmerized, her eyes darting back and forth between Trotsky and Goldman as if she were watching a ping-pong match.

"This is my experience, not my opinion," Lev said, red with rage.

*   *   *

That night when Lilly fell asleep, she dreamed about Gertie—or was it Frida? She and Gertie were sitting on the stoop in Brownsville. Lilly tasted root beer as the glass shards smashed into their faces. Gertie screamed. But she wasn't wearing a white sweater, she was wearing a long ruffled skirt with ribbon appliqués, hand embroidery and a red and green *huipil*—it was splattered with blood and glass shards.

"Don't touch your eye!" Lilly cried grabbing her hand. Her eye was full of blood. Lilly yelled, "Mama, Mama, hurry it's Gertie!"

*   *   *

Two days later Kate and Lilly sat on a stone bench in the garden taking a break after lunch. A billow of drowsy air rustled the foliage around them. Orange bird of paradise plants with foliage resembling banana leaves stood in planters fashioned from tiles or clay pots with blurred painted designs that fused slightly with the glaze.

"How did you like the blue corn quesadillas at lunch?" Kate said, turning to look directly at Lilly.

"I loved them." Lilly smiled remembering the taste. "I really liked the ones with chicken and mushrooms."

Kate tilted her head and said, "I thought you might be upset by the cheese in it." The tiny diamond stud earring that sat on her fleshy ear lobe glistened as it caught a ray of sun. *An indulgence*, Lilly wondered, *or a gift perhaps*? She wondered if there had ever been a man in her life—other than Dewey.

"No, I've decided I can't stick to what I'm used to here," Lilly said. "It's a relief actually. I want to be adventurous and taste Mexico."

"Catholics can't pick and choose like that," she said.

"Jews aren't supposed to either, but I'm not religious."

"You mean you're *not* Jewish?" Kate asked twisting her face in confusion.

"I'm Jewish, I'm just not religious," Lilly said casually, as if it was obvious rather than a nuance particular to Jews.

"I don't understand," Kate said. "If you're not a practicing Catholic, you're not Catholic. It's a religion; you either practice it or you're not a Catholic."

"It's different with Jews," Lilly said, realizing this was more complicated to explain than she originally thought. "Being a Jew is not just about religion, it's about a culture—food and Yiddish and a certain kind of humor." She'd never articulated that before. But it felt right to her.

"Shh. Look over there," Kate said jabbing Lilly's arm. She pointed to a bird with a green, red and orange beak half the length of the body that sat on one of the short stalks of a huge papaya tree. Smooth-skinned green fruits hung in clusters directly from the branchless trunk beneath the shady umbrella of giant leaves at the top.

Dewey emerged from the house with both hands on his lower back and said, "I'm so glad to get off my carcass."

"Shh," Lilly said, looking at Dewey with her finger across her lips. She put her hand over her mouth, simultaneously horrified that she told John Dewey to "shh" and trying to stifle a laugh at Dewey discussing his carcass.

"Wonderful," Dewey smiled as he looked up at the bird.

"What an amazing bird," Lilly whispered.

"I think it's a toucan," Dewey said. Lilly was surprised Dewey would take interest in a bird. But then he gestured toward the house and blurted out, "It's hard to imagine this man as a bloody revolutionist."

"What did you imagine a revolutionist would look like?" Lilly asked him, suppressing a chuckle. Dewey, it now seemed to her, was full of surprises.

"I guess I imagined someone more dour-looking. He looks so earnest and he has a sense of humor."

How amazing, Lilly thought, *the brilliant Dewey has such a childlike image of a revolutionary*. But then she wondered to herself what her image of a revolutionary was—she thought of Manny. He wasn't dour-looking, but it was true that he didn't have a sense of humor when it came to Stalin.

"He lives with such bad deeds," Dewey continued, thinking out loud, "and yet he seems to have such good intentions in his heart."

*   *   *

On the fourth day, Frida Kahlo was wearing a sea green striped skirt and a bodice of red silk gauze with blue embroidery. Lilly thought it was an unusual combination of colors—she'd never think of putting them together. But Frida was dazzling—even Trotsky glanced over at her during some of the duller moments of the hearings.

Dewey asked Trotsky what reason he had for thinking the dictatorship of the proletariat in any country wouldn't degenerate into a dictatorship of the secretariat of the party.

"That is a very good question Professor Dewey," Trotsky responded. "You are a man of unshakable moral authority."

110

Lilly wondered if Trotsky really meant it or if he was just buttering him up; but then she noticed his eyes were watery.

"In fact, I warned Lenin of the danger." He broke into a smile or maybe it was a smirk. "I'm sure you must have read about that Professor Dewey. The answer is that Stalin's dictatorship resulted from Russia's backwardness and isolation."

Lilly's head moved back and forth between Lev and Dewey. In between, she wrote as fast as she could. "The idea of socialism in one country," she scribbled, "is the result of Russia's backwardness and isolation. Leads to dictatorship."

"Can you explain that?" Dewey asked without responding to Trotsky's provocation.

Even I can explain that, Lilly thought, She remembered the arguments about Trotsky vs. Stalin in the alcoves of the City College cafeteria.

"Yes," Lev responded. "The dictatorship of the proletariat can only happen in more advanced and less isolated countries."

Lilly smiled to herself. She knew that.

Dewey removed his glasses and nodded his head as Trotsky spoke. He looked transfixed by Trotsky. Lilly wondered why—Trotsky wasn't saying anything new.

On the fifth day Dewey asked Trotsky about the Soviet Union using brute force to create a state- controlled economy.

"You are the personification of American idealism," Trotsky answered. "I am as opposed to brute force as you are, but the Soviet state's ownership of the means of production makes it the most progressive country in the world."

Most of the questions asked by commission members Otto Ruehle, Benjamin Stolberg and Suzanne La Follette, centered on Trotsky's written materials and never seriously challenged him. She wrote them down so she would have a record of the proceedings for Dewey, but Lilly felt their questions were facile. She could have answered them herself by citing pages in Trotsky's works because she'd become so familiar with them during the train ride with Dewey. She felt proud of herself, realizing that she had become quite an expert on Trotsky's ideas. Lilly looked over at Trotsky and noticed Natalia glancing at Frida in the onlookers' gallery. She thought, *If looks could kill, Frida would keel over.* She wondered why Natalia hated Frida.

Distracted, Lilly glanced at the three fortified, covered French windows. She couldn't see the garden. She remembered the smirking policeman searching her purse for weapons and finding a sanitary napkin. She had developed a way of numbing herself—when he put his grubby hands in her purse each day she focused on a crack in the adobe wall, watching a spider crawl inside it or an ant scampering past it; or she counted the veins in a leaf on the ground. When she looked at the adobe brick and sandbag barricade against the windows, she felt a flash of anger toward Sidney. *Did he know about the security problems and change of venue before we left New York? What was he thinking when he encouraged me to come here?* She had been naïve, but he must have realized the danger.

Commission member Carleton Beals, a Latin American specialist, stifled a yawn. With his mouth open the brown crust on the side of his lips looked like the beginnings of a scab growing on a wound. Lilly thought he looked like a soup chicken, plump with yellow-tinged skin, all the flavor drained out of him. He took a package of Camels from his shirt pocket and lit a cigarette.

"We must have no smoking," Suzanne La Follette scolded him. "Trotsky doesn't like smoking."

Lilly wondered what Beals might say to La Follette in response, but to her surprise he put out his cigarette, replacing it with piece of gum. His lifeless skin hung loosely around his jowls. He looked bored, Lilly thought, watching him steal looks at his watch faced inside his wrist while other commission members asked questions.

"You must throw away your chewing gum as well," La Follette told him sharply.

Lilly wanted to stand up and yell, *Good for you Suzanne. The guy is such a schmuck.*

"I'm trying not to smoke, for God sake," he blurted out like a schoolboy being castigated by the teacher. Lilly was tickled by his comic gruffness.

"Did you send a Soviet agent to Mexico in 1919," he asked Trotsky, "to foment revolution?" He sat silently waiting, his cheeks imploded as if he was sucking a lemon, waiting for Trotsky's response.

It was clear to all present that this was an attempt to get Mexico to deport Lev. Lilly caught Van's eye across the room as she was writing and they shared a look. Diego and Frida sat a few rows in front

112

of Lilly in the onlookers section. Diego let out a bark and then he and Frida whispered to each other in rapid-fire Spanish, both clearly angry at Beals' provocation.

The room got darker. Outside, black clouds extinguished the sun. Lev was a man accustomed to being on guard. Yet now his face turned red like a little boy whose face had been slapped. His posture stooped. "Your informant is a liar." He folded his hands in front of him and looked straight ahead as if he was trying to control himself from punching Beals.

The next day Beals resigned from the Commission announcing that it was a "whitewash" and "show trial." Dewey's face was flushed, his jaw tense and his posture rigid as he listened, probably horrified at being accused of being Lev's pawn. After days of listening to Trotsky's testimony, Dewey had become just as convinced of Trotsky's innocence and brilliance as Sidney Hook, but he had done everything possible to remain neutral during the hearings, avoiding any contact with Trotsky outside the hearing sessions to avoid any suggestion of impropriety.

*   *   *

Although Manny wrote to Lilly weeks before the Commission of Inquiry began, she didn't receive the letter until the hearings were in process because it was delayed. Someone had to smuggle the letter to France to be mailed to Brooklyn (as it was illegal for an American to be a combatant in Spain), and then the post office forwarded it to Mexico.

March 15, 1937

Dear Lilly:

Thanks for the socks and the cigarettes.
Ramon thanks you too, since he's always
mooching cigarettes—like Mooch. But he's
not a Trotsky lover like Mooch.

There's so much death around us that our
only escape is at the Museo Chicote, our
favorite watering hole (definitely not a

museum!), on the Gran Via. Ramon cooks
there sometimes because he used to be an
assistant chef at the Ritz in Barcelona. He
says it relaxes him. Ernest Hemingway loves
his cooking, can you believe it? "The coward
dies a thousand deaths, the brave but one."
I'm definitely the former. He's here to replace
John Dos Passos on a film about the war. He
has a wife in Key West, but he's clearly
having an affair with Martha Gellhorn, a
correspondent for *Collier's*. Now they're both
covering the war. She's the only female
correspondent here. Zeus sent out two eagles
to fly across the world to meet at its center.
When he's had his fill of martinis and
absinthe (can you believe he even mixes
absinthe with champagne), Papa says his wife
is a rich fashion editor who's a Fascist. He's
quite full of himself—a macho guy just like
the heroes in his novels. He and Martha are
fixtures at the Chicote. Papa claims Dos
Passos left Spain because he was scared, but
he's a great story-teller. He just wrote a short
story called, "The Chauffeurs of Madrid"
about Tomas the dwarf driver. Now he says
he's working on a novel.

The four of us (Papa, Martha, Ramon and I)
have great arguments about everything from
art to how the war is being reported (or not) in
the States. Papa loves this guy Miro. He
bought one of his paintings and showed us a
picture of the painting. It's called "The
Farm." He won it in a dice game. Papa's very
dramatic when he talks about it: "It has in it
all that you feel about Spain when you're
there and all that you feel when you're away.

No one else has been able to paint these two
opposing things.'

Ramon knows a lot about art and agrees with
Papa about Miro. He told us about one of
Miro's paintings that he saw called: "Man and
Woman in Front of a Pile of Excrement." I
think it sounds grotesque, but Ramon says it
communicates the sense that the world's
collapsing. It does nothing for me. I suggested
to Papa that he cut up his Miro and frame
each piece. He didn't appreciate that.

We argue about everything like why isn't
there more support from France and England,
how to deal with the anarchists, and whether
the Soviet Union is going to keep up its level
of support. Ramon and I are sure that Stalin
will support us until Fascism is defeated, but
Hemingway is skeptical.

How are you and your family? What does
your sister the art critic think of Miro?

Best,
Manny

It was exciting to think that Manny was sipping scotch with
Ernest Hemingway. Lilly had read all of Hemingway's novels—*A
Farewell to Arms* was her favorite.
The world breaks everyone ... those that will not break it kills. It
kills the very good and the very gentle and the very brave impartially.
Lilly thought she and Manny were both fighting battles and
both in danger, although she knew the death and destruction in Spain
couldn't be kept at bay with sandbags and adobe bricks.
Lilly put off responding to Manny's letter. When there are
things you don't want to say, it's hard to think of anything at all to say.
She didn't want to tell him she was a Trotsky lover like Mooch –that

indeed she was in Mexico with Trotsky. She didn't want to tell him that she knew from Sidney (another Trotsky lover) that Dos Passos wasn't a coward. He'd been distraught over the execution of his friend Jose Robles, a left-wing Republican, by the Stalinists and left Spain for good reason—he was getting death threats for investigating the murder. But most of all, how could she tell him she was in Coyoacán with the Dewey Commission?

She kept dithering. Writing to Manny felt like shoveling snow: it's light and fluffy, until it becomes heavy and weighs you down. She wondered if she was trying to protect Manny because he was in such a dangerous place or trying to protect herself from his judgment.

That night Van invited her to dinner. "I would like to take you out for a traditional Mexican meal," he said, "before you leave Mexico."

She was taken aback—he was quite a bit older than she. But she had been admiring him from the onlookers' gallery, wondering if such a cosmopolitan man could be interested in her. What if he was? She felt a fluttering between her legs. She wondered what she would do if he made a pass at her.

Lilly tasted the idea, first feeling a twinge of guilt about Howie, but then submitted to its gastronomic—and other—possibilities. She told herself it was just a friendly dinner with a mentor—nothing for Howie to feel jealous about. But she only half believed it. "Why that would be lovely. Thank you."

"I want to take you to a Tizatlan restaurant before you leave. That region is known for wild mushrooms that grow in the woods. It's not what you usually think of as 'Mexican food.'"

"Great. Let's go," she said with as much nonchalance as she could muster to cover her excitement; but she could feel the tic in her eye again.

Van smiled and guided her through the garden to the Roadster that was parked on the street. They drove past cows stretched out on the grass chewing their cud and avoided donkeys braying on the road as they shook off flies buzzing on their faces. Lilly looked at Van and noticed the creases on his cheek and the tension in his neck. The trees looked pink in the light of the setting sun. Parking in front of a gate that was surrounded by walls, they walked into what looked like someone's house rather than a restaurant. But when Van opened the gate, there was a lush Mexican garden with tables and chairs throughout.

Van greeted the owner, a stocky man with a bulbous nose. Lilly nodded hello and smiled to herself, thinking his skin looked like fried salami. He chose a secluded table for them. Van thanked him and ordered various Tizatlan specialties in Spanish. It was the first time since Lilly was a child that someone ordered food for her without asking. She was surprised that she liked it. And she wasn't worried about whether there would be mole sauce or if they were going to mix meat and cheese. She knew they would. She was only going to be in Mexico a little longer, so she was going to taste everything. They sat under a full moon that was partially obscured by clouds. When their margaritas arrived, Van seemed to take a breath and relax. As he lifted his glass, Lilly noticed the bulging vein running like a swollen river from his wrist all the way to his muscular upper arm.

"So, Lilly, tell me about yourself," Van said.

How could I do that? Lilly wondered. *It's such a boring story.*

"I'm from New York—Brownsville in Brooklyn, to be exact, and…"

"I know Brownsville," he interrupted. "I visited New York before coming to Mexico and I had this suit made in Brownsville." He pointed to the gabardine suit he was wearing.

"Oh!" she said. "I probably know your tailor."

"I grew up in Paris…not as colorful as Brownsville," he laughed.

Lilly laughed with him and then decided to take a risk and ask a personal question as casually as she could. "But your name isn't French, is it?"

"No. My father was Dutch. But I never met him. I grew up in Paris with my French mother." He tapped his fingers on the table as he spoke.

She wondered if his absent father had anything to do with his strong attachment to Lev, but she kept it to herself. She didn't want to be like Gertie and make facile psychoanalytic interpretations.

"What was it like growing up in Paris?" she asked.

He hesitated for a moment as if he was deciding which version of his childhood he was going to share with her. Then he said, "The

French taunted me when I was little. They called me *sale Bosch*—dirty German because I was blonde and my last name sounded German."

Lilly made a face, an exaggerated pout, to silently express her sympathy. She patted his hand.

"I was an outsider, a Dutchman in France, a boy surrounded by women." He took his hand from under hers, looked away and changed positions in his chair.

Lilly folded her hands on the table, trying to ignore his withdrawal. *Why did I touch him?* She chided herself, *I don't even know the man.*

"What turned you into a revolutionary?" she asked.

"Hmm," he raised his brows and stroked the skin under his chin. She put her hands on her lap trying to control the impulse to touch him.

After a few pensive seconds, he nodded his head. "I think it was a combination of things. My mother was a chambermaid and I was angry that she had to clean rich people's toilets," he said clenching his fist. "Also, I hated the arcane French school system and wanted to overthrow it. I guess I saw the destructiveness of nationalism and that attracted me to Trotsky, to internationalism." He looked Lilly directly in the eyes as if to say, *See, I understand what I'm about.*

Do I know what I'm about? Lilly wondered. *Here I am with this older man when Howie's waiting for me in New York and Manny's off fighting in Spain.*

The owner brought to the table a clay pot filled with chicken and a dish of mushrooms with green leaves.

"This is chicken with amaranth seeds—it's native to Tizatlan." Van pointed to the clay pot. "And these are wild mushrooms with a wild herb called *epazote*."

When they finished their food and second round of margaritas, Van turned to the salami-faced man with a smile and asked for the check. By the time they left, the clouds completely covered the moon and the air was heavy with humidity. They walked to the car. Van opened the door for Lilly and she noticed his broad shoulders. They were both quiet as he drove to her hotel. She wondered if he was sorry he had confided in her. She knew that when you tell someone something too personal, sometimes you avoid the person in order to avoid the shame. He walked Lilly into the magnificent Art Nouveau

118

lobby and looked around. Then he smiled at her and said, "Wow, capitalism is seductive, isn't it?" He kissed her on both cheeks, said "Goodnight." No one had ever kissed her on both cheeks before: it seemed so gallant. As she walked toward the elevator she turned and looked back at the hotel entrance, wishing he was still standing there watching her, wishing he had kissed her on the mouth, wishing he would change his mind and follow her.

*   *   *

A few days later, when the Commission was about to leave Mexico, Van called the hotel and asked if Lilly could have lunch with him. She was delighted, hoping he might ask for her address to correspond or visit if he ever returned to New York. Van was usually quite fastidious, but when Lilly met him in the lobby, his clothes were wrinkled and he was unshaven. He looked, she thought, like one of the men who sleep on benches in Union Square. She waited for him to speak. Finally he groaned, "Jan Frankel is going to resign as Trotsky's principal secretary and go to New York. The stress of all this has gotten to him and he can't take it anymore. Plus he has been telling Lev that his affair with Frida is dangerous; it could undermine everything, but Lev won't listen to him. I'm going to take over as first secretary." He pressed his hands together as if he were measuring them.

Lilly covered her eyes. The world was falling apart and looking to Lev for guidance and he was *schtupping* Frida? Like Dorothy, she had followed the yellow brick road to Emerald City and found the Wizard and he was just a man. But still he was a revolutionary, she thought. *How could he do such a thing?* She felt betrayed—he was old enough to be Frida's father. And right under Natalia's nose? No wonder she'd been giving brusque glances at Frida during the hearings.

Frankel was Trotsky's right hand man. Jan's gray stubble and slumped posture made him look haggard and old, although he was only 32. He had been with "the Old Man" since 1930 and he was one of the people with whom the usually charming and polite Lev felt comfortable enough to be prickly, like his beloved cacti.

Lilly had once seen him ask Frankel for a document and when he said it wasn't ready, Lev slammed the door so hard that all the panes of glass fell out. Now Lilly understood Lev was angry at Frankel not just for the late documents, but for his comments about Frida.

"What will happen when Frankel leaves?" she asked.

"I'll take over many of his duties," Van said. The muscles in his neck strained.

"How do you feel about Lev's affair with Frida?" Lilly asked.

"It's irrelevant," he said in a steely tone.

Lilly felt a chill in the air.

Then he softened and added, "I feel bad for Natalia…but we need to focus on larger issues. We need someone who speaks and writes English. Would you consider staying in Coyoacán and working for the Old Man?"

Lilly's stomach tightened as if she were walking up a steep flight of stairs. Van was inviting her to be the internationally famous Leon Trotsky's secretary! Despite realizing that he could be difficult, the idea of living at *Casa Azul* with Leon Trotsky was tantalizing.

Lilly loved Mexico—the bracingly strong *café con leche* in the morning; the sweet *agua de sandia* watermelon juice at lunch and the margaritas with salt around the edge of the glass every night before dinner. Most of all, she loved how she felt about herself. When she looked in the mirror she saw a sexy young woman with dark eyes and long wavy brown hair. In New York, she always wore black. In Mexico she had taken to wearing colorful low-cut embroidered blouses, bought from the Indian women with chiseled faces in the Coyoacán market. She imagined herself dancing to a mariachi band with cymbals in her hands, swirling her long flared peasant skirt. She also wondered if Van wanted her to stay for more than working for Trotsky. He was tempting, but she didn't want to cheat on Howie. She didn't want to be like Miriam.

There was no way she could stay in Mexico. She'd promised Howie she would only be gone for the Dewey hearings. He expected her to come back to him. And she missed him: she missed him whispering "My Lilly" in her ear and kissing her hair. She wanted to tell him about everything she'd heard and seen and tasted. She wanted to continue working on the report with Dewey. Besides, it was dangerous to stay in Coyoacán. And she didn't want to be part of the drama of Lev and Frida cheating on Natalia and Diego. And as much as she loved Mexican food and margaritas every evening, she longed for a corned beef sandwich on rye with half-sour pickles and Dr. Brown's cream soda. And she missed *Shabbos* dinner with her parents and Gertie and Sol.

She looked at Van and felt a rush. She crossed her legs.

"Thank you. I'm very flattered, but I can't do it," she said, pressing her fingers to her mouth as if she wanted to control the words that came out.

"Don't be so fast to answer. It's a big decision, why don't you take a day or two to think about it," Van suggested.

The next day when Lilly got back to the hotel the concierge handed her a letter. She didn't recognize the handwriting. The writer's strokes were economical—no wasted motion. She sensed it was bad news. A weight pressed down on her chest; she could barely breathe. She got a big glass of purified water from the lobby, walked to the hotel garden and sat on the ground under the fig tree. There were patches of sunlight in the garden and a crow made a recurrent noise that sounded like someone screaming, "Ow." The sky was an ocean of blue so intense that it made her think of something she once read about the color blue warding off the evil eye.

April 10, 1937

Dear Lilly:

I have some terrible news for you. I found your letters in Manny's things so I had your address. Our beloved Manny was killed in the battle of Guadalajara. His battalion suffered direct hits from Nationalist shells. Manny became separated from his unit and spent two days alone behind the Nationalist lines. Eventually he gallantly rejoined his men, but he was wounded too badly and drowned in the river.

Manny told me a great deal about you and I feel very sad to have to tell you this terrible event. He was such a wonderful man—and he

could be so funny. I loved his stories about
City College.

He died to save the working class and to
defeat fascism. He was a devoted communist
and was willing to die for what he believed.

Yours sincerely,
Ramon Mercader

Lilly couldn't conjure up Manny's face. Her hands trembled. She shivered and hugged herself as if she'd been caught in a windstorm without a coat. He had been so young, so alive. How could someone so young die? Dying was for grandparents.

She felt his hand on the small of her back, on her hip as they walked in the Botanic Garden. She smelled the rosemary and the lavender and felt the breeze blowing her hair, the taste of his kiss and the smell of his skin.

She ran back into the hotel. Who could she call? Kate would never understand—for all Lilly knew she might have supported Franco. So she called Van.

"Please, please," she sobbed, "he's dead."

"Who is this, is this Lilly?"

"Yes, Van. It's Lilly, please come."

"Who's dead? Did your father die?"

"No, no, my friend was killed in Spain…"

"I'm so very sorry. I'll get there as soon as I can."

"Thank you. Thank you so much," she sniffled, wiping her nose with her hand.

She sat on the couch, clutching the letter, waiting for Van. Outside the sky was darkening. *What would have happened between us,* she wondered, *if Manny had survived and returned to New York? Would I have left Howie? Would I have married him?* About half an hour later, Van knocked. She was still wobbly when she opened the door.

"How are you?" he asked.

The groundswell came back with renewed force. She was crying so hard she couldn't talk. She handed him the letter. He stood

122

there with the door open reading it. Then he walked into the room, closed the door behind him and took her in his arms. "It's so horrible, so fucking horrible. Lilly. I'm so terribly sorry," he said as he stroked her hair.

They stood there for a few minutes until she realized that his shirt was wet from her tears. She moved away from him and straightened her limp hair.

"He was my close friend from New York. He was so fucking committed," Lilly said, not caring about her foul language. "We've been writing since he left last fall. I've been sending him socks and books…" She didn't want to tell him Manny was a Stalinist. What did it matter? He was willing to die to defend Spain against Franco. She didn't want Van to say something mean about Stalinists. Not about Manny.

"That's too bad." His head tilted to one side and his chin dropped. He was quiet for a few moments. Then he asked, "So who was this man? Were you lovers?"

She was quiet for a few moments. "No we weren't lovers. But I thought we might be."

"Don't you have a boyfriend back in Brooklyn?" He raised his eyebrows.

Lilly felt accused. "Yes, I do," she said in a whisper as if that wouldn't sound as bad, "but I wasn't sure what was going to happen between us when Manny came back."

"Aah," Van nodded as if he understood the conundrum. "And who is Ramon Mercader?"

"His friend. A Spaniard he met in Madrid. They fought together."

Lilly walked over to the couch and sat down. She thought about her mother and how she would react if she or Solly or Gertie died. *She would never get over it. Not Tateh either*, she thought, *no matter what we died for.*

"How can I go home to New York and live my life as if I'm in a bubble, untouched by the dying in Spain and the betrayal of the revolution in Russia?" She turned to Van. "Manny was willing to die for what he believed." She thought about Manny floating in the river. "Are you willing to die for Lev?"

Van sank into the upholstered chair next to the couch. He didn't answer reflexively; he was silent for a few moments.

"Yes. Lev is a prophet who is ahead of his time. Prophets are always persecuted. People are afraid of change and of the unknown. But Lev is not afraid because his revolutionary intuition allows him to see beyond the present moment—not like a future-teller, but a visionary."

"Like Elijah," she said with a smile.

"He's not a prophet like Elijah, he can't perform miracles."

She was surprised at his knowledge of the Old Testament prophets. She thought Christians only knew the New Testament.

"But I believe he's like Moses." He paused. "And he will free us from the slavery of capitalism and win back the Promised Land from Stalin."

She smiled in appreciation.

"So I'm willing to die," he said no longer smiling, "not just for Lev, but for everything he stands for. I'm willing to die for the revolution. Yes," his resolve strengthened, "I'm willing to die."

Suddenly, as if there was someone else inside her, she saw herself get off the couch and walk over to Van's chair. She bent down and kissed him. He pulled her on top of him and kissed her hard. She wasn't thinking; she didn't want to think. He put his hand under her dress and found his way to her inner thighs. All thoughts of Manny or Howie fell away as they tumbled onto the floor and he kissed her neck, lifting her dress. She was pounding and wanted him inside her, wanted to feel him hard and strong. But then she realized what she was doing and managed to say, "Wait, wait, do you have a rubber?"

"Yes, yes," he said rolling over onto the carpet, unzipping his pants and pulling them off. His erection was larger than Howie's and his penis looked different because he wasn't circumcised. He took his wallet from the back pocket of his trousers and found a condom. She recognized the wrapper from her days handing out rubbers on Pitkin Avenue—it was a Sheik.

He pulled her dress and slip over her head. Then he unsnapped her garters and pulled her panties down, throwing them on the couch. He undid the hooks on her bra and threw it on the upholstered chair. She unbuttoned his shirt and helped him take it off. They were lying on the floor naked and he climbed on top of her. He kissed her neck and

124

licked her ear, circling it with his tongue. Then he put his tongue deep into her ear and moved his hand between her legs until he felt her wetness and pressed his fingers in a circle as she writhed beneath him moaning, wanting him. She was a wounded and hungry animal. He slipped the rubber on and entered her harder and deeper than she had ever experienced, so deep inside, making her gasp. He was completely in control of her, moving inside her. She heard herself moaning as she was filling up and then yelling as she was ready to burst, "Oh! Oh!" Finally she burst and he let out a huge groan and stopped moving. They both lay sweaty and spent. Tears ran down her cheeks. Her back hurt, but she didn't want to move. Through the window she saw a crescent moon with just a dim outline of its full self.

Van snored, his face buried in her wet neck. Their clothes were strewn around the room. *How can I marry Howie now?* Everything had changed. *What did I just do?* Her inner brakes had failed completely and now she was careening out of control. She couldn't go back to Brooklyn. She knew at that moment she had to stay in Mexico and work for Trotsky.

*   *   *

Two days later Van helped her move her things from the hotel into one of the rooms in the guard house—two doors down from his. The room had whitewashed adobe walls, a small desk and a single bed on a metal frame. The first night she laid on the lumpy mattress in the empty room, harsh rain swept across the window as though someone was hissing at her. She remembered a line from Faulkner's *As I Lay Dying*. "In a strange room, you must empty yourself for sleep...And when you're emptied for sleep, you *are* not." On that first night in the guard house, Lilly did not want to *be*, she hungered for sleep.

*   *   *

Lilly's job was to transcribe Lev's dictation from the Ediphone and reshape it into well-written English. She had never seen one of those machines before. There were three parts to it: the recording machine, the reproducing machine and the utility shaver. The recording machine had a horn that looked like the *shofar* Jews blow on Rosh Hashanah—it was attached by a metal hose. When Lev was ready he switched the stick with the red knob to "talk". Then he leaned all the way back in his chair, put the *shofar* close to his mouth and spoke. Lev pressed the button on the horn and the wax cylinder started to spin. His voice was engraved on the cylinder. When he finished dictating, he listened and used the utility shaver to erase anything he didn't like the second time around. Then he gave Lilly the wax cylinder and she inserted it in the reproduction machine next to her black Royal Deluxe typewriter. When she put on the earphones, there was Lev dictating in his heavily accented voice. She controlled the reproducing unit with two buttons: "speak" and "repeat". With the "speak" button she could start or stop the cylinder and by pressing the "repeat" button, she could hear the last seconds of speech again if she missed something or wasn't sure she got it right. Sometimes Lev confused words—i.e., "impel" when he meant "expel." Other times he used words that were technically correct, but didn't work in a particular sentence structure or context—i.e., "I thrust you" rather than "I urge you."

Almost every day Lev made a point of having an informal conversation with her. He didn't act like "The Commissar," just an older man taking a fatherly interest in a young person. With each conversation, Lilly's anger at him for his relationship with Frida faded more and more.

"Lilly, sit here," he pointed to the seat next to him on the bench in the garden. A bird swooped down into the bird bath. Lev said it was a barn swallow. It had a steel blue head, a brownish-red forehead and throat and a broad dark blue breast. The outer tail feathers were elongated making it look like it had a forked tail. The shadows transformed the usually white stone to a greenish color. Lev stretched his legs out and leaned back on the bench.

"You know, the first day I attended secondary school in Odessa, I walked proudly down Uspenski Street in my new school uniform and one of the boys spit at me." He coughed, but Lilly felt it was to cover his emotion rather than clear his throat. "The other boys yelled profanities at me. It turned out boys in the preparatory class were not supposed to wear full uniforms," he took out his handkerchief and covered his mouth with it to cough. Then he continued, "but no one told me. When I got to school the principal tore off the badge, braid and my belt buckle." Lev covered his mouth with the handkerchief again. Then after a few moments, he said, "I was humiliated."

126

Lilly was silent, touched that Lev was sharing this poignant story with her as though she were a friend. She wanted to hold his hand, to comfort him.

"Tell me Lilly, what kind of work does your father do?" he asked.

Jolted by the change of focus, she didn't want Lev Trotsky to know what her father did. "He owns real estate," she whispered wishing he wouldn't hear.

Lev smiled, but looked straight ahead as he spoke rather than facing her. Wrinkles fanned out from the corner of his eye.

"One day my father was yelling at a barefoot peasant whose cow had strayed on to our field." A band of sunlight lit up his face. "He wouldn't give the cow back despite the man's pleading that he was sorry." He turned his searing eyes to look at Lilly directly.

"Were you ashamed?" she asked. Her father was always polite and respectful to his tenants; he would never be so cruel.

"Yes, I cried and cried," he nodded, looking away. "Another time my father didn't object when a foreman whipped a peasant for leaving the horses out late…" Lilly was shocked by his father's brutality. Tears filled her eyes. Then a surge of pride. Leon Trotsky was explaining to her, Lilly Abramovitz from Brooklyn, how he evolved into a revolutionary. Lev paused and then his tone of voice changed as he turned to face Lilly with a sly grin. "It made me understand what needed to be done."

* * *

Two weeks later Bob Harte, one of Lev's guards, brought in the mail. He was tall and lean with kinky red hair and an acne-scarred face with a cleft so deep it looked like he'd been shot in the chin. He sat at the kitchen table, as he did every day, sorting the mail into piles, always in a state of cheerful readiness. Bob was about Lilly's age, but seemed younger to her. He was usually quiet, but he liked to talk to Lilly about his short stories—maybe because he knew she had worked at *Partisan Review*. "I'm trying to communicate how revolutionary consciousness develops." His Adam's apple bobbed up and down as he spoke and he shook his foot in the same annoying way Mooch did. "But it has to be demonstrated through my characters. It's a struggle to not make it read like *The Communist Manifesto*."

Bob handed her a letter. He was sweating profusely and a drop fell on the envelope making the ink bleed. It was a letter from Sidney. When Dewey had returned to New York, he called Sidney to tell him Lilly was staying in Mexico to be Lev's secretary.

May 1, 1937

Dear Lilly:

Congratulations! What an honor! Leon Trotsky's secretary! But I'm not surprised. Dewey came back raving about how smart and competent you are. Wherever you go people quickly realize you're bright and talented.

I hope you're well and enjoying the good weather. It's cold and nasty in New York.

As you probably know, Miriam has gotten an apartment in Paris and is trying to find meaningful work. She is working at a few different part-time jobs teaching English and doing translation.

William, Phil and Dwight Macdonald are re-establishing *PR* without any Party connection. The "editorial office" is in Dwight's apartment so they can run on a smaller budget, but also George Howie is funding it. He's a painter who is a friend of Macdonald's from the old days at Yale. I'm delighted. With the Dewey Commission hearings, it's another important milestone in anti-Stalinism. The new *PR* will not measure art with any political yardstick; they will publish Ezra Pound and T. S. Eliot; James Joyce and Franz Kafka. They have even planned on two articles by Trotsky that they will publish next year. You will probably be working on those very articles!

I'm delighted you've decided to stay in Coyoacán. It will be a great experience for you and invaluable to the "Old Man".

Best,
Sidney

Sidney's letter filled her with pride: staying in Coyoacán was a great career decision. She'd be editing Lev's articles for the new *Partisan Review*. How could that be wrong?

But then she got a letter from Howie. She was afraid to open it. She felt so far away from him—as if they were living on different planets. Her throat felt parched and closed up. She went into the garden; it was drizzling. The air was humid and the path was muddy. She breathed in the smell of magnolia, sweet and almost fruity. The wind picked up and the white blossoms fell to the ground. She sat on a damp stone bench, shivering as she opened the letter.

May 5, 1937

Dear Lilly:

Congratulations. You must be very flattered to have been asked to be Leon Trotsky's secretary. But I must confess I'm deeply disturbed that you're doing it. I'm concerned for your safety. Unquestionably, the GPU is scheming to kill him and I don't want you to be with him when it happens. I don't understand why you didn't return with Dewey and work on the report of the Commission. Don't you want to be with me? Why are you putting yourself at risk like this?

I visited your parents and they are very proud
of you, but beside themselves with worry.
Please come home Lilly.

I love you.
Howie

She turned away from his pleas the way one avoids looking at
someone missing a limb—first in shock, then avoidance, then guilt. She
couldn't tell him that she was staying because Manny was killed. It was
so crazy anyway. How could anyone understand the logic? She was
staying to work for Trotsky because she wanted to live up to Manny's
ideals, but Manny had hated Trotsky. And she was so upset that Manny
died that she had sex with Van! How could anyone possibly understand
that? She certainly didn't. She felt like she was looking into a cracked
mirror and she didn't recognize the reflection. She didn't love Van. But
it couldn't be undone. Things had gone too far. Who was she now?
    She took some writing paper and sat in the shade in the garden,
inhaling the intense candy-like smell of the lilies. She felt nauseous.
How could she explain this to Howie when there was so much she
couldn't say? She couldn't tell him why she was staying in Mexico or
that Van was coming to her room each night. What could she tell him?
She could tell him about Lev. Yes, that she could tell him.

May 25, 1937

Dear Howie:

This is the chance of a lifetime. Lev is
brilliant and I get to actually see his mind
work. We have long talks in his office. He
stops dictating into his machine and leans
back on his chair when he's thinking.
Sometimes he tells me what he's thinking and
even asks me what I think about it. Other
times he comes out to the garden to smoke his
pipe and asks me about my family.

130

The other day he started talking to me about
the new *Partisan Review*. Of course, he was
shocked to find out that I knew the editors and
had worked for them. Lev was quite critical of
William and Phil. He said they were
publishing their "peaceful little magazine" in
a "cultural monastery." He feels they are not
anti-Stalinist enough. I told Lev that he was
wrong about them. They are anti-Stalinist.
After all, that's why they stopped publishing
the magazine originally. They wanted to be
independent of the Party and now they are.

I think about you all the time, but I can't leave
now.

Love,
Lilly

*   *   *

In the middle of June Lilly was sitting in the garden hoping to
get some relief from the sweltering heat. As perspiration dripped down
her blouse, a small, gray dove landed on the path in front of her. She
thought about the blue birds that nested in the bird house her father put
on the beech tree in his garden. She imagined the autumn leaves falling
and floating in a puddle. Then her mind turned to Manny floating in the
river. She and Manny would never go to the movies or walk on the
boardwalk in Coney Island. She was never going to make love to him.
She had been typing one of Lev's letters to Dwight Macdonald,
the current editor at PR. Feeling a little dizzy from listening to Lev's
wordy run-ons, she heard Natalia screaming in Russian. Lilly assumed
she must be screaming at Lev. He was paying increasing attention to
Frida and Natalia had been acting more and more withdrawn, looking
increasingly frangible in the past month. She was used to losing people
she loved, but she was not ready to lose Lev. Poor Natalia. A flower in
blossom when Lev met her, over the years she had been pressed tight in
a book and put away on a shelf. Lilly thought about the 23-year-old

Jewish farm boy turned revolutionary from Ukraine seducing the aristocratic Natalia in Paris so many years ago. He had been Jacob rolling the well stone to impress Rachel; now she was Leah trying to get Jacob to love her. Just then, Van came and sat next to her on the stone bench. He looked exhausted. His short sleeved shirt was saturated with sweat and Lilly could smell his pungent body odor.

"What's she yelling about?" she asked, although she thought she knew.

"She knows about what's been going on with Frida," he said, sadly shaking his head. "She'd have to be deaf and blind not to notice, don't you think?"

He was right. Lev and Frida flaunted their relationship. When Lilly first saw it, she was shocked; she expected more of a man out to save the world.

Perhaps as a compensation for her scarred leg, Frida had developed sharp elbows and she was pushing Natalia out of the way. Frida was soaked in self-admiration and enjoyed showing off her intimacy with Lev by openly calling him "*piochitas*, little goatee" and speaking English at dinner knowing full well that Natalia, sitting like an ice statue, could not understand the conversation. Poor Natalia. She had a whiff of mold and self-righteousness about her, but she was trembling inside like a scrap of windblown paper.

Lilly had studied the marriage and family laws that had been established by the October Revolution. She wrote a paper on it for a history class at NYU. The Bolsheviks created unconditional freedom of divorce in the name of liberating women from bourgeois notions of family. But Stalin had rescinded all that. Lilly remembered talking about it one afternoon sitting on Miriam's fire escape. Miriam sat in her shorts fanning herself with a newspaper.

"It's a disaster for women," she'd said. "The way it was before, the woman didn't have to face the man—she could just send her husband a postcard: 'I've had enough. We're divorced.'"

They'd both laughed.

"No kidding," Miriam continued. "All those fat pigs full of vodka will be back to raping their wives again."

"It's because he wants women to make more babies," Lilly had nodded, wiping the sweat off her forehead. "He's outlawing abortion too."

132

But now, Lilly was unsure of the position she'd taken for granted—it was naïve. What would become of Natalia if Lev divorced her? What became of his first wife who he left behind in Siberia? When he met Natalia in Paris he probably sent his wife a postcard to announce they were divorced. Sometimes Lev and Frida had dinner alone together when Natalia gave an empty smile, claimed to have a headache and disappeared like a speck of dust whisked off a shoulder. Lilly didn't understand why she gave up so easily. Why didn't she fight back? Other times Lev and Frida took the Roadster and drove to the country for a picnic. Or they went to her sister Cristina's house on Calle Aguayo. Cristina's cook told Carlos and he told Lilly.

"What is he saying back to her?" she asked Van.

Van put one hand over his eyes as if to spare them the shame of their public display and squeezed Lilly's hand with the other, "She's not yelling at him. She's yelling at Frida."

Lilly smiled to herself thinking about what her father might say, *"When a man is too good for the world, he's bad for his wife."*

*   *   *

On December 12, after months of anticipation, the Commission of Inquiry announced its verdict—the trials were a frame-up and Trotsky was innocent. The Old Man was euphoric; his eyes sparkled. He grabbed Natalia and kissed her full lips, as if there had never been a field of thorns between them. Diego and Frida ordered a Mexican fiesta to celebrate the victory. Extra kitchen help was brought in to help Lupe Rodriguez, the cook, and Carlos and Pedro her assistants. Lupe was a short, squat, red knuckled woman with arms so fat her elbows were covered by dimples of flab. With dark, almost black eyes and naturally pouting lips, she walked like a penguin, shifting her weight from one foot to the other. Lupe had prepared oyster soup, a big pot of *carnitas* perfumed with oregano, orange zest and cinnamon, *salsa caliente, salsa verde; guacamole*, prawns *veracruz*, stuffed chilies in broth, and chicken *mole pueblo* style. Van and Lilly and Bob Harte were invited as well as friends and colleagues of Diego and Frida. Musicians played marimbas and they sang song after song. First they sang the *Internationale*:

Debout! les damnés de la terre
Debout! les forçats de la faim
La raison tonne en son cratère,
C'est l'éruption de la fin.

Then Diego stood up, blood coming to his face, in his wide-brimmed hat with a peacock feather, and laughed his fat laugh. Frida looked up at him, pink flowers and ribbons in her hair, her red lips smiling. He sang the song of the Mexican Revolution and they all joined in:

Soy soldado y la patria me llama
a los campos que vaya a pelear,
Adelita, Adelita de mi alma,
no me vayas por Dios a olvidar.

They danced in a line, Van's hands on Lilly's hips. She was flying high and thoughts of Howie felt like the tail of a kite far behind. She loved being part of the celebration; it was like dancing the hora at a Mexican bar mitzvah.

La cucaracha:
La cucaracha, la cucaracha,
ya no puede caminar,
porque le falta, porque le falta,
mariguana que fumar.

She had asked Carlos what the words meant and now that she knew, she wondered why this song about a cockroach was considered a revolutionary song.

Everyone made tequila toasts in between songs until they were all drunk. The room was spinning and Lilly had to hold on to a chair to steady herself, but then her eyes locked on Van standing next to Lev and looking at Frida laughing and dancing with Diego. Lev had amused lines around his eyes, but Van's back was tense and he had the same sad look of disappointment that she'd seen on his face the day Natalia screamed at Frida. *Was Van in love with her too? Didn't she have enough men?*

Lilly felt jealous of Frida and then ashamed that she had so much *chutzpa*. Who was she to compete with Frida Kahlo? And she had no claim on Van, she told herself, but felt angry at him for wanting Frida anyway. She felt a surge of sympathy for Natalia, who probably felt she couldn't compete with Frida either.

Just then Frida walked over to Lilly and put her hand under her chin as if she knew what Lilly was thinking.

"Don't look so wounded. He's married you know," she said with a smirk, "Fook him. All men are the same. He and his wife Gaby have a three-year-old son."

"What are you talking about?" Lilly gasped in disbelief.

Frida looked into her eyes for a moment, then turned away.

Lilly had never been that drunk before. Her head pounded. She stumbled to her room and fell into bed with her clothes on. When she woke up her mouth felt like the bottom of a scorched pot. She remembered Frida's words: "He's married you know." She turned on her side and her tears dripped from the pillow to the sheet. *What have I become? Not only did I betray Howie,* she thought, *but I had sex with a married man.* She'd been so outraged at Miriam for having an affair with Sidney and now she'd done the same thing. *What would Mama and Tateh think of me?* Eventually, she dragged herself out of bed and walked over to the mirror on the back of the door. She put her face close to it, looking to see if the change in her was visible on her face. She knew that she had become unmoored, her image of herself shaken. Tracing the outline of her cheek with her forefinger, she recited Shakespeare's sonnet 94:

"Lilies that fester, smell far worse than weeds..."

Then she took a breath, satisfied that her face had not changed, and walked out the door, through the garden to the house.

The dining room table was scattered with newspapers—the first stories about the verdict. Lupe and Carlos poured coffee and put out plates of food for breakfast. Carlos glanced over to Lilly with a look of concern, but she couldn't look him in the eyes. Lev had his arm around Natalia's shoulder and she whispered something in his ear and he laughed. Diego was sitting next to Frida and rubbing her back as he read the front page of one of the papers. Frida looked up at Lilly with a knowing smile, but said nothing. Van was reading and sipping his coffee. He looked up.

"You look like you were hit by a car," he said with a laugh.

She wanted to yell at him. *How could you have done this to me? Why didn't you tell me? You betrayed your wife, your child. And now I'm a party to it. What's wrong with you?* But she didn't say any of that. She shrugged and said, "You don't look so great either."

"Quiet everybody, Dewey is about to make his broadcast," Lev said.

The ceiling fan hummed as they all waited.

"A country that uses all of the methods of fascism to suppress opposition," Dewey said, "can hardly be held up to us as a democracy, as a model to follow against fascism."

The room was quiet. Diego breathed loudly, as if he wanted to blow Dewey's house down. Van tapped his fingers on the table.

"I disagree more than ever," Dewey said slowly, enunciating each word, "with Trotsky's ideas and his defense of the USSR."

They were completely aghast.

But then the final punch arrived. "The next time anyone says we have to choose between communism and fascism ask him: What is the difference between Hitler's Gestapo and Stalin's GPU?"

"What?" Lev roared like a wounded lion. He slumped in his chair, his cheeks hollow and his white mane tousled as if he had a heart attack. Dewey, the "man of unshakable moral authority," was saying Trotsky was as bad as Stalin and Stalin was as bad as Hitler. Lev looked like a castigated schoolboy. Lilly thought of the story about school in Odessa that he had told her in the garden.

Van burst out of his chair like a match flaring up. His cheeks looked hot. In a booming voice he bellowed, "What a bastard!"

Lilly was conflicted: she respected John Dewey, but she was angry at him for hurting Lev. She didn't understand why Dewey felt the need to make this speech immediately following the Commission's conclusion that Lev was not guilty. He could have waited. *Why did he need to go so far out of his way to separate himself from Trotsky?* It seemed beneath him—she was disappointed. She thought about Carlton Beal's accusations against Dewey at the trial and wondered if Dewey was responding to that—trying to make sure no one thought he supported Trotsky.

136

Later that day, Van came and sat next to her in the garden. The sky was gray and the air was heavy with humidity. "Dewey's an egotistical bastard," Van said.

"He's not a bastard," she said, feeling the need to defend Dewey. Her disappointment in Van trumped her disappointment in Dewey. She stared straight ahead at the bare lilac tree—she could feel her temples pulsating with rage. She wanted to tell him that he was the bastard, not Dewey. But she didn't feel she had the right to criticize him for cheating on his wife when she was cheating on Howie. So she sat on all those feelings and said calmly, "He's a Liberal in the true sense of the word."

Van listened with one eyebrow raised.

"He believes in the right to defend yourself at a trial, free speech and representative government," she continued. "But he wants to make it clear that exonerating Lev from the crimes he was accused of doesn't exonerate communism."

Van shook his head, not looking at her. She noticed the hair on his ears and the creases next to his ear lobe.

"He believes," she said, taking his chin and turning his wooden face to look directly in his eyes, "that communism inevitably leads to the oppression of the proletariat as well as the bourgeoisie."

"But that's all bullshit, Lilly." He jerked his face away from her hand and waved her away. "Liberalism is just capitalist ideology. Dewey doesn't care about the proletariat." Van got up from the bench and went back into the house. With the slamming of a door, her relationship with Van was over.

10

January 18, 1938

Dear Miriam:

I'm sure you will have heard the news about Dewey by the time you get this. Poor Lev was really undone. He expected vindication and he got an eruption of molten lava instead. The attack from Dewey has made him even more aggressive than usual.

He asked me to edit a letter to Dwight Macdonald for him. It was incredible. He wrote: "You defend yourselves from the Stalinists like well-behaved young ladies whom street rowdies insult." I couldn't believe he actually wrote that! I told him it was outrageous, but he insisted on it. Then I had to edit his letter to the secretariat of the League of Nations demanding that the League investigate the GPU. He called it "a centralized Mafia of terrorists," at work in various countries killing and kidnapping active opponents of the Stalin regime. Mafia? He's confusing Sicily and Stalingrad. Not just that, he hates to throw things away. He has file cabinets full of old passports and used ferry tickets, tattered photographs of rented rooms he once lived in. Natalia yells at him to get rid of things. But he won't. It's strange.

I'm still unable to fathom how Manny could be dead. I feel like I'm standing in the ocean and sinking deeper and deeper each time a

wave recedes. I don't know how Lev can
stand the deaths of so many people he loves.

I got a letter from Howie signed "Howard."
Only his mother called him that! He sounds
frustrated and angry—even bitter. It makes
my stomach hurt to think I could lose the one
person who really loves me and is devoted to
spending his life with me. But I can't leave
Mexico now. I'm at the top of a mountain
with a 360 degree view of world events. How
can I leave?

Tell me about your apartment and everything
you're doing in Paris.

Love,
Lilly

The sun was breaking through the storm clouds when Lilly put
down her pen and looked out at the bare trees from the fly-specked
window of her room in the guard house. She stretched her arms, feeling
lighter and more energetic having unloaded so much angst on the page.
She opened the drawer of her tiny desk looking for an envelope and
addressed it to Miriam.

Walking out into the garden, she breathed deeply and smiled at
the puddles of water shimmering and glistening in the morning light.
Then she noticed Frida swaddling herself in a cranberry red *rebozo*,
sitting on a wet stone bench. A strong current of anger rushed through
her as she remembered the way Frida had relished telling her about
Van's wife. She felt caught in a whirlpool of guilt, for her affair with
Van, for having acted holier than thou during Miriam's affair with
Sidney, and again when Miriam cheated on him. She imagined Howie's
pain, the horror on Mama's face and the disbelief on Tateh's if they
ever found out what she'd done. The alchemy of the guilt and anger
combined yielded empathy: Lilly sat down next to Frida.

While tears had been dripping down Frida's face when Lilly
approached, now she bawled. She heaved and yelled in her inimitable

139

mix of Spanish and English curse words, "Fook him, fook him. *Le odio. Cabrónonacabrona.* Bastardo!" When the cursing stopped, Frida sat whimpering with her head on Lilly's shoulder.

Opposite the sun, the arc of a rainbow covered the sky: red, orange, yellow, green, blue and purple.

"Fook Diego," Frida whispered. "Fook him." Then the storm returned; a vein bulged in her temple. Pointing her finger in the air as if Diego was standing in front of her she yelled in Spanish, "*Son of a bitch! Who gave birth to you! How dare you cheat on me, pig? Go to hell!*"

How can she be furious at Diego for cheating on her, Lilly thought, *when she's cheating on him?* But then she realized that she would feel angry at Howie for cheating on her even though she'd been having an affair. In fact, it wouldn't be "cheating" if he had a relationship with someone else. But she'd still be angry. What had been black and white now blurred like ink on wet paper. She squeezed Frida's shoulder and sighed. After a few minutes of silence, Frida wiped her dripping nose with her hand, like a little girl, and said, "I'm sorry I was a beetch to you. I'm sorry." She started sobbing again.

"I understand," Lilly said softly, patting Frida's hand, like a mother comforting a child who lashed out and now feels guilty. Lilly knew she wanted her to suffer the way she suffers from Diego's lying and cheating. It wasn't personal. She felt sorry for Frida and then felt jolted, realizing she was feeling sorry for Frida Kahlo. *Who am I*, she thought, *to feel sorry for Frida Kahlo?* But she did.

*   *   *

In the following weeks, Frida's attitude toward Lilly shifted from disinterest with a splash of sadism to seeking her out. One morning she stopped by Lilly's desk outside of Lev's office to chat. Lilly was wearing large earphones listening to the wax cylinder machine next to her typewriter. Lev's heavily accented voice was droning on so she was delighted when Frida interrupted her.

"André Breton is coming to visit soon," Frida said. "To visit Lev. Do you know who he is?"

"No, not really, just that he's a French intellectual," Lilly said, looking up from her desk. She knew the name, but that was all.

"Yes, yes you know—the leader of the Surrealists," Frida smiled. "Essays on literary criticism and art."

Lilly's face turned red. Gertie probably knew who he was, she thought.

"Oh well," Frida sighed as she turned to walk away, but then added, "You'll get to know who he is soon enough."

As soon as Frida walked off and Lilly returned to typing, Lev came out of his office and handed her two letters addressed to her, one from Miriam and the second from Gertie. He started to talk to her and she was annoyed that she had to put off reading them until he was finished.

"I heard Frida telling you Breton is coming," he said.

Lilly tried looking down at the letters to decipher the handwriting, but Lev was looking directly down at her, demanding her attention. She felt compelled to look up at him while he spoke.

"I don't know why he is coming," Lev said. "He has a conference in Mexico so he decided to visit me. I think Surrealism is like mysticism. Garbage." He winked at her and added, "She's all excited about it," he nodded in the direction of Frida's exit, "because she hopes he will like her paintings. We'll see."

Lilly was relieved when Lev went back to his office because she could finally look at the letters. She felt a surge of excitement: one was from Miriam and the other from Gertie. She went into the garden and found a sunny spot to savor them. She sat Buddha style on a bench, saying: "Eenie, meenie, miney, mo…" and finally decided to open Miriam's first.

February 15, 1938

Dear Lilly:

I keep thinking about Manny's death too, so I
can imagine how you're feeling. All these
crazy political shenanigans impact real
people—they die as a result. It makes my
head hurt to think about it. Everyone in Paris
is upset Anthony Eden resigned—because of
his opposition to Chamberlain's appeasement

policy, no doubt. Yet the Duke and Duchess
of Windsor are on the front page of *Paris-Soir*
smiling as they return from three weeks on
the Riviera. No thought, I'm sure, of how
many people their beloved Nazis will murder.

I don't know what "Howard" represents, but I
doubt Howie's going to give you up. He's just
angry. You can't blame him.

I've been getting a few interviews, but if I
don't get a regular job soon I'll be on the
street selling apples. The most interesting
interview is with Nancy Cunard (you know
the shipping company!). The job is as her
personal assistant, but she's into so many
things it's hard to know what the job would
be. She created a shelter that serves hot meals
to Spaniards fleeing the Fascists who landed
in concentration camps across the French
border. But she's also written articles
exposing the whole situation in the
international press. So if I get the job I might
end up a social worker or I might end up an
editorial assistant. I'll let you know what
happens.

Love,
Miriam

By the time Lilly read the whole letter, her initial excitement
had turned to gloom. *That's the problem with letters*, she thought, *by
the time you get a response to what you've written you're on a different
planet than when you wrote them.* She didn't want to be reminded of
Manny's death and Howie turning into Howard—whatever that meant.
She opened Gertie's letter in hopes of a diversion from those thoughts.

February 18, 1938

Dear Lilly:

I love the colorful huipil you sent me! It's just
like Frida's! Mama and Tateh are fine, except
they are worried sick about you. Tateh walks
around the house cursing Stalin and the
Fascists. Mama does her best to console him
and herself by saying: *"The just path is
always the right one."*

I'm so jealous of you being in Mexico and
Miriam in Paris while I'm stuck in Brooklyn.
Especially you—seeing Frida every day.

I want to travel and experience life; I think
that's a much better education than sitting in
my room studying. I don't want to go straight
to college. I want to take off a year and travel.
Tateh tries to discourage me. He says: *"The
world is big, its troubles still bigger."* He
thinks a war is going to break out in Europe
very soon. He's so worried about you he
doesn't want to have to worry about me too.
But still, I wish I was there!

Love,
Gertie

Lilly thought about her parents—Mama always seeing the glass
as half full and Tateh always the gloomy one, seeing it as half empty.
She missed them. She smiled remembering when she was little and sat
on Tateh's lap facing him, begging him to wiggle his ears, a talent he
often displayed to her delight. Then her thoughts turned to Gertie. Poor
Gertie was stuck in Brooklyn. Lilly understood why she didn't want to
go straight to college; she wanted to do something exciting.

*   *   *

That night Lilly dreamed about Gertie. She and Gertie were sitting on the stoop. Gertie screamed, "I'm dead, I'm dead!"

"Don't touch your eye!" Lilly cried grabbing her hand. Her eye was full of blood. Lilly yelled, "Mama, Mama, help, it's Gertie!"

Gertie sobbed, "My life, my life!"

Lilly's heart pounded. "You'll be all right. Gertie, I love you. You'll be okay I promise."

*   *   *

André Breton arrived at the house on a clear April day. He was a middle-aged man—older than Van but younger than Lev. His wavy brown hair was brushed straight back revealing a high forehead and accentuating his Gallic nose. He wasn't handsome, but he was an attractive man with full shapely lips and a slight cleft in his chin—the kind of man who is used to seducing women with his intellect and wit more than his looks.

One sunny afternoon when the moon was high in the clear blue sky, he joined Lilly sitting in the garden among the palm trees, red hibiscus and yellow wisteria growing in huge pots. A green parakeet with a yellow beak sat on a lilac tree watching the two of them.

"Bonjour," Breton said putting his hand out. Lilly put her hand out to shake it, but he bowed slightly and kissed it instead. "I am Andre Breton."

"I am Lilly Abramovitz," she said. "I'm Lev's English language secretary."

He took a deep breath, as if he were inhaling her as well as the scent of the oriental lilies.

"Do you mind if I join you?"

"Please do," she said, moving over on the stone bench between two pre-Columbian sculptures, "I'd be delighted."

"Ah, Mexico City is such a surrealist city," he said in French-accented English as he sat down. "I got lost the other day and it was wonderful."

Lilly could smell his after-shave—it reminded her of crushed mint leaves. She was not sure she understood what "surrealism" was: how could a city be surrealistic? She was embarrassed and yet felt this

144

was a great opportunity. In the end her intellectual curiosity trumped her embarrassment. "What is surrealism, exactly?"

"Such a good question," Breton said. The green parakeet nodded its head vociferously as though he agreed yelling, "ack, ack."

Breton took out a blue pack of cigarettes with a picture of a truck on the front from his shirt pocket and hit it against the back of his hand. She noticed the strength of his wrist and hands as he slid a cigarette halfway out of the package. "Surrealism is the expression of the true functions of thought in the absence of all control by reason or aesthetic preoccupation." He smiled broadly, his mouth stretching wide like a rubber band.

Lilly wanted to say something to impress him. She remembered Santayana's essay on Aesthetics and wished she could recall it. She knew there was some connection, but it had been stored in the attic of her mind for so long, she couldn't retrieve it. "Would you like one?" he said turning to face Lilly with the cigarette extending from the pack. His amber eyes looked directly into hers.

She took the cigarette, hoping it would make her seem older and more sophisticated. She didn't want to say no to him, although she had only smoked cigarettes a handful of times when Mooch had taunted her to try one. She didn't know how to inhale. *He's flirting with me. But then, what if he makes a pass? What if...?*

"Frida is a naive Surrealist," Breton said, leaning toward Lilly with his lighter.

She looked down at her blouse to see if her cleavage was showing. The gathering at the top of her blouse exposed about a half inch of her white breasts beneath her tanned chest. She pulled the top of the blouse up a bit. *This was just what Frida had hoped for*, Lilly thought. She inhaled and immediately coughed, feeling foolish and exposed. But Breton said nothing, as he inserted his cigarette in his cigarette holder, put it in his mouth so that it tilted up the way FDR's did and lit it. He inhaled deeply, exhaled a focused stream of smoke and crossed his legs. The green parakeet flew from the lilac tree to the fig tree as if it wanted to get a closer look at what was happening.

"Why is Frida's work naïve Surrealism?" Lilly asked, holding the cigarette away from her and leaning toward Breton so that her arm brushed his. She blushed, not sure whether she had wanted to touch him or not. *I'm flirting with André Breton*, she thought to herself. *It's ridiculous: I work for Lev Trotsky, share confidences with Frida Kahlo, and now I'm flirting with André Breton!*

"Because her work gives you a window into her unconscious." Eyes lit up, a few strands of his slicked-backed hair fell on his forehead. "It's like a ribbon around a bomb. She's not trying to be a Surrealist. This painting she's working on now: *What the Water Gave Me*," he said raising his eyebrow, "she's floating on the water of her bathtub, blood or a scar on her foot."

Lilly felt a surge of jealousy at Breton's excitement about Frida. *So many men are in love with her, isn't it enough? Does Breton have to fall for her too?* She tried to shake it off. *What do I care? I don't want to have an affair with him. Frida wants him to promote her work— she's desperate.*

"Frida is drowned in her imaginings," Breton said, the crease above the bridge of his nose deepening, "but she didn't start out trying to say that... She didn't even know what she was saying. And that is the essence of Surrealism. You are not trying to *be* anything, just express something."

"So you're saying it's the spontaneous generation of pictures," Lilly said haltingly, trying to put her jealousy aside, "without any conscious control."

"Yes, yes." Breton nodded his head and so did the parakeet with its long tail feathers bobbing up and down.

She breathed in the smoke from both their cigarettes and coughed. When the coughing passed she remembered something from her Wordsworth class at NYU: poetry is the spontaneous overflow of powerful feelings. Her eyes widened as if she had seen something for the first time. "Can it be written," she asked, "as well as painted?"

"Yes, Yes," Breton said, waving his hands and moving just a bit closer to Lilly on the bench. "Surrealism is about poetry as much as painting. Beauty is convulsive or it will not be at all. The form doesn't matter."

'Beauty is convulsive.' Lilly liked that phrase. She wanted to remember it.

"I'm going to set up a solo show for Frida, yes, yes. I must go," Breton said, "but it was such pleasure to meet you." He smiled and turned to go into the house as the green parakeet flew out of the garden.

146

Lilly sat for a moment after Breton left—taken aback by the abruptness of his departure. After a while she went back to her desk, still smelling the Gauloises. She had a smile on her face as she put on her earphones to continue hammering on the black glass keys. Lev came out of his office leaving the door slightly ajar. In the moment before he closed it, she could see Breton slumped in a chair smoking a cigarette.

"Freud and Marx do not go together," he said standing in front of her desk and gesturing toward the door. "The focus on the individual in psychoanalysis drains away the energy for collective change. Incompatible. You either want to change the individual or you want to change the society."

"Why can't changing individuals release energy for social change?" Lilly asked. Howie would think Marx and Freud were compatible. He'd say: "You can't change society without changing individuals. If individuals don't control their selfish and destructive impulses and take responsibility for themselves, they can't hope to change society." Howie believed people had to *be* good to *do* good. She felt a rush of admiration for him.

"You sound like him!" Lev yelled at her, pointing to his office door.

Lilly didn't want to argue with him. Jan Frankel had argued with Lev and he ended up leaving, so she just turned around and continued to type. Lev walked back into his office and she could hear him and Breton talking in loud voices behind the door.

She thought Lev was right that focusing on individuals reduces one's devotion to the revolution, but she was starting to feel that allegiance to the revolution was used to justify a lot of destructive behavior toward people.

Just as she put on her earphones to continue typing, the ribbon got tangled and she tried to straighten it. Frida came limping toward her desk as Lilly stood over the typewriter with her blackened fingers.

"He's setting up two shows for me," she said with a wide grin, ignoring the fact that Lilly was struggling with the ribbon.

"A solo show in New York—my first one! And I'll be in a Mexican show in Paris later." She did a little dance around the small office—raising her hands high in the air and twirling her blue skirt with white ruffles. Her limp was hardly noticeable when she danced, but as

147

she twirled her long skirt, Lilly could see the bottom of her disfigured leg.

"My sister will be so excited," Lilly said, trying to ignore the white scars on her withered brown leg where the streetcar hit the bus and the iron lodged in her leg. The handrail had pierced her the way a sword pierces a bull. She had been sitting next to her boyfriend Alex, who was unhurt. But he wasn't able to protect her just like Lilly had not protected Gertie from the bottle flying in the air, breaking into a million pieces.

"She loves your work," Lilly finally managed to say.

"Tell her come to the opening. Yes, of course, she must come." Frida laughed. "First solo exhibit you know," she said with tears of happiness. "No more Mrs. Rivera," she yelled. "Finished, Fook that. I am Frida!"

Lilly smiled, delighted that Frida was so happy and also thinking about how happy Gertie would be to meet Frida.

Suddenly, Frida's face darkened as though a cloud had covered up the sun, "Gringolandia," she said solemnly.

Lilly looked puzzled.

"I hate it there," Frida said. "I don't know a person there. No one."

"Don't worry," Lilly patted her arm, "people will be after you in droves. You'll get all kinds of invitations and lots of attention."

When Frida took leave, Lilly hurriedly fixed the ribbon, but she didn't return to the letter for Lev. She took that piece of paper out and typed a letter to Gertie. Her heart was beating fast as she typed. She told her about meeting Andre Breton and about Frida's coming shows in New York and Paris.

When she finished typing the letter, she sat back and smiled to herself thinking about the time she took Gertie and Solly to a game at Ebbets Field. Gertie had a crush on Harry Eisenstadt, so Lilly got tickets for a game in which he was scheduled to pitch. Harry was a Brooklyn boy who had gone to James Madison High School. The obese man sitting next to Gertie had pushed his hotdog into his mouth letting the mustard drip down his chin. Though his mouth was full, he still wouldn't shut up. He kept explaining the game to his wife and he was the kind of person who speaks in novels rather than sentences. Finally,

Gertie blurted out in Yiddish: "*An empty barrel reverberates loudly.*" Sol and Lilly had cracked up. Sometimes Gertie was such a hoot.

Lilly thought she had a great idea. Since the school year would soon be over, maybe Breton could get Gertie a summer job at the gallery hosting Frida's exhibit in New York? Wouldn't that be great for Gertie's resume? It would certainly help her get a job in a gallery when she finished NYU. As she typed the address on the envelope, Breton walked out of Lev's office.

"Hello again," he managed a smile, but his eyes looked tired. Arguing with Lev about Freud versus Marx was draining. He had handwritten pages in his hand.

"What are you working on?" he asked.

"I'm happy to type that for you," she said extending her hand.

"Yes, thank you, these are the notes from my discussion with Lev."

"Yes," Lilly said, thinking that "discussion" was an understatement.

"But tell me," he asked, "what are you working on now?"

"Actually," Lilly wiped the sweat from the back of her neck with her cotton handkerchief, unsure if she should admit she wasn't working, but decided to tell him the truth. "I was writing a letter to my sister in New York—telling her about Frida's exhibit."

"Is your sister interested in art?"

"Yes, she's very interested in art and particularly in Frida's work. She's thinking of studying art history—either that or psychology."

"I like your sister already," he winked at her.

Lilly's right eyelid fluttered. She was conflicted about enlisting Breton to help Gertie get a summer job in the gallery: she didn't want him to think she was aggressive or opportunistic. But this was a perfect opportunity for Gertie and she didn't want to let it pass.

"Do you think," she faux coughed, "that you might be able to get my sister a summer job at the gallery—setting things up for Frida's exhibit?" There—it was out. Now she held her breath waiting for his response.

"But of course," Breton smiled, "I will write them and ask. It will be my pleasure. I will let you know when I hear from them."

"Thanks so much!"

*   *   *

A few weeks later Lilly sat in the garden listening to the fig tree
groan with the weight of the plump fruit. The sun beat down on the
burro-tail succulents and the hot dry air parched her mouth and drained
her energy. She held a letter from Howie in one hand and a glass of
water with the other. The excitement of Breton's visit and her new
relationship with Frida made her glad she was in Mexico: she was at
the center of the universe and Howie was in some other solar system.
She took a sip of water, put the glass on the ground next to the bench
and opened the letter. The green parakeet sat on the fig tree nodding its
head.

June 16, 1938

Dear Lilly:

I've gotten promoted and I'm now Director of
the Teaching Project and my salary is now
$50 per week. I can afford to buy a car and do
some cultural things in NY now. The other
night I went to hear Benny Goodman at
Carnegie Hall and I saw two good movies
"The Life of Emile Zola," and "The River,"
which is about the history of the Mississippi. I
want to do these things with you Lilly. I'm
tired of being a third wheel with my friends
and their girlfriends. I'm tired of living with
my mother.

I'm thinking of getting my own apartment. I
saw a nice place for $25 per month near
Ebbets Field. Johnny Vander Meer threw his
second no-hitter in a row last night. Such
irony—the first night game at Ebbets Field
and the bums couldn't manage a hit. The Reds
have 82 wins this season so far and the
Dodgers are in the toilet with 69. Only the

Phillies are worse. The Dodgers made Babe
Ruth the first base coach. I hope that helps the
poor bastards.

I feel a million miles away from you. I don't
want to live this way. I can't look at any other
women. I go to bed thinking about you, dream
about you all night and wake up wondering
how long it will be until you're lying next to
me. Please come home Lilly.

I love you,
Howard

She didn't want to lose him—she wanted him to be like a
perennial bulb that comes back every year, no need to fertilize it, it's
there in perpetuity. She sat with the letter in her hand for a few
moments, facing the magenta bougainvillea with sharp thorns draped
over the southern wall of the patio. Picking up the glass, she walked
back into the house and sat down at her desk to type a response to him.
Before putting the paper in the typewriter, she put his letter back in its
envelope and slipped it into her desk drawer.

"June 25, 1938

Dear Howie:

Congratulations on your promotion!"

She pulled the paper from the typewriter carriage and crumpled
it. Staring at her typewriter for a few minutes, she listened to the
whirring of the fan in front of her desk. Then she got up and stood
directly in front of it, letting the hot air blow her skirt. But it offered no
relief.
    "What are you doing?" Frida said as she came down the hall.
    "Oh, nothing. I was just trying to cool off, but the fan doesn't
help."

"I'm leaving," Frida said with a big smile and hands extended as if she had just finished a dance.

"To New York for the exhibit?" Lilly asked with a smile, feeling a mixture of excitement for Frida and sadness at her leaving.

"Yes, and I will meet your sister when I get there."

Lilly felt proud that she had been able to set up a meeting between Frida and Gertie. Thinking about Gertie's excitement brought tears to her eyes. Part of her wished she was going with Frida so that she could see her family and Howie.

"Give my love to Gertie," Lilly said.

"Of course, I will give big hug from you."

After Lilly and Frida embraced and said goodbye, she went back to her desk and finished the glass of now warm water. Then she sat down at the typewriter again. She took another sheet of paper and rolled it into place.

"June 25, 1938

Dear Howie:

Congratulations on your promotion! I'm
proud of you! Getting your own apartment is
a great idea."

Twirling her hair, she tried to think of something to say to him. She didn't want to tell him Frida was going to New York. No, then he'd ask her why she didn't come to New York. Sweat dripped between her breasts and under her arms. She read what she had written and shook her head, rolled the paper out of the typewriter, crumpled it and threw it on her desk. Then she got up, walked out to the garden and sat on the stone bench, her arms and legs crossed, staring into space.

The green parakeet was back on the limb of the lilac tree. "Ack, ack," the parakeet chirped, nodding its head furiously as if it was trying to tell Lilly something. She tried to imagine what the parakeet was trying to say. Maybe, she laughed to herself, *you dope, Breton is leaving, Frida is going to New York for her show, Gertie is getting a job at a gallery, and Howie has gotten a promotion and is getting his own apartment. What are **you** doing?* She thought about how boring it

152

was to listen to those wax cylinder recordings of Lev's voice all day and type them. A bird with a golden olive body and a black bill landed on the pedestal bird bath a few feet away from where Lilly was sitting. She had learned so much about birds since she'd been in Mexico. But she'd never seen that kind of bird. It had a yellow and white face and the back of its head was red. She smiled thinking she had to look it up in Frida's bird book.

She got up from the bench, walked over to the rose bush and leaned over to pick one of the apricot-colored blossoms. Seeing the thorns, she assured herself she could place her fingers carefully between the spikes and break off a stem to bring inside. "Ouch!" she yelled as she was pierced by an unseen thorn. She sighed. "That was incredibly stupid," she said out loud to herself. Licking the blood off her forefinger, she went back into the house empty handed and sat at her desk. Once again, she rolled a piece a paper into the carriage of the typewriter. She felt a tightness in her chest, as if someone were squeezing her.

June 25, 1938

Dear Howie:

Congratulations on the promotion! I'm really proud and happy for you. I understand how hard it is for you to feel your life is standing still because you're waiting for me to return. I cannot ask you to do that. I don't know when I'll be ready to leave Mexico. I don't want to make promises I can't keep. I love you, but I can't turn my back on Lev and everything I believe in. I'm at the center of the most important historical and philosophical debate of the century. I cannot walk away from that.

Love,
Lilly

Putting her head on her desk, she cried for a few minutes. Then she took a deep breath, got up and looked out the window at the garden. The bird with the golden olive body was gone. Clouds covered the sun and the humid air was heavy. Lilly went back to her desk and continued typing Lev and Breton's joint manifesto. It was going to be published in *PR*. It called for an International Federation of Independent Revolutionary Artists with local branches and eventually national branches. *This is important*, she told herself. *The typing is boring, but the content is exciting. I can't go back to Brooklyn now.* Lev and Breton had finally collaborated despite their differences. Lev agreed to put Diego Rivera's name on the manifesto because he was supposed to be part of the collaboration. But he didn't participate.

"The man is impossible," Lev told Lilly one afternoon as he handed her more pages of the manifesto.

"Breton?" Lilly asked.

"No, Breton is okay. It's Diego. He's a great artist but a horrible man. He insists on writing this with Breton and me and then he never shows up to do any work."

"So why are you making him a co-author?" Lilly asked, trying not to sound insubordinate.

"Because we are living in his house and I don't want to start a big fight. I'm not possessive, I can share the credit," he said and then laughed. "I'm a communist for God's sake

Lilly remembered what Carlos had told her about Diego and Lev: Trotsky was living at the Blue House rent-free and Diego was paying for most of the cost of his security.

*   *   *

Months passed without any letters from Howie. Lilly tried writing to him. Before going to sleep each night she sat at her desk with fountain pen in hand and started a letter: "Dear Howie:" But then she didn't know what the next line was. "I miss you but I'm not coming back now" or "I'm so sorry for all the pain I've caused you" or "I'm so sick of typing letters and manifestos." The little trash can next to her desk was filled with papers with one line. Nothing felt right. Finally, one morning she got a letter from him. She sat at her typewriter looking at it. Sweating. She imagined what it might say: I met someone else; I am engaged; I don't want to have any more contact with you. She took the letter up to her room. It was dark, the dirty window filtered out what little light got past the clouds. She put the letter down on the duvet and covered her eyes with her hands for a few moments, trying to gather the strength to open it. Finally, she took a deep breath, sat on the edge of the lumpy bed and put the envelope to her nose. It wasn't the same scent that she remembered from years ago. It reminded her of the scent in the barber shop when her father got a haircut. She opened the letter.

November 15, 1938

Dear Lilly:

Your last letter was so cold. I don't even
know why I'm writing to you. You probably
won't care, but I got an apartment in the City
on Rivington Street. It's a one bedroom that's
close to the subway and within walking
distance of Ratner's. I go there after work. I
sit and cry eating my bowl of borscht or
cheese blintzes.

The world is coming apart. First Chamberlain
capitulates to Hitler and dooms
Czechoslovakia. Then the Nazi troopers and
hooligans destroyed the Jewish shops and
burned synagogues. Now they've thrown all
the Jews out of the colleges and high schools
and forbidden them to sell their stock. The
Polish Jews are being expelled from Germany
no matter how long they've lived there and
they have no place to go. The British won't
let them go to Palestine. And the Gallup poll
says 77% of Americans oppose an increase in
the quota of German refugees allowed to
come to the United States. That's why
Roosevelt won't do a damn thing. I don't
understand why the Jews think he's so great.

Europe is moving inexorably toward war and
the Communist Party can't distinguish
between Nazism and western democracy.
They say all war is about imperialism and
refuse to see any moral imperative. They
don't distinguish between liberals and
Fascists. And *PR* is filled with articles
attacking Stalin, but there is nothing about
what the Nazis are doing to the Jews.

I thought I knew you. Once I knew you. But
who are you now? Trotsky is no more
concerned about the Jews than the Stalinists.
Even Sidney is disgusted with Lev's silence.
It's astounding to me that Lev can be so
incredibly oblivious to what is going on. How
can you stand it?

Lilly, I miss you so much. You're the only
woman for me. But I don't know how long I
can stand this. I'm still hoping you will decide
to come back to me soon. I love you.

Howard

She asked herself, *why don't I run back to Brooklyn to marry
him?* Remembering the conversation with Van after she found out
about his wife, the contrast between the two had never been more
obvious.

"I know you're married," Lilly had said as they sat in the garden
on a wintry afternoon surrounded by bare trees.

"So?" he said lighting a cigarette.

"How could you do that to me?" She turned to look at him
directly.

"I didn't do anything to you, Lilly," he said looking straight
ahead. "Don't do the naïve girl from Brooklyn act with me."

"What do you mean?" Lilly stammered, feeling as if she had
been slapped across the face.

156

"You were the one who invited me to your hotel room and threw your arms around me. Not the other way around. You didn't ask if I was married that night in your hotel in Mexico City. You didn't care."

He was right…She sat on her bed holding Howie's letter to her nose. She found herself saying out loud, "Howie would never cheat on his wife. He would have pushed me away in that hotel room. He would have protected me from myself." *He's a mensch,* she thought. *How long can I be Trotsky's secretary? Is this really the life I want?*

She closed her eyes and dozed with the letter in her hand. She dreamed about Manny. He was being dragged down a raging river by the current, a bloody mass careening from boulder to boulder, with his head occasionally jutting out as he screamed for help. "Lilly," he yelled. She woke up with a start, her head jerking and her heart racing. It took a minute for her to realize where she was, to orient herself. Did Manny die for nothing? Franco won, after all. No, she decided. She couldn't go back to Brooklyn and marry Howie. No. She couldn't. Not yet.

She got up from the bed and looked out the dirty window. Deciding she couldn't stand the dirt anymore, she went to the bathroom down the hall to get a rag and some soapy water. She came back to her room and washed the inside of the window, drying it with newspaper so that it wouldn't streak. Opening it to clean the outside panes, Lilly shivered as the cold winter air rushed in. After a trip to the bathroom to wash her hands, she returned to her room. The clouds had cleared and a streak of sun glared through her shiny window. She sat at her desk and penned a letter to Howie that talked about everything except the most important thing: leaving Mexico.

December 4, 1938

Dear Howie:

Your apartment sounds great. What a wonderful location, near Ratner's! I can smell and taste the blintzes with a big dollop of sour cream on top.

157

You're right about the Trotskyists and the
Stalinists not speaking out about what the
Nazis are doing to the Jews. Lev has written
about the Jewish question, but his conclusion
is always that the salvation of the Jews is
completely tied into the overthrow of
capitalism. I've talked to him about it a lot
and I have argued that racism and anti-
Semitism don't just wither away. But Lev
says the reason anti-Semitism has not
withered away in the USSR is because of
Stalin.

Diego and Lev are like Laban and Jacob. Juan
O'Gorman the architect of Diego's house,
painted a mural for the terminal building in
the airport with a caricature of Hitler and
Mussolini. Good for him! But the Mexican
government is selling oil to Italy and
Germany and they didn't want to insult them
so they destroyed it. Of course, Diego
identified entirely with O'Gorman (remember
Rockefeller Center) and assumed Lev would
agree. Van and I both assumed he would too.
But, Lev said the government was acting "in
its own national independence." He was
trying to stay clear of Mexican politics. Diego
is furious.

Lev is yelling for me. I have to go.

Love,
Lilly

*   *   *

Sitting in the garden one morning, watching Lev feed the chickens, Lilly said, "Lev, why did you argue with Diego about the O'Gorman frescoes?"

"Mexico is an independent country," he said with a surprised look on his face.

"Yes, but they're selling oil to Italy and the Nazis. How can you support that?" Carlos told her that Diego said Lev was more interested in his asylum than his principles.

"Mexico is an independent country," he yelled, red-faced. "The British and American imperialists cannot determine Mexico's domestic policies." He threw down the dried corn in his hand and walked off into the house.

Lilly was shocked. Her whole body stiffened. It took a few moments for her to let out a breath. *Howie was right*, Lilly thought. *Why am I staying in Mexico with Lev?*

*   *   *

Later that day at dinner, as Van, Lilly and Natalia chatted, Lev said, "I cannot live in Diego's house any longer."

Natalia looked at him with eyes wide. Lilly wondered if she might be pleased to finally have her own house and get Lev away from Frida. She was in New York, so she was not there to protest. Van sat nodding silently as though he knew this was coming

On a cloudy morning as she packed up the books in her room, Lilly's back was aching. She wondered why she was moving to another house with Lev instead of going home. Teary and lonely, she decided to take a break and write a letter to Miriam. It felt easier to admit the uncomfortable truth to Miriam than to Howie.

March 25, 1939

Dear Miriam:

Things here have been crazy because of the
conflict between Lev and Diego. Van found a
new house a few blocks away on Avenida
Viena and we're moving there in a few weeks.
I hate to go. I love it here. I was packing some

of Lev's books the other day and found letters
from Frida to Lev tucked in the books. It's all
very sad. It makes me think now is the time to
leave Mexico.

Thanks for letting Gertie stay with you in
Paris. My parents would never have allowed
her to continue working for Frida otherwise
and she would have missed out on this
incredible opportunity. My mother read about
a professional dancer from Brooklyn, Jean De
Koven, who went to Paris a year or two ago
with her aunt and was murdered by a
charming man who offered to translate for
them. But they trust (silly them) that she will
be safe with you. The exhibit in NY was very
successful. Frida sold half the paintings on
display! I hope her luck holds out in Paris.

Love,
Lilly

On the day of the move, flat-bed trucks were lined up outside
the house and men were running back and forth moving books and
clothing. In the midst of the chaos, the mailman arrived and handed
Lilly the mail. She went into the garden and looked through the pile of
letters and manuscripts. In the middle of the pile was a letter from
Gertie postmarked in Paris. Lilly put the pile on the bench next to her
and tore open the letter.

April 1, 1939

Dear Lilly:

You won't believe this. When we arrived in
Paris in February we found Frida's paintings
were still in crates. You know how
combustible Frida is—she screamed that it

was all Breton's fault and that he was a son-of-a bitch. Then she went off on the Parisian Surrealists in general as "coo-coo lunatic sons of bitches". It was pretty horrible considering she was supposed to be staying at his house! You know how she can be when her coil unwinds—every other word is a curse. Then she got really sick and the doctor hospitalized her—she had a kidney infection.

Come to think of it, this whole experience has been like trying to pass a kidney stone. (Remember when Tateh had one?) When we got the crates to the gallery and unpacked them, the exhibit curator said all but two of her paintings were too "shocking" for public view. You might have heard her cursing at him in Mexico! Eventually Duchamp convinced the curator to show 17 of her paintings. The exhibit opened on March 10th but she hasn't sold any paintings yet. She's very upset and not at all impressed with the French.

She's obsessing over Nickolas Muray and just wants to get back to NY. He's a great party-giver and she's afraid he's so handsome and debonair he will cheat on her while she's in Paris. He's a fencing champion, how romantic can you get? And best of all, he has taken a portfolio of photographic portraits of Frida. She's not at all self-conscious about having an affair with him while she's still married to Diego. She thinks about men the way other people think about the Whitman's Sampler. It's incredible.

Miriam introduced me to a very nice man named Jacques. He came to the exhibition several times. He's a student at the Sorbonne and kind of a Renaissance man—very fluent in English. I'm always surprised at all the people he knows and the breadth of things he knows about—politics, art, history and even food and wine. He loves to cook. He's very handsome—tall and lean with a burnt-sienna complexion, blue eyes that twinkle in the light and curly black hair. I'm kind of shocked that he is so interested in me. I'm expecting him to pull a Houdini. In the meantime it's fun, but, unfortunately, I'll be leaving for NY with Frida pretty soon.

Love,
Gertie

PART II

11

"The results are going to be published in the 1939 *Left Review*," Miriam said, "as 'Authors Take Sides on the Spanish War.'"

Gertie took in Miriam's outfit: black bolero-style jacket with wide lapels over a black and white print dress. Then she looked down at her high-waisted dress with ruffles around the neck that Mama had sewn for her. She felt childish next to Miriam's Paris chic. *I liked this dress in Brooklyn*, she thought to herself, *but it doesn't work in Paris.* In Brooklyn she was a girl and in Paris she wanted to be a woman.

Miriam explained her new job. "The questionnaire was sent to 200 writers and asked them: 'Are you for, or against, the legal government of Republican Spain?' There were 147 answers and 126 supported the Republic."

Gertie noticed Miriam's thin ankles, accentuated by the narrow flaring skirt that reached just below her calf. She envied women who had prominent bones in their ankles, as the bones were invisible in hers, which made her feel fat.

"Did any of them support Franco?" Gertie asked nonchalantly as they settled in at a cozy table in the corner of a bistro on Rue Vaugirard. At the next table, two older women dressed in elegant but well-worn suits likely purchased in St. Petersburg or Moscow sat chatting in Russian.

"Yes, it's amazing," Miriam said excitedly. "Five writers were explicitly in favor of Franco. It's unbelievable

"Who?" Gertie's eyes opened wide.

"Evelyn Waugh, Edmund Blunden, Arthur Machen, Geoffrey Moss and Eleanor Smith."

Gertie grimaced. "I never heard of any of them. Stupid Fascists..."

"Come on, you've heard of Evelyn Waugh," Miriam insisted. "And H.G. Wells, Aldous Huxley, Ezra Pound and T. S. Eliot were 'neutral.' Can you imagine?"

"No, actually." Gertie shrugged her shoulders. "I can't imagine."

"Get this," Miriam leaned forward as if she was telling a secret and laughed. "George Orwell wrote back: 'Will you please stop sending me this bloody rubbish?' He spent six months fighting in Spain and was shot there, but said he didn't want to 'blab' about defending democracy." She shrugged.

"He's a schmuck," Gertie blurted out. She covered her mouth and looked to see if the Russian ladies had overheard. The thin one had rice paper skin and a blue vein on the side of her neck that bulged as she talked excitedly. Her friend listened intently, with her chin falling into her fat throat. When she was sure they were not listening Gertie added, "By the way, do you know that 'schmuck' in German means jewel? So the penis is a jewel in Yiddish. Tateh used to say, 'Don't sit on the family jewels' when I sat on his lap." For Gertie, aphorisms were like family histories with aunts and cousins and intermarriages through the generations.

"You're funny," Miriam smiled, adjusting the sleeves of her jacket. "You should be a cultural anthropologist or a linguist or something."

"I'm pretty sure I'm going to major in art history."

When they finished their blinis, they walked down Rue Pierre-le-Grand on this mild April day scouring the pawn shops and galleries overflowing with Russian antiques and artwork.

In the spring of 1939, Paris was a refugee camp. Some people had been there for years, but lived as if a bell might ring at any moment and they would be able to return home. There were White Russians running from the Bolsheviks; Jews who had escaped from pogroms in Poland and Russia; Armenians fleeing Turkish persecution; and Italians who came after Mussolini's accession. Then there were the newer arrivals—Jews fleeing the Nazis and anti-Franco Spaniards who had poured over the border since the Civil War began. Everyone on the street spoke a different language. You couldn't ask for directions, but you could send a telegram in six languages.

Passing a cast iron structure plastered with advertisements for BYRRH, an aperitif wine, Gertie thought it was a newspaper kiosk adjacent to the entrance to the Metro, but there were no newspapers. "What's that?" Gertie asked. Then she noticed a man's feet at the bottom of the kiosk. "What's he doing

"It's a *pissoir*, silly."

"A what?"

"A *pissoir*. It's for men to pee," Miriam said nonchalantly.

165

"They're peeing in the street?" Gertie gasped.

"Yes," Miriam laughed. "Why not? You can't actually see them."

"Right in the middle of the street? Do women use it too

"No, you can't sit down or anything. They just stand up and pee."

Miriam pointed to the languid female nudes in a shop window. "Father Coughlin wouldn't approve of that," she laughed.

"No," Gertie agreed, "killing Jews is fine with him, but no nudity. Do you believe there were 20,000 people at the Bund meeting in Madison Square Garden screaming *heil Hitler?*"

"New York is full of anti-Semites—haven't you been in Yorkville?" Miriam said.

Gertie nodded. She knew that East 86th Street was a German neighborhood. It was lined with restaurants, cabarets, theatres, beer halls and *Konditoreien* with delicious pastries filled with *schokoladecreme*. When she was younger, before Hitler came to power, Mama and Tateh used to take the family to the Heidelberg for Wiener Schnitzel or sometimes just for pastry at Kleine's on a Sunday afternoon. Now her parents didn't want to spend any money in that neighborhood. The last time she had made a reference to how delicious Kleine's apple strudel was, Tateh mumbled in Yiddish, "*May no evil eye avoid them.*"

"I was in New York last year visiting my parents." Miriam's face turned ashen. "Mooch and Irving Hillman, you know them? They went to City with Howie."

"I know Mooch. I think I met Irving once, he's the one who looks like he must have been fat when he was a kid."

"Ha! Exactly. They were going to a Hitler birthday rally at the Yorkville Casino with a bunch of guys," Miriam continued, "and I went with them. It was wild."

"Why did you go?" Gertie asked. "You were asking for trouble."

"I thought it would be interesting."

Interesting?" Gertie winced.

"The doorman was dressed in long socks and short leather pants held up with suspenders. It was a huge auditorium and it was filled to the brim with pro-Nazi Germans—over 3,000."

166

"Weren't you scared?"

"The guy who was speaking said Jews and communists are trying to overthrow the government of the United States," Miriam said. "Irving stood up and yelled that wasn't true."

"He must be crazy!"

"Mooch and several other guys got up to help him. They beat the hell out of them. It was terrible." She shook her head. "Seven guys went to the hospital—Mooch and Irving among them. Nazi bastards."

"Oh my God," Gertie covered her mouth.

"These guys in Nazi uniforms," Miriam continued, gesturing with her hands, "attacked him with their blackjacks and belt buckles."

Gertie was stunned. "How horrible." She took Miriam's hand. Tilting her head, Gertie looked at Miriam as if she had not fully taken her in before. She suddenly understood what Lilly had said about Miriam living on the edge of the tracks, just waiting to see if the trolley would hit her.

Miriam let go of Gertie's hand and opened her purse to take out her make-up compact. Turning the mirror from one cheek to the other, she dabbed on face powder.

"What do you think of Vassilieff?" Miriam asked, pointing to one of the paintings in the window that maintained bodily proportions but used extreme colors.

"I like Cubism, but if I had to choose, I'd take home the Kandinsky and the Chagall," Gertie said, happy to turn to a lighter subject. "These are almost like folk art. There's something uniquely Russian about them. Maybe it's the strong colors and bold patterns."

"Don't you have two Chagall's in your dining room?" Miriam asked.

"Yes, my father bought them years ago."

"Are they paintings or prints?" Miriam asked.

"Paintings, why?" Gertie asked.

"Your father's so rich," Miriam said, shaking her head in mock disbelief.

Gertie stepped back, looking quizzically at Miriam with her bad eye closed. "What?" "Come on, he is," she teased. "That's why you're so shocked about having to share a bathroom with your neighbors…That's what I had to do growing up, and what your father's tenants still do."

167

Gertie blanched. She thought back to the conversation at Miriam's apartment the day she arrived.

"Why do they have two toilets?" Gertie had asked her after going to the bathroom for the first time.

"The second one isn't a toilet, it's a *bidet*. Since you have to pay for a bath, you wash up in there after sex or a bowel movement and then it's easier to put off taking a bath. The French are so smart."

Gertie had felt foolish mistaking a bidet for a toilet. Now, she felt cut by Miriam's sharp edges. She gestured toward the window display of the belongings of the White Russians who lived in the neighborhood. "They inherited their estates, murdered Jews and flogged peasants. My father is a self-made man. He left Russia to escape those bastards."

"Yes, but he exploits his tenants."

Gertie winced but said nothing.

They continued walking dodging a tall man on a bicycle with two baguettes tucked under his arm who yelled, "zut alors," as he sped past them. The tension was broken when Miriam grabbed Gertie's arm trying to avoid the bike. They both broke into giggles at the bizarre almost-accident. Still arm and arm, Miriam pulled Gertie over to look at another shop window. "I love the posters," she said, pointing to the ones for performances of the Russian Opera and the Ballet Russe.

Gertie was still shaken. She had never been critical of her father the way Lilly was and it was a shock to realize that Miriam judged him so negatively. But then again she was Lilly's friend, Gertie thought, so she shouldn't be surprised. And she was staying in Miriam's apartment, so she didn't want to provoke her.

Next door, a store displayed samovars made of copper, silver, brass and bronze. Eyeing one in a dark chocolate patina with a conical shape, ornate handles with flutes and a spigot decorated with tiny rose buds, Gertie said, "I'd love to bring that samovar home for Mama."

"Doesn't your mother already have a beautiful samovar that's always on the dining room table?" Miriam asked.

"It's nothing like that." Gertie felt the weight of Miriam's judgment of her family's excesses and was relieved when Miriam didn't respond. Gertie was keenly aware that she was jealous of Miriam: she felt unfinished and uneasy around her because Miriam was so cool and classy. But she was surprised that Miriam was jealous of

168

the Abramovitz's material possessions. Gertie had never thought of her family as rich or privileged. For the first time the realization hit her. She felt a wave of guilt, not just for having a home full of precious possessions, but for being oblivious of it.

After a few moments of silence, Miriam stiffened and looked around as if to make sure no one was within hearing distance.

"Don't worry," Gertie said, seeing Miriam's concern, "they don't understand English."

"It's weird to see this stuff," Miriam whispered disregarding Gertie's reassurance. "The people who owned these things were White Army officers and Cossacks." She grasped Gertie's arm as if they were in danger. Gertie was happy Miriam saw her as an ally instead of her class enemy.

"These are the kind of people," Gertie said, putting her free hand over her mouth, "who burned down my great-grandfather's factory in Kiev."

*   *   *

Two days later, Miriam dropped in to see Frida's exhibit at the Pierre Colle Gallery. Gertie felt fortunate to be there—even in a menial capacity. After all, it was the place that a few years earlier had shown the works of a pantheon of surrealist artists: Salvador Dali, Marcel Duchamp, Max Ernst and Man Ray. As soon as Miriam walked in and greeted Gertie, she saw someone she knew.

"Jacques," Miriam called to him across the gallery. She took Gertie's arm and walked her over to where a thin but well-built man, about 5'10" with black wavy hair and an olive complexion, was standing.

"How are you?" Miriam asked.

He smiled at Miriam and kissed her on both cheeks.

Miriam introduced them, and Gertie smelled his scent, a combination of Gauloise cigarettes and cologne. Warmth welled up inside her.

Miriam said, "Jacques, Gertie is Frida's assistant."

"Ah, yes," he said in accented, but perfect, English. "Gertie, is that a nickname? I have not heard it before."

She thought his accent sexy and noticed that although he spoke English fluently, it was formal, without contractions.

"My real name is Gertrude."

"Such a beautiful name," he said, looking her directly in the eyes. Turning to one of Frida's paintings, *"My Nurse and I,"* he furrowed his brow. "It is such a painful experience she is telling us about. Do you think so?"

"Hmm," Miriam said, moving closer to the painting to read the title.

"Yes, that's very insightful!" Gertie said. "Frida told me that her mother was unable to breastfeed her and she was fed by a native Indian wet-nurse who needed the money and whose only real concern was running home to feed her own child."

"Really," Jacques said, looking intrigued. "That is amazing."

"And why do you think the baby has an adult face?" Miriam asked.

Jacques nodded: "Hmm. That is a good question."

"If your mother can't feed you and your wet nurse just wants to go home, maybe you have to grow up fast," Gertie said.

"Yes, of course," Jacques said, looking at Gertie with eyes that refracted all the light in the room. "You are so perceptive."

After a few moments he turned and stood looking at the painting thoughtfully with two fingers on his lips. He had piano fingers and, in that position, with his large thumb bent outwards with pronounced musculature, his hand reminded Gertie of Rodin's *The Hand of God.*

She felt like she was standing on a swinging bridge.

Miriam turned to Jacques and said, "You know Gertie knows a lot about art—her parents own two Chagalls."

Gertie felt stung. Why did Miriam insist on bringing that up again?

"Really?" Jacques said, his eyes widening as he turned to Gertie, "That's wonderful, I love Chagall."

"Oh, well, I have to leave," Miriam said, looking at her watch. "I need to get back to the office." She kissed Jacques on both cheeks and said to Gertie, "I'll see you later."

Gertie smiled, glad Miriam was leaving.

When she was gone, Jacques said, "I like Chagall because the trees and the houses and the people all seem to dwell in a space that's removed from the world."

170

"Yes," Gertie said, feeling her heart racing. "It's removed from the world but looks directly at it."

"It is nice to meet someone who is interested in art."

"Yes," Gertie said, grinning. "I feel the same way."

"You have a wonderful smile. I like your dimples."

Gertie blushed and felt heat in her cheeks. She felt his gaze examining her and wondered if he was deciding if she was a big enough fish to keep or should be thrown back in the river.

"I would like to show you some of Paris, if you would like that… Gertrude. Would you?"

"Of course, I'd love that," Gertie gushed and then worried that she'd been too eager.

"Can I pick you up at Miriam's? Is that where you are staying?"

"Yes, do you know where she lives?" Gertie wondered how they knew each other and how well.

"I know where Miriam lives, yes. May I pick you up at 10 tomorrow?"

"Yes, that would be wonderful." Gertie tried to contain her excitement.

When she put her hand out to meet his, he bent over and kissed the top of it. She noticed a few gray hairs peeking out above his ears. He gently turned over her hand and looked at her palm. Her pulse quickened.

"Ah, you have two fate lines," he said. "One is broken very early and another starts running parallel to it. Something happened when you were very young that changed your fate." She felt transparent. Catching her breath, she said softly, "You're very good at this…"

"Thank you," Jacques said, looking intently into Gertie's eyes.

She wondered what he thought of her bad eye. "I'll look forward to seeing you tomorrow," she said. She fingered the gold chain of her heart locket.

"Yes, as will I." He grinned and turned to leave.

*   *   *

The next morning, Jacques arrived at Miriam's house at 33 Rue de Verneuil in the 7th arrondissement, two blocks from the Seine, and bolted up the stairs to Miriam's apartment. When Gertie answered the door, he said "Bonjour!" and kissed her on both cheeks. They left the apartment immediately and headed to Picasso's exhibit at the Galerie Paul Rosenberg. As soon as she slipped into the seat next to him in his yellow Citroen she noticed the bulging muscles pulling his slacks tight over his thighs. Turning onto the Rue de Bac, he told her he was studying history at the Sorbonne and that his father was a high-ranking Belgian diplomat.

Passing the Gare d'Orsay and the National Assembly, they crossed the Seine on the Pont de la Concorde. Jacques pointed to the Obelisk of Luxor turning onto the Champs-Élysée.

"Wow," Gertie said looking down the street toward the Arc de Triomphe. It reminded her of the arch at Washington Square. "I've never seen a wider, more elegant boulevard. It makes Fifth Avenue look scrawny by comparison."

Jacques smiled. "I'm pleased that you think Paris surpasses Manhattan." Passing a heavily guarded palace with a monumental gate, he pointed and said, "That is Élysée Palace, it's the French version of the White House." *The White House beats this,* she thought. But she was enchanted that this sexy man was making so much effort to give her a tour of Paris.

Arriving at the Rosenberg Gallery on Rue de Boétie, Jacques parked, got out of the car and opened the door for Gertie. No one had ever opened a car door for Gertie before. She wondered if men were this gallant in Mexico. *Did anyone open the car door for Lilly?* A wave of delight passed through her. *This is the first time in my life,* she thought, *that I'm experiencing something before Lilly—maybe even better than Lilly.*

"Picasso was so upset about what was going on in Spain," Jacques said with his hand on the small of Gertie's back as they walked into the gallery, "that he didn't paint for two years, 1935 and 1936."

She felt the heat of his hand on the small of her back. No man had ever touched her there.

"He hasn't had an exhibit for three years." He opened the door of the gallery for her. "This is the first."

Once in the gallery, they stood looking at the array of small oils-on-canvas paintings in a luscious palette of purple and white that were, with only one exception, still-lifes of candles and flowers, fruits and pitchers, bird cages and oil lamps, knives, forks, figurines and doves.

"These paintings don't look like Picassos at all," Gertie whispered to Jacques.

"I know what you mean," he replied, putting his hand on his chin. "Did you ever see *Guernica*?"

"Yes, I've seen pictures of it. How could this be the same artist?"

"He did a series of nightmarish etchings too—*Dreams and Lies of Franco.*"

When they left the exhibit, Jacques drove Gertie back to Miriam's. She hoped he would want to come upstairs with her. Or, at least, kiss her goodbye.

"That was fun," Jacques said, smiling at her once he turned off the motor. He got out of the car and again came around to open the door for her.

When she got out of the car, Jacques did not kiss her. He said, "Would you like to do some more sightseeing tomorrow?

"Yes, that would be lovely." Gertie was disappointed there was no kiss, but elated that he wanted to see her again.

*   *   *

When Jacques arrived the next day, Miriam answered the door and Gertie heard them speaking and laughing. When she entered the living room, Jacques smiled broadly.

"Bonjour," he said kissing her on both cheeks.

"Would you like to join us?" he asked Miriam. "We're headed for the Marais."

Gertie felt a pain in her chest. *Oh no*, she thought, *please don't come. Why did he ask her?*

"No, thanks, I've got some work to do for Nancy," Miriam replied.

"Then we will be off, *au revoir*," Jacques said kissing Miriam.

"Bye," Gertie said to Miriam.

"Have fun," she replied.

They drove to Rue de l'Université, crossed the Boulevard Saint Germaine where she had walked with Miriam, and passed the Palais Bourbon across from the Place de la Concorde. The sleeves of Jacques' shirt were folded well above his wrists and as he moved the gear shift Gertie noticed that he didn't have any hair on his arms, which made his veins more pronounced. They continued along the Rue Fabert alongside the Esplanade des Invalides.

"What's that?" Gertie asked.

"Hotel des Invalides," he said. "It has museums and monuments, all relating to the military history of France."

"Why do they call it 'Hotel' des Invalides?"

"It was originally conceived by Louis XIV as a hospital and a retirement home for war veterans," he said, "but what I really want to show you is the École Militaire."

"Oh, why?"

"This is where Alfred Dreyfus was publicly stripped of his rank and uniform," Jacques said, "following a sham trial in which he was convicted of treason and sent to Devil's Island based on forged evidence. I thought you might like to see it because I understand you are Jewish—like Miriam."

He isn't Jewish, Gertie thought. *Too bad. No future.* She had never considered the possibility of marrying a man who was not Jewish.

"Yes, thank you," Gertie said. She didn't want to make Jacques feel self-conscious for explaining the Dreyfus Affair to her.

Arriving in the Marais, Jacques parked the car on the Rue des Rosiers and they walked side by side, not touching. She could smell body odor and garlic breath as men with *yarmulkes* rushed by talking loudly in Yiddish, Russian or other Eastern European languages she couldn't identify. They passed advertisements for Yiddish boarding houses, posters for Yiddish theatre productions and a bistro where bearded and wrinkled old Jews with trembling hands ate plates of chicken and boiled potatoes at a table near the window. Gertie felt surprised that she was so comfortable in Paris.

She wondered if Jacques was going to hold her hand.

"This has been a Jewish neighborhood," Jacques explained, "since the Middle Ages. It was known as 'La Juiverie.' Now they call it Marais or Pletzl." Gertie looked at the signs and noticed the names of the narrow cobbled streets that ran at angles were different on either side of the street like the streets in the Greenwich Village.

174

Finally taking her hand, Jacques continued, "It was a thriving and fairly self-sufficient community even then with synagogues, cemeteries, and kosher food manufacturers."

Jacques had a strong grip like someone who knew where he was going. She wondered how he felt about her moist palms. Walking down the street with such a smart and attractive man made her proud—she wanted to shout out, *Look everybody. He chose me*! She wondered if Miriam was jealous.

"By the way," Gertie said as nonchalantly as she could, "how do you know Miriam?"

"She works for a friend of mine, Nancy Cunard. She lives in Paris now, but she used to run a shelter for Spaniards who were put in camps at the French border. She got them out of the camps. I was lucky I never got put in one of them when I came back from Spain. Most of them were women and children, old people and wounded civilians, but the rightist French officials think they're all communist 'scum,' so they make them wait days for food and then they give them a piece of bread and a little bit of rice. I used to volunteer there sometimes," he said.

She was about to ask Jacques more questions about his experience in Spain when she noticed graffiti on the side of a building. Gertie knew enough high school French to understand: "*Juifs rentrent chez eux*" meant "Jews go home." Her back tensed; she had never seen anti-Semitic graffiti before. Jacques didn't say anything about it and she wondered if he didn't notice it or he was used to it.

They passed the Speiser bookstore where Jews from places like Bydgoszcz, Zlatana or Milowek slipped between piles of books. They browsed with eyes deep and lost, some with backs bowed, others limping and squinting, ignoring the rubbish in the gutters and the unwashed children playing on the narrow streets.

Jacques pulled her toward the Rue Pavée. "I want to show you *Agudath Hakehilot*—it's an Orthodox synagogue designed by Hector Guimard," Jacques said excitedly. "He is the architect and decorator who designed the entrances to the Paris metro stations with decorative wrought iron and glass. He is probably the father of Art Nouveau."

"He's Jewish?" Gertie blurted out, surprised because Guimard didn't sound like a Jewish name. She realized that she was so comfortable with Jacques that she forgot he wasn't Jewish—he was just interested in medieval ghettos and synagogues. She covered her mouth and looked around to see if there were any gentiles on the street who might have heard her. But, there were no obvious ones: only men with *tsitsis* and large black hats, others with beards and *yarmulkes*; there were women with kerchiefs and others with hats. The neighborhood was overflowing with Jewish immigrants: there were 150,000 Jews in France in 1919 and 300,000 in 1939. Most of them settled in this crowded neighborhood, congregating here as if there was safety in numbers.

A paunchy man with gray hair and a *yarmulke* was standing in front of *Boucherie Père et Fils*. The awning was decorated with a menorah and Hebrew letters. He must be the father, Gertie thought. On the wall in the alley near the shop was a hand-painted sign: "*Juifs bellicistes sortir*." This time she understood the first and last words only.

"What does that mean?" she asked Jacques.

"Warmonger Jews get out," he said, grimacing.

"Why warmonger?" Her stomach tightened and she felt sweaty.

"The anti-Semites in France think the Jews are set on a war with the Nazis," he said.

"I didn't realize the French were anti-Semitic," Gertie said, biting her nail.

"Ever since Blum became Premier in 1936, the *Action Française* has used him to connect Jews and the Left. It is like the Dreyfus Affair, but without Dreyfus!"

Next door at the bakery, a line of people formed at the entrance, waiting for their baguettes, croissants and challah. Two young women stood arm and arm laughing and speaking in Yiddish. Did they know she was Jewish and Jacques wasn't? Could they tell? A young couple waited patiently. His pants barely covered his socks and her skirt looked like it once belonged to her mother.

Gertie felt guilty. They were probably from Germany or Poland or Russia and had fled from the Nazis with only the clothes on their backs. They were not affluent tourists like her.

"Guimard's wife is an American Jew," Jacques explained. "In fact, they have fled France and gone to the United States, afraid the appeasement of the Nazis is not going to prevent a war."

176

"And what do you think?" Gertie asked. Tateh was sure the war was going to start any day. That's why he made her promise to come home as soon as Frida's exhibit ended.

"I think France and England are willing to feed the sharks in order to protect themselves. Is that the right expression? They do not care what countries Hitler swallows as long as he does not attack them," Jacques said, his eyes narrowing.

Gertie squeezed Jacques' hand. What would happen to her if the war started while she was in Paris? And what would happen to him? They turned onto Rue Pavée and there was Guimard's synagogue wedged in between other buildings. The narrow windows accentuated the height of it.

"That is really inspiring," Jacques said, looking up at the building.

"Yes, it's quite beautiful and unlike any synagogue I've ever seen." *This man is interested in the architecture of synagogues?* She looked at the delight in his face as he looked at the building.

"Why are you so interested in things Jewish when you're not Jewish?" she asked.

"I am interested in Jewish history and culture. I had a close friend in Spain who was Jewish and my friend Yvette is Jewish."

When they got back to Rue de Rosiers, Jacques insisted on introducing Gertie to Yvette. The steps groaned as they climbed the indented wooden stairs to her third floor apartment. When they got to the first landing, they heard the sounds of a sewing machine starting up, in operation and then stopping. A door creaked open and they saw bolts of fabric piled on a cutting table. With a thump something dropped on the wooden floor. A woman's voice yelled in Yiddish, "*Oy! What's the matter with you?*" A boy with a yarmulke came out of the door with a package wrapped in brown paper and slammed the door behind him. He ran down the stairs without looking at them. On the second floor, Gertie smelled the familiar scent of onions browning in chicken fat. She smiled to herself thinking this was more like Brownsville than Paris. Then, panting as Jacques walked one step ahead holding her hand behind his back, the buttery smell of fresh pastry overtook her. *No, this is not like Brownsville after all*, she thought. *No croissants in Brownsville.*

"She's a baker," Jacques said.

When they reached the third floor, Yvette opened the door, "*Bonjour mes amis. Ca va?*" she said, kissing Jacques French style on both cheeks. She turned to Gertie, who was gasping for air, and kissed her on both cheeks as well.

"Gertrude," and then in Yiddish, "*Beautiful girl, it's so nice to meet you.*" Gertie wondered if Yvette could hear her heart pounding, surprised and flattered that Jacques had told Yvette about her.

Yvette was a small, plump 50ish woman with a round face, blond hair and warm hazel eyes. She seemed more like a beloved aunt than a past lover, and Gertie liked the idea that Jacques had a Jewish aunt. In thickly accented English Yvette said, "Would you two like some coffee and chocolate croissants? I just made them."

"Of course," Gertie smiled.

Yvette ushered the couple into the dining room. On the far wall was a pair of green painted arm chairs with scrolled arms and red damask silk upholstered seats on either side of a large parcel-gilt mirror. The mahogany dining table, with a turnip-shaped samovar in the middle, was surrounded by a set of eight mahogany chairs with green velvet seats.

Gertie found the French custom of bread and chocolate in the morning exceedingly strange and fattening; she was used to Kellogg's corn flakes. But it was too delicious to turn down. When they settled down at the table, Gertie took her first bite of the warm croissant. She savored the way the melted chocolate mingled with the flaky pastry. It was a pleasure that, like the champagne she drank at Frida's exhibit openings, must not be rushed, but rather taken slowly and deliberately, each bite remaining in the mouth until the full richness was tasted.

After Gertie oohed and aahed about the luscious croissant, she noticed the portrait on the wall of the dining room. "Is that a painting of Tolstoy?" Gertie nodded in the direction of the painting.

"Yes, it's Lev Tolstoy." Yvette looked at Jacques and smiled. "But it's not a painting. It is pokerwork –it is made of wood using heated pokers to create pictures," she said. Yvette hesitated as if she were deciding whether to explain it further to Gertie. After a few moments, she said, "Like the wood burning that was practiced by the ancient Egyptians and some African tribes."

"How interesting…Where are you from originally, Yvette?" Gertie asked.

"Kiev."

"Really? My mother's parents were from Kiev."

"When did they leave?"

"After the assassination of Alexander II. My great-grandfather's factory was burned to the ground. He wasn't physically harmed, but he was never the same."

"I am so sorry, Gertrude," Jacques said putting his hand out to take hers. "That is so horrible."

Yvette was silent but nodded knowingly as if this was a story she had heard many times before.

"The other day I saw something amazing," Yvette said after a few moments of silence. "I saw Count Cassini, the former ambassador of Holy Russia to France, running through the rain on the Place de la Madeleine to board a bus, probably to take him to the *taudis,* the word *en Anglais,* Jacques, *s'il-vous-plait,* the French government has provided him."

"He lives in a slum," Jacques said, turning to Gertie, "what we call a *quartier misérable.*"

"Good for him, *le bâtard,*" Yvette bellowed, hitting the table with her hand. "The only ones worse than the White Russians are the Nazis."

Noticing the deep crevices between Yvette's eyes, Gertie thought they made her look permanently skeptical.

"Gertrude and I were just talking about the chances of a war breaking out," Jacques said.

Gertie felt her face flush. She noticed that Yvette did not ask what they had discussed or what each of them thought about the chances of war. Yvette was quite definite in her opinions. "The English and the French won't resist Hitler in the east," she said, making a fist with her hand. "They're encouraging Germany to attack Russia."

When they left Yvette's, Gertie wanted to ask Jacques how he knew her, but felt it was too intrusive. They continued walking on the Rue de Rosiers. He took her hand and kissed it. Tears came to her eyes.

"I'm going to have to go home soon," Gertie blurted out.

Jacques put his arms around her; she could feel his strength. Then he loosened his hold and put his hand under her chin, smiled reassuringly and said, "We can talk about it later. I've got a surprise for you. Let's have lunch at a little Italian restaurant I know on Rue Bonaparte near Saint-Sulpice."

When Jacques and Gertie walked into the restaurant, Pablo Picasso was sitting at a table flirting with the waitress.

"*Hola, cómo estás?*" Jacques greeted him.

Gertie's eyebrows raised and her mouth dropped.

"*Hola,*" Pablo Picasso responded, smiling. Picasso had piercing eyes with dark leathery pouches under them.

Gertie managed the only word she knew in Spanish, "*Hola.*"

"*We were just at your exhibit yesterday,*" Jacques said in Spanish.

"*Not what you expected...was it?*" Picasso replied and turned away, continuing to flirt with the waitress.

Jacques and Gertie sat down at a table suitably distant from Picasso.

"You're fluent in Spanish too?" she asked.

"Yes, my mother was Spanish. You know, Picasso has a spaghetti lunch every day before he starts working at about 2 P.M. He has an enormous, factory-like studio at the Rue des Grands-Augustins."

Gertie noticed that he used the past tense. "Is she dead? Your mother?"

"Yes," he said matter-of-factly, "she died three years ago."

"I'm sorry..." Gertie imagined how she would feel if Mama died. She would be devastated. Maybe it's different for a man. But she thought Solly would be devastated too. "How did she die?"

"Suddenly."

He seemed elusive. She felt as though she was trying to catch a firefly and it kept flying away.

She wanted to continue asking questions; she wanted to know everything about him. But she felt his abrupt answers meant *don't ask.* She changed the subject.

"Isn't it interesting that both Spanish painters, Miro and Picasso, are painting still-lifes for the first time since the Spanish Civil War started? Why would war and destruction engender painting objects?" Gertie whispered.

"Maybe there is something about death and still-life. Life stands still only in paintings," Jacques said.

Gertie was moved. Jacques understood something about death that she did not want to know.

"Miro's still-life isn't like Picasso's," she said after a short silence. "It's full of tragic symbols like an old shoe and an apple pierced with a fork and a crust of bread. That makes more sense to me as a response to the Civil War than Picasso's fruit and flowers…" Without waiting for a response she asked, "By the way, how do you know Picasso?"

"I have met him at many Popular Front parties to raise money for the Republicans."

"Is that how you know Yvette?"

"Yes, I have met a lot of interesting people because of the Popular Front. People I would probably never have the opportunity to know. Yvette is opinionated, but she has a good heart and she's very smart. I have also become friends with the Chilean poet Pablo Neruda. Do you know his work?"

"Yes, of course, *Twenty Love Poems and A Song of Despair.* I can't believe you know him.

> Lovely one,
> just as on the cool stone
> of the spring, the water
> opens a wide flash of foam,
> so is the smile of your face,
> lovely one."

Jacques reached over and took Gertie's hands in his and recited:

> "Lovely one,
> with delicate hands and slender feet like a
> silver pony,
> walking, flower of the world,
> thus I see you,
> lovely one."

He kissed her hand and then smiled, looked in her eyes and said simply, "Gertrude."

Gertie melted like snow on the first day of spring. Something inside her was peeking through the grass for the first time.

*   *   *

A few days later Jacques and Gertie took the Metro to République and walked down the Rue de Fauborg du Temple to the Canal Saint-Martin and watched the bridge open at Rue Dieu. They gasped with pleasure, like children, as the swing bridge opened to allow a barge to pass. They ran along the side of the canal as the water lowered under the barge and filled the next lock like a giant bathtub. When the barge passed out of their sight, they sat on a bench and Jacques pulled Gertie's legs over his lap. They snuggled for a while and then walked aimlessly until they found a café that seemed suitable for lunch. Jacques suggested they both have *oeufs en meurette*. A simple dish, Jacques told her, just eggs poached in red wine with onions and mushrooms. He chuckled with delight as Gertie lapped it up with a fresh baguette.

That night Jacques took Gertie to hear Louis Armstrong. Wearing a calf length skirt and tight sweater, she felt sexy, like Lana Turner.

"You look wonderful tonight," Jacques said.

"Thank you," Gertie replied with a wide grin.

They danced to "Blue again, blue again. You darned well know it's you again…."

Gertie felt a buzz from the three glasses of Moet and snuggled against Jacques' chest. Rubbing against him as they moved rhythmically to the music made her wonder what it would be like to have sex with him. What did a naked man look like? She wondered if Jacques could feel her pulsating when the music changed.

*   *   *

It was almost morning when Jacques and Gertie walked arm and arm to his apartment on Rue de l'Université—a few blocks from the jazz club. Taxis passed them on the empty street, but they preferred to walk along the uneven cobblestones. They didn't discuss whether she was going to spend the night with him, but she knew she would.

She was hopeful that tonight was the night she was going to have sex for the first time, but nervous about whether it would really happen. Would it hurt? She had never discussed that with Lilly or

182

Mama, but she read that it was supposed to hurt the first time. And how would it feel to have sex with him and then leave Paris? She couldn't stay much longer—a war was going to start soon. Her mind veered, as it often did in times of anxiety, to one of the many pieces of information about aphorisms that she loved knowing. "Do you know the term 'bury the hatchet'?" she asked, trying to mask her anxiety. The needle skipped on the Billie Holliday record Jacques had put on the phonograph upon entering the apartment, but she was singing one of Gertie's favorites, "What a little moonlight can do."

"No."

"I read that the origin of that saying is that many American Indian tribes used to have a war pole and when a war ended, the chief would bury the hatchet halfway between the pole and the ceremonial fire and that indicated the war was over."

"That's really interesting...," he said raising his eyebrows. "I don't know anything about American Indians."

Gertie worried that Jacques thought she was an idiot. She realized "bury the hatchet" was a strange association to be having when she was on the verge of losing her virginity. *What would Freud say? Maybe it is a "reversal into the opposite,"* she wondered, *or some phallic imagery? Or,* she thought, *it could be related to Jacques being a goy.* She was about to have sex with Jacques although she knew her father wouldn't approve, not only because of the sex, but rather because she was getting involved with someone who wasn't Jewish. Maybe she hoped her father would bury the hatchet if she became involved with Jacques. *Yes,* she thought, *that sounds like the right interpretation.*

When he opened the door, she was taken aback by the heavy smell of old cigarette butts. Dappled light and a diaphanous breeze came through the ancient-looking windows in the living room. A worn leather couch with heavy wooden claw feet sat in front of a wall of home-built book shelves filled to overflow. There were records divorced from their sleeves on the floor near the phonograph. Recognizing some of the names on the album covers, she was delighted that they liked the same kind of music: Ella Fitzgerald, Louis Armstrong and the Mills Brothers. She honed in on one of her favorites—"Summertime" by Bing Crosby. Gertie smiled and felt the muscles in her back relax.

Jacques went into the kitchen and said, "I'll be back in a second." Gertie could hear him fumbling around in a drawer. She wondered what he was doing—perhaps looking for a rubber.

She sighed in delight. Nothing in her past experience had prepared her for this. She'd made out with Norman in the first months of her junior year, and petted with Jeffrey on her parents' couch in Brooklyn in her senior year of high school. But they were boys, and Jacques was a man. She had felt aroused when they had lain on top of her and rubbed against her in just the right way. But she knew this was going to be entirely different. She sang along with Billie Holiday: "Ooh, ooh, ooh, What a little moonlight can do, Ooh, ooh, ooh," stopping when he put a corkscrew and a bottle of red wine on the coffee table in front of the sofa, and continuing when he went back to the kitchen to get glasses.

Sitting at the edge of the couch, she noticed a well-read copy of the communist paper *L'Humanité* lying near the record sleeves. She smiled thinking Lilly would approve: he loves art and literature and has the right politics. What a heavenly man she had found!

Jacques opened the bottle and poured the wine into two mismatched glasses. He pulled her to the couch, handed her a glass, lifted his to touch hers and said, "*Salut*." He took a sip and put the glass down on the table. Then he put his arms around Gertie and slowly licked her earlobe. She worried about whether she had cleaned her ears—would he taste wax? His tongue worked its way down her neck and up to her chin. He whispered, "Gertrude." No one else called her "Gertrude" and the way he said it gave her chills. The slowness of his movements made her tremble in anticipation; her breathing quickened.

"Sorry for the mess," he whispered.

"Don't worry." She was throbbing.

He unbuttoned the top buttons of her dress and slipped it down to her shoulders, exposing the straps of her full slip and bra. Then he took her glass from her hand and put it on the table next to his.

Gertie worried about what he would think when he discovered her lightly padded bra. And what should she do with her hands?

His tongue started at her neck and worked its way slowly to her shoulder. Then he returned to unbuttoning her dress. He opened it to look at her, rubbed his face against her breasts, motioned for her to stand up and helped her step out of her salmon-colored slip and dress.

184

The clothing fell to the floor a few feet from the records. He held her face in his hands and kissed her bad eye. Gertie cried. He kissed her tears.

He took her hand and placed it below his belt. She could feel the firmness of the bulge. But what was she supposed to do now? She had never been with a man before, only boys. And she had never seen an adult man's penis, only Sol's. As if he heard her, Jacques put his hand on hers and moved it around slowly. He made an "aah" sound as her hand began to grip him.

Jacques followed the outline of her mouth with his tongue, finally slipping it into her mouth so that she was hungry for it. He unhooked her long-waist bra and licked her erect nipples, twirling his tongue around each one. Then he worked his way down to her belly and lingered. She wondered if he thought she was fat. He removed his shirt. She was relieved that he did not seem deterred. She'd never seen a man with so little hair on his chest. He put his hands into her panties and put one finger deep inside. She gasped—shocked that he knew this secret passage and was so comfortable entering it. He moved another finger between her wet lips and she began to ripple. Her back arched as he gently moved his hand back and forth. A wave built inside her. When he pressed harder and faster, Gertie moaned as it swelled, grunted as it surged and then almost yelled, before it crashed. She was drenched with sweat. She wondered what it was going to feel like when he entered her. How big was his penis? And what would it look like?

Jacques unsnapped her garter belt and rolled down her nylon stockings. He kissed her inner thighs, took off her underpants and then his own in one motion. He was big, protruding like a giant anteater ready to suck up his lunch. She was shocked at his size. She gasped and then she was embarrassed. He laid her on the couch. She was afraid she was going to bleed on his couch and she was worried about birth control.

"Are you using something?" she whispered.

"Don't worry," Jacques responded as if he were calming a child who was afraid of a swing. "I've got everything under control."

He entered her while his fingers and tongue filled every other orifice. Hearing a cry, Gertie realized it was hers.

*   *   *

The next morning, Jacques walked into the kitchen naked to make coffee. He had two pinkish sacks that hung unevenly as if they were weighted down by different sized potatoes. Seeing a man naked took her aback—everyone wore robes in her house. She loved his bare chest and muscular thighs, but wished he'd put on a robe. He ground the coffee beans, put the ground beans into a glass carafe and added boiling water. After a few minutes, he used a plunger with a screen to compress the coffee grounds and separate them from the liquid.

"What is that kind of coffee maker called?" Gertie asked. "I've never seen one like that." Her family used Maxwell House ground coffee and brewed it in an electric percolator.

"It is a *cafetière à piston*," Jacques smiled proudly, as if he invented it.

"Hmm. Ingenious."

While the coffee was brewing, Jacques put a towel around his waist and went down the hall to wash up. While he was gone, Gertie wondered if he was using the bidet. She got up and checked to see if there was blood on the sheets. She was both relieved and confused that there was no stain. Returning to bed, she thought about how it felt when he entered her, the feeling of being filled up to the brim and then exploding. She got out of bed and walked over to the mirror behind the door. Had sex changed her? Was she still Gertie?

When she heard Jacques come back to the apartment, Gertie got back into bed. He came into the bedroom and walked over to the bed to kiss her cheek. "Bonjour," he said smiling and stroking her hair.

"Bonjour," Gertie smiled and kissed the palm of his hand. She got a whiff of their combined aroma from the night before. Part of her was pleased he was holding on to the scent of their having been together, but then she remembered that everyone in Paris had body odor. Jacques casually slipped into his pants and put on a shirt.

"I have an appointment. I'll call you later," he said kissing her.

Once Jacques left, Gertie peeked out the door first to the left and then right, checking to make sure no one was in the long narrow hall, and then took a run for the bathroom wrapped in one of Jacques' thin white towels. Having to share a bathroom with strangers was bad enough, but after having sex, having to go down the hall to urinate was like carrying a poster: She straddled the bidet facing the wall with a

186

large tank near the ceiling. She giggled, remembering the first time she used one at Miriam's and didn't know which way to face.

*　　　　　*　　　　　*

The following week, Jacques announced he was going to take Gertie to the Tour d'Argent. She often borrowed clothes from Miriam while she was in Paris, but when Gertie told her where Jacques was taking her, Miriam insisted that Gertie wear the dress she had worn to Frida's gallery opening. It was peach colored, ankle length with a crossover neckline, wide shoulders and a narrow waist. That night Gertie parted her hair in the middle with finger waves like Jean Arthur and stood in front of the mirror practicing her throaty voice. She couldn't do it for more than a few minutes without her throat getting sore. Jacques wore a double-breasted blue suit with wide padded shoulders.

When they arrived at the restaurant, the tuxedo-clad *maître d'* greeted Jacques as if he were an old friend, shaking his hand warmly—Gertie felt like she was with a celebrity. The dining room was on the 5th floor, with floor to ceiling windows that overlooked Notre Dame Cathedral. Wide-eyed at the sight of the Gothic church lit up like a million candles against the Paris sky, Gertie thought it was like watching the fireworks at Coney Island. As soon as they reached their table, a tall waiter with curly black hair greeted them, pulled Gertie's chair out for her, lifted the napkin and flicked his wrist, spreading it over her lap. It felt rather intimate to Gertie, and Jacques laughed at the shocked look on her face.

"You're funny," he said.

Her embarrassment was washed away when Jacques leaned across the table to take her hand in his, looked into her eyes and said, "I love being here with you."

Gertie believed him. No one had ever been so attentive to her. For the first time in her life she felt she was a sexy woman capable of delighting a man and being loved by him. And he was everything she had ever hoped for—handsome, debonair, well-educated, wealthy and seemingly crazy about her.

Jacques ordered champagne for two from the attentive waiter. They sat holding hands inhaling the view of the moonlit Seine. After a few silent moments, an elderly waiter arrived and put down the flutes.

Jacques touched his glass to Gertie's and said, "To us." Then he took her hand and kissed it. Gertie smiled broadly.

"You know Jews don't click glasses," she said.

"Really, why?" Jacques asked with furrowed brows.

"It was a Roman custom. They clicked wine cups so that some of the wine from each cup would spill over into the other. It was protection against being poisoned."

"Interesting." Jacques looked directly into Gertie's eyes. "But I still do not understand why Jews do not do it."

"Jews never want to do anything that the Romans did—on principle."

Jacques smiled.

The tall waiter returned and gave Gertie a menu. When she glanced at it, she noticed it had no prices. She thought that was strange.

"Can I choose a few of my favorite things for both of us?" Jacques asked.

"Of course," Gertie readily agreed. It was a relief—she didn't recognize any of the items on the menu.

"*Foie gras d'oie des Trois Empereurs*," Jacques said looking up at the waiter who nodded as he took the order without writing it down, "with two glasses of sauterne and then the Caneton Tour d'Argent for two and a bottle of '29 Cheval Blanc."

"What is *foie gras*, exactly?" Gertie asked as soon as the waiter left the table, tilting her head to the side.

"Just wait," Jacques laughed, taking her hand again, "Goose liver. It's like nothing you have ever experienced before. And they are famous for their duck. The restaurant raises them on its own farm."

"I've never had goose liver. The only kinds I know are chicken or calves liver," Gertie shrugged and blushed.

The elderly waiter returned and brought two small plates. He explained to Jacques in French what they were. Gertie only understood the word "*bouche*"—mouth.

Jacques explained, "This is called an *amuse bouche*. A playful little preview of the meal. It is a lobster tart. Will you eat lobster?"

"Sure," Gertie laughed. She felt touched by his concern about whether she would eat non-kosher foods. She thought to herself, *if I can eat goose liver, for God's sake, I can eat lobster*. It was the strangeness of the food that made her uncomfortable, she realized, not whether it was kosher.

Just then another waiter, a middle-aged man with caramel eyes and graying side-burns, came over to their table and put down two glasses of sauterne.

The *amuse bouche* waiter returned, removed the empty plates and explained the next course to Jacques.

When the waiter left, Jacques translated, "The foie gras is mixed with black truffles and scooped out of a pot with a spoon, like ice cream."

The idea of liver and ice cream struck Gertie as nauseating, but she tried to push it away. When the *foie gras* was served, Gertie was unsure if she was going to be able to eat goose liver-flavored ice cream with chocolate chips. Worse yet, it was served with brioche and salted butter. *Liver and butter?* But she wanted to be open to the things Jacques loved; she wanted to be open to life. She waited for Jacques to begin and followed his lead. Once she forced herself to taste it, she savored the velvety texture and rich silky taste.

Once the *foie gras* was cleared, a waiter opened the red wine, smelled the cork and poured the wine into a crystal decanter. Gertie thought he looked like a scientist doing an experiment. He poured a small amount in a goblet, lifted the glass to the light and squinted at it, rolled the wine around a few times, and put his nose deep into the glass almost touching *their* wine as Jacques watched impassively. Then, to Gertie's outrage, he sipped the wine, *their* wine. He gurgled it in what seemed to Gertie a most disgusting way. Finally he looked at Jacques and nodded his head. Jacques nodded as well as if they had made some secret agreement. Gertie did not understand what was going on. With his left hand behind his back, the man poured the wine into Gertie's goblet, careful to fill less than half the glass. After pouring wine into Jacques' glass as well, he said, "The waiter will explain about the duck momentarily."

As soon as he walked off, Gertie made a confused face.

"He is the sommelier. He smells and tastes the wine to make sure it is right. The waiters serve the food."

Gertie nodded silently. She felt like Margaret Mead, but not in a primitive society.

The elderly waiter returned to the table. "Your duck," he explained in heavily accented English, "died by strangulation so as to preserve its blood for the sauce. No more than twenty-four hours later, the chef roasted the dressed carcass, set aside the liver for the sauce, and removed the legs and breast. What emerges is a sauce the color of dark chocolate, with the unmistakable tang of blood." The waiter inhaled, closed his eyes and smiled in ecstasy. Then he continued, "The breast is served in slices and covered in the blood and juices of the crushed duckling. The next serving is the duck legs that are cooked in a different style."

"They strangled a duck?!" Gertie raised her brows and widened her eyes.

When Gertie tasted the slices of duck, she didn't care how they killed it. Sublime, the duck was rich, yet primitive, and the sauce was wild, salty, iron-like. Her mouth had never experienced so many textures and tastes simultaneously. It felt like only a few minutes had passed before it was all gone.

Afterwards, Gertie felt uncomfortably full in her tight-waisted dress. If she were home she would slump in her chair and hold her stomach. She smiled to herself thinking about how Mama stuffed derma pushing the filling into the casing. The elderly waiter wheeled a cart of cheeses to their table. There were twenty different types of cheese on the cart. Gertie opened her mouth, letting out a gasp. Jacques laughed.

Her hand nervously picked at a pimple on her neck that she'd discovered that morning. She was used to eating cheese at breakfast—farmer cheese or cream cheese on a bagel. She had never heard of cheese served as a course after dinner. The waiter stood there attentively, waiting for Gertie to choose.

Some of the cheese looked like it had been left in the icebox too long—covered with mildew and mold. Some had blue veins leading to little infected wounds. She swallowed hard, smiled weakly at the waiter and pointed to a few of the least spoiled-looking specimens.

"Take the Brillat-Savarin, too," Jacques said. "It's a triple cream, very rich. It cuts just like butter. You'll love it."

No mold. Okay. The waiter put four dainty pieces of cheese on her plate.

190

Jacques pointed to six different cheeses, three of which were full of mold. He smiled lustily as his forefinger danced from one level of the cart to the next.

By the time Jacques requested the bill, they had been eating and drinking for over three hours. The tall waiter put what looked like a leather-bound book on the table. Inside was the bill and a watercolor drawing of a duck on a heavy silver tray. There was also a printed certificate that said "Caneton Tour D'Argent #142,032."

*   *   *

Gertie began staying at Jacques' apartment and occasionally going back to Miriam's place to pick up a book or an article of clothing. She got accustomed to running down the dimly lit hall in her robe, using a wash cloth to clean herself rather than bathing, taking care that her pubic hairs were carried down the drain by the gurgling water, finishing quickly before one of the neighbors, usually old Madame Boucher, knocked on the door impatiently shouting, "*Dépechêz-vous!*" But when she had to move her bowels, the anxiety provoked by someone knocking seemed unbearable. She looked around the tiny cubicle with dark green tiles and yoke-colored paint, unevenly layered from years of painting over the cracks, and tried not to breathe in the smell of urine. She wondered how the French could be so elegant and cultured on the surface and so primitive beneath. Saying a prayer to hurry her bowels, she worried about leaving an odor and the person following knowing it was her. Imagining the look of disdain on Madame Boucher's wrinkled face made her shudder.

At the end of the first week of staying with Jacques, Gertie made her run to the bathroom and was dressed by the time Jacques returned from the bakery. She put the croissants he bought on a plate while he made an omelet for the two of them. She'd never had eggs like this before. He put herbs in the mixture and poured it in a pan, waited a minute or two, folded the sides of the eggs so it looked like a blintze and effortlessly flipped it on to a plate and divided it in two equal parts.

How will I go back to being Gertie, she wondered, *now that I know what it's like to be Gertrude?*

When they were finished, Gertie cleared the dishes and stood at the small sink, imagining what it would be like to live with Jacques.

She would put pictures on the bare walls and make curtains for the windows. Jacques got up from the table and walked over to his desk.

"Did you touch anything on my desk while I was gone?" he asked, squinting at the piles.

Gertie scanned his face for a clue to his shift in mood. "No, I just tidied it up a bit while you were out." She realized with a flutter in her stomach that she had stepped in emotional quicksand and was sinking quickly.

"Don't touch my desk." His eyes flared up, his face contorted in a rage. "Ever. Do you understand?"

"I don't understand why you're so angry. I just neatened it." She looked down at the table, holding her breath, the color draining from her face and her chin collapsing.

"I don't like anyone touching the things on my desk. That's all."

"I'm sorry, I won't do it again," Gertie said, sinking into a chair.

"No, no," he said, his demeanor changing entirely, "it's not your fault." The flames went out. He went over to her chair and bent down, put his arms around her and held her. "It's nothing. Don't worry about it. I'm sorry I got so angry."

Gertie's heart pounded: maybe she was outstaying her welcome.

*   *   *

The events of that morning were quickly forgotten when he took her to the Comédie-*Française* production of *Cyrano de Bergerac* with brilliant costumes by Christian Berard. It was a play that Gertie knew very well so the language was not a barrier. The theatre was filled night after night, but somehow Jacques was able to get tickets.

"I wonder what it is about this story," he said, "that resonates so deeply with the French who have behaved in the most un-Cyrano-like fashion. After Munich they wanted to make Chamberlain the King of France. They all bought umbrellas for God's sake."

"It's strange to me that Cyrano is seen as a selfless hero," Gertie responded.

"Why?" Jacques said, jerking his head.

Why is he angry at me for questioning Cyrano's altruism? "The play is about deception. Isn't deception for a good cause still deception?" She tried to explain something that seemed obvious to her.

She didn't understand how he could not see it. "There's no justification for deception. I never understood the play."

Jacques looked startled. "No," he yelled, "I don't agree." He shook his head and squinted at Gertie as if he were taking her measure.

Gertie's eyes widened. She held her breath.

"Cyrano is a moral hero," he said pointing at her. "He is willing to sacrifice his own happiness for something outside himself." He paused and took a deep breath, continuing in a calmer tone. "But I do not understand why the French love the play since they are willing to let the world fall apart around them and live with the illusion that their lives will not be touched."

Maybe that's what I'm doing, Gertie thought. *A war is about to start and Jews are trying to get out of Germany, yet I'm having a wonderful fling in Paris.*

*   *   *

Jacques accompanied Frida, Miriam and Gertie to Duchamp's party celebrating the hanging of Frida's self-portrait, *The Frame*, at the Louvre. It was the only one of her paintings sold at the *Mexique* exhibit, but it was the first work by a 20th century Mexican artist to be purchased by the Louvre.

Duchamp's apartment was a shock. It was his studio as well as his home and he had made no attempt to clean before the guests arrived. People milled around drinking champagne among the open drawers of bureaus and put their drinks on lamp tables covered with dust. But most shocking was the shiny porcelain urinal hung over a doorway.

"It's a pigsty," Miriam said.

"Yes..." Gertie replied, looking around at the snow shovel suspended from the ceiling and the upside-down bicycle wheel resting on a stool. A coat rack sat in the middle of the room—the most inconvenient place because they had to make their way through throngs of guests to get to it. Once there they realized it was a permanent installation: nailed to the floor.

"He's not a slob," Jacques said, amazed as he looked around the large room. "These are selected objects in chosen positions. They're exhibits!"

Just then Frida came over to greet the three of them. She was dressed in one of her Mexican Tehuana outfits: a sea green striped skirt and a bodice of red silk gauze with blue embroidery. Everyone turned to look at her as she worked her way through the crowd.

"The French are all coo-coo lunatic sons of beeches," she said, sipping her champagne.

Gertie, Miriam and Jacques burst out laughing.

"She thinks," Gertie whispered to Jacques, "in order to breathe you have to break a window."

Jacques smiled and squeezed Gertie's hand.

Duchamp came and joined them, kissing Frida on both cheeks and nodding at Gertie. She had met him when he set up Frida's exhibition at the Pierre Colle Gallery. He was a tall man with a high forehead and a long nose. He held a cigar in one hand and a glass of champagne in the other. Gertie introduced him to Jacques and Miriam.

"Perhaps you three can convince Frida to stay in Paris a little longer?" he said.

"I hate the French," Frida said. "I have to go."

"Why? We gave you an exhibition at the gallery; we sold one of your paintings to the Louvre and put you on the front page of *Vogue*. How can you hate us?" His deep set eyes seemed genuinely puzzled. "Schiaparelli even created a dress in your honor."

Frida shrugged and walked away.

Duchamp, Miriam, Jacques and Gertie stood speechless for a few moments.

"Don't be upset," Gertie said in a reassuring tone to Duchamp. "It's not about you or the French, it's about Nickolas Muray. She wants to go back to New York before he starts up with someone else."

Jacques and Miriam stared at each other with astonishment; Gertie was comforting Marcel Duchamp!

*   *   *

When Frida was leaving for New York, Miriam encouraged Gertie to remain in Paris. "You can't leave now," Miriam said. "Anais Nin says, 'The day came when the risk to remain tight in a bud was more painful than the risk it took to blossom.'"

"My parents are furious at the possibility that I might stay in Paris when Frida leaves. Solly wrote me that my father is incensed. If I don't go back and register at NYU for the fall, it will mean delaying college for another semester. What will I do here anyway? Once Frida goes back I have no income or reason to be here other than not wanting to leave Jacques. And I *do* want to start college. I hate hurting my parents."

Miriam sighed and handed Gertie a two letters. "And this came for you. I'm sure they won't help my cause to keep you here."

Gertie recognized her father's handwriting and opened it immediately. She read it aloud to Miriam.

April 18, 1939

Dear Gertie:

Your mother and I agreed to allow you to take this year off from school and work for Frida. Then we agreed to allow you to go to Paris with her. But we are very upset that you are prolonging your stay there. You promised to return and get ready to enroll at NYU in the fall. It's too crazy to be in France now. The war is coming. Appeasement will not prevent war. No Jew will be safe.

You must come home. NOW!

Love,
Tateh

"Oy," Gertie said and ripped open the second letter. Again, she read it aloud to Miriam.

April 22, 1939

Dear Gertie:

I can't sleep at night. We read the newspapers every day and worry that war can break out at

any moment and you will be stuck there. I
can't stand it. Hitler keeps making threats
against the Jews. The situation is getting
worse. It's not safe to be in Europe. Please
come home.

I love you.
Mama

"Poor thing. She sounds like she's really scared," Miriam said,
"Aren't you scared?"

"No, not really. I know I can get out whenever I want. This is
France. The Nazis aren't going to invade France. Anyway, Nancy can
always get out and I'll be able to go with her. She's not leaving yet, so
I'm staying."

"Nancy's not a Jew, Miriam." Gertie thought of Miriam's story
about going to the Nazi rally at Madison Square Garden. She wondered
if Miriam was naïve or crazy.

Gertie was scared: not just about staying in Europe, but about
Jacques. She remembered the storm when she neatened his desk.

"You know, there's something I want to tell you," Gertie said,
taking Miriam's hand.

"Sure, what?"

"Jacques, he's very secretive. I straightened his desk and he had
a fit. As if I was going to see something. And he has a wicked temper."

"Really?" Miriam raised her eyebrows in surprise. "I didn't
know that. We've all got our little idiosyncrasies. These are tense
times. He's probably worrying about getting drafted into the French
army. Who knows?"

Gertie liked the idea that Jacques' rage might have been about
his own anxieties and not about her. Maybe he wasn't being secretive,
just weighed down by the threat of war. She climbed on the idea, like a
child mounting a swing and let her doubts be momentarily suspended.

*   *   *

She kept the letters in her purse so that Jacques wouldn't find
them in the apartment. She couldn't bear leaving him, but she was
frightened about the war and pained by defying her parents. She had

never defied them before. Lilly had stayed in Mexico working for Trotsky against their protestations. At the time Gertie couldn't imagine doing that. But now she was in Europe on the verge of war. Her vision of herself in the world had changed from bucolic to a grand landscape where she was surrounded by towering rocks and raging waterfalls.

"Guess what?" Jacques said arriving home late one afternoon as the sun streamed through the living room windows of his apartment.

"What?" Gertie got up from the couch to kiss him.

"I have found a job for you. They want weekly synopses of books on psychology."

"Come on," Gertie said suspiciously. It sounded too good to be true. "For who?"

"A French newspaper. They want a sample. The editor suggested Karen Horney.

The next morning Gertie went to Shakespeare and Company on Rue de l'Odéon and bought a copy of Horney's *The Neurotic Personality of Our Time*. She found a bench on the river's edge and settled into reading the book. Horney argued that environmental and social conditions, rather than the instinctual or biological drives described by Freud, determine much of personality. But Gertie was more interested in Horney's description of neurosis than in her view of the origins of it.

The neurotics may feel hurt, for example, if someone does not accept their invitation, does not telephone for some time, or even only if he disagrees with them in some opinion. This sensitivity may be concealed by a "don't care" attitude. Furthermore, there is a marked contradiction between their wish for affection and their own capacity for feeling or giving it.

What a perfect description of Frida, Gertie giggled. She read the whole book in one sitting and felt delighted that she was going to get paid to summarize books like this one.

But her parents kept sending her letters pleading with her to come back to New York and go to college and the American Embassy kept sending frightening warnings for all Americans to leave Paris. She never saw the published newspaper for which she wrote. Jacques always had a ready excuse for not having a copy. She began to sense that her "job" was a way for Jacques to keep her in Paris. So, with great sadness, Gertie decided it was time to go home.

197

"I need to leave, you know." Gertie bit her nail as she sat across the breakfast table from Jacques. She was expecting him to protest, to put up a fuss, to beg her to stay.

He sat looking at her silently for a moment and then nodded, "I know."

Gertie's head jerked as if she'd been slapped. She wanted him to protest, to say he couldn't live without her. Didn't he want to be with her? Wasn't he in love with her? But she nodded. She was also relieved that there was no fight, no accusations.

"It is dangerous for you to be here," he said, getting up from his chair and walking over to her. He kissed her bad eye and then stood behind her with his arms around her chest. "You have to go. I will follow as soon as I can."

"Oh," she sighed. *He does love me; he wants to be with me. He wants me to leave because he wants to protect me.* She got up from her chair and turned to face him. He held her close to him and she whispered, "I love you."

"I love you too," Jacques said.

12

"*Oy, Gut in Himmel*," Tateh said with tears in his eyes grasping a sugar cube between his teeth. He put his glass of tea down on the kitchen table next to the *Forward*. The pounding rain sounded like waves smacking against the windows and roof of the house. The smell of eggs left too long on the burner wafted through the air. "What happened?" Gertie asked with a start as if shaken from a dream. She sat in her cotton nightgown twiddling her hair, eating a bowl of oatmeal before going to work. She had been back from Paris a couple of weeks and a letter of recommendation from Frida to Alfred Barr, the director of the new Museum of Modern Art on West 53rd Street, had landed her a summer internship.

Tateh read the headline out loud, "18 Refugees Enter Cuba; 922 Others Wait While Their Cases Are Being Studied."

Mama sighed, "I pray to God they don't all end up in concentration camps." Putting her cup down, she tapped her ring against it, like a drum beat until, jolted by a crash of thunder, she almost spilled the coffee on the red and white checked oil cloth.

Gertie thought about the German Jewish refugees she saw when Jacques took her to the Marais. At least they got out. They would be safe in Paris, she imagined, just like Yvette. But she worried, what about the ones who weren't allowed to leave Germany or Austria?

"*If it would help to pray to God, then people would be hiring others to pray for them,*" Tateh replied in Yiddish. He put his hand on the back of his neck, his fingers searching for a cyst just below his right ear. Once his forefinger found the spot, he rubbed it for a few moments and then his hand returned to the half empty glass of tea.

Sol had hung a map of Europe in his room and he and Tateh put thumbtacks in areas occupied by the Nazis. There was a thumb tack in Austria and another in Czechoslovakia. A series of calendar pages papered Sol's bedroom walls. He had only started the project in the last year, but Mama helped him find old calendars so that the timeline could begin in January, 1933 when Hitler was appointed Chancellor of Germany. Important dates were circled in red with explanations written in: April 1, 1933: "Nazis stage boycott of Jewish shops and businesses"; May 10, 1933: "Burning of books"; September 29, 1933:

"Nazis prohibit Jews from owning land"; July 22, 1934: "Jews are prohibited from the legal profession"; November 15, 1935: "Nuremberg Race Laws Decreed"; March 7, 1936: "German army occupies the Rhineland"; November 16, 1937: "Jews are prohibited from getting passports to travel abroad"; March 12, 1938: "Hitler announces Anschluss with Austria"; September 30, 1938: "Munich Agreement dooms Czechoslovakia"; November 9-10, 1938: "Kristallnacht: destruction of synagogues and shops"; March 15, 1939: "Germany invades Czechoslovakia"; May 27, 1939: "MS St. Louis arrives in Havana with over 900 European Jews on board."

"The Cubans will take the people from the boat," Sol bit the inside of his cheek and pushed his cereal bowl away, "won't they Tateh? They have to..."

"I doubt it," Tateh said, slumping in his chair, his hand searching for the right spot on his neck again, as if finding it would situate him. "The Nazis and the Franco supporters in Cuba tell everyone that the Jews are all communists."

"They don't want communists or Jews or any refugees," Gertie said. "It's not just about Jews." She remembered Jacques telling her about the horrific conditions in the Spanish refugee camps in Southern France. They weren't Jews, just anti-fascist Spaniards running for their lives. Her thoughts turned to the smell of Brilliantine in Jacques' hair and the way his tongue in her ear made her squirm.

Sol sat in a sullen stoop, shaking his head. "Why do people hate us so much?"

Gertie felt tears welling up. She felt bad for fantasizing about Jacques during such an emotional discussion.

Mama got up, walked over to Sol, put her arms around him and kissed the top of his head. Sol was almost 15 and taller than Mama, but everyone wanted to protect him from the reality of what it meant to be a Jew. Gertie knew the story of Abraham and Isaac made Mama wild with rage. She was not going to offer up her son. Over her dead body.

"We don't know yet," Mama said, stroking Sol's face. "Maybe they'll let them in."

Sol kissed his mother's cheek but then he moved her arms, freeing himself from her embrace. "Stop already," he groaned, "I'm not a child, you know."

Mama pulled a cotton handkerchief from her bosom and wiped a tear from her eye.

Gertie sighed. She knew exactly what Sol was talking about. It was difficult to adjust to being a child in her parents' house after her weeks with Jacques in Paris: she was tired of Mama overcooking the eggs; she was annoyed when her father asked what time she'd be home; she wanted her *café au lait* in a bowl, not a cup; and she wanted croissants for breakfast, not bagels or cereal.

"No," Tateh shook his head with his eyes closed, gripping the bridge of his nose as if he had a headache. "They had a large anti-Semitic demonstration in Havana a couple of weeks ago, days before the *St. Louis* sailed from Hamburg. They organized a demonstration against letting them in."

Gertie noticed her father's jowls and the dark half-moons under his eyes. She leaned over and stroked his hand, her fingers tracing the bulging veins. Both her parents had aged in the weeks that she was away. She wasn't sure if it was a response to all the bad news about the European Jews or if she was seeing them differently since her return from Paris. Mama looked slimmer and Gertie noticed the tiny paper cut creases on her upper lip. For the first time, she thought about her parents dying.

"It's not likely that Roosevelt will let them in," Tateh said leaning forward on the table. His face looked like papier mâché. "Not if the Cubans say no."

"Those polls last year showed most Americans don't want to help the refugees," Gertie said, closing her bad eye as if it would help her concentrate. "What was it I read? About seventy-five percent said they don't want them here."

"They're anti-Semites," Tateh sighed. "Let's face it. They don't even want a one-time exception to allow children to come. I was lucky to get here before 1924."

"Do you think the Joint Distribution Committee will be able to get them visas somewhere else?" Mama asked.

"Oy," Gertie sighed, "I have to go to work." She went to sit on her unmade bed and picked up Jacques' wrinkled letter. She thought about being engulfed in his arms on the wooden walkway of the Pont des Arts, holding hands in the Louvre and the sweet taste of his lips. Then she reread the letter.

May 15, 1939

Dear Gertrude:

I think about you from the moment I wake up
until I go to bed. I saw Yvette last week. She
invited me for dinner—she sends her regards.
She was talking about how stupid it was to
exclude the Soviet Union from the Munich
conference. She says Blum wants to go to
visit Stalin and try to improve relations, but
he can't get any support for it. Things are
getting worse for the Jews here, not just
Blum. It is a good thing you left—although I
can hardly stand it.

Pablo Neruda is leaving Paris and going to
Mexico City—he's been appointed Chile's
Consul General to Mexico. His words echo
my feelings perfectly:

> That is all. Someone sings far off.
> Far off,
> my soul is not content to have lost
> her.

Love,
Jacques

Gertie moaned and put the letter to her nose, hoping to smell
Jacques' body. She imagined his voice reading Neruda's words. He
missed her. Maybe he would come to the United States to be with her.

When she got into the bathtub, Gertie thought about how lucky
she was that Jacques missed her and wanted to be with her. She soaped
her washcloth and stroked herself, imagining his arrival in New York.
Her father could help him find an apartment and she would help him
decorate it. She pictured them in the little kitchen together: Jacques

202

making *soupe à l'oignon gratinée*, the rich smell of caramelized onions and melted cheese floating on the air like a warm breeze; teaching him how to make a sweet noodle *kugel* with raisins the way Mama made it.

When she got out of the bath, Gertie walked over to the full length mirror behind the door, standing sideways, the way she always did, so that her good eye faced the mirror. She held her pear-shaped breasts in her hands remembering Jacques circling each nipple with his tongue.

She remembered the day she met him at Frida's exhibit—how impressed she was at his analysis of Frida's paintings. He was so smart. And the day they met Picasso having lunch! She wanted to take him to the Museum of Modern Art and show him her favorite painting in the Picasso exhibit, "*Jeune fille endormie*." A portrait of his lover, Marie-Thérèse Walter, it was bursting with color. There was an intimacy to it, despite the abstract technique. Gertie wondered what it must be like to have a lover so enamored he paints portraits of you. She wasn't sure how it would feel to stand naked for hours while Jacques looked at her. How would he feel about the thickness in her thighs? He might not have noticed it in bed, but posing nude felt more exposing than just being naked in bed. As she stood in front of the mirror she imagined Jacques standing in the bathroom looking at her, and felt a spasm between her legs.

Before she left for work, Gertie sat at her desk to write to Jacques. She put his letter on the desk so she could look at it while she was writing.

May 23, 1939

Dear Jacques:

I think about you from the moment I get up to
the moment I go to sleep as well. I think about
every day and night we spent in Paris. I miss
your touch, the warmth of your body next to
mine. I miss your voice whispering
"Gertrude. "I miss your moist omelets with
herbs, and the way you put your face into a
wine goblet to smell it before you taste the

wine. (I don't know anyone else who does that!)

The job at the Museum of Modern Art is working out very well. There's a Picasso retrospective there. I visit it every day and think of the day you took me to meet him.

I'm worried about you. If the war starts will you be conscripted to fight the Nazis? I realized I don't know if you're a Belgian or French citizen. I don't really care. I just wondered if you can be conscripted by the French army. Why don't you leave now? Why don't you come to New York?

Say hello to Yvette for me. Have you seen Miriam? I haven't heard from her.

I have to go to work. I just wanted to respond quickly to your letter.

Write soon.

Love,
Gertrude

*   *   *

One summer evening Gertie came home from working at the museum and found her father sitting at the window in the living room reading the afternoon newspaper and sipping tea.

"Who *is* this Jacques person?" Tateh asked narrowing his eyes as if he were trying to read what was hidden in the small print.

Gertie had tried to hide Jacques' letters from her father. But as Mama always said, Tateh was like a cow—he could detect a smell five miles away. He picked up the pile of mail in the morning and noticed a letter to "Gertrude Abramovitz" with Jacques' return address. He was not happy—he assumed anyone named Jacques was a *goy*.

Gertie asked Mama not to tell Tateh about Jacques. Mama agreed, Gertie thought, because she thought it was a passing thing and there was no reason to upset Tateh.

"I remember the first time I was in love—with Abe Rabinowitz," Mama had told Gertie. "I was 14 and he lived down the street from us. He used to wait in front of my apartment house in the morning," Ida sighed, "to walk me to school. He had curly black hair and blue eyes—he looked like a *goy*. But he was Jewish. I often wonder what became of him."

He was no Jacques, Gertie had thought.

Gertie knew Mama wondered if she had had sex with Jacques. Usually Mama was so outspoken, but Gertie realized she didn't feel comfortable asking her. Lilly she might have asked, but Mama had always been more reticent with Gertie, more afraid of hurting her. Lilly had been the one to talk to Gertie about birth control. Mama had once told her that you love all your children, but not exactly the same way. One might feel like a newly hatched egg, warm in your hand, but you can't grasp too hard or it breaks. Another one might feel hard boiled. You don't have to worry about damaging it; you can throw it up in the air and catch it. Even if you miss, it's just the shell that breaks.

Gertie sat down across the dining table from her father as he folded the newspaper and put it aside on the table. She felt weightless as if she were floating underwater, waves breaking above her, the sun refracted. Her heart pounded.

"Gertie," he said shaking the letter, "you're a good girl and you're home now and I want this to be the end of it. I don't want you getting any more involved with a *goy*. Soon they won't let Jews into America or Palestine. Don't you get it? I won't have it."

Gertie looked down at the table silently.

"My daughter is keeping company with a *goy*? You have to choose a side: your own people or the *goyim*. If there ever was a time that being with a *goy* would be okay, this is not the time…And stop looking like somebody died. You're going to meet lots of nice Jewish boys at NYU."

It felt like a spanking, although Tateh had never raised a hand toward her. She didn't want to get into a fight with her father—there was no point to it. She had witnessed the endless fighting between Lilly and Tateh and Lilly never changed his mind. But she wanted to yell, *I don't want a Jewish boy, I want Jacques; he doesn't think I'm a damaged bird like you do!* She flew up from her chair, glared at her father and then rushed out of the room.

*   *   *

Toward the end of the summer the letters from Jacques stopped coming. Gertie ran for the mail each day and couldn't understand why—he had seemed so in love with her in Paris. His first letters were so romantic. She felt thrown away like yesterday's paper. By September, when the Germans invaded Poland and the British and French declared war against the Germans, she imagined Jacques might have gotten conscripted into the Belgian army or joined the French army to fight the Nazis. She feared this, but guiltily thought it would also mean his lack of communication wasn't a rejection of her. She yearned for Jacques, but also ached to see Lilly.

September 30, 1939

Dear Lilly:

No one can speak about anything other than the German invasion of Poland and the beginning of the war. There are lots of marches in Union Square, but the American government is not likely to interfere. If they won't even let refugees into the country, they're certainly not going to get involved in a war to protect Poland.

I haven't heard from Jacques. I don't know if he got out of France or if he was conscripted. It's depressing. I was a fool to think I really meant something to him.

I hope you're settled in by now with Lev and Natalia. I feel like a river about to enter the

206

ocean. I'm taking Introduction to Art History and we're starting with ancient through medieval. It's one of those large lecture classes so there's not much discussion, but the professor is a great storyteller. At first I was upset that there was so much sculpture as opposed to paintings. But it turns out I love all the Egyptian stuff—the sculpture as well as the hieroglyphics. I've been spending so much time at the Met looking at the Egyptian collection with my friend Hannah who always sits next to me in lecture class. She says I have to forget about Jacques and move on. She says thinking about Jacques all the time prevents me from meeting another boy. I'm sure she's right, but I just can't stop thinking about him.

Have you heard from Miriam? I wrote to her, but I haven't gotten a response.

Love,
Gertie

In October, Gertie finally received a letter from Jacques. Mama put the letter on Gertie's bed and Gertie cried when she saw it. A flood of excitement and a surge of anger flowed together. She propped her pillow against the wall and sat back on her bed to rip open the envelope.

October 13, 1939

Dear Gertrude:

I am sorry I haven't written. I've been very busy. I left Paris in mid-August, just before the invasion of Poland, and moved to Toronto just in time for Canada to declare war. There

are very few young men around—it seems
they have all enlisted. Women are driving the
buses and trains.

I have a great job. I am assistant to Robertson
Davies, the literary editor of *Saturday Night*.
It's an arts, politics and current affairs journal
and I'm very excited about the opportunity.

I am living near High Park in a picturesque
neighborhood with gently rolling hills,
winding streets, and towering oak trees. I
wish you were here with me, but I know how
important school is to you.

Love,
Jacques

Gertie felt like the popcorn in one of those machines in movie
theaters that blow the kernels fiercely. She was happy to hear from him
and glad he was out of harm's way. But she was embarrassed that all
the letters she had written to him were so unguarded and his was so
cool and distant. *Why did he go to Toronto instead of New York?* Part
of her wished that he had enlisted in the Belgian or French or Canadian
army and committed himself to fighting the Nazis rather than being the
only healthy young man left in Toronto.

"Gertie," yelled her mother from the kitchen, "it's Hannah."
Gertie ran to pick up the phone. The smell of onions browning in
chicken fat filled the air, which felt stagnant. She looked around to
make sure her father was not in earshot.

"You won't believe this," Gertie said.

"You finally got a letter from Jacques?"

"Yes, how did you guess?"

"Because that's what you live for, you're *meshuganah*."
Hannah was only 20 years old, but she had the skepticism of a much
older woman. Although they were in a large lecture class together, and
Gertie wouldn't dare raise her hand, Hannah never hesitated to ask the
professor for evidence of his point of view.

"He's in Canada," Gertie said with a pout.

"So he's not coming to New York?"

"I guess not. He got a job there." Gertie gnawed her lower lip.

"He's a *shmuck*, what can I tell you? To go to Canada when he could be with you?"

*   *   *

Gertie continued to run to the mailbox each morning in hopes of a letter, but she didn't receive another one until after Thanksgiving. She could hear the sound of shovels scraping the pavement outside as she sat on her bed. The pure white blanket of early snow would be piles of gray by morning with treacherous patches of ice.

December 1, 1939

Dear Gertrude:

I hope you had a nice Thanksgiving. The Canadians celebrate it on November 6 and it was a special one because Canadian troops are departing for Europe in droves. For many families it may be the last time they ever see their husbands/fathers/brothers.

Work at the magazine is going very well. I'm getting great experience. Bill Davies is a novelist and playwright as well as a critic and he is helping me with my writing.

How is school going? What do you hear from your sister in Mexico?

Love,
Jacques

Her tears blurred the ink on the card. She heard the whirling wind outside and saw the flurries blowing against the window. It was not even a real letter, just a note. All his passion, for her and for the state of the world, seemed to have drained out of him. She wished Lilly was there—maybe she wouldn't feel so alone. She missed her in that moment more than she had for months. She took up a pen and paper to write her a letter. Then she hesitated for a moment, unsure of how much of her unhappiness to share with Lilly.

December 28, 1939

Dear Lilly:

Jacques writes me notes every once in a
while. They're friendly, but cool. Absence, in
this case, did not make the heart grow fonder.

She stopped writing and went to the bathroom to get a tissue. She dried her eyes and returned to her bed to continue writing:

I feel like a fool. I obviously mistook a sexual
fling for a love affair that was going to turn
into a life together. How stupid and naïve I
am.

She felt angry and had to stop again. Shame and embarrassment flowed through her.

After a few minutes of heaving, she calmed down and continued the letter:

Mama and I went to see "Gone with the
Wind." It was incredible. Vivien Leigh is the
embodiment of Scarlett—so selfish and
tackling life with both claws. She reminds me
of Frida with a Southern accent.
She smiled at the thought of it: Frida with a
Southern accent. Then she continued:

We are all in a state of shock from Stalin's
invasion of Finland. He's such a scoundrel.
How come Lev isn't saying anything?

I'm busy with school and still working part
time at the museum. I just wanted to send you
a note to tell you about the movie.

Love,
Gertie

*   *   *

For New Year's and Valentine's Day Jacques sent Gertie cards,
but they were as colorless as a winter day. The cards never included
any mention of what was going on in the world or anything personal
about Gertie. In April he sent a note wishing her a happy Passover. She
hugged herself after she read it—it was clear he didn't want her. He
could have called her. She accepted their relationship had not meant the
same thing to him as it had to her. By May, Gertie's first year at NYU
was almost completed and in response to much prompting from Mama,
Tateh and Hannah, she started dating.

13

Lev's new house was at the end of Avenida Viena next to the Churubusco River which was more like a creek than a river, and a dry one at that. They moved there early in May 1939.

The house was the former summer home of a merchant family—solid and spacious with a garden wall draped with blood-red bougainvillea surrounding it. In the center were orange and fig trees and there were a variety of paths lined with yuccas and agaves. The one-story house was shaped like a T—the stem of the T jutted out into the patio and housed Trotsky's study and Lev and Natalia's bedroom. Three tall windows enclosed by iron grillwork looked out onto a barbed-wire fence.

When Van found the house, it had been unoccupied for a few years. The owners were renting it at a rock bottom price because it was in ruins. To make it habitable and safe a series of repairs were necessary, and it also had to be painted. For security purposes, a young Trotskyist named Melquíades Benitez was in charge of the painting and repairs. Melquiades and his crew raised the height of the walls and created a steel entrance door. They installed an electric device to open it and an alarm system.

Avenida Viena was not paved and Lilly often walked along the path, passing modest adobe houses on both sides surrounded by corn fields. On the southeast end of the property, the police built a guard booth outside the walls. Ten policemen working two shifts of five each were assigned to guard Trotsky. Inside the walls there was a guard house, and the living quarters for Lilly, Van, Bob Harte and four other volunteer American bodyguards.

Ever since they moved to the new house, Lev's temper had become increasingly volatile. When Lilly threw away a letter, he had banged his desk with his fist and yelled, "What did you do that for? What is the matter with you?"

"You told me the woman was stupid and you weren't going to respond to her," replied Lilly, shocked at his anger.

"It doesn't matter," he yelled. "Do not throw things away!"

No one had ever yelled at her like that. But Lilly was even more offended by Lev's lack of reaction to the Nazi-Soviet pact in August 1939, followed a week later by the invasion of Poland.

One of the first disturbing letters challenging Lev's position on Hitler and Stalin came from Sidney Hook.

October 15, 1939

Dear Lilly:

As you can imagine we were aghast at Lev's reaction (or rather non-reaction) to Stalin's treaty with Hitler. How in the world can he say it is "of secondary importance"? And now he's silent on Stalin's occupation of eastern Poland and his demand that Latvia, Lithuania, and Estonia give him the right to establish military bases there. What's wrong with the Old Man? For years he predicted this would happen and now that it has he's quiet.

He uses the dialectic as an excuse for passivity. Dewey says it's no different than believing in "God's will." I must say I agree with Burnham's article in *Partisan Review* that Marxism needs the intellectual equivalent of an appendectomy—it has to have the dialectic removed.

I'm looking forward to hearing your views on all this.

Best,
Sidney

Lilly crushed Sidney's letter in her hand. She agreed with him. She didn't know how to respond. She didn't want to write a letter defending Lev's positions—they were indefensible. Yet, she felt protective of him.

In November Lev asked her to start working on his scathing attack on the American Trotskyist dissenters, "A Petty-Bourgeois Opposition in the Socialist Workers Party." She was offended by it and increasingly conflicted about working for him.

They sat in the garden and argued about it. He picked one of the last oranges on the tree with his tanned arms and started peeling it, carefully putting the peels in a pile on the ground next to him. Lilly noticed the swollen joints on his fingers.

"The dissenters are all clerical workers, not factory workers, believe me," Lev told her. The Old Man's eyes smiled when he slowly articulated the play on words, "Petty-bourgeois."

"That's ridiculous, they're all intellectuals—like you," Lilly smirked.

Lev didn't answer.

"And how can you defend the invasion of Finland?" she asked, so angry that she didn't care if Lev got angry at her.

"The Red Army was engaged in the expropriation of Finland's capitalists," Lev insisted, "while the Finnish Army was defending them against the workers and peasants."

"Come on, Lev," she said waving her hand. The discussion reminded her of talking about the birth control movement with Tateh. She knew her father understood the importance of birth control—he just didn't want to say it publicly. And now there was a *prima facie* case against Stalin. How could Lev possibly deny it? He knew it, he just wouldn't say it.

Lev smiled, patting Lilly's arm.

"Good," he chuckled. "I like when you argue with me. I used to love to argue with Jan Frankel. He is in Los Angeles now. He disagrees with me on everything—part of that ridiculous group that started the Workers Party. I wish I could sit down with him and argue it out."

"Okay, good." *If he gives me permission to argue I will.* "Can you tell me why you are silent about the European Jews?"

"Let me explain," Lev said. "The issue isn't just what Hitler is doing to the Jews. That is terrible. But Jews aren't the only ones who are murdered by fascists."

214

"But you are a Jew. Your parents were Jews. Why are you so nonchalant about the hideous things happening to European Jews?"

"Lilly," he put down the orange, took off his glasses and wiped them with his handkerchief, "my parents didn't speak Yiddish. I didn't go to a Jewish school. I didn't have Jewish friends. I am a Russian, not a Jew. Ivan Grebon, the farm mechanic who almost cut off his thumb with an ax, was my friend. He had a red mustache and beard." The Old Man smiled at the memory. "And he could fix anything. He could repair steam engines and tune a piano. He built my first bicycle. Ivan Grebon built a pigeon loft and I fed and watered the pigeons. I climbed the ladder a dozen times every day to give them water and seed. I went to a Christian secondary school in Odessa. My best friend was a German named Carlson. My people are the workers, not the Jews, Lilly."

What's this nonsense? Lilly wanted to scream at him, *Hitler thinks your people are the Jews!* Instead, she got up from the bench and said, "I better get back to the office and get to work."

*   *   *

December 2, 1939

Dear Lilly:

No one here understands how Trotsky's "ABC of Materialist Dialectics" has anything whatever to do with the invasion of Finland. Lots of people are outraged at his put-down of those of us who disagree with him as "petty-bourgeois." And how can he claim there was a civil war in Finland? The Finnish masses don't support Stalin's invasion of their country. It's ridiculous.

School is good. I have the same professor you had for English 1. He's a tough grader—I've gotten only B's on my papers so far.

Jacques wrote me that he is in Toronto
working for a magazine. I guess that's the end
of that. He doesn't seem to have thought
about coming to New York to be with me, so
I guess it's time for me to try to forget about
him and move on.

We missed you at Thanksgiving. We just miss
you! I hope you come back soon.

Love,
Gertie

Gertie's letter made Lilly homesick; she wished she was in
Brooklyn to comfort her. She sat on her bed in the tiny room she had in
the guard house and sighed, thinking about home: going to the movies
with Gertie and Sol; taking them for an egg cream; going to a concert
with Howie; putting her arms around Tateh and feeling his embrace;
cuddling on the couch with Mama while she stroked her hair. She
imagined sitting in her parents' kitchen laughing with Gertie and Sol,
the afternoon light streaming in, peeling potatoes or shelling peas for
dinner. She craved Mama's borscht with sour cream. She yearned for
fresh bagels with smoked salmon and cream cheese. She longed for
corned beef on rye bread with coleslaw from the delicatessen. And she
didn't understand what the "ABC of Materialist Dialectics" had to do
with the invasion of Finland any more than Gertie did.

*   *   *

December 15, 1939

Dear Lilly:

Hitler sent Stalin a birthday card! And Lev
claims the Nazis and the Allies are all just
capitalists cut from the same cloth. How can
you continue to work for him? He is no better
than Stalin.

Shachtman and Burnham are demanding that
the Trotskyist Socialist Workers Party
condemn the Red Army invasion of Finland.
As you can imagine, "Little Finland" trying to
defend itself against Stalin is drawing
enormous sympathy in the United States—a
lot more outrage than the wholesale murder of
the Jews. Lev is supposed to be the most
important critic of Stalin. When is he going to
speak out?

I don't understand you Lilly. It was one thing
to stay and work for Lev when you believed
he represented the major opposition to Stalin.
But it's clear that he doesn't. He's not
interested in saving the Jews or saving Poland
or Finland. How can you continue to help him
write ridiculous letters and arcane articles
about the dialectic? I feel you've cordoned off
part of your consciousness. What are you
doing? I've had enough. This is crazy.

I love you, but I cannot take it. I cannot waste
any more of my life waiting for you to come
to your senses.

Howard

Who is this other person—"Howard"? She was frightened by
his threat to end their relationship if she didn't stop working for Lev
and return to New York. Howard, she felt, might actually end it. She
didn't want that. She liked the security of knowing Howie was there in
New York whenever she decided to leave Mexico. But "Howard" was
not going to wait much longer. And she was choking from having to
swallow her own thoughts and feelings when preparing manuscripts for
the Old Man.

A week after Lilly received the letter from Howie, she argued with Lev while he fed the rabbits and the chickens in the morning. He was most relaxed when he was doing his gardening and feeding the animals. He often spoke to them in Yiddish: "Come on *bubbela*, eat your breakfast." She enjoyed seeing this pre-revolutionary part of Lev.

"I thought your parents didn't speak Yiddish."

"No, they didn't, but my cousins in Odessa did." Changing the subject, he asked, "Do you know where I learned about literature?"

"No." Lilly thought she saw a tear in his eye.

"When I lived with Moshe and Fanny in order to go to school in Odessa," he said, nodding his head. "They used to explain things to me and give me books to read. They introduced me to Charles Dickens. Imagine that." He smiled at the memory. "And they bought a copy of Tolstoy's play *The Power of Darkness* even though it was banned."

"Lev, you have so many positive memories of your time with Moshe and Fanny when you lived with them in Odessa and they spoke Yiddish and you suffered at that St. Paul's because you were Jewish, so I just don't understand why you say you're not a Jew."

"Being a Jew means you believe in God," he lectured, "and you think the Jews are the Chosen People. I don't believe any of that rubbish."

Lilly groaned. "Lev, Hitler doesn't care if you keep kosher or you believe in God or you think Jews are the Chosen People. Hitler doesn't care if *you* don't think you're a Jew. To the Nazis, you're a Jew."

Lev smiled. "Enough," he said, as he got up and walked to his study. After his breakfast break he returned to his study and spent most of the day working.

Lilly sat at her desk thinking about Bubby and Zayde Shmuel escaping from Russia after his father's factory burned. How they had packed up their silver flatware, bone china, crystal, linens, and four children and left Kiev. She wondered how many Jews were now trying to escape from Germany. She thought about the story Zayde had told so many times—how they paid an agent to arrange overland transportation to the German border. When they got close to the border, they waited in a lodging house until a guide put together a large enough party to make it profitable to pay off the border guards. They were afraid they would be robbed—or murdered. But the smugglers shipped their baggage via

218

wagons to Hamburg. Then at night the guide led the emigrants across the border by foot.

Lilly thought about the fact that Zayde Shmuel couldn't practice medicine legally when he arrived in New York. He had some patients who knew him from Kiev and didn't care if he had a license. But he wasn't able to work very much and then he became ill with asthma and spent most of the day at home laboring to breathe. They had an apartment that was too small for their growing (and growing and growing) family. So, although the plates were bone china they had little to put on them for their children.

Late that afternoon, Lev came out of his office and talked to Lilly about the response to a letter from a supporter that she was working on. He stood next to her, looking over her shoulder.

"Why do Americans say 'I've gotten…instead of 'I've become…?'"

"I don't know. I never noticed it actually. I'm American," Lilly responded haltingly. *Who cares about such details*, she wondered to herself, *when the issues at hand are so major?*

*   *   *

On the night of May 23, 1940, Lilly fell asleep reading in her bedroom in the guards' house. The window was open because it was a hot humid night. She was dreaming about Friday night Shabbos dinner in Brooklyn when the loud banging began. "Go away," she mumbled wanting to hold on to the smell of chicken soup and fresh baked challah. She turned over, trying to return to her grandfather telling the oft-told story of how he and Grandma tried to convince their parents to leave Russia. He always had a vacant look in his eyes as if he were talking to someone who wasn't at the table and his hand shook so much she thought he might spill his seltzer. "They wouldn't come," he cried. "As frightened as they were to stay, they were more frightened to leave." Lilly tried not to look at Gertie so they wouldn't start to laugh.

She woke to a pounding sound that got louder and faster. She thought it was hail stones beating against the tin roof. Putting the pillow over her face and ears, she tried to block out the hammering, but she could feel the floor shaking beneath the bed. There were flashes of light out the window, so she thought it must be thunder and lightning. No matter how she turned or contorted the pillow, she could not go back to Shabbos. Finally, she gave up and pulled herself up from bed and walked toward the window. There was screaming along with the hammering and it started to dawn on her that what she was hearing was machine gun fire.

She opened the blinds and saw two men in police uniforms in the garden. One of them saw her and turned a flashlight in her direction. *They're here for Lev and we're all going to die! What's wrong with me, why didn't I listen to Howie and go home? What have I been waiting for?*

A group of about twenty men with machine guns got through the police on duty outside the house, cut the telephone cables, forced the guard on duty to open the gate and entered the patio. One of them turned the light in her direction and the other fired a submachine gun splattering the window. Screaming, she hit the floor hard, falling into a pile of glass shards which turned pink and then red. Her body shook with fear and pain. Was she going to die now?

One of the "policemen" yelled in Spanish, *"Get back in your room and you won't get hurt."* Her mother's face flashed before her. *I don't want to die, Mama.* She began dry heaving, but nothing came up except some liquid that burned the back of her throat. *Help me, I don't want to die.* Bullets ripped through the windows and doors of the main house. She covered her ears, smearing her face with blood. The shooting continued for five minutes that felt like a lifetime. A loud blast sounded like a bomb and she smelled smoke. More gunfire, then a lull. Crawling to the window sill, she peeked out the bottom of the broken window and screamed when she saw flames coming from the main house.

Lev and Natalia's thirteen year-old grandson Seva's bedroom was at the base of the T-shaped house. Marguerite and Alfred Rosmer, old friends of Lev and Natalia, had escorted him to Mexico from France in August 1939 after his uncle's death since his mother had committed suicide years earlier. Sure that Lev, Natalia and Seva were dead, Lilly sat on the floor sobbing and hugging herself. She heard the cawing of crows and then Van yelled, "It is okay. It is clear. You can come out now." When Lilly stood up, she had cuts on her hands, forearms and knees.

She ran towards Lev and Natalia's bedroom to see if they survived. Natalia had ice on her hands. She had burned them trying to smother the flames from the grenade the assailants used to break down the bedroom door. Seva's foot was bleeding from a gunshot wound; they had shot through his mattress when he was hiding under the bed. Lev stood in his cotton pajamas. He had some small scratches on his face from the flying glass. When he showed the others the bullet holes in the walls he laughed. He was exuberant that he and Natalia and Seva were still alive and that even though it had been scrupulously prepared and executed, the attack had failed.

When Lilly returned to her room, a dreary rain tapped at the window as she cleaned up the bloody shards of glass by the window. She lay down on her bed, shaking, and thinking about the loud blast and the smoke. To calm herself she imagined being held tight in Howie's arms, his voice whispering, *"You're safe with me."*

*   *   *

Two days later, they still couldn't find Bob Harte. It wasn't clear if he had been taken as a hostage or an accomplice. It was hard for her to imagine him as part of an assassination attempt. But someone had turned off the alarm.

May 25, 1940

Dear Howie:

Of course you've heard the news by now. We were all sleeping when they opened fire. Natalia pushed Lev under the bed and protected him with her body. Seva, Lev's grandson, was under his bed also, but the bastards shot through the mattress. Miraculously, he was only slightly wounded. Thinking they had killed the Old Man, they escaped taking the two cars from the house.

The local Stalinist newspapers are saying Lev organized this event himself. It's so ridiculous. The police captured some of the assailants, who were active members of the

Mexican Communist Party. The ringleader was Diego's friend David Alfaro Siqueiros, but he got away. The attacking party was composed of men who had served under Siqueiros in the Spanish Civil War and of miners from his union.

Since the murder attempt, the house has become a fortress, the surrounding walls have been made higher and the windows blocked off. The alarm system has been improved. The Old Man says the house is a medieval prison and every morning he says: "Damn it, we have survived another night without being murdered ..."

I'm so happy that Lev and Natalia are safe. But I don't think I can stay any longer. I feel like I'm on the Titanic and it's just a matter of time. The house is gloomy. I am constantly arguing with Lev about his positions that are splitting the SWP and his attacks on the minority. I can't continue to help him with his incendiary position papers when I completely disagree with him. He doesn't just criticize the opposition, he calls us "petty-bourgeois" and even "Mensheviks." My head feels like an anvil that's being hammered every day.

I'm coming home. Stress is good for grapes, but it's bad for me. I've had enough. I realize now that I'm one of those people Thoreau was talking about: I've been fishing all my life and I don't even like fish. I'll see you soon.

I love you.
Lilly

14

May 26, 1940

Dear Gertrude:

I have wonderful news! I will be arriving at
Pennsylvania Station in NY around 4:00 in
the afternoon on June 1. I will be staying with
Neruda's friend in Manhattan. I can't give
you the details now, but I have a great job
opportunity and I want to tell you in person.
Remember Anais Nin:

> Do not seek the because –
> in love there is no because,
> no reason, no explanation,
> no solutions.

But I don't agree. The solution is to be
together. See you soon.

Love,
Jacques

Gertie sat on her bed trembling, stunned. Jacques was finally
coming back to her. He loved her after all. But she immediately had
anxiety about what to say to Herb Cohen, the law student she had
recently started dating. The first time he touched her breasts he had
said, "I don't want you to do anything you'll regret later."

"Don't worry," she said laughing to herself, "it's okay."

All the doubts that had risen while she read Jacques' prior
letters—about her parents' disapproval, about Jacques' devotion—
dissolved like honey in hot tea.

She arrived at Penn Station at 3:00PM, wearing a print dress
that showed off her breasts and hips; she felt like Scarlett O'Hara
waiting for Rhett Butler. She remembered one afternoon in Paris when

she had asked Miriam "How could someone as handsome and charming as Jacques be in love with Gertie from Brooklyn?"

"Don't torture yourself," Miriam had said with a shrug. "Love is not about handsome or beautiful or where you're from. It's about unconscious chemistry. That's why it's so difficult to fix people up. The superficial aspects of people are not what make them click."

"But look at him. He's so much older and more sophisticated than I am."

"Yes, but anyone can see that he is totally involved with you. He wants to please you and teach you things." She had put her arm around Gertie's shoulder reassuringly and Gertie believed her. Miriam could be nasty about her father's money, she had thought, but not about Jacques.

When Jacques walked from the subterranean platform into the crowded lobby area and saw her, his face lit up.

"I can't believe you're here!" Gertie said, running toward him.

Jacques was carrying two leather suitcases and wearing a pair of wide-legged white cotton pleated slacks and an open-collared shirt that exposed the top of his chest. His smile began at the corners of his eyes and spanned out to the rest of his face. He put the bags down and kissed her deeply, whispering her name in her ear: "Gertrude."

As they walked to the taxi stand, she noticed some new gray hairs on his sideburns and a few wrinkles under his jaw. Was she enough of a woman for him? Would she be able to make him stay? What had he been doing all this time since she left Paris?

When they put the bags in the cab and started to drive downtown toward Horatio Street, she thought about the argument she'd had with her father when she told him Jacques was coming to New York.

Tateh said, "Something just doesn't add up. I don't like it."

"Tateh, don't talk about Jacques that way. Just because he's not Jewish doesn't mean he's a Nazi or something."

"Why didn't he stay in France and fight them?" Sol asked, mindlessly picking his nose.

"Maybe you can't believe that a bright, handsome, debonair man like Jacques could be in love with me. Maybe that's it."

"Debonair, shmebonair," Tateh said with a smirk, "who cares?"

Tears had trickled down Gertie's face as she abruptly got up from the table and went to her room.

The pain of her father's words and Sol's question had hurt all the more because it resonated with Gertie's own doubts; she also wondered why he wasn't fighting.

Now Jacques was back—she convinced herself that this was what mattered.

Since she left Paris, Gertie had a deep thirst and sitting next to Jacques in the taxi she felt herself filling up. She kissed his cheek. He turned to her, took her hand and kissed it.

*   *   *

A few days after Jacques arrived in New York, he walked through the heavy wooden door of the Abramovitz house for the first time. Tateh seemed aghast at this dapper Frenchman, or Belgian or whatever he was, whose well-developed chest and muscular arms showed through his tight short-sleeve shirt. It wasn't just that he was a *goy*. Gertie watched his face as Tateh saw him. She imagined him thinking, *what's he doing with my Gertie? She's very bright, but she isn't pretty. And, of course, there's her eye.*

Tateh didn't seem to know how to talk to Jacques. Finally he managed to smile and say, "Bonjour, it's nice to meet you. Gertie has told us a lot about you. This is my wife, Ida."

Jacques shook Tateh's hand, then turned to Ida, kissed her hand tenderly, looked up at her directly and said, "It's very nice to meet you both. Gertrude has told me a lot about you as well."

Tateh seemed impressed that Jacques called Gertie "Gertrude." Gertie knew it was the kind of thing that indicated respect and authenticity to Tateh. But Mama looked suspicious. Gertie thought Mama suspected she was sleeping with Jacques. Mama had even remarked to Gertie when she saw the envelope of a letter Jacques had written that "Gertrude" sounded like a woman, not a girl. But Mama seemed charmed nevertheless.

Gertie glanced at her father and smiled to herself thinking she saw his posture relax slightly.

When they sat at the large dining room table and Mama and Gertie served tea, Jacques looked thoughtfully around the room and said, "Your home is so lovely. That's a beautiful menorah in the breakfront."

"Thank you, it was my mother's," Mama said.

"Who is that handsome couple?" He pointed to the framed photo on the side table. It was a formal picture. The expressionless couple sat side by side and stared at the camera. The man, with a neat beard and mustache, was dressed in a suit, collarless shirt and tie. The woman, her curly hair pulled back in a bun, was wearing a black dress with a high collar and white lace around the bodice.

"They're Tateh's parents," Mama said.

They aren't exactly a handsome couple, Gertie thought. She imagined Tateh might think Jacques' comment odd.

"Those are Chagalls aren't they?" Jacques said with surprise. "Mmm, I love the dreamy imagery and the kaleidoscope of colors. The paintings are so full of life..."

Gertie noticed that Jacques had forgotten Miriam had told him about the Chagalls. *Why did she do such a bitchy thing?* But Gertie stopped herself. She had not gotten a response from Miriam although she had sent her two or three letters since leaving Paris. *Where is she?*

Tateh agreed, "Yes, the paintings are full of life, but the newspapers are full of death. They're shutting off the only escape. Hitler will kill all the Jews if they don't get out." He tried to expand the conversation. "So what do you think of the Non-Aggression Pact?"

"Would you like a rugelach?" Mama passed the plate to Jacques.

"To be honest, it was a shock. That is for sure," Jacques replied.

"It's all about Hitler getting insurance against a two-front war," Tateh said. "He doesn't want to make the same mistake as last time and split his forces. Stalin is so stupid."

"He's not stupid," Mama said. "The Nazis and the Stalinists are cut from the same cloth. Stalin wants to expand just like Hitler. It isn't a non-aggression pact at all. It's the opposite—it's an aggression pact. My God, Stalin invaded eastern Poland two weeks after Hitler started the war."

"Yes, yes, you are so right," Jacques nodded strenuously. "Stalin and Hitler are cut from the same cloth. And Stalin doesn't like the Jews any more than Hitler."

226

Sol looked like he was about to say something and Gertie was holding her breath, worried that he was going to confront Jacques and ask him why he wasn't in the French or Canadian armies fighting the Nazis. Sol was obsessed with the Nazis. Not only was his room papered with the dates of Hitler's every move, but after *Kristallnacht* he also started to buy *The Day* and bring it home for Ida or Tateh to translate because it had the most complete coverage of the plight of the German Jews. He felt the American papers were not giving it enough coverage and even the *Forward* was more interested in covering labor disputes than what the Nazis were doing to the Jews.

"I wonder why Trotsky didn't say a word," Sol said, "against the pact or about the invasion of Finland."

Gertie exhaled with relief.

"Good question, Sol," Jacques said.

Gertie felt a surge of warmth rise up in her. She and Jacques were so different and their lives had taken such different courses in the year since they'd been in Paris together. But salt water and fresh water mingle at the mouth of the river.

"Yes," Gertie said, smiling at Jacques and Sol. "Trotsky used to say Stalinism and fascism were totalitarian twins, now he argues for an unconditional defense of Russia no matter what Stalin does. Lilly can't understand it either. It's ridiculous. But Stalin tried to kill him anyway. Even if he shuts up, Stalin wants to kill him."

"Lilly was completely terrified by the Siqueiros raid," Mama said. Her left eyelid fluttered as if she had a tic. "I want her to come home as soon as she can. Enough is enough."

"She promised she's coming home," Tateh said tapping his foot on the floor. "She's not completely *meshugge*."

*   *   *

The next day when Gertie came home and joined them for dinner, she was relieved when Tateh said, "He's a bright fellow. Nice enough." But then he added, "Too bad he's a *goy*."

"Johnny One Note, all you ever think about is whether someone is a Jew or a *goy*." Gertie said.

"From you," Tateh's eyebrows rose and his eyes widened, "I never expected this."

She was silent for a moment. "You make life so simple." She looked her father directly in his eyes and said in a calmer voice, "you're either this or that. Period. Life is so much more complicated than that." She stood up and made a fist. "Jacques is an anti-fascist; he fought against Franco; he worked with the Civil War refugees that were put into camps in Southern France."

"I'm glad to hear he's not a fascist. That's a relief. But that is not the point. He's not a Jew. Period. He's not one of us."

Feeling that it was pointless to argue about this with her father, Gertie turned away from the table and went to her room.

*   *   *

The next day she met Jacques at Union Square Park. An oval set within a square, the park was an elongated wheel with six spoke-like walks that all led to the flagpole in the center.

Gertie had been to many demonstrations at the park, often with Sol, protests against Stalin invading Poland, marches against Hitler rounding up the Jews, rallies against the Neutrality Act. But on this splendidly sunny day in June, there were no speakers' stands or soapboxes, no protest for or against anything. A dark haired young woman with full lips and almost-black eyes sat on a bench, enjoying the sun, holding hands with her boyfriend. Men were sprawled out on the grass reading newspapers in Russian, Yiddish, Polish and Italian, while others read *The Daily Worker* in English. The men read with intense concentration, some of them moving their lips or saying the words out loud.

The park was surrounded by staunch and reliable icons of capitalism–Guardian Life, Apple Savings Bank, Central Savings, Union Square Savings Bank. Along the walks were small groups of men talking or arguing politics, swinging their arms to drive their point home.

As Jacques and Gertie passed the arguing men, she turned to him and asked, "What do you think? Do you think Stalin will do anything to avoid having to fight the Nazis?"

"Stalin doesn't want to support the capitalists in their wars against each other." His demeanor was cold. "Maybe he doesn't want the Soviet proletariat to spill their blood to fight the capitalists' battles."

Gertie was thunderstruck. *Oh God, how could he justify the pact between Stalin and Hitler?* At her parents' house he had said Stalin was as bad as Hitler, now he was justifying Stalin. Maybe this change is what happened to his feelings about her. In Paris he couldn't live without her and then, instead of coming to New York he went to Canada. Does he have a split personality? She thought of his anger when she tidied up his desk and when she questioned Cyrano's heroism. Jacques took her hand and kissed it, but this time she pulled it away and scowled.

"I was just kidding." He waited a moment and then kissed her bad eye.

As wonderful as it felt, Gertie could not fully accept that he was kidding. But she wanted to.

When they left the park, Jacques suggested they stop and have a glass of wine and Gertie felt lucky to be with him again.

The waiter brought two glasses of wine and Jacques clicked her glass and said, "To us."

She smiled and thought of that spectacular meal in Paris, the *foie gras* and the decanted wine. She looked in his eyes. "Remember, Jews don't click glasses."

"Oh, sorry," he laughed.

When they left the restaurant, they walked toward Neruda's friend's apartment on Horatio and Hudson where Jacques was staying. They made love and lay in bed, intertwined, her face snuggled against his neck, arm across his chest and thigh resting on his penis. Gertie was enjoying the wetness on her leg, the smell of them together and she felt serene again like fresh snow. But then she grew anxious. Who had he been sleeping with while he was in Canada? Why were his letters so cold, so infrequent?

"There are some things I need to tell you," he said. His shoulders relaxed and his voice softened. "I got a fake passport. I was afraid if I applied for a real one, I would get conscripted. So I've got a Canadian passport with my picture."

"What? That's crazy." The color drained from her face. She stared at him with her mouth open. "Can't you get arrested for using a false passport?"

"Gertrude, don't worry. People do it all the time," he took her hand. "When all those people were trying to get out of Spain and into

France, a lot of them didn't have passports and they had to get false papers once they were in France. It's easy. Shh." Jacques stroked her hair.

Her head jerked brusquely and she stared at him. "It's illegal; you could get arrested."

He put his hand under her chin and lifted it so he could look at her directly. "I thought you'd be happy for me. I have a great new job." He smiled.

"What?"

"It's a journalism job. In Mexico City," he continued, ignoring her concern.

"Mexico City?"

"Yes. I've actually been down there briefly." Jacques replied casually. "Don't you want to see your sister? And meet Trotsky? It's perfect. I applied because of you. Don't you want to come with me? Just for the summer, until September. You could be back for the beginning of the fall term."

Gertie was silent. She felt divided. Part of her was bubbling over with excitement. She'd be spending a few days on the train with Jacques, seeing parts of the United States for the first time, visiting Lilly while she was still in Mexico, and, of course, meeting Trotsky. But the thought of telling her parents filled her with anxiety. She knew they would object. After all, they wanted Lilly to come home as soon as possible, so they certainly wouldn't want *her* to go to Mexico City. And she had her own anxieties as well. What about the months when he said he was in Toronto? Was he really there? He was so distant and confusing. She was a moth attracted to a flame, but she was afraid if she went with him she would get burned.

"What is the matter with you? I thought you were sophisticated," Jacques said icily.

"This doesn't have to do with being sophisticated," she said, sitting up in bed and squinting with her bad eye. "It has to do with getting arrested. Just being afraid. These are normal feelings!"

"You are so pedestrian," he mumbled as he got out of bed.

"No, I'm not," she said scrambling out of bed, trying to pull him back. "Don't say that to me. You're so condescending."

He shoved her away. "What's the matter with you? I thought you wanted to be with me."

She began to cry. "I do. I do want to be with you." Tears streamed down her cheeks.

She embraced him but his arms remained at his sides.

"The fake passport is under the name 'Frank Jacson,'" he said, "That's the name I will have to use in Mexico."

"What? I can't call you 'Frank'," she yelled, pushing away from him. "Are you crazy?" Her hopes were unraveling and she didn't know how far it was going to go.

"Fine, you can call me 'Jacques' and if anyone asks about it we'll say it's your pet name for me because my last name is Jacson. 'Jac' and 'Jacques' sound exactly the same, don't they?" He kissed her bad eye. "But don't worry," he said putting his arms around her. "It isn't definite. I haven't been told if the job is permanent, so I'm going to be doing freelance work for a while."

Jacques now seemed even more mysterious than he was in Paris. Away from him Gertie was a little girl who lived with her parents and sat at the dinner table every night talking about whether whatever was going on in the world was good or bad for the Jews. With him she was the woman he couldn't stay away from, the woman he wanted to make love to in every room. When she and Jacques were together it was as if they lived in the tower of the abbey of Mont Saint-Michel, at the highest point of an island surrounded by an immense bay, protected by the highest tides in Europe. But the abbey was often cut off from the land by relentless tides. And there was so much they didn't say to each other—she, because of her fear the tides would turn and he, she would find out later, because of the skeletons in the tomb.

15

On a hot morning at the end of June, Jacques and Gertie drove down an expansive tree-lined street toward the Hotel Montejo on the Paseo de la Reforma. The taxi driver pointed out all the historical sites. Gertie gushed that some of the monuments in Mexico City reminded her of Paris, particularly the arch and the Palacio des Bellas Artes opera house.

"Funny you should say that," the driver said, unable to stifle a laugh. The dictator Porfirio Diaz spent all the people's money copying the monuments in Paris; like Napoleon."

When they arrived at the hotel, they registered as Mr. and Mrs. Frank Jacson. Gertie turned her class ring around so it looked like a wedding band. Jacques bit the inside of his cheek and lip waiting for the clerk to fill in the information needed to register. The paunchy Mexican clerk with buck teeth took his time and Gertie walked around the lobby examining the pots of cacti and orchids. The exuberance she had felt in expectation of this moment was suffocated by the lies—and her nausea.

The next morning Jacques was gone when Gertie woke up. She called to him thinking he might be in the bathroom. But there was no answer. She pulled herself out of bed, calling his name, "Jacques? Jacques?" Then she felt a surge of nausea and ran into the bathroom. She didn't throw up: it was a false alarm, but she felt queasy. Where did he go? By the time she showered and got dressed, Jacques had returned.

"Where were you?" Gertie asked.

"I went to the new office at Plaza Río de Janeiro," Jacques said, sitting on the unmade bed, "to meet everyone."

"How was it?" Gertie asked toweling off her hair. She was mildly annoyed that he'd left without leaving a note, but excited that he was starting his freelance article for *Hoy*, the Mexican version of *Life* magazine.

"Fine. Everything is fine," Jacques said lighting a cigarette. "They gave me a car for my own personal use—a Buick sedan," he said smiling. "Isn't that great?"

"Yes," Gertie agreed. "That's terrific. We can drive to Coyoacán." She walked over to the bed and put her arms around Jacques. But he turned away and stood up. She felt foolish and rejected.

"Do you want some breakfast?" Jacques asked. "I had huevas rancheros downstairs already."

"What's that?"

"Eggs with green chilies and cheese and tortillas."

"No," Gertie said making a face. "Let's just go. I'm not really hungry."

*   *   *

The sky was cobalt blue and the sun was vibrant and piercingly hot when they arrived, just before noon, at the entrance to Trotsky's new house. Jacques left the car idling outside the guard booth while a policeman with a large birthmark on his cheek inspected the car, while another with a bulging belly and sweat dripping down his neck, asked Gertie and Jacques for their identification papers. They both showed their passports and Gertie held her breath as he looked first at the picture on Jacque's passport and then at his face. Once he returned their passports, two gruff policemen, wearing uniforms that smelled like they had been washed in the river, gave them body checks. Gertie winced as one of the policemen smiled slyly beneath his large mustache.

Once the policemen were satisfied that they were not carrying weapons and that there were none hidden in the car, Gertie and Jacques were escorted to heavy bolted doors that led into the garage and through another set of doors to the patio garden. They found Lev feeding, what seemed to Gertie, about fifty rabbits and dozens of chickens which she found out later were Leghorn, Plymouth and Rhode Island Reds. The garden was planted with tall and leafy trees, surrounded by daisies, lilies, nasturtiums, and climbing yellow and red roses. Abundant varieties of cacti that Lev had collected mainly from El Pedregal and the sierra of the State of Hidalgo crisscrossed the stone paths. Gertie grabbed Jacques' hand; she had never seen such a fecund garden.

Lev greeted them, *"Buenos días, señor and señorita."*

Gertie felt overcome—how could she, Gertrude Abramovitz, be facing Leon Trotsky in his garden? She was standing in the Holy of Holies.

"*Buenos dias señor Trotsky*," Jacques said, offering his hand to the Old Man.

Gertie managed to repeat Jacque's words:

"*Buenos días señor Trotsky.*"

"And who are you?" Lev asked

"I'm sorry, I don't really speak Spanish," Gertie responded, "I'm Lilly's sister, Gertrude. And this is my friend," she hesitated for a moment, "Jacques Monard."

She felt a wave of panic realizing the policeman saw the passport saying "Frank Jacson" and she just introduced him as Jacques Monard. But she glanced at Jacques and he showed no sign of being upset. The policeman just wanted to make sure he had a passport, she consoled herself—he won't remember his name.

"Ah, yes. I'm delighted to meet you both. Lilly told me you'd be coming. You are as lovely as your sister. Two Mensheviks from Brooklyn, I presume," Lev said with laughing eyes.

"No, I am neither a Menshevik nor from Brooklyn," Jacques smiled.

"Oh, where are you from?" Lev asked.

Gertie held her breath and felt tension in her shoulders.

"I'm from Canada originally, but I lived in Paris for many years."

Gertie wondered why he was lying to Trotsky?

"I met Nata in Paris," Lev smiled. "Lovely city, so romantic. We will have to talk about it some time. Let me show you where you can find Lilly."

Gertie recognized Lev's heavily accented English from his recorded speeches. Her heart beat furiously. The Old Man led Gertie and Jacques through the garden indicating the plants he particularly liked.

"I love cactus," he told them, "and this variety is my favorite. He pointed to an elongated cactus covered by white threads that looked like a beard.

"Isn't that one called *los Viejitos,* 'the old man'?" Jacques inquired.

"Why yes," Lev responded, surprised. "How did you know that?"

234

"I don't know. I guess I've seen it someplace else." Jacques had a look of satisfaction on his face.

Gertie suspected Jacques's question was premeditated, like one of those painters whose works appear to be spontaneous. Why would he do that? Had he done the same when he was surprised to see the Chagalls in her parents' house?

When Lev, Jacques and Gertie reached the dining room, Lilly was there to greet them. The dining room was rather undistinguished; a shiny multi-colored plastic table-cloth covered the table. In the front office, where Lilly sat, there was a wooden-cased GE shortwave radio and wax cylinders containing Lev's dictation.

"Oh my God, it's really you! I've missed you so much," Gertie blurted out, running to embrace Lilly with a rush of tears. Lilly looked older; her hair was longer than Gertie had ever seen it and her body more shapely than Gertie remembered. Lilly was wearing a colorful ruffled skirt and a white *huipil* that accentuated her tanned skin. *What a sexy woman she's become*, Gertie thought. Perhaps, if Jacques were not standing there with her, Gertie might have felt jealous of Lilly, her attractive older sister who always had Howie.

"I've missed you so," Lilly hugged Gertie tightly. She stroked her hair and kissed her cheeks several times with tears streaming down her cheeks. Then she stood back a few feet and smiled as if to say, *You're a woman.* Gertie unlocked herself from Lilly's embrace and pointed to Jacques. "And this is Jacques."

"*Buenos dias señorita,*" Jacques said, kissing Lilly's hand and then looking directly into her eyes.

"Hello," Lilly said haltingly, "it's so nice to meet you."

Jacques immediately moved closer to Gertie, put his arm around her shoulder and kissed her cheek. Even though Mama had written Lilly about how handsome and charming Jacques was, she was still stunned. Here was Gertie with a man who looked like a Spanish toreador with his well-developed chest and muscular biceps. She imagined him waving a red cape at the bull.

When Lev and Natalia were toiling in the garden, Lilly took Gertie and Jacques for a tour of the house. On Lev's desk were old copies of *Pravda* and books in Russian, English and German. Jacques stood behind the desk and put his hand on a pile of books in Russian. A desk calendar lay next to the Ediphone recording device behind the desk. The windows, bricked up halfway on the outside, were stained glass so only a slice of light peeked through.

"The glass is lovely," Jacques said. "It's a shame they had to brick it up. But I guess that's the level of danger now."

"Yes," Lilly replied. "It's like an armed camp here since the Siqueiros raid.

It's horrible, the police just found the body of Bob Harte. He was a young kid who was a volunteer from New York. They must have kidnapped him during the raid. Lev thinks he let them in, but I can't believe he had any part in it," Lilly said, shaking her head.

*   *   *

The next morning Gertie woke up and Jacques was gone again—she called for him, but there was no answer. She got out of bed feeling queasy and looked for a note, but there was none. She felt angry and thought that might be why she was feeling nauseous. She showered, dressed and dithered about wondering what she should do, *Should I call Hoy? Or should I just sit in this room and wait until he decides to come back or call me?* She decided to go down to the lobby and ask the clerk where *Hoy*'s office was located. She could take a walk and surprise him.

"Libertad, between República de Chile and Calle Allende," the day clerk with the dried prune skin and large gray mustache replied in English.

"Oh, is that near Plaza Río de Janeiro?" Gertie asked, now recalling that was what Jacques had told her.

"No, no. That's a different area."

Gertie felt shaken, a tidal wave of nausea overtook her and she had to get her balance. *What is going on*? She felt immobilized by uncertainly and barely found her way back to their room.

*   *   *

A few days later Lilly met Gertie for lunch in Mexico City. They sat at a table in a lush shade garden under a cloud-studded sky drinking *aguas frescas*.

Lilly broke the silence. "Jacques is very attractive. How are things going with the two of you?"

Gertie found herself blurting out the truth. "I love him, but he's been very moody since we arrived." She couldn't stop fidgeting with

236

her napkin. "Sometimes he opens up briefly like a daylily, but then he's gone. He can make me feel that I'm the only woman he's ever loved and that the most important thing to him is to be with me, but other times he's distant and cold." She hugged herself, looking down at the table. "He goes for long walks by himself and he never tells me where he's going or where he's been."

"Distant and cold? And where do you think he's going?"

"I have no idea. Maybe he's just roaming the streets." Gertie did not want to tell Lilly that *Hoy's* office was not where Jacques had told her or that when Jacques looked at her, his attention was elsewhere and he wasn't interested in having sex.

"Come on," Lilly said, "why would he be roaming the streets aimlessly?"

"I don't know," Gertie said putting her head in her hands. "Leave me alone," she said, "I just don't know."

"Sorry, I didn't mean to upset you." She sipped her drink quietly and then said, "How long do you think you'll be in Mexico City?"

"I don't know. He says his assignment should be over soon, but he hasn't given me an exact date." Gertie dug her nails into the palms of her hand to try to control her tears until a rotund waitress with sleepy eyes and full lips came over to their table and took their order.

"I'm not hungry," Gertie said. "I'll just stick with the *aguas frescas*." She noticed a spider web on one of the legs of the next table.

"*I'll have the chalupas with refried beans, thank you*," Lilly said in Spanish. When the waitress left, she took a deep breath and closed her eyes. "I hate to tell you this, but I told you in my letter, I'm leaving and going home. I only stayed this long because you and Jacques were coming. But now it's time for me to go back to Howie and get on with my life."

Gertie felt like a fly caught in a spider web. Jacques had released a single thread into the wind in Paris and it caught on. Then he released another and wove it beneath the first, then another and another. Now she was caught in the web. Her eyes welled up with tears. "Oh, no, do you have to?"

"You know Lev's reaction to Stalin has been very disappointing and he keeps calling anyone who disagrees with him petty-bourgeois or

Mensheviks. And I can't stand the way he refuses to speak out against what Hitler is doing to the Jews. He's a Jew for God's sake."

"You know what Tateh would say: *No answer is also an answer.*"

They both laughed.

"I can't keep working for him in good faith," Lilly said. "I'm editing papers that take positions I completely reject. It's an impossible situation." She shook her head.

"I understand," Gertie nodded. "But can't you stay a little longer now that I'm here?" She wanted to tell Lilly what was really happening. She wanted to tell her that Jacques was ignoring her. She wanted to tell her that she had missed her period and felt nauseous every morning and was afraid she was pregnant. She was bloated like one of those dried figs that Mama soaked in hot water until they were soft and doubled their size. Of all people, Lilly was the one she could tell—the one who would know what to do. But the words stuck in her throat.

Lilly took Gertie's hand. "I just can't do it anymore." She looked her directly in her eyes and whispered, "And I'm afraid it's only a matter of time before Stalin gets to Lev. He was just lucky last time with Siqueiros. It's too scary to stay in the compound. I'm leaving next week."

When Gertie returned to her hotel, she felt more alone than she had ever felt in her life. Lilly was leaving and Jacques had grown increasingly distant and difficult to be with. She was afraid to tell him about her period. Suddenly drained of energy, she lay down on the bed and cried.

Massaging her aching breasts and then, feeling bloated, stroking her stomach, she wondered what she was she going to do. She thought about the night before with Jacques. She'd gotten into bed while he stayed up reading. She wanted to tell him she felt sure she was pregnant, but she didn't think it was the right moment. After a few minutes, her mind wandered to something she had read about the history of England. She had said, "You know the word "curfew" dates back to the 11th century when William the Norman became the King of England. Within the city walls a bell would ring and the people had to cover their fires at night. In French it was "*couvre de feu*" and the English bastardized it to "curfew.""

Jacques put his book down and took his reading glasses off. His earlobes were bright red. He said, "You are an idiot. Who gives a damn? You're always talking about these sayings. Who cares?" At that, he put his glasses on and went back to his book.

Gertie had seen Jacques's contempt before and she cried in her pillow. But Jacques did not move to comfort her or to apologize. Gertie imagined being in Brooklyn with Mama sitting on the bed. Mama would kiss away her tears, "*Shana maidela, shana maidela*, my beautiful girl."

The next morning Gertie called Frida from the hotel and asked if she could visit her at the Blue House.

"I am in bad shape," Frida said. "That bastard Diego. I hate him. Fook him. I divorced him."

"I'd like to visit you. I need to talk to someone. Would that be all right?"

"Of course," Frida said, "of course."

When Gertie got off the bus at the Coyoacán market, the morning fog still lingered like gray gauze. A ghost of gnats surrounded her, swarming around her head for almost half a block. When they moved on, she noticed a large peasant woman with rawhide skin sitting on her heels with a blanket spread out in front of her displaying appliquéd baby quilts of butterflies and flowers in bright reds, oranges and blues and the tiniest sweaters of pink and tan donkeys on a white background. Gertie smiled and put her hand on her stomach. It would be fun to make clothes for a little girl...But it might be a boy. She stopped herself. She wasn't sure if she was going to have this baby at all. If things with Jacques didn't improve pretty soon, she might have to find out about having an abortion. The air felt heavy, like a weight on her chest.

Gertie needed to open up about Jacques, but was fearful that Lilly would be too judgmental. She thought perhaps she would be able to talk to Frida—she wouldn't judge her. She wanted to tell her about Jacques's tantrums. She couldn't figure out what started his fits of rage or what ended them just as abruptly, but they had increased in frequency and intensity since arriving in Mexico City. And he was no longer interested in touching her.

When Gertie arrived at the Blue House, Carlos answered the door and greeted her.

"*Buenos días, señorita,*" he smiled.

"*Buenos días, señor,*" she smiled back. "I am Lilly's sister. It's nice to meet you."

"Ah, yes, you are Gertie. Lilly told me about you. I am happy to meet you. Are you here to visit Frida?"

"Yes, I am."

"She is in bed," he said nodding his head. "She has not been well since Diego said he was divorcing her and she came back to live here."

"I'm sorry to hear that." Frida had told her she divorced Diego, but now Carlos said Diego divorced her! Gertie believed Carlos's version: maybe Diego found out about her affair with Nickolas Muray. She had been critical of Frida's behavior in New York and Paris, but now she felt sorry for her. Under these circumstances, how could she tell Frida about her problems with Jacques' bizarre behavior or being pregnant?

Gertie walked into the bedroom where Frida was lying on a single four-poster bed with an easel set up so that she could prop herself up and paint while lying down. A shelf of books was within arm's reach.

"Death is not the greatest of evils," Frida quoted Sophocles without saying hello. "It is worse to want to die, and not be able to."

"Oh come on Frida," Gertie said, trying to stay calm, "it's not as bad as that."

She looked around at Frida's latest paintings which reflected her distraught emotional state. One was a little girl wearing a skull mask.

"That's the mask they wear at the annual Mexican festival "*Day of the Dead,*" Frida explained.

Gertie looked at the girl holding a yellow flower and standing alone on a vast empty plain under a stormy sky. *That's how I feel*, she thought to herself.

The painting Frida was still working on was "Two Fridas." Frida just pointed to it, she didn't talk about it. She didn't need to, Gertie understood immediately. On the right, was the part of Frida loved by Diego—the Mexican Frida in a Tehuana costume. On the left, was a more European Frida in a lacy white Victorian wedding dress—the Frida abandoned by Diego. The hearts of the two women lie exposed; Frida's pain was palpable. The unloved Frida's heart was broken while the other Frida's heart was whole. Pondering the painting silently for a few minutes, Gertie began to cry. There were two Gertie's as well: there was Gertrude, the woman Jacques had loved in Paris and Gertie the damaged girl from Brooklyn that he didn't want.

"Watch out, *mi amiga*," Frida said, "remember what Pablo Neruda said: 'Love is so short, forgetting is so long.'"

*   *   *

The following Sunday, Gertie and Jacques joined Lilly and the Trotskys for a cactus expedition and picnic. On Sundays, Lev and Natalia frequently took his secretaries, guards and friends on trips to the countryside. It was a nice distraction for Lev—he was obsessed with the threat of death and he devoted himself to cactus hunting with the same energy and enthusiasm he had for his work. A favorite spot was in the Lagunas de Zempoala in the mountains above Cuernavaca. The area had forests of oaks, cedars, pine trees and firs, and falcons, sparrows and hummingbirds were plentiful. They traveled in three automobiles. Lev and Natalia were in the Dodge; the guards and secretaries in the Ford; and American or Mexican visitors in the third car. Lilly had gone on many of these excursions. When Lev told her that he wanted her to come on their last outing before she left for New York, but that they were having trouble finding a third car and driver, it seemed natural to her to ask Gertie and Jacques to come along so that Jacques could drive.

"I hope he drives better than he writes," Lev told Lilly.

"What do you mean?"

"He gave me something to read the last time he and your sister visited. He says it is a defense of my position on the dialectic, but it's not very thoughtful."

Well, Lilly thought to herself with a laugh, *he's a bullfighter not a Jewish intellectual. What do you expect?*

Lilly sat in the back seat of the third car with Jacques driving and Gertie in the passenger seat. They stopped at Huitzilac to buy some barbecued mutton, turkey mole and fruit-flavored *pulque* for the picnic. Lev insisted that Jacques and Gertie visit the San Juan Bautista church with its inscription dating from 1690. A little boy stood in front of the church with his dirt encrusted hand extended. He smiled broadly, "Tour, tour." That must have been the only English word he knew. He wore stained shorts and an oversized shirt that looked like it belonged to his older brother or his father. Lev gave him a peso.

Gertie wondered how old the boy was—seven or eight she supposed. He was a handsome boy, though skinny, with dark magnetic eyes and a beauty mark on his high cheek bone. She wondered if her baby was a boy. Would he have Jacques's dark wavy hair and olive complexion?

After a brief look around the church, the group got back in the cars and headed for the Zempoala lagoon.

"Can we go for a hike?" Gertie asked. "The hills above the lagoons are supposed to be beautiful."

"Yes, that would be fun," Lilly said.

When the three cars arrived at the picnic area, Lilly, Gertie and Jacques helped the four guards who had been in the second car set up the tables and chairs. Lev walked over and pointed to a bush with waxy green leaves and yellow flowers. "Look at this," he motioned to Gertie. "The Mexicans call it *hediondilla*, which means 'little stinker.' In English it's called 'creosote' because it smells like coal when you rub it," he smiled. "The Indians made a medicinal tea out of it to cure the flu and coughs or colds."

"He's so knowledgeable," Gertie whispered to Lilly.

"Yes, he loves to lecture," Lilly said under her breath.

Before lunch Lilly told Lev, "We're going for a short hike and we'll be back in time to eat."

"Of course, of course. After all, you won't be spending your Sundays here anymore after today."

Lilly led Gertie and Jacques toward a trail that Van had shown her on a picnic the prior year. They passed fields of wild grass, heather in flower and yellow clover on the way to the trail. A butterfly settled on Gertie's shoulder, fluttering its wings as if a welcoming gesture. Gertie's face was aglow like bright sunshine on the snow. Entering the woods, dead leaves silenced the noise of their steps. Jacques offered Gertie his hand as they stepped over the trunk of a fallen tree with moss covering it. Gertie smiled, feeling hopeful: maybe Jacques *did* care about her, but he'd just been worried about starting his new assignment. She pointed to a wild orchid, reddish purple in color, growing out of the rotting wood. Rays of sun filtered through the branches of the trees. Lilly eyed an oval-shaped stone, smooth and black. She picked it up

242

and ran her finger around the cold surface and slipped it into the pocket of her shorts as if it were a talisman from Eden.

"Look at that," Jacques said, pointing to a brown lizard about five inches long with cream-colored stripes, each paralleled by a precise line of tiny, yellow dots. Its hind legs were larger than the front ones, and its tail disproportionately long. The lizard scampered away waving its tail back and forth like a whip.

"That's a whiptail lizard," Lilly explained. "When a predator tries to catch it by its tail, the tail just comes off. Can you imagine?"

"Remember when we used to take hikes in the Catskills?" Gertie asked Lilly.

"And Solly would always lag behind," Lilly laughed.

"How about the time we couldn't find him because he stopped to look at a snake? Tateh and Mama were afraid a bear had got him," Gertie giggled.

"It sounds like you had a lot of family activities as children," Jacques said. "My family never did things like that…"

"What was your family like, Jacques?" Lilly asked.

"Oh, I'm an only child and my father is a Belgian diplomat and he was away a lot," he said. He crossed him arms and continued, "When I was three, father was sent to the Congo for six months and when I was five he went back there for a year." He shook his head, "Then when I was eight he was sent to Ruanda-Urundi. My mother was not the outdoor type. We didn't go hiking or camping or anything like that," he said, looking at the ground.

"We took hikes, but we never went camping overnight. And Gertie always had to relieve herself and would complain that it wasn't fair that Tateh and Solly could do it anywhere." Lilly laughed at the memory. "Talking about that, I'm going to find a spot up ahead. I'll come back and join you in a few minutes."

The sun disappeared behind a cloud as Lilly walked away. She felt a chill as she searched for a place in the trees that offered cover for her. She crouched down noticing a rotting tree stump with fungus growing on it and red ants crawling around it. She was disgusted, but her shorts and underpants were already around her ankles and her bottom just above the ground. She struggled to position herself so she wouldn't have to look at the ants and shuddered as she finally relieved herself. She could hear Gertie and Jacques talking.

"I'm so tired," Gertie said.

"You're such a pain in the ass," Jacques retorted. "And that's one of the most common places people have pain," he mimicked, "right?"

"Don't make fun of me. I don't feel well."

"You'll be fine. After all you're an experienced hiker," Jacques snickered.

When Lilly returned, Gertie was sitting on a large rock, her arms crossed over her chest, embracing herself, her face colorless.

Lilly wanted to scream at Jacques, *You bastard, don't you dare talk to my sister like that!* But she decided to contain herself until she could speak to Gertie alone.

Smiling broadly, Jacques offered his hand to help Gertie get up from the rock, "Let me help you."

When they returned after the trip, Lilly had a few minutes alone with Gertie back at Lev's garden. She tried to offer Gertie her support without letting her know what she'd overheard. Lilly wanted to tell her outright that this guy was from the bottom of the pot, but she could feel Gertie's defensiveness about him even as she opened her mouth to speak.

"Gertie," Lilly said putting her arms around her and kissing her cheek. "You can come back to Brooklyn with me. You don't have to stay here."

"No, I don't want to do that," Gertie said, stiffening. "Jacques' just been moody and the moods change so rapidly."

Lilly tightened her grip on Gertie. She wanted to pick her up and scoop her away as if she were a little girl playing too close to the street. Gertie gently separated herself and sat down on a bench.

She looked down at the ground twisting her hands; her head was pounding. She didn't want to tell Lilly how much Jacques had changed since they arrived in Mexico City. She thought about the night she woke up and put her arm out to caress him and he wasn't there. She yelled for him and there was no answer. She got out of bed and checked the bathroom, but he was gone. When he came back in the morning he refused to tell her where he'd been. If she told Lilly that, what would Lilly say when she and Jacques returned to Brooklyn and announced their engagement?

244

Lilly knew it wasn't moods. This was something else—Jacques was putting on a performance. When people were watching, he was hyper-considerate to Gertie and when they were alone he was abusive. He never looked at Gertie when he thought she wasn't paying attention the way Howie used to do with her, or Tateh did with Mama. *Maybe Jacques has a girlfriend in Mexico City? Maybe he's cheating on Gertie or involved in some nefarious business.* Lilly was at a loss for words.

Gertie looked into Lilly's eyes. "Something's just bothering him. I'll stay a while longer and see how things go." She bit her lip to control the voice screaming inside her: *Don't go, don't leave me, what will I do if he doesn't want me now?* She wanted to tell Lilly that she was sure she was pregnant, but the words were stuck someplace just below her throat. She could feel them, like a lump, but she couldn't get them out.

16

Lilly sat on the front steps waiting for Howie. The morning sun was high in the sky. She was excited, but her stomach was filled with worry. After all, three and a half years had passed since she'd gone to Mexico with Dewey. Lilly had changed in so many ways; she wondered how much Howie had. Did they have a future together? Who was this new person, Howard? How would it feel for her body to be under his?

Howie caught a glimpse of her and ran toward her. "You're so beautiful," he said, out of breath from running. "Let me look at you." He stood at the bottom of the steps in order to take her in—all of her. He was like a gaslight responding to a flame. Howie was a man who loved light.

Lilly was wearing a colorful striped skirt and a red *huipil* that accentuated her chest. She had left a girl and returned a woman with shapely hips and full breasts. Wearing a turquoise necklace and silver bracelets, this was a distinctly different Lilly.

"Wow," Howie said, holding his hand to his cheek. Lilly wondered if he might be thinking: *Who did she sleep with in Mexico?*

Lilly looked at Howie and felt like she was waking up to a sunny morning the night after a thunder storm. Howie's hair was thinner, his forehead higher, and his stomach leaned a bit on his belt. But the gleam in his eyes when he looked at her was the same.

They embraced; they didn't kiss. He held her tightly in his arms, nuzzling his face between her neck and shoulder. Lilly wondered if he had another woman in his life. Was this just visiting an old friend? But then Howie said, "I'm so happy you've come back to me. I love you, Lilly." He kissed her deeply and she knew there was no other woman to worry about. She recognized his tongue, but his mouth was harder on hers than she remembered. She liked it.

Mama came to the door, followed by the smell of cinnamon. She wiped her hands on her apron and put her arms around Howie, kissing his cheek. "It's so good to see you." She took his hand and led him into the living room. "Come sit down and tell us what you're doing. Would you like a cup of tea? I have some warm babka. Hershey,

Hershey come, Howie's here," she yelled down the hall toward Tateh's study.

Sol came out of his room and hugged Howie. "It's good to see you again," Sol said.

"God, you're all grown up. Taller than me," Howie replied. "It's great to see you again." Then he turned to Lilly, took her hand and put it to his mouth kissing it. "See, another benefit of having you home."

Howie and Lilly sat on the couch facing the grand piano. The sheet music on display was "A Foggy Day" from the movie *Damsel in Distress*. Fred Astaire's smiling face and George and Gracie Burns were on the cover. Mama and Sol settled onto the carved settee. When Tateh joined them in the living room, Howie stood up to greet him.

"Hello, Mr. Abramovitz, it's so nice to see you."

For the first time, Lilly noticed the creases next to Howie's ears that looked like a gathered piece of cloth. He put out his hand to shake Tateh's, but Tateh ignored it, walked around the mahogany drop leaf table in front of the couch and put his arms around Howie.

"It's so good to see you," Tateh said, his eyes twinkling with pleasure as he hugged Howie. "So tell us what you've been doing, Howie."

"Mostly, I've been missing Lilly," Howie said, putting his arm around Lilly and kissing her cheek. Lilly noticed he was wearing a Jewish star around his neck. The gold chain was tucked into his undershirt, but tumbled out when Tateh hugged him. "But aside from that," he continued, "I've been spending most of my time working for the American Jewish Congress." He turned to Lilly animatedly. "The *Congress Bulletin* is the only Jewish publication that's paying attention to the Nazi atrocities." His face grew red. "It's crazy. Stephen Wise keeps praising Roosevelt and even the Zionists only focus on Palestine and not on the rescue of refugees."

"Wait, I'm confused," Lilly said. "Isn't the whole purpose of Palestine to create a place for Jews to go?"

Sol didn't wait for Howie to answer. "Yes, but it's a matter of priorities. First you have to get the Jews out of Germany and Poland; then you worry about Palestine." He looked at Howie who nodded. Lilly looked at Sol. He wasn't a child anymore. He had stubble on his cheeks and he had a man's voice. She had missed the transition between his childhood and adolescence while she was in Mexico. She felt remorseful that she wasn't there the first time he had a crush on a girl or went to his first dance.

"We've been giving money every week to the United Jewish Appeal," Mama said. "We understand we have to save the refugees first."

"They don't tell you," Howie said, "half the money's going to Palestine."

"*What's wrong with that?*" Tateh asked in Yiddish, making a face.

"You can't fight on two fronts, Mr. Abramovitz," he said softly with a smile. "We can't fight the British and get the Jews out of Europe at the same time."

Tears welled up in Lilly's eyes as she turned to look at Howie speaking so respectfully to her father. He said "we," "we the Jews." She felt a warm rush. Howie put saving Jewish lives ahead of Zionism, ahead of making a proletarian revolution. She was happy to be home.

17

"What's wrong? What's the matter with you?" Gertie begged Jacques to open up.

It was 5 P.M. and she was sitting on the bed next to him in the hotel room they had shared since arriving in Mexico City. The shutters were closed tight, blocking out the fresh air as well as the sun. The ceiling fan whirred, but it circulated stale air that smelled from sweat, Gaulois and Jacques' last diarrhea attack. Jacques' socks, shoes and underwear were strewn about. Each time Gertie had bent down to pick them up he had yelled, "Leave them alone."

Gertie was desperate. *I have to tell him I'm pregnant*, she told herself. *I can't wait any longer.* She had been about to tell him before he took to his bed a few days before. But Jacques wouldn't talk to her; he turned away and put the pillow over his ears. She took his hand, but it was cold to the touch. He had been looking haggard for days. He didn't shave or take a shower. He had a nervous twitch in his bloodshot eye, and his fingernails were bitten down to the quick.

"Jacques, we need to talk....please," she begged.

Jacques still didn't answer. His complexion mildewed, he stared at the clock.

"I have an important meeting," Jacques said. Dragging himself to the bathroom, Jacques looked like an unmade bed. Gertie sat with her head in her hands sobbing. He ignored her as he stood looking in the mirror shaving for the first time in days. When he finished, he rinsed the shaving cream from his face and turned on the bath. When he emerged from the bathroom, he dried himself with a towel, dropping it on the floor when he was finished, and put on a suit and tie.

"Where are you going?" Gertie asked.

"No place, just a meeting, it's nothing." His eye was twitching as he picked up his raincoat.

"Why are you carrying a raincoat? There's no chance of rain," she said as she opened the shutters. "The sun is out." She touched his arm.

"Leave me alone. Just leave me alone," he said, looking at her with scowling eyes. He grabbed his new gray fedora and an envelope with some papers in it and slammed the door behind him.

She walked to the bed, passing the mirror and felt a jolt when she caught sight of the pall on her face. She climbed into the bed, curled up in a fetal position and began to bawl. "Mama, what am I going to do? What am I going to do?"

*   *   *

Gertie was in a deep sleep when intense knocking on her door woke her. At first she thought she was dreaming it, but as she got her bearings she realized it was not a dream.

"Open up, police," a man's voice yelled in Spanish-accented English through the door. Gertie's heart pounded and her shoulders ached; her first thought was that Jacques had some terrible accident. She scurried to open the door: two Mexican policemen stood there. They were wearing navy blue short-sleeve shirts and carrying machine guns.

"You under arrest," the short stocky policeman with a round face said while his taller colleague with narrow set eyes stepped into Gertie's room and shoved her out the door into the hall.

"For what?" she yelled, in fear for her life.

"Trotsky. Murder of Trotsky."

250

18

"The program of St. Louis Blues has been cancelled tonight. The world," said Eric Sevareid, "trembles…"

Tateh, Lilly, Howie and Sol sat around the dining room table listening to the CBS World News report about the attack on Trotsky's life. The air was heavy. Sol half-heartedly thumbed through the current *Life* magazine. Mama, too tense to sit in a chair, listened from the kitchen as she put away the last of the dinner dishes. Lilly sat wrapped in a red and purple wool rebozo she'd bought the year before at the Coyoacán market. A gust of wind shook the windows of the dining room. Although it was August, the house felt damp and cold.

Lilly chewed her fingernails and mumbled to no one in particular, "I just can't believe it. Security was so tight there…" In the hours since they woke up to the headlines about the assassination in *The Brooklyn Eagle*, she had been in shock.

"No, no. Oh my God!" Lilly had shrieked in disbelief. "It's not possible. How could anyone get to him? Fucking Stalin!"

Mama had been standing next to her when Lilly picked up the paper. Her eyes welled up with tears and she sat down to steady herself. Tateh rushed over to look at the paper.

"*Oy Gut in himmel,*" he said. He covered his eyes as if he didn't want to know.

"What's going on," Solly asked.

"Look," Lilly said as she handed him the *Eagle*.

Lilly had remembered sitting next to Lev in the garden—the tears in his eyes when he talked about his father's foreman whipping a peasant. She saw the disappointed boy still stirring in the old man. She had wanted to hold his hand and comfort him, but held back because he was Lev Trotsky. Now she regretted it; she wished she had comforted him. Suddenly, her head jerked as if she had been awoken from a dream. She shivered. Lev was attacked with an icepick. He was so protected after the raid in May. Who did it? Did she know the attacker? And then her thoughts took another sharp turn: could she have stopped it if she had stayed in Mexico? And where was Gertie for God's sake? Why didn't she call and tell them what was going on?

"I'm going to get the *Times*," Lilly had said. She grabbed an umbrella from the stand by the door and headed for the newspaper stand on the corner. It was hot and humid. Lilly was wet from sweat and drizzle when she reached old Mr. Fleishman sitting in his kiosk as he did every day from 6 A.M. until 6 P.M. A fleshy man without a neck, Mr. Fleishman had been a fixture on the corner since the day Tateh and Mama bought the house in Brooklyn Heights.

"Good morning Mr. Fleishman," Lilly said as she picked up the *New York Times*.

"*Guten morgen*, Lilly," he said. He smiled at Lilly but his eyes were teary. "It's not such a good morning…"

"No…," she said. She was not looking at him. She stood reading the front page of the *Times*, trying to take it in: Trotsky had been struck several times with an icepick and it pierced the brain and he was not expected to live. The assassin was Frank Jacson.

She did not look up to see the pigeon-toed girl holding her father's hand as he cried. She didn't pay attention when the girl kept repeating, "What's wrong Daddy?" She didn't notice the woman who bought an *Eagle* and murmured, "He deserved it." Lilly was in a world of her own: she didn't notice smell of burnt rubber or the clanking streetcar, the people rushing across the street against the light, or the cars honking their horns at the man in the black Ford who stopped with window open and hand out to pick up a newspaper from Mr. Fleishman.

When Howie tapped on her shoulder, she was shaken out of her trance.

"Hi," he said. "I thought you might like some company after you heard the news."

"Yes," Lilly had said.

He wore glasses with black frames instead of the rimless ones he used to wear, but his tender eyes had not changed. He hugged her. She put her head on his shoulder and felt like a little girl. In a minute, Howie broke the embrace just enough to look at her face.

"Would you like me to walk back to the house with you?"

"Yes, thanks," Lilly said. She noticed the way the breeze toyed with his hair. His dark wavy hair was thinner than it was when she left for Mexico, but Lilly thought it made him look more adult—like a man rather than a boy. She had taken his hand as they walked back to the house.

Now, at the dining room table, Howie sat with Lilly and her family.

"I just can't believe how thoughtless she is," Lilly said covering her face with her hands. "She must realize how upset we are about Lev. Why doesn't she call for God's sake? It's been twenty-four hours already."

A thunder bolt made Mama drop a plate on the linoleum floor in the kitchen.

Tateh and Sol ran to check on her. Seeing Mama on her knees picking up the chards of porcelain, Tateh warned, "Don't touch it, you'll cut yourself." He bent down to help her stand and pulled her away.

"Sol," he said, "please get a broom." Mama and Tateh joined Lilly and Howie at the dining room table.

"Are you okay, Mrs. Abramovitz?" Howie asked. He had been spending a lot of time at the house since Lilly returned the month before. They did not explicitly discuss what their relationship was or where it was going, but had silently agreed to find out what their relationship was about now: were they old friends or lovers?

"Yes, thank you, I'm fine," she patted Howie's shoulder as she sat down next to Sol's empty chair.

Lilly smiled appreciatively at Howie. *You're such a mensch*, she thought. But what about her? She had been lying to him since before she went to Mexico. She didn't deserve him. And now Gertie had gone silent. She was flooded with anxiety and guilt about Gertie.

"It's so thoughtless of her not to call us," Lilly said. She turned to look at her mother. "Where is she?!"

"She's probably traumatized," Sol said, sitting down after cleaning up the mess in the kitchen. Putting his worksheets and textbook in a neat pile, he said, "She's probably trying to help out, to comfort Natalia or Frida. She's busy."

Tateh sat silently looking at the table, hands gripping the arms of his chair.

"Yes, of course, you're right Sol," Mama said nodding, her arms folded across her chest, "She's probably trying to help everyone deal with the shock of it."

Tateh shook his head and the muscles in his jaw tightened.

"*Hoping and waiting makes fools out of clever people,*" he said staring at the floor.

"I'm going to try to get her at the hotel," said Lilly. She got up and went to the phone on the wall in the kitchen.

She picked up the receiver and dialed the operator. "Hello operator, I want to place a person-to-person call to Miss Gertrude Abramovitz at the Hotel Montejo in Mexico City... Abramovitz," she enunciated slowly. "ABRAMOVITZ."

Despite the static on the line when the operator connected to the concierge at the hotel, Lilly could still hear him tell the operator that there was no Gertrude Abramovitz registered at the hotel.

"Try Jacques Mornard," Howie yelled from the dining room.

"Operator can you ask for Mr. Jacques Mornard?"

The operator repeated the name to the hotel concierge, but once again he said no, there was no one by that name registered at the hotel.

Hanging up the phone, she cursed her sister silently: *Where the hell are you?*

"Leon Trotsky, the 60-year-old former Soviet War Commissar and one-time close associate of Joseph Stalin has died of his wounds in a Mexico City hospital," Eric Sevareid announced.

Lilly stood silently by the phone, her hand still on the receiver. Lev was dead. How was it possible? She remembered the smile in his eyes the first time he invited her to sit next to him on the stone bench in the garden. The *Eagle* and the *Times* had said he was dying—she had been expecting it all day. But she felt an electric shock shoot through her nevertheless. Hail tapped on the windows.

"The assassin," Sevareid said, "has been initially identified as Frank Jacson."

"Did you know him?" Sol asked.

"No." She shook her head, and draped her hands to her side.

"I think," Howie said, getting up from the table, "we should call the embassy and see if they can help us find Gertie." He put his hand on Lilly's shoulder silently.

"Yes, yes," Mama said. "Turn off the radio," she said to Sol.

"Do you think," Sol asked Howie, "they will know anything about her?"

"I don't know," Howie said. "But she's an American citizen so they may know her whereabouts. Or at least help us find her."

"I'll get the phone book," Sol said, getting up from his chair.

Tateh sat white-faced, biting the inside of his cheek.

"No," Howie said. "It's not going to be in the New York phone book." He smiled at Sol. "We need to get the number of the State Department in Washington, D.C. and they can call the embassy in Mexico City or tell us how to do it."

"Yes, yes," Tateh agreed. He took Mama's hand and put it on his cheek, closing his eyes. Mama got up, put her arms around his neck and held him tightly.

Howie called the operator and asked for information in Washington, D.C. Lilly chewed on her nails as Howie was transferred from one operator to the next. After speaking to several people at the State Department, he reached someone who agreed to call the embassy in Mexico City and find out if they knew Gertie's whereabouts. But, the man warned Lilly, they would only know if she had registered with the embassy.

They all sat at the table silently waiting for the State Department to call back. Finally Tateh looked at his watch, turned to Sol and said, "Put on Lowell Thomas."

Sol got up to turn on the radio and changed the station from CBS to Lowell Thomas on NBC.

"Good evening everybody…" Lowell Thomas began. "Russia's exiled Commissar has been pronounced dead. The initial reports were that the assassin was a Frank Jacson, but we have learned that his real name is Jacques Mornard."

Lilly's mouth dropped. There was a collective gasp at the table. It felt as if a huge wave had knocked Lilly off her feet and thrown her under the water.

She had introduced Jacques to Lev. She had asked him to fill in as a driver for Lev's household. *She* had given him the access he needed to murder Lev.

Mama covered her mouth with her hand and the color drained from her cheeks.

Tateh sat shell-shocked with his eyes squeezed shut whispering, "Oy my Gertie."

Sol's eyes glared with hatred. "That bastard. He attacked him like a wild dog. He must have been a Stalinist agent. I hope they hang him…"

Tateh davened back and forth, "*How could I have let her go? What's wrong with me?*" Tears streamed down his cheeks, the salt stinging his lips. Sol put his hand on Tateh's arm.

"He sat at this table," Mama shrieked, pulling her chair back as if she could distance herself from him. "What did we do?"

"*You let a pig in the house,*" Tateh replied with his face full of regret, "*and he'll crawl on the table.*"

Gertie brought a murderer into our house! Lilly felt a wave of nausea.

Just then the phone rang. Howie went into the kitchen to answer it.

"Yes, this is the Abramovitz residence. Thank you for returning our call…" "Where is she?" Lilly asked, straining to hear the man through the receiver Howie held. Howie shook his head. "She's an American citizen, you must know what happened to her!"

Howie put his finger to his lip while he listened to the Embassy person on the line. But Lilly couldn't help herself. "Where is she? For God's sake, where is she?"

"Well thank you anyway," Howie said. He hung up the receiver.

"Well?" Lilly asked.

"Gertie didn't register at the embassy," he said. "They don't know where she is."

Lilly's heart was pounding. Her temples hurt as if something was squeezing her head. She left Gertie in Mexico to fend for herself, she thought, and now there was no telling what had happened to her. Lilly remembered how pale Gertie looked when she arrived in Mexico. She'd been living with a murderer. Suddenly it dawned on her—*he might have killed Gertie. She might be dead.* Lilly's face took on a chalky color. Another wave of nausea rose up inside her and she ran to the bathroom.

"Let's go find her," Sol exclaimed, jumping from his chair.

"No, no you have to stay here and take care of Mama," Tateh said waving Sol off.

Lilly returned from the bathroom. Howie handed her his glass of water.

"My bubela, my poor Gertie. Lilly and I will go," Tateh said.

"What are you talking about? I'm going," Mama said. She got up from her chair as if she was going to pack.

"And I'm going too," Sol protested, banging his fist on the table.

"Forgive me for saying it, but I don't think that's a good idea," Howie said. He shot a glance at Lilly. "We don't know how long it will take to find her."

"I shouldn't have let her go," Tateh said, his voice shaking with tears again. "It's my fault—I looked right at the snake without seeing him."

"No, no," Mama tried to console him. "It's not your fault. He sat here and I offered him tea. I didn't see through him either."

Lilly cleared her throat. "Howie is right." She could barely get the words out. Her head hurt. *How could I have left her? What's wrong with me? I knew there was something wrong with him,* she thought, *I knew it. Why was I so selfish? I could have stayed with her or insisted she come home with me. That's what I should have done. Insisted.* She took a deep breath.

"Howie and I will go," she said. Putting her arms around her father she continued, "We don't know how long it will take to find her. And maybe," she said, turning to put her arms around her mother, "she will call home and you need to be here."

"I want to go with you," Sol said. He stood up and looked at Lilly with pleading eyes.

"I know you do," Lilly said. She looked at him tenderly, putting her hand under his chin. "But it will be better if you stay here with Mama and Tateh. Howie and I go. They will need you here."

*   *   *

Lilly and Howie boarded the 20th Century Limited from New York to Chicago at 6 P.M. the next afternoon. The gateway to the Century's platform was peopled with passenger agents, Pullman conductors and New York Central Railroad conductors posted on the crimson carpet, which had been rolled out on the platform by red-capped attendants at Grand Central station. Women stood sweating in their mink stoles, brought to contend with the air conditioning on the train. Men wearing business suits shook hands and chatted as they wiped their brows with monogrammed handkerchiefs. Porters greeted them by name and rushed to take their bags.

"This is a little too much, don't you think?" Howie said.

"Yes, it's the capitalist express," Lilly smiled.

Lilly and Howie were taking one of the world's most luxurious trains at Tateh's prodding because, with its newly streamlined equipment, it made the 960 mile journey to Chicago in 16 hours.

They stood on the carpet, feeling contemptuous of the Hollywood atmosphere.

"The minks smell like wet dog," Lilly whispered.

"Yes, it's the mix of Schiaparelli and sweat that does it," he laughed.

An elderly porter with white hair and caramel-colored skin asked if he could take their bags.

"Oh?" Howie said in surprise. Howie whispered to Lilly, "For God's sake he's too old to be carrying our bags."

Lilly felt a tinge of guilt but then said, "It's his job. Let him do it. Just give him a tip."

Howie blushed and took out some change.

The porter acted as if he hadn't heard what they said or seen Howie's embarrassment. He took their bags and helped them board.

Once on board, another porter asked them to follow him to their cabin. They walked through the observation car with its glass ceiling and the bar with oak walls and blue leather upholstery.

Their compartment was a suite with two separate rooms and toilet facilities.

Lilly thought about how much more luxurious this was than the train she had taken with Dewey and Kate three and a half years earlier. She wasn't going to have to worry about who she would meet on the line to the bathroom, but she wasn't sure what the sleeping arrangements were going to be with Howie. They had not had sex since she returned from Mexico. As soon as she wondered about it she had a pang of guilt. How could she think about sex when Gertie might be dead?

"Cocktails," the porter announced, "are being served in the lounge or in the observation car."

"Thank you," Lilly said.

"My name is Porter Alfred and I will be happy to help you with anything you would like. Just ring this bell," he said pointing to a button on the wall.

"It's a pleasure to meet you," Howie said. He put out his hand.

"Yes sir," Porter Alfred said in a surprised tone extending his white-gloved hand. Then turning to face Lilly he added, "and Ma'am. You may want to visit the observation car—there's a lovely view of the sunset over the Hudson."

"Thank you," Lilly and Howie said in unison.

Once Porter Alfred left their cabin, Lilly said, "You want to hear something funny? The first time I took this train I didn't know if "Porter" was the man's first name or his title," she said with a chuckle.

Howie smiled.

"Every major capitalist between New York and Chicago must be on this train."

"Remember," Howie said, taking her hand. "We're just doing this to get to Mexico faster. You don't need to feel guilty. You may as well enjoy it because we're not going to be having much fun once we get there."

Yes, Lilly thought. She took her hand away from Howie's and bowed her head. *Where is Gertie? Is she alive?* Lilly felt a shooting pain in her chest. *Did he hurt her? Even if she's physically safe, she must be in a desperate state. Where would she go?*

An hour later, Lilly and Howie were at a table for two having the 20th Century Dinner: canapé of Russian caviar, filet mignon, and apple pie topped with French Vanilla ice cream.

"We didn't eat like this when I took the train with Dewey and Kate, I can tell you that," Lilly said, holding her stomach. She closed her eyes for a moment and felt the relaxing rhythm of the train.

Howie smiled and put his hand across the table in search of hers. She smiled back and put her hand in his, thinking *this is what it must feel like to go on a honeymoon.* But immediately, their real purpose for the journey jerked her back to the present.

"There's something I want to tell you," Lilly began. She put her hand to her forehead as if she were checking for a fever. "I had doubts about Jacques. There was something peculiar about him. He showered attention on Gertie when the three of us were together. But once when he thought I was out of earshot, he was horribly nasty to her. And not only that, she told me he was acting strangely."

"Well, none of that adds up to him being a murderer. How could you have known?"

Lilly didn't answer. She just looked down and shook her head.

"Look," Howie said softly, "you didn't understand what was happening. You couldn't have."

Lilly looked up at Howie—he had fans of tiny wrinkles at the corners of his eyes that made it always seem that he was on the brink of a smile. But there was so much he didn't know about her. So much he might not *want* to know.

They went back to their suite and hugged for a long time, but then Lilly went to the bathroom to put on her nightgown and robe. When she returned Howie was in his bed in the adjoining cabin. She said good night and so did he. She wondered what he was thinking. Was he thinking about her refusal to come home from Mexico despite his pleas? Was he wondering who she had slept with while she was away? She climbed into her own bed and her thoughts turned to Gertie. She closed her eyes and prayed—something she only did under dire circumstances. She didn't think about God very often. *Please keep her safe. Don't let anything happen to her,* she prayed silently. Then she felt foolish—something terrible had already happened to her. She must be devastated by Jacques' betrayal. *He used her to get to Lev. He must have planned the whole thing from the beginning in Paris. He made it a point to meet her and have an affair with her because she was my sister,* she thought. *It was all about access to Lev.*

She heard Howie snoring and her thoughts turned back to him. She was a different person before she went to Mexico, she thought. She was a naive adolescent who thought she could change the world. There was so much she had to tell Howie. But she wasn't ready and wasn't sure when she would be. Eventually she was lulled to sleep by the cadence of the train's wheels clicking on the tracks.

Arriving at LaSalle Street Station the following morning, they boarded the Missouri Pacific "Sunshine Special" from Chicago to El Paso—the same train Lilly had taken with Dewey and Kate. When they found their sleepers, Lilly was sorry to find their porter was not Porter Lawrence, but Porter Joseph—a tall horse-faced man with a gullet that hung like wet clothes on a clothesline.

They spent the next day trying to relax, looking for any excuse not to think about the ordeal lying ahead in Mexico City. They lapsed into soulful reminisces of the old days at City College, speaking of current or former friends caught up in the anxieties caused by the inexorable drift towards war. They were desperate to talk about anything but the two most pressing subjects—Gertie's fate and their relationship.

When Howie walked Lilly back to her cabin, the bunk bed was pulled out and made.

"Thank you," Lilly said. She took Howie's hands in hers and looked him in the eyes. "Thank you for coming with me. Thank you for being who you are. Thank you..."

Howie pulled her toward him and put his arms around her. He didn't move. He just held her. She felt he was waiting for her to give him a signal: What was their relationship going to be? Was he just a good friend? Were they going to be lovers? She felt it was her decision.

She pulled back from him, looked up at him with a smile and then kissed him on the mouth. She felt his body melt into hers. He kissed her hair and her neck and swooned, "Mmm..." She moved away from him and unbuttoned her blouse, letting it fall on the floor. He smiled and kissed her shoulders and the tops of her breasts. She turned to lock the door and then unbuttoned her bra: she had made her decision. She expected him to pull her down on top of him and kiss her passionately. Instead, he pushed her away.

"I still love you," Howie said red-faced, and breathing hard. "I still want to marry you. But I don't want you to come back to me because you're so distraught about Gertie."

Lilly stood half-naked in front of him, gasping for breath, trying to understand.

"I want you to want me," he said with eyes filled with tears.

"But..."

"No, don't..." Howie said. He shook his head and waved her away.

She tried to hug him, but it was like trying to hug one of Lev's cacti. Lilly was shocked into silence.

She pulled the covers down on the lower bunk and climbed into bed half dressed. Howie unlocked the door and went down the hall to the bathroom. Lilly's tears wet the foam rubber pillow and she lay there feeling humiliated and also angry at Howie for humiliating her. She looked at the dark outside the train window and felt a blackness inside herself. She heard Howie return and the door of his cabin shut. *You bastard*, she thought. *You made me think you wanted me to make the decision and when I did, you pushed me away.* She grudgingly fell into a fitful sleep, but awoke several times during the night overcome with self-loathing and desire for Howie. *I've been so selfish*, she thought. *I ignored his pleas to come back from Mexico; I cheated on him and lied. What did I expect? I might have lost the two people I love most in the world.* She wished she could shed her old self like a snake sheds a skin and leave it on the train.

The next morning, while Howie slept, Lilly sat looking out the window at the fresh grasslands swaying like soft hair blowing in the wind. She remembered sitting with Dewey, reading and filing Lev's writings and the documents from the Moscow trials and trying to understand Kate. That seemed a lifetime ago. All the moral righteousness she had felt had been swept away like silt in a river.

There was a knock at the door.

She yelled, "Come in."

"I'm sorry I hurt you," Howie said, standing in front of her. "I love you. But..." He scrunched up his face.

"You don't need to apologize," Lilly said, looking up at him. "You're right. After all I've put you through, I can understand if you want to take things slowly and make sure I'm not going to run off somewhere."

"No." He sat down next to her and looked intently into her eyes. "It's not that. I want to make sure that you really want me and you're not just settling because things are in crisis. I need to know you want to marry me and have a family."

"I understand," Lilly said. The look in his eyes made her want to embrace him: to feel his unshaved face next to hers, to feel his hairy chest against her breasts. She wanted to feel his arms around her, his erection pressing against her. But she knew that would be a mistake. He wanted to be more than a comfort to her. She thought he was, but she realized her credit was not good—it was better to wait.

*   *   *

After two nights on the train from Chicago, they reached El Paso where they had to change to the Texas-Mexican railroad at Union Depot. Lilly pointed to the six story bell tower topped with a tall spire and said to Howie, "Pancho Villa used that as a lookout position during an attack on Ciudad Juarez just over the border."

"No kidding," he smiled.

Emerging from the train the sunlight streamed through the large semi-circular windows which ringed the upper level of the Depot.

"Don't they remind you," Lilly said, "of the pictures of the Roman baths we saw at the Metropolitan Museum?"

Howie stood looking around taking in every detail: the patterned marble floor, the Neo-Classical pillars and pilasters.

The last time she was there, she had wished he was there to see it. Now he was and it felt like they were on a small island of respite on their way to a sea of misery.

Once on the train, they were given private compartments. Lilly remembered the mix of houses as the train passed through the Mexican villages: flimsy structures made of corn stalks or bamboo with thatched roofs; more substantial adobe tile-roofed houses; and some large Spanish-looking houses made of brick or stone that were surrounded by outer walls.

"The people who live in those thatched-roof houses," Howie said, probably work for the people in the stone houses. Don't you think?"

"Yes," she said. It was uncanny; he said exactly what she remembered thinking all those years ago.

They passed newly planted fields amidst shrub growth that looked like it had been there for years without any visible trails or roads. They saw solitary houses of stone or reed with thatched roofs with one or two scrawny cows. Occasionally they passed a burro carrying a large load being pulled by a peasant. Passing through the city of Chihuahua, they admired the spectacular stone cathedral. Heading south paralleling the Sierra Madre Oriental, they saw the snow-capped Pico de Orizaba in the distance—the highest peak in Mexico.

"Wow," Howie said.

"Yes, isn't it amazing," Lilly said. "The first time I saw it I missed you so much. I wished you were there to see it," she said, taking his hand and putting it on her cheek. "And now you're here." She kissed

263

his hand and put it back against her cheek. Lilly felt a rush of emotion; she was teary.

That night when they returned from the dinner car to their compartment, Lilly locked the door behind them, put her outstretched arms on Howie's shoulders and looked into his eyes.

"I love you," she said. "It's not just because I'm so worried about Gertie."

"Are you sure?" Howie asked.

"Yes, I am sure. I want to be with you."

"I'm not a revolutionary or ..."

"I know who you are," she said. She put her fingers on his lips and pulled him closer to her. She felt the hair on his chest under his shirt and the familiar smell of his aftershave.

"I love you, Lilly," Howie said. He tightened his grip on her.

"I know..."

He pushed her blouse to the side and kissed her shoulder.

"There are things I have to tell you..." Lilly whispered.

He unbuttoned her blouse and kissed her collarbone. "Not now...it can wait..." he said. Her blouse fell to the floor. He undid her bra and it fell on top of her blouse. He held her hand as he took a few steps to the bunk and pulled her toward him.

*　　　　*　　　　*

When Lilly and Howie arrived at the Buenavista railroad station in Mexico City, they were assaulted by the blinding sun just as she had been the first time she had arrived with Dewey and Kate. Skinny children with mud-caked bodies still clamored with their grimy hands extended, begging for change.

"This is horrible," Howie said.

"Look at that statue," Lilly said with a smirk. "It's Christopher Columbus!" Kate had not understood the irony of its presence, but Lilly knew that Howie did. She hailed a taxi and they set out for the Hotel Monejo on the Paseo de la Reforma, the only address Lilly had for Gertie. As they drove down an expansive tree-lined street toward the hotel, Howie was mesmerized by the sights and the Mexican workers with faces like dried prunes carrying large boxes, piles of wood or huge pieces of furniture on their backs.

"They're like beasts of burden, for God's sake!" Howie said.

Lilly was lost in memories. A pigeon on the sidewalk reminded her of the way Lev's hens shook their fat feathered bodies when he threw them corn. She remembered the childlike glee on his face as he watched them gobble up their food and the way he used to close his eyes and feel the sunshine on his face.

"Tell him to wait so we can leave the bags in the cab," Howie said when they reached the hotel.

Lilly asked the driver to wait and the two of them got out of the taxi and went into the hotel. The short pudgy concierge with a name tag that said "Pablo" smiled and greeted them, "Hola."

There was a couple sitting on a frayed couch in the lobby chatting in Spanish. They swatted a few flies as they sat in front of the fan. Their luggage sat next to them as if they waited for their room to be ready.

Lilly explained in hushed Spanish that they were looking for Gertrude Abramovitz. She didn't want the couple to overhear her—she felt as if she were inquiring about Mr. and Mrs. John Wilkes Booth. Pablo shook his head and said he never heard of her. Then she asked him about Jacques Mornard. No, he told her, he never heard of him either.

"Frank Jacson?" Howie asked.

Pablo scowled and said in loud rapid-fire Spanish, *"Yes, he and his wife were here. But they killed Trotsky."*

The couple sitting in the lobby looked up at Lilly and Howie nervously as if they might be dangerous.

"What?" she said in English, her breath catching in her throat. Then she said in Spanish, *"Where is she? Where is my sister?"*

"I don't know," he replied shrugging with a disgusted look on his face.

"What did he say?" Howie asked.

"He said they killed Trotsky and he doesn't know where Gertie is."

"Shit," he winced. "We better go to the embassy right away."

They hurried out of the hotel into the waiting taxi. The air was hot and humid and the low moon looked like it was on fire. Lilly asked the driver to take them to the American Embassy.

"It looks like a castle on the Rhine," Howie said when they arrived at the huge gray-stone edifice with battlements. They showed their passports to the guard at the entrance to the embassy and then climbed the flat stone steps on the winding staircase that led to the embassy's consular offices. A pert woman who reminded Lilly of Kate, sat at a small desk at the top of the staircase guarding a suite of offices. The name plate on her desk said: "Carolyn Billingsley."

"We'd like to speak to someone about the whereabouts of my sister," Lilly said.

"Is she an American citizen?" Carolyn Billingsley asked. She continued typing.

"Yes," Howie said in an annoyed tone. "This is an emergency. We need to speak to an embassy official immediately."

"About what?" Carolyn Billingsley asked. She stopped typing and looked at them. Her dark hair looked like the rollers had just been removed.

"My sister's boyfriend assassinated Trotsky," Lilly said, "and we can't find her."

"Oh," Miss Billingsley said. She seemed finally interested. "You'll need to speak to Mason Smith. Why don't you sit over there?" She pointed to a tufted brown leather sofa. "I will see if he is available." She called Mason Smith and told him in a whisper who was sitting in the waiting area.

A few minutes later a heavy set man, red-faced as if he had dragged a dry razor across his cheeks, walked out of his office and introduced himself.

"I am Mason Smith, political attaché and assistant to the ambassador." He extended his arm to indicate a direction. "Please come into my office."

"We are looking for my sister Gertrude Abramovitz," Lilly said. She sat facing his desk. A portrait of President Roosevelt hung on the wall behind him. The book lined office was air conditioned, but Lilly felt sticky as she sat on the upholstered Queen Anne chair.

"She has been arrested," Mason Smith said in a sympathetic voice. His cat green eyes looked sadly at Lilly.

"Why?" Lilly blurted out. She was conflicted. Part of her was relieved: *at least she's alive*, she thought. *He didn't kill her*. But the relief quickly turned to outrage. Howie leaned over and squeezed her hand.

"They think she was a co-conspirator. We have not been able to contact her. We only found out from the newspapers. Mornard or Jacson or whatever his name is, is at Lecumberri Prison and we think that's where she is as well. But the Mexican authorities are not cooperating with us at this point."

"That's crazy," Lilly said. "My sister didn't have anything to do with it. She was used by him. She's a victim." It came out as a protest.

Mason Smith was silent.

"She was naïve—he knew she was my sister and I worked for Trotsky. It was a set-up."

He did not say a word.

"Can we visit her?" Lilly asked.

"You can try," Smith said.

"What does that mean?" Howie asked.

"Can't you help us?" Lilly pleaded.

"I'm afraid we can't do anything until the Mexican authorities inform us that they have an American citizen in custody." He put his folded hands on his desk in front of him as if to indicate the conversation was over.

"That's ridiculous," Howie said. Lilly nodded agreement.

"I'm sorry, but those are the rules."

"This is my sister we're talking about. Don't tell me about the rules."

"Is money the issue here," Howie said taking his wallet out of his back pocket.

"No…Please put that away," Smith said. He waved Howie off and looked insulted.

"Then just exactly what do we have to do to get to the bottom of this?" Howie asked.

"You have to understand, this is Mexico. Things take time here. You can't push these people. Things have been sensitive since the oil expropriations."

"My sister's in some horrible prison. God only knows what she's going through. Don't tell me we have to take our time," Lilly yelled at Smith.

"Do you understand that your sister was living with an assassin? What was she doing here? Why didn't she register at the Embassy?"

"Are you implying that her sister had something to do with the assassination?" Howie said, narrowing his eyes.

"I don't know if she had anything to do with it or not… But for now, until the Mexican government tells us they have an American citizen in custody for the assassination of Trotsky, the embassy cannot do anything."

Howie got up and extended his hand to Lilly. "Let's go. There's nothing more to be done here." They walked out of Mason Smith's office without thanking him.

"Lecumberri Prison," Howie said to the cab driver as they got back into the car.

"Bad place," the stocky cab driver said scratching his head with dirty fingernails. "Who there?" he asked.

"My sister," Lilly answered.

The driver had a round Mayan face and straight black hair. He put his hand on his cheek and shook his head sympathetically the way his ancestors might have when someone else's daughter or sister was chosen for sacrifice.

Once they got to the tall brick walls crowned with barbed wire, the driver pointed to the entrance of the prison where a fleshy peasant woman with her arms folded across her bountiful breasts stood arguing with a guard, her three dirty children pulling at her skirt. An old man with stained clothes was lying on the grass babbling incoherently. Six guards were posted. Howie took the Mexican pesos out of his pocket that he had exchanged for dollars at the El Paso train station. Lilly chose the appropriate bills from his outstretched hand and put them into the calloused hands of the driver. Leaving the taxi, they had to fight a dark howling wind.

"We are here to visit a prisoner," Lilly said to a guard with a meaty build and a bloated face. His shirt was stained in the armpits and he smelled of sweat and nicotine. In an ugly voice, he asked for a name.

"Gertrude Abramovitz," she said.

He wet his thumb with his tongue to turn the pages of a listing of prisoners and when he found her name, he looked up at Howie and then Lilly suspiciously. He ordered her to put her bag on a table for him to search. Another guard searched Howie. When they were through security, they were led down a hallway to a wide, high, circular room at the center of the compound. The prison had a central circular room and

268

several long, corridor-like extensions extending on all sides from the main, domed hall. Like Dante and Virgil, Lilly and Howie were taking a journey to the underworld and passing through the circles of suffering at the prison. As Howie and Lilly walked past tiny cells with peeling paint, reeking of sweat, urine, feces and vomit, a short man with a round head and broad face banged his fists on the bars of his cell and yelled at them in Spanish, "*Besa mis huevos.*" Another Indian-looking man yelled, "*Chinga tu madre*" and a tall man with olive skin and curly black hair grasped the bars tightly and begged in heavily-accented English, "I am a political prisoner, please help me."

Trying to stifle heaves, they were ushered to a small windowless room that reeked from nicotine where a straight-lipped policeman with a large mole under his right eye sat sweating behind a desk. The guard said something to him in rapid-fire Spanish. The only words that Howie and Lilly caught were: "Gertrude Abramovitz." Lilly's posture stiffened. The man behind the desk nodded, rubbing his chin. Then he gestured for Howie and Lilly to sit down.

"I have ...bad news... for you..." the policeman said in heavily accented English, his eye twitching above the mole. "Visiting hours are over. You will have to come back tomorrow."

"You mean she's here, but you won't let us see her?" Lilly said. Her face was contorted. The policeman looked at her—blank, expressionless.

"This is crazy," Howie said. "After all we've been through. Why can't we see her?"

"Too late. Hours are over," the policeman said. He was looking above Howie's head, as if the person who asked the question was standing behind him.

"That's impossible. I demand to see my sister," Lilly said. "She had nothing to do with Trotsky's murder. She doesn't belong here."

"Too late. I'm sorry," the policeman said.

"Okay," Howie said standing up and again extending his hand to help Lilly out of her chair. But we will be back tomorrow...and the day after that if necessary." Then he turned to leave and said to Lilly, "Let's go. There's no point arguing. We'll just come back."

Walking out of the prison, Howie was puzzled. "Where shall we go?"

"I don't know," Lilly said. She knew only two hotels in Mexico City—the Gran Hotel de la Ciudad de Mexico, the luxurious hotel where she had stayed with Kate during the Dewey hearings, and the Hotel Montejo where Gertie and Jacques had been.

She decided immediately that the Hotel de la Ciudad was too expensive and thought for a moment about how it would feel to stay in the same hotel where Gertie and Jacques had stayed. Would it feel ghoulish? Or would it feel comforting? She wasn't sure. Finally she decided she would like to stay where Gertie had stayed.

"Let's go back to the Montejo," she said.

"Are you sure?" Howie asked.

"Yes...I think that's what I'd like to do."

They waited for what seemed much longer than the fifteen minutes it took before they could hail a taxi passing by the prison.

"Hotel Montejo," Lilly told the driver."

*   *   *

When they arrived at the hotel, Pablo was still on duty. The look on his face said, *Not you again.* But Lilly ignored it and asked him in what room Mr. and Mrs. Frank Jacson had stayed. He made a face full of disdain for them but answered the question. She asked if that room was available and when it was, she asked if they could have that room. She hoped there would be some sign of Gertie left behind: a bottle of shampoo she had used, leftover soap, something. But there was nothing of hers left in the room. Lilly picked up the pillow on the side of the bed closest to the bathroom and smelled it. She thought that would be Gertie's side because at home her bed was the one closest to the bathroom. But there was no scent of Gertie.

"We better call your parents," Howie said putting their bags down.

"Yes," Lilly replied absentmindedly.

"They'll want to hear from you, not me," he said.

"Yes, of course," Lilly put down the pillow and picked up the phone. "Mama," she cried, "Mama it's me. Can you hear me? There's so much static. We're here and we've found out where Gertie is." She could hear Mama calling Tateh and Sol to come to the phone.

"So where is she?" Tateh said.

"It's not good. She's in Lecumberri Prison."

270

"Where?" Tateh asked.

"Prison," Lilly said louder over the static. "She's in prison."

"Where?" Mama asked.

"She's in a horrible prison!" Lilly cried.

There was a chorus of gasps on the other end of the phone.

"Why? That's crazy," Sol yelled.

"They think she collaborated with Jacques," Lilly said.

"So did you see her?" Tateh asked.

"No," Lilly replied, digging her nails into the palm of her hand. "They wouldn't let us see her today. It was too late when we got there. But we're going back tomorrow."

"*Oy veh*, my poor Gertie," Tateh said with his voice cracking.

*   *   *

The next morning after a restless night, Lilly and Howie left the hotel. The sun was hidden behind a cloud when they hailed a taxi to go to the prison. It was hot and humid and they were both sweating when they got into the cab.

"*Hola*," Howie said. "Lecumberri Prison." This time the driver made no comment. The brick walls surrounding the prison were baking in the morning sun, the driver once again pointed to the entrance to the prison. Visiting hours had just begun so there were no relatives sitting on the grass or showing their identification papers. Six guards stood talking and laughing in front of the large iron gates.

"We are here to visit a prisoner," Lilly said to a fat guard with body odor. Gertrude Abramovitz."

"Where do you think the women are?" Howie said to Lilly, while holding his nose. Once again they were searched and ushered to a small windowless room where the same straight-lipped policeman sat behind his desk.

"Ah you are here to see Gertrude Abramovitz," the policeman said gesturing for Howie and Lilly to sit down.

"She is in the women's wing," the policeman said.

"Can we see her now?" Lilly asked.

"Yes," the policeman half smiled. He opened his desk drawer and pulled out a large metal ring of keys. Then he got up and gestured for Lilly and Howie to follow him.

He led them to yet another circle of suffering down a long corridor with a locked door at the end. Unlocking it, he gestured for Lilly and Howie to walk through. They heard women's voices for the first time. The stench was the same as it was in the men's wing. A fat Indian woman with dirty hair and stained clothing screamed from her cell and shook the iron bars.

"*Tu madre es puta y pendeja*," she yelled at the policeman.

"What does that mean?" Howie asked Lilly.

"It's not a compliment, put it that way," Lilly said.

"*El mayate*," the others yelled and laughed.

Ignoring them, the policeman turned to Lilly and Howie and said, "Your sister is in the last cell at the end of this hall."

Lilly walked faster, repeating her sister's name under her breath, "Gertie, Gertie…" Her heart beat so fast she felt it would burst out of her chest. There was no answer. Her head pounded. She started to run, "Gertie, I'm here…Gertie..!"

As she approached the cell Lilly saw a dark shadow on the wall. She stopped abruptly, afraid to take another step. "Gertie, Gertie…" Howie caught up to her. He took her arm and nudged her to take the next step. Gertie was hanging from a torn sheet she had tied around her neck and to the iron grill of the window.

PART III

19

Lilly thought he must know. After all, Gertie's name had appeared in the newspapers along with Jacques' for over three weeks since Lev's murder. Her suicide felt like an open wound at the center of herself and the prospect of talking about it felt like pouring hydrogen peroxide on it. That's what Mama did when she or Gertie or Solly fell down. Lilly used to wince as the white substance mixed with blood bubbled up from the lesion.

"He was wearing a trench coat when it wasn't raining." Her fingers tapped the arm of the chair. "Why didn't anyone notice that? Joe Hansen, the head of the security detail was right there with Melquaides, the handy man. They were so careful about searching people. I once asked Joe why he went to such lengths when the police guards provided by the Mexican government searched all visitors first."

"What did he say?" Dr. Bloom asked, as if he was interested in hearing all the details although most of them had been in the *Times*.

"He didn't trust the police. He wasn't sure who they worked for." Lilly felt as if there was no air in the room. "Can you turn the fan on?"

"Of course, Lilly." He had a German accent that made him sound like he had a hair stuck in the back of his throat.

Dr. Bloom got up, walked across the office and flipped a switch on the wall behind his large mahogany desk. His consulting room was a large L-shaped space with high ceilings and tall windows. The desk and chair were tucked in the alcove. The doctor was wearing baggy chinos, heavily creased around the crotch from sitting all day.

The ceiling fans made a whirring noise and blew some of the papers off his desk. He bent down to pick them up and stuck them under a book to anchor them. Lilly noticed he had a bald spot with a birth mark on top of his head. Her palpitations grew stronger as she waited for him to settle back into his arm chair.

"The murderer walked right in to the house," she said as if she didn't know him. "He said he wanted Trotsky to read an article he wrote in response to the minority that had criticized the Old Man's position on the war and the USSR…Do you always have such a messy desk?"

274

Dr. Bloom smiled politely, "I'm afraid so. The journals pile up on me. Please continue."

Her eyelids drooped as if they were weighted down. "He was well-dressed in a summer suit and tie. I bet it wasn't a bow tie like the one you're wearing. Bow ties remind me of little boys. Are you taking notes?"

"I was jotting a few things down."

She felt a surge of nausea. "Who's going to read it?"

"No one will read it. It's just for me," he said gently. "I would never discuss a session without your permission." He shook his head to convey that the idea was unthinkable. Dr. Bloom was an "Old World" gentleman, the kind who opens the door for women and doesn't sit down until the women in the room are seated.

She exhaled and only then realized she'd been holding her breath while he answered.

"The *Times* said he wore a gray hat and carried a tan raincoat over his arm although it was a sunny day."

"Yes?"

She felt pressured. He wanted her to make sense of it, but she couldn't.

"Why wasn't he searched by the police guards?" she asked rhetorically. "The *Times* said the assassin waved to them and they waved back. Schmucks. Maybe Joe was right about the police."

She hated rooms with cracked plaster. Colonies of ants could be in the cracks, she thought, or dust mites or worms. She was afraid she would vomit, but it passed.

"And Lev never brought a visitor into his study without a guard or a secretary present. He was so careful. Why were they alone? Lev had a gun on his desk, why didn't he use it? Can you stop touching your face? And there was an alarm button right in front of him, they installed it after the Siqueiros raid, but he didn't push it."

Her blouse was wet; she wasn't sure if it was sweat or tears. Her feelings bobbed up and down like a cork in the ocean. She was afraid that if she settled down and focused on what she was feeling, she would sink and drown in the horror of it all. She wanted distraction. The doctor had stubby fingers; he bit his nails. *An anxious shrink*, she thought. *Great*.

"Do you know it takes two eyes to discern depth up to 20 feet, but for longer distances you only need one eye for depth perception?"

"No I didn't know that. What made you think of that?" He wrinkled his brow and there were two deep creases like trolley tracks between his eyes.

"Why did he take the time out to read this article with the author right in front of him? He didn't even like the man. Lev told me he read an earlier version of the guy's article and it was banal and unoriginal. He could have taken it and asked him to come back in a week. But he didn't. Lev sat down at his desk and started reading it while he was right there. Can't you stop scratching your ear?"

"I'm sorry, Lilly. I didn't realize I was doing it." He clasped his hands.

She stared at the ceiling and was quiet.

"Lilly?"

She didn't answer.

"Can you say what you're feeling?"

She shook her head silently and grimaced. Suddenly she looked straight at him and yelled, "Don't you get it? He plunged an ice pick into the back of the Lev's head." But that was not the only thing Lilly felt Dr. Bloom didn't get. She couldn't bring herself to speak of the larger thing he didn't get: *I didn't protect my little sister and now she's dead.*

20

Lilly entered Dr. Bloom's office from the waiting room through the padded sound-proof double doors. Sitting down on one of the two beige and brown upholstered armchairs facing each other, she noticed that the brown and cream Persian rug in the center of the room had a diamond shape forming the medallion and a border of similar smaller medallions. Glancing at the analytic couch with a slightly raised headrest on one side and a tapestry velvet throw on the other, she remembered Diana Trilling talking about her Stalinist psychoanalyst so many years before at Yaddo.

"When did you emigrate?" Lilly asked Dr. Bloom. She wanted to talk about him rather than her.

He didn't answer immediately. Putting his hand on his chin, as though he were deciding whether or not to answer, Dr. Bloom continued doodling on the pad he had on his lap.

She waited, wondering what he was doodling and if he was going to answer directly or, like the caricature of a Freudian, say: "What do you think?"

She imagined he had left soon after Hitler took power.

"I left Vienna in 1934," he said, "but I went to Holland, not the United States. I didn't come here until 1938."

"Vienna," Lilly said with a smile, glad that Dr. Bloom had answered her directly and that he was from Vienna, the cradle of Nazism, Zionism and psychoanalysis.

"Yes," Dr. Bloom smiled and nodded.

"I heard that Hitler was rejected as an art student by the Academy of Fine Arts in Vienna," Lilly said, hoping to keep the conversation away from Lev and Gertie, "and went on to become a house painter."

Dr. Bloom was quiet.

Lilly knew from Diana as well as her reading that Freudian psychoanalysts often didn't say anything, so she worried that she might be looking at the ceiling for the whole session and he would be silent. But she soon realized the silence was hers, not his. There was so much she didn't want to say. They both sat silently for quite a while until Dr. Bloom said very softly, "We're going to have to stop for now."

When Lilly got up to leave she looked at Dr. Bloom's pad. He had been doodling Jewish stars.

*   *   *

The next session, after several minutes of silence during which Lilly sat staring at the ceiling, Dr. Bloom said, "Lilly, I think there is a lot you don't want to say and if you come once a week it will take a very long time for you to feel better. I think it would be best if you came frequently, four times a week, and used the couch."

She was quiet.

"What are you feeling?" he asked.

"I once knew someone who went to analysis five times a week. Diana Trilling. Years ago before I went to Mexico. It didn't seem to help her much: she was giving up on a career or even having children to devote her life to the care and feeding of Lionel, but I'm willing to try anything."

So reluctantly agreeing, Lilly got up and walked over to the couch. Dr. Bloom positioned his armchair next to the headrest. But she didn't speak; she tried to focus on a crack in the ceiling and not let anything enter her mind.

*   *   *

The next session Lilly lay motionless on the couch with her arms at her side humming, trying to block out her thoughts of Gertie and Lev with the low frequency noise:

> "Oh, the Cloakmakers' Union is a no-
> good-union,
> It's a company union for the bosses.
> The right wing cloakmakers and the
> socialist fakers
> Are making by the workers double
> crosses."

"What's that you're singing?" the doctor asked.

She continued humming. He waited a few minutes for her to respond and then, when he lost the scent, he tried a new approach.

"What are the double crosses?"

278

Lilly was impressed that he was listening carefully. But she ignored the question anyway.

"I had a dream about Lev. Jacques stabbed him with the icepick and Lev doesn't fall over on to his desk. He stands up straight like one of those phallic cacti he loved and lets out a piercing scream. Natalia comes running to the Old Man's side and Lev turns his bloodied cheek toward her and says, 'Lilly, why did she do it?' That's what woke me up."

"What did you feel when you woke up?"

"Oh, the Cloakmakers' Union is a no good union..."

"Lilly, what did you feel when you woke up after the dream?"

"What the hell do you think I felt? I felt terrified!" She immediately felt sorry for raising her voice to this kindly man who was trying to guide her through a dark tunnel inside herself.

"I'm sorry. I didn't mean to upset you," he said gently.

"I know. I'm sorry."

"No need to be sorry." He smiled. "Freud said, 'The first human who hurled an insult instead of a stone was the founder of civilization.'"

"'Footfalls echo in the memory down the passage which we did not take towards the door we never opened into the rose-garden...'"

"T.S. Eliot, isn't it?"

"Yes." His recognition increased the tension between her shoulders. You're a "pain in the neck" she said silently, smiling to herself. The thought made her think of Gertie and her aphorisms. Oh Gertie. Tears dripped down her cheeks.

"Lilly, what is the path you didn't take, the door you didn't open?"

She felt him getting closer to what she didn't want to tell him, to the wound that was still bleeding. She hesitated. Finally, she said, "I could have stayed in New York and married Howie. Instead I told him I was just going away for a couple of weeks with Dewey and then I told him I was going to work for Trotsky for a while. I kept putting him off. I knew he loved me and I left him waiting for me to get it out of my system."

"Get what out of your system?" He picked up the scent; his nostrils had been trained by Freud.

"Wanting to change the world, save the masses..."

"Anything else?" He prodded gently.

She didn't want to tell him what else. She felt only loosely tethered to her sense of being a decent person and she didn't want to cut the last thread. She held her breath, trying to control what was coming out of her.

"Lilly?" The doctor nudged.

She looked at the ceiling and tapped her foot against the wall next to the couch.

"Lilly, you have things on your mind that are causing you great pain. Keeping them secret is not going to make the pain go away."

"Okay, I had sex with Van Heijenoort when I was in Mexico." *There, I said it*, she thought. Van was such a serious man; never a joke in his eyes. But for Lilly there was a magnetic field around him—the air was charged. She was drawn to him with uncontrollable force, electricity coursed through her body when he touched her. She could still conjure up the smell of his sweat at the end of the day.

Dr. Bloom said, "So? What's the problem with that?"

She didn't understand how the doctor could be anything but horrified. "Howie was waiting for me in Brooklyn. He wasn't having sex with anyone. He was waiting for me to come back." It seemed so obvious to her that she had betrayed Howie.

"Were you engaged? Had you promised not to have any other relationships?"

"No, I didn't overtly promise. But it was an understanding we had. I know he expected that. I expected it of myself."

"Okay," he said like a tug boat gently prodding a barge on the East River, "so you slept with someone else when you were in Mexico. Why is that so terrible?"

"You don't understand…" She couldn't bear to hear the words coming out of her mouth. "He was married and had a child."

"Did you know?" he asked in a soft, neutral tone.

"I didn't know at first, but then Frida told me. His wife and son were in Paris. I felt so ashamed of myself. His wife, Gaby, and his son actually came to Coyoacán in November of 1937."

"Were you still involved with Van then?"

"No, I ended the sexual part of the relationship before they arrived." She thought of the autumn night she and Van sat on a stone bench in the garden of *Casa Azul*. "Van said he was sorry he didn't tell

280

me something," Lilly told the doctor. "I couldn't imagine what else he could have omitted. I already knew he was married. What could be worse? When he said the words 'wife and son coming' I felt like my mother was arriving. How could I face her? And his son yet? They came to live at the house soon after that."

"What happened?" the doctor asked.

"She was a beautiful woman and was used to being at the center of things. She didn't pay any attention to me, but she was living in Natalia's house and the two of them got into a terrible fight."

"Yes?"

"Lev broke it up and told Gaby he'd call the police if she didn't leave the house."

"And what did Van do?" Dr. Bloom leaned forward in his chair, eager to know.

"Nothing, absolutely nothing." Lilly thought Dr. Bloom was getting interested in the saga. "I lost all the respect I'd had for Van and by then I didn't have a lot left. He didn't defend his wife; he didn't resign his position." She remembered the moment when her remaining feelings for him were snuffed out like a candle. "The Old Man told his wife to leave and Van acted like an obedient little boy. It was clear when she walked out of the house that he was never going to see her or his son again and he just let them go."

"What are you feeling?" Dr. Bloom asked.

"I'm thinking about Howie. He would never have acted that way. He would have resigned and walked out with me."

"So Van had some kind of idealized father relationship with the Old Man?"

"Yes," Lilly laughed. "He said Lev was a prophet, like Moses, but I think he was more like Jeremiah."

"Why Jeremiah?"

"Jeremiah enunciated some key ideas that completely changed the nature of the Jewish faith and of monotheism as a whole."

"Really, what were they?"

"The universality of God and the non-existence of other gods. And Jeremiah said the Israelites could worship their God even in exile."

"I guess that sounds like Lev." He laughed.

"Personal responsibility too. Jeremiah rejected the idea that the sins of the father were visited on the son. And he believed in human action as the way to redeem the world. Jeremiah is the originator of the great rabbinic concept, 'One does not rely on miracles.'"

"So there are actually a lot of parallels between Jeremiah and Lev. Is that what you're saying?" the doctor asked.

"No, I don't care about Jeremiah and Lev. I'm talking about Van and Lev—their relationship had all the earmarks of the Oedipal Complex."

"How so?"

"Well, on the one hand, Van let his wife and son leave because Trotsky ordered them out. But on the other hand, I'm sure he had an affair with Frida or wanted to. He was overflowing with desire for his Old Man's lover. Isn't that classic?"

"What makes you think he had an affair with Frida?"

"Well he knew that Lev was having an affair with her and I could see that bothered him."

"Perhaps because he thought it inappropriate for someone of Trotsky's stature. Or maybe he felt sympathy for Natalia?" Dr. Bloom offered Van the benefit of the doubt. But Lilly had no doubt.

"No, it wasn't just those things. He was dejected at the Dewey Commission celebration while he watched Frida dancing with Diego. I remember feeling jealous of the way he looked at her. And he was obedient in finding Trotsky another house, but he was clearly upset when Lev broke with Diego because he wouldn't see Frida anymore. I think I arrived in Mexico expecting the Garden of Eden…"

"And what happened?"

"It wasn't just Adam and Eve, there was Frida and Diego and Lev and Van… and me…"

"Yes?"

"Everyone ate the apple, not just Eve—all of us."

"So what does that mean?"

She wondered if Dr. Bloom was confused by her metaphor or he just wanted her to make sense of her feelings.

"Each of us sinned; we all sinned. Lev cheated on Natalia; Frida sinned against Diego; Diego betrayed Frida with her sister and others; Van betrayed his wife and Lev….and I betrayed Howie."

"So?"

"It means that we all lied to ourselves and each other. We all acted as if we were doing it for some cause greater than ourselves. But that's a *bubbameister*. Do you know what that means?"

"Yes, of course, it's an old wives' tale."

"Yes...We all felt so self-important. We were saving the proletariat; we couldn't be bothered by bourgeois values like loyalty and fidelity. I was contemptuous of my father for collecting rents, but he never cheated on my mother. He wouldn't have left his wife and children in Siberia the way Lev did with his first wife. He wouldn't have allowed someone to order his wife and son to leave the way Van did."

Dr. Bloom said with great sadness, "Sometimes you have no choice."

Lilly was taken aback. She could taste the bitter regret in his words. She was talking to a man who had run for his life. He was responding from some dark place inside himself, not to what she was saying.

"Did you leave people you were close to in Vienna?"

"Yes...in Vienna and in Amsterdam," he said, his thick voice cracking.

"Who did you leave?"

His chair squeaked as he changed positions in his chair. She felt he was deciding how much he should tell her.

"I left my parents in Vienna. The Nazi party was growing in Austria, but my parents didn't believe they could take over the government or that Hitler would invade the country. My father had a business; they had a house; they had relatives and friends..."

The revelation was slow to sink in... He feels guilty for having left his parents in Vienna.

"Do you know what happened to them?" Lilly asked softly.

"Yes," he cleared his throat to stifle his emotion. "During Kristallnacht, most of the synagogues in Vienna were destroyed, burned while the fire department and the public watched in glee. Jewish businesses were vandalized and looted. Thousands of Jews were arrested and deported to Dachau—my parents among them."

Lilly was speechless. She knew Austria had always been a hotbed of anti-Semitism. She had read that Jews were held responsible for the stock market crash of 1873 and for any and every other setback

283

that occurred. There was even a Viennese saying: "Who's to blame?" "The Jew." "Why?" "Because that's the way it is." Jews were seen as parasites.

They sat in gruesome silence for what seemed like hours. *He fled*, she thought to herself, *and they stayed and were probably sent to a concentration camp. He left someone behind too. They're very likely dead. He can't forgive himself*, she thought, *and neither can I.*

Finally he said, "What are you feeling?"

"Sorry, so sorry." She felt weighted down as if someone was sitting on her chest and the air was pushed out of her.

"Thank you. But you didn't do anything wrong." His voice was soothing. She felt the weight lifting, but then her mind took a turn and tears streamed down her cheeks.

"I *did* do something wrong. I continued to work for Lev when Hitler's intentions for the Jews were clear and he refused to speak out about it. He kept insisting that fascism is the most developed stage of capitalism and that there was no difference between the fascists and the British or Americans. He was a respected world leader and a Jew himself and yet he refused to condemn what the Nazis are doing to the Jews. Howie and my father kept writing to me and pleading with me to leave and I brushed them off and made excuses. I argued with Lev, but I stayed for over a year after Kristallnacht—typing his articles, editing his grammar."

And, of course that wasn't all of it...She could feel her heart break afresh every time her mind went near it.

21

Lilly sat in Dr. Bloom's waiting room ruminating about Gertie's last letter. She still carried it in her purse and read it over and over the way one compulsively picks at a scab. What did the last line mean? Was it about her disappointment in Jacques? Or was there something else she felt ashamed of?

August 1, 1940

Dear Lilly:

It's really hot in Mexico City. Jacques promised that we can leave in a few weeks. I want to be able to go back to NYU next month. He just has to finish his work here and we will be on our way. He is as eager to leave as I am. His temper bubbles up like a shaken bottle of seltzer. He has trouble sleeping and says it's because he is having stomach problems. But I think he has bad dreams. He tosses and turns during the night and mumbles. But when I ask him about it in the morning, he says it's because of his stomach.

Lev is in a terribly nervous state. He feels he could be assassinated at any moment. There are ten Mexican policeman on guard outside the house. There are sentries at the gate. Five men in the guards' quarters. There are electrified doors and wires everywhere. His friends, the Rosmers, have left—Jacques drove them to the station. Lev's only respite is when he and Natalia go on picnics in the countryside where he can relax and gather cacti for his garden. Jacques is still filling in as the third driver.

The Old Man has stuck to his view that the
Soviet Union is still a "workers' state." He
thinks that Soviet foreign and domestic policy
should be thought about separately. Jacques
agrees with him. He's writing a paper to
justify it and mentioned it to Lev the other
day. But he won't show it to me. I don't
understand. It's ridiculous.

I will see you in NY by the end of August. I
have so much to tell you. As George Meredith
said: "We live but to be sword or block." I
thought I was a sword, but I am a block.

Love,
Gertie

The letter was sent a few weeks before Gertie killed herself.
    When Dr. Bloom came out of his consulting room and greeted
her, she walked straight to the couch and lay down. After a few
minutes, she started to tell him the repeating nightmare that woke her
nightly:
    "She stood on a chair which she had dragged over to the
window. She calmly tore up the sheet from her bed and tied it to the
window bars. She climbed on the chair and tied the sheet around her
neck. Then she stepped off the chair and the weight of her body made
the sheet tighten around her neck." Lilly put her hands over her eyes,
but continued to talk. "She struggled just a few inches above the floor
when she started suffocating"—Lilly was crying hard and it was hard to
get the words out—"as the noose constricted her airways. She writhed
in pain for a few seconds before going limp."
    Lilly slapped the side of her head trying to knock out the image
of Gertie's body. Unsuccessful, her hands dropped to her lap. She
stared at the wall.
    "What's in the cracks?" she wondered out loud.
    "What do you mean?" the doctor replied, confused.

"All sorts of things fall into the cracks. They stay there. But they can come out at any time." She wanted to scrub her brain with kosher soap, wash away the image of Gertie hanging in a cell. She hugged herself, trying to generate warmth.

"What might come out?" the doctor asked.

"Her face turned blue. In my nightmare there are little blood marks on her face and in her eyes and her tongue's sticking out. ..There are rope marks and bruising on her neck."

Lilly put her hands around her throat to indicate where the marks were on Gertie's neck and *davened* back and forth on the couch as if she was saying the Mourner's *Kaddish*.

"I read that sometimes the person pees or even shits because the muscles become deprived of oxygen and relax. It was in my dream. My image of Gertie hanging in her own shit is preserved in amber. I'm afraid to go to sleep and have the dream again."

There was a pause and then Dr. Bloom asked, "Do you feel responsible?"

"Of course!" she yelled. "I was her older sister. I introduced Gertie to Frida and supported her going to Paris. What was I thinking? She had never been anywhere but Brooklyn. Even the subway signs say, '*To the City*.' She was naïve and trusting." The image of Gertie standing on the elevated platform gripped her like a rope around her own neck.

"But she was set up by the GPU. You're not responsible for the plot to murder Trotsky," the doctor said calmly. "It was a Stalinist plot. First Siqueiros tried and then the second time Frank Jacson got him."

"Sidney came over yesterday," Lilly said. "He tried to convince me it wasn't my fault. I told him he shouldn't have come. I wondered why he came to visit me. He had never been to my parents' house, not even for Gertie's *shiva.*"

"Hmm…" the doctor said. Lilly felt he was critical of Sidney for not paying his respects. She felt encouraged to continue.

"I asked him why he came," Lilly said. "I asked him if it was pity or just curiosity. He said he wanted to come. He said how sorry he was about Gertie's death and the horror of the assassination...He should be sorry. He got me into the whole thing."

"Tell me more," Dr. Bloom said.

"He *did* tell me something I didn't know. He told me that when Jacques was in New York he was staying in a safe house provided by the GPU. It was the apartment of Louis Horvitz. He's a long-time Party member who fought with the Lincoln Brigade in Spain."

"Yes?"

"Gertie visited him in that apartment. She thought it was Neruda's friend's apartment—that's what Jacques told her. I bet Horvitz knew Manny from the Brigade and maybe Jacques too. Gertie told me he fought in Spain. I killed my sister." She put her hands over her face and bawled, "I killed my sister, I killed her..."

She cried for a few minutes, and was brought back by Dr. Bloom's voice. "Don't you think," he asked "they would have found another way to get access to him?"

"Maybe, but I'm the one who gave him access to Lev. He was my sister's boyfriend. I'm the one who asked him to drive the third car for the picnic. That gave him his access."

"But you are not responsible, the Stalinists are," he said.

"Yes, I am. They used Gertie because she was my little sister. That's what set up Jacques' access." Lilly remembered the way Gertie smelled after she took a bath. She regretted yelling at her for sprinkling talcum powder all over the floor.

"How did they find out your sister was going to be in Paris and he could meet her at Frida's exhibition?"

"I don't know. I never thought about that." Lilly felt as if the blood was draining out of her body.

"I don't want to act like Poirot, but the GPU had to know Gertie was going to be there. It was set up perfectly. Who knew?"

Lilly sat pondering his question, her face ashen and her mouth open from the shock of it.

"Frida knew. My parents knew. But Frida would never help the Stalinists. Frida wouldn't want to kill Lev. No. No. She's a nut, but she'd never do that. Not Frida."

"Did anyone else know?" The doctor seemed intrigued.

Lilly hit herself in the head with her hand as if she were literally trying to wrack her brain: *my parents, no; Sol, no; Howie, no; Miriam, no.*

"Did Manny know you were in Mexico with Trotsky?"

"No, I hid it from him because he was a Stalinist. He would have been furious if he knew. He was angry that I studied with Sidney Hook and worked for *Partisan Review,* never mind Trotsky."

"Is it possible that Manny knew even if you didn't tell him? Could someone else have told him?"

"I had always been careful to give the letters to someone who was going to mail them from the States. So Manny wouldn't know where I was… but, when I got the letter from Ramon Mercader….It came to Coyoacán. The letters from Manny had always been sent to my parents and they forwarded them to me. But the one from Ramon was to Coyoacán. It wasn't forwarded by my parents. I was so upset Manny was dead that I never thought about the postmark on the letter."

"Yes?"

"Someone must have written to Manny and told him I was with Trotsky in Mexico."

22

"I'm a hypocrite."

"Why is that?" Dr. Bloom seemed surprised.

"I suppressed what I knew about Trotsky the whole time I was there. I stored it in the attic. Dewey didn't. He defended Lev's right to a fair trial when Stalin accused him of collaborating with the Nazis. But he also castigated him for being guilty of being just as dictatorial as Stalin."

"You didn't speak out against Trotsky. So?"

"I stayed and worked for Lev when Dewey left even though I *knew* Dewey was right about him."

"Yes?"

"It's complicated; I don't know how much you know about Russian history. About the Kronstadt Rebellion and all that."

"Tell me."

"Okay. In June, 1937 there was an announcement from Moscow that Marshal Mikhail Tukhachevsky and seven other top ranking officers of the Red Army had been tried in secret and executed for conspiracy with a Nazi-Trotskyist plot to overthrow Stalin. Tens of thousands of Army officers, most of whom had been civil war commanders, were also executed. Trotsky was sentenced to death in absentia for treason."

"So?" he said, impatient for her to explain why this was important.

"Sure the 'conspiracy with Nazi Germany' part was ridiculous, but I knew the Kronstadt sailors had played a pivotal role in the revolution and had pledged their allegiance to Lev. In 1921, when they demanded an end to the Communist monopoly of power, I knew it was *Lev* who ordered Marshal Tukhachevsky and the Red Army soldiers over the ice in the Gulf of Finland to assault the sailors on the island fortress. Most of them were killed and the rest were executed without trial. That's what made Emma Goldman and Alexander Berkman leave Russia. I knew that…I knew what Lev did."

"Yes? So what does that mean?" His whole face squinted when he was confused.

"You told me to explain it, so I'm explaining it."

"But I still don't get it."

"What did your father do for a living?" Lilly asked.

"He was a furrier," he said quickly—eager to get to the point. His thin lips pursed when he was impatient. Knowing he was annoyed did not discourage Lilly from circling around; she knew she was stalling.

"Did he belong to the union?" she continued her tangent.

"No, he owned a shop." He was trying to comply, but wanted her to stop digressing. "What are you feeling, Lilly?" The trolley tracks between his eyes seemed to reappear whenever he was confused.

"I feel sad," she said, taking a deep breath. "I've spent all these years trying to save the world and, instead, caused the death of my sister and Trotsky and brought agony to my parents and my brother." She imagined her mother's face when she heard that Gertie had hung herself—her face was white as chalk, as if all the blood had been drained out of her body. She fainted on the phone when Lilly told her and Tateh caught her just before she hit the floor.

"You didn't kill your sister or Lev. You didn't benefit from their deaths. You only suffer."

"She was my little sister. When we sat on the stoop and I saw those Irish boys laughing at us, I should have..." Lilly's chest was heaving and it was hard for her to catch her breath, "I should have protected her...I should have covered her with my body or pulled her over and put her face in my lap."

"How could you have known what was going to happen?" he said softly.

"I knew they were dangerous." Her face was stinging from the salt in her tears. She took a tissue from the box he had on the table. "In the winter, they ran after us screaming 'the Jews killed Christ' and threw snow or ice balls at us. Once one of them caught up to me and washed my face in the snow. I knew they were bad. I should have just grabbed her and ran into the house as soon as I saw them."

"When you look back everything is so clear—20/20 hindsight." She heard remorse in his words.

"But it's not only that..."

"Yes?"

"I betrayed Howie too."

"What about that?" he asked gently.

"I cheated on him, with a married man yet. How can I tell him that? He could never forgive me."

"It sounds like you can't forgive yourself."

"No, I can't. And he won't be able to either." Tears rolled off her cheeks onto her blouse.

"I don't think you know if he will be able to forgive you. From everything you've told me about Howie, he loves you very deeply and despite the pain of being apart, he was willing to wait until you were ready to commit yourself to him."

Lilly felt relieved for the first time in a long while. *It might be true*, she thought, *that Howie was willing to wait until I was ready to come back to him. Maybe he will be able to forgive me.* She was grateful to Dr. Bloom for understanding the depth of Howie's feelings for her. But she wasn't sure Howie's devotion could withstand her having an affair with another man.

"What are you feeling?" Dr. Bloom inquired.

"I'm feeling grateful to you for appreciating that Howie is a wonderful man. But I'm also feeling hopeless that such a transgression could be forgiven."

"I think it's hard for you to imagine Howie forgiving you because you can't forgive yourself. "

"What about working for Trotsky when I knew he ordered the murder of the Kronstadt sailors? Dewey was right about him. What about my parents? Why did I leave Gertie in Mexico? She begged me to stay. Aren't there things for which there is no forgiveness? That even God can't forgive? How can we be forgiven?"

He was silent. Lilly was afraid she had gone too far. *Maybe Dr. Bloom can't forgive himself*, she thought. But then after a few minutes he answered in a voice that seemed to come from some deep place inside him.

"There are things which cannot be forgiven. I agree. I hope, and believe, God does not forgive Stalin for murdering millions of his own people or the Nazis for murdering Jews. I don't believe God will forgive Jacques for what he did to Trotsky or your sister. I am not Christian. I don't believe in 'turning the other cheek.' But I don't think what you did as a little girl or leaving Gertie in Mexico when you had no idea who Jacques was or what you have done to Howie are things that cannot be forgiven."

292

"Is it God who has to forgive me, or Gertie and Howie?"

"Good question. What do you think?"

"I don't know if I believe in God. Do you?"

He was quiet for a few moments.

"Jews were quite assimilated in Vienna. We weren't religious. If the Nazis hadn't come to power we would not have thought about God or being Jewish."

"My family is not assimilated," Lilly said. "My parents speak Yiddish; we celebrate Shabbos and go to *shul* for all the holidays. On Yom Kippur, there is a prayer that says the wrongs between humans are not atoned for by Yom Kippur, until the wronged one is appeased. 'Even the day of death does not atone for such sins.' You forgive anyone who has wronged you on Yom Kippur 'whether in person or property, even if they slandered me, or spread falsehoods against me.' But that doesn't mean the other person will forgive you. It kind of leaves the Jew in the lurch."

"Yes," he laughed, "it isn't easy being a Jew for a lot of reasons." He shifted in his chair. "There are times, it's true, when the other person can't or won't forgive you. Then you have to find a way to forgive yourself..."

Lilly felt she could hear him thinking as he spoke, weighing his words, deciding if he believed what he was saying to her. "It's not easy to do." She knew he was speaking from experience. Something frozen inside her began to melt.

*   *   *

A week later, Lilly walked into the kitchen of her parents' house and saw a letter addressed to her sitting on the table. The handwriting was familiar—it was Miriam's. She felt a surge of excitement—she hadn't heard any news about Miriam since Gertie returned from Paris. The initial excitement was quickly replaced by relief—the postmark was from London—at least she got out of Paris. She took the letter into her bedroom and sat Indian-style on her bed.

November 1, 1940

Dear Lilly:

I am so sorry about Gertie. It came as a
terrible shock to read that Jacques was
Trotsky's assassin! But it was more wrenching
to read about Gertie's suicide. Poor thing—
she was swept up in a Stalinist conspiracy! It's
taken me this long to screw up the courage to
write to you because I feel partially
responsible for her death. I introduced her to
Jacques and encouraged her involvement with
him, never dreaming the whole thing was pre-
planned. Jacques was a friend of Neruda's and
I met him at one of Nancy Cunard's parties—
she was close to Neruda from their days in
Spain. Jacques was so charming. I must have
mentioned to him that I had a friend who was
the English secretary to Trotsky in Mexico
City and her sister was coming to Paris to
work at Frida's exhibit.

Lilly felt struck by a bolt of lightning. Her body stiffened,
almost paralyzed. She sat catatonic for what seemed like a long time,
tears fell slowly down her face and then she heard the sound of a
wounded animal and realized it was her. By the time she looked at the
letter again, it was damp from her tears.

He was very excited, eager to visit the gallery.
I didn't give it a second thought. What did I
care about Stalin vs. Trotsky? You know I
never cared about politics. It was all so boring
when Sidney went on and on about Trotsky
and Dewey. I wanted him to read poetry to
me. It's clear now, of course, that Jacques was
looking for access to Trotsky and I
unknowingly provided it.

"Oh God, Miriam," Lilly shouted, "how could you be so stupid?!"

> She was so much younger than Jacques and so naive. But I didn't question his interest in her, I thought it was romantic. I couldn't imagine the fall of France either—or the census of Jews or the restrictions on business activities for them. Not in France, I thought. That could never happen in France. When I finally got the message and left Paris with Nancy, I felt I'd escaped. I could go back to reading poetry and thinking about free love. Instead, the bombs fall every night, the sirens wail, we run to shelters amid the explosive booms and crashing buildings. Fires consume the city. We emerge from our caves to the crackling of fire and the shouts of desperate firemen.

Lilly's rage started to mingle with fear for her. She grabbed her pillow and hugged it as she continued to read.

> The Luftwaffe doesn't just blast docks and railways, but whole neighborhoods. They're targeting civilians! The other night the greatest of all the fires was right in front of me. Flames whipped hundreds of feet in the air, there was a giant balloon of smoke—they had bombed St. Paul's Cathedral! People stood on the street in shock for hours, but slowly the smoke receded and the gigantic dome was still standing. People started to clap as if it renewed their faith in God that it was still there. But not me. Such savagery. If there were a God, how could he allow it?

I've been in denial for so many years, Lilly,
caught up in my petty jealousies and self-
righteous contempt for convention. There was
a time when I wanted to help people, so many
years ago on Pitkin Avenue, remember, and
it's taken all this darkness for me to finally see
the light.

With great sadness...

Love,
Miriam

Lilly sat squeezing her pillow, crying and clutching the
letter...When she woke up, the letter was crumpled in her hand and the
pillow was wet.

23

"A man must have a minimum of three masticating teeth above and three opposite them below and three natural incisor teeth above and opposite them three natural incisor teeth below," Howie read the letter from the Selective Service out loud. He added, "Well, I've got twelve teeth." He continued reading, "A man must be at least 5'4" tall and weigh at least 105 pounds."

"Can you imagine a man who is 5'4 and weighs 105 pounds? That's less than I weigh," Lilly said and they both laughed.

"They say they're not being fussy now," Howie said. "They have looser standards for a peacetime draft." It had been almost two months since President Roosevelt signed the Selective Service and Recruitment Act. Howie had registered with the local draft board and was waiting for his number to be called. They were trying to joke about it, but they were both terrified: they didn't know how long they had before he was called up.

It was four in the afternoon and Howie and Lilly had not gotten out of bed except to put up coffee, cut up bagels to munch on and go to the bathroom. Being in Howie's apartment was much nicer than the old days when they made love on the couch in his mother's living room. Here they had a bedroom to themselves and didn't have to listen for the key in the door. Lilly had been gone over three years, but bodies have muscle memory. Within a few minutes of their first time together all of the anxiety about what it would be like to have sex with Howie had passed. It seemed comfortable and natural. They sat naked in bed with sections of the Sunday *New York Times* mixed in with the bed covers.

"I heard Arnie got drafted," Howie said, "and may refuse to go if we get into the war. He is sticking to Browder's position that good Communists must refuse to fight their proletarian brothers."

"He'll go to prison, won't he?" Lilly asked.

"Yes, he can't even claim to be a conscientious objector because he doesn't object to all wars, only ones in which Stalin is on the other side." Howie smirked.

"What about Fritzi? You think she's going to let him go to jail?"

"She's just as much a Stalinist as he is. You know how they are," Howie said. He paused and added, "Speaking of Stalinists, you haven't looked inside the first section, but there's an article saying that the Mexican police found out that Frank Jacson is actually a Spanish Stalinist agent named Ramon Mercader."

"What!" Lilly screamed.

He squeezed her hand. "The paper said he fought in the Spanish Civil War and was recruited to kill Trotsky if the Siqueiros raid failed."

Lilly felt like a giant wave had knocked her off her feet and she couldn't catch her breath. She had started to steady herself after getting Miriam's letter and now she was being thrown against jagged stones, when she righted herself, she realized Howie was holding her. She could hear her heart beating.

Howie was silent for a few moments and then her gasping stopped, he asked, "What does this mean, I don't understand."

Slowly, as her breathing slowed down, she whispered, "It's all my fault…"

"What are you talking about?" Howie turned her face toward his.

"It's such a long story," she said.

"I want to hear it. Tell me. Tell me the whole thing."

"Oh Howie, it's so bad…" Tears ran down her cheeks.

"Tell me, please."

Lilly moved away from him so that she could face Howie. He took both her hands. "Tell me."

"Just before Manny left for Spain I was developing a crush on him. I saw him at the John Reed Club and once he called me to take a walk in the Botanical Garden." She waited for his response. *Does he hate me now?* He bit his cheek, but said nothing. Lilly continued, "Nothing happened between us, but I wrote to him when he went to Spain." Again she paused. Howie was silent. "I didn't tell him that I was going to Mexico because I knew he hated Dewey and when I stayed on to work for Lev, I didn't tell him that either. I knew he hated Trotsky even more than Dewey. So I asked other people passing through to mail my letters from New York. But when I got the letter saying that he died, it was mailed to me in Mexico. It was a letter from his friend…." She paused and put her hands over her eyes. "It was from Ramon Mercader…"

298

"What?!" Howie jerked as if an electric shock had passed through him. He let go of her hands and screwed up his face. "So Ramon Mercader knew about where you were even though you didn't tell Manny. But, of course, other people were writing to Manny while he was in Spain and they all knew you went to Mexico with Dewey and stayed to work for Trotsky—any one of them could have told him. It was no secret. Arnie might have told him."

"Yes, I was so stupid…I never told anyone to keep it a secret."

"It wouldn't have done any good. You couldn't control who knew you where you were".

"But it's worse than that. I set it up…I encouraged her to go to Paris."

Howie took her hand and put it on his cheek. "How could you have known?"

They sat quietly finally comprehending the plot of a tragedy they were part of but had not fully understood until now.

A wave of fear washed over Lilly. Howie was going to be called up. It was inevitable that the United States was going to enter the war and he didn't have the kind of job that would get him a deferment, or a wife and five children. And he had more than 12 teeth.

"Howie," she said, starting to feel the undertow, "I couldn't bear it if anything happened to you, if you didn't come back to me."

"Don't worry, nothing will happen to me. After waiting for you this long, I'll be damned if I'm going to let myself get shot."

"Manny died."

Howie put his hand on her chin and turned her face to look him directly in the eyes. "I won't die, but I have to go. I won't be able to live with myself if I don't go."

"I know, but there are things I need to tell you, Howie."

"No, you don't need to tell me anything. You came back to me. That's all I need to know. I love you and I want to spend my life with you."

"But…"

He put his finger on her lips. "Shh! You don't need to tell me anything." He kissed her neck and rubbed his nose on her ear. "Remember what we say on Yom Kippur? '*We* have sinned.' You told me you needed to do what you thought was right. Every Jew has his Egypt and I was yours."

"You're so funny," she said and kissed his cheek.

"And you did that and you came back to me," Howie continued. Then his smile disappeared. "Now I have to do what I think is right. I will come back to you."

Lilly squeezed her arms around him and nuzzled into the space between his neck and shoulder.

"Howie, I don't believe in God. How can there be a God when Hitler is sending the Jews to concentration camps, Jacques killed Lev, and Gertie killed herself? How could God have allowed that? How could there *be* a God who would allow my parents to suffer so. My mother won't eat anything and my father sits and stares at the walls all day. So I can't pray to God for your safety. I have no faith. Do you believe in God?"

"I think so. I don't believe he's an old man in a chair somewhere. And I don't think he tinkers with our lives or determines our fate. But I believe there's something greater than our individual lives that matters—something bigger than we are. I don't know what to call it, maybe God."

Lilly thought about Dr. Bloom. *How could he believe in God when the Nazis probably killed his parents and so many other relatives?*

"You know I never understood the story of Abraham and Isaac," she confessed. "I could never understand how God could ask Abraham to sacrifice his son. How could you believe in a God who would ask that? And worse, Abraham was willing to do it. It used to make me angry when the rabbi told that story in synagogue."

"I understand it, I think," Howie said. "It's about the sacrifices that Jews have to be willing to make. God didn't ask Abraham to do it, but he was willing. We circumcise our sons even though it hurts and it identifies them as Jews. We are willing to fight and die for Palestine and to stop the Nazis. Jews have to be willing to sacrifice their sons. I think I understand why the story is taught and told over and over."

"What about our daughters?"

Howie kissed her cheek. "Yes, our daughters too."

"I mean *our* daughters."

"Yes, I know."

Lilly held him tightly and said, "Howie I love you, will you marry me?"

300

"Yes, I love you too. But not until I come home."

"No, I don't want to wait for you to come home. You want to wait because you're not so sure you will be coming home. No, I want to marry you now and I want to have our baby."

"Really?" Howie took her face in his hands and looked into her eyes.

"Yes," Lilly said, nodding and laughing.

"I think that can be arranged."

HISTORICAL NOTES

Two Sisters of Coyoacán takes place between 1932-40. It begins in Brownsville, Brooklyn which had the largest population of Jews in New York City at the time—predominantly immigrants from Eastern Europe. They had fled 25-year conscription into the Russian army, pogroms following the assassination of Czar Alexander II in March of 1881 and restrictive anti-Semitic laws in Russia and Poland. Persecution under the Czars and encounters with poverty and factory labor in America inspired many Jews to look for radical social change.

Many American Jews supported the overthrow of the Czarist regime in 1917. Some were left-leaning, but most simply hated the Czar. Joseph Stalin and Leon Trotsky were the heirs-apparent to Vladimir Ilyich Lenin. Tensions between Stalin and Trotsky increased when Lenin's health began to fail in 1922. In 1924 when Lenin died, Stalin emerged as leader of the Soviet Union. He believed that despite the failure of the communist revolutions in Germany and Hungary in 1917-21 and despite the backwardness of Russia's economy, "socialism in one country" was possible and that the Soviet Union needed to focus on internal development. Trotsky, on the other hand, believed it would be impossible to achieve socialism in a country with an agrarian economy. He argued that it was not possible to have a "proletarian revolution" in countries in which there was little or no proletariat. Calling for a continuing world revolution ("permanent revolution"), he claimed this was the only way societies which had not achieved advanced capitalism could have successful socialist revolutions—by harnessing the technology and wealth of more developed capitalist countries. In response, Stalin and his supporters launched a propaganda counterattack against Trotsky. Trotsky criticized the new regime for suppressing democracy in the Communist Party. But in 1925, he was removed from his post as head of the War Commissariat and in 1927 he was expelled from the Communist Party. In January 1928, Trotsky began his internal exile and the next January was expelled from the Soviet Union outright.

In the early 1930's, while the sons of Jewish immigrants argued about the virtues of Trotsky vs. Stalin at places like City College in New York, Hitler became Chancellor of Germany and the dictatorship of Primo de Rivera in Spain was overthrown. The monarchy was abolished—Spain became a republic. Manuel Azaña was the Prime Minister, but he was opposed from both the Left and the Right. Parties of the Left came together to form the Popular Front, which organized strikes and riots. The Right opposed him because he abolished Church-operated schools and charities, and greatly expanded state-operated secular schools. He was forced to resign in 1933. In 1934 coal miners in the Asturias went on strike but were ruthlessly put down by the army led by Franco. In a last minute attempt to avoid civil war, a general election was called for February 1936. In this election, the Popular Front won and Azaña became prime minister once again. But General Franco and the military took control of Spanish Morocco after overthrowing the civilian government there. Next Franco invaded mainland Spain, establishing a military government and ridding the country of everyone who had been involved in left wing politics. The civil war started in July 1936.

Supporters of the Popular Front poured into Spain from all over Europe and the United States. The Abraham Lincoln Brigade was a group of approximately 2,800 American volunteers who served in the Spanish Civil War. They were anti-Fascists of all left-leaning political stripes: anarchists, socialists, Stalinists, Trotskyists and social democrats. Approximately 800 of them were killed in action or died of wounds or sickness.

At the same time that the Spanish Civil War was being fought, Stalin was orchestrating the Moscow Trials directed at purging the Old Guard Bolsheviks and the Nazis seized Czechoslovakia. One year later, Mexican Stalinists attempted to assassinate Leon Trotsky, but failed. The second attempt, by Ramon Mercader, succeeded in August 1940.

AUTHOR'S NOTE

The events in this novel are based on real events. However, Lilly and Gertie are fictional characters based on Ruth and Sylvia Ageloff—two young women from Brooklyn who were the daughters of a real estate developer. Ruth *did* go to Mexico with the Dewey Commission and Sylvia *was* romanced by Ramon Mercader in order for him to gain access to Leon Trotsky. However, Sylvia was older than Gertie. She was a social worker when she met Ramon Mercader in Paris and it was not until years after the assassination that Ramon Mercader was definitively identified as a Stalinist agent. He went to Mexico rather than Canada when he left Paris and came to New York to reconnect with Sylvia after the Siqueiros raid failed to assassinate Trotsky in May, 1940.

Miriam and Howie, the boys from City College, Dewey's secretary Kate, and many other minor characters are fictional. The basic facts about historical figures such as Sidney Hook, John Dewey, Leon Trotsky, Jean Van Heijenoort (Van), Frida Kahlo and André Breton are accurate, but the relationships between them and the characters in the novel are entirely fictional. Ruth Ageloff did not have an affair with Van; Sylvia Ageloff was not pregnant when she went to Mexico; and she did not commit suicide. Rather, she was released by the Mexican police after a few days once they were convinced she had not collaborated with Frank Jacson (Ramon Mercader) and returned to New York. Ruth Ageloff became a psychoanalyst and had a practice in Manhattan.

ACKNOWLEDGEMENTS

It was a lucky day for me in 2009 when I realized that Ruth Poulos, a fellow member of the National Psychological Association for Psychoanalysis, had been Leon Trotsky's secretary. My husband, Richard, and I had visited Trotsky's house in Coyoacán a few years earlier. I recalled that the docent mentioned that the boyfriend of Trotsky's secretary's sister was the assassin. *Could Ruth Poulos be that secretary?* That question was the beginning of a great adventure. I discovered that Ruth Poulos' maiden name was Ruth Ageloff and her sister, Sylvia, was seduced by Ramon Mercader in order to gain access to Trotsky! I also found out that the sisters were Jewish and had been brought up in Brooklyn and their father was a wealthy real estate developer.

I was gripped by this story. Perhaps it's because Ruth Poulos was a fellow psychoanalyst or because I am also Jewish and brought up in Brooklyn. Or maybe it was because I have several friends who were "red babies"—the children of wealthy communists. And also, I had been obsessed by Russian history in college and wrote my undergraduate honors thesis in political science about Trotsky. Although I had written a trade book, I had never written a novel. But I felt this story needed to be written as fiction—and I had to write it.

Many people have helped me make this novel happen. My writing group: Zeeva Bukai, Geri De Luca and Julia Hirsch encouraged me to write a novel despite my lack of training. They read every chapter many times and their feedback and encouragement gave me the incentive to continue the project through years of frustration.

I'd like to thank Jennifer Gilmore, my first (and only) writing teacher for teaching me the basics of writing fiction and being generous with her feedback on the earliest versions of the book. Julie Miesionczel was extremely helpful as the editor of the post-Gilmore draft.

Most of all I'd like to thank my husband, Richard Wool, who edited multiple drafts of the book, proofread it, and painstakingly checked every historical and geographical reference. He has encouraged me through years of frustration and self-doubt.

Bertrand M. Patenaude's, *Trotsky: Downfall of a Revolutionary* was an excellent and indispensable source and I have liberally drawn from it in the Prologue and Chapters 8, 9, 10, 13, 15 and 17. Other sources from which I have drawn information are: Terry A. Cooney, *The Rise of the New York Intellectuals: Partisan Review and Its Circle, 1934-1945*; Janet Flanner, *Paris was Yesterday, 1925-1939;* Arthur Granit, *The Time of the Peaches*; Alfred Kazin, *A Walker in the City;* Alter F. Landesman, *Brownsville: The Birth, Development and Passing of a Jewish Community in New York*; Anita Burdman Feferman, *From Trotsky to Goedel;* Leonard Q. Ross, "Union Square" in Louis Filler, editor *The Anxious Years: America in the Nineteen Thirties,*

Irving Howe's *World of Our* Fathers, Harcourt, Brace, and Jovanovich, New York, 1976 (pages 283-286); Irving Kristol's "Memoirs of a Trotskyist," New York Times, January 23, 1977; and Eric Hoffer's chapter: "City College in the Thirties" in Charles H. Page, *Fifty Years of Sociological Enterprise*, University of Massachusetts Press, 1982 (pages 56-104) were a great help in Chapter 3. Diana Trilling's *The Beginning of the Journey* described the atmosphere of Yaddo which was useful in Chapter 5. Christopher Phelps, *Young Sidney Hook: Marxist and Pragmatist* was helpful in Chapters 4, 5 and 8.

CPSIA information can be obtained
at www.ICGtesting.com
Printed in the USA
BVOW03s1746010817
490792BV00001B/5/P